ILLUSION OF TRUTH

Also by James L'Etoile

DETECTIVE EMILY HUNTER SERIES
Face of Greed
River of Lies

OTHER NOVELS
Little River
At What Cost
Bury the Past
Black Label
Dead Drop
Devil Within
Served Cold
Sins of the Father

ILLUSION OF TRUTH

A DETECTIVE EMILY HUNTER

MYSTERY

JAMES L'ETOILE

OCEANVIEW PUBLISHING
SARASOTA, FLORIDA

ISBN 978-1-60809-649-7

Published in the United States of America by Oceanview Publishing

Sarasota, Florida

www.oceanviewpub.com

10 9 8 7 6 5 4 3 2 1

ILLUSION OF TRUTH

CHAPTER ONE

"ALL AVAILABLE UNITS, report of a large crowd and 459s in progress at the corner of Rio Linda and South Ave.," the dispatcher's voice called out over the radio.

Sergeant Brian Conner clicked the microphone in his patrol unit. "1-Sam-12 responding."

"Hey, Tommy, isn't there a church on South Ave?" Conner asked.

Tommy Robinson, a Black rookie officer assigned to Patrol District 1 in North Sacramento, turned in the passenger seat, checking for cross-traffic at the intersection. "Yeah. It's one of those pop-up, God-in-a-box churches. You know—no denomination, takes all comers."

"Why would a church be a target for looting at midnight?"

"It's right on the edge of Tru Heights Bloods territory. Could be gangbangers after the food pantry and the donations the church's brought in."

"Tommy, let me ask you something. You've been married a while, so you've got this whole relationship thing down. When Emily says she isn't ready to move in together, what does that mean?"

"Um, Sarge, you think I'm the one to answer that? Shouldn't Emily—I mean Detective Hunter—tell you why?"

"I mean, sure, but I thought everything was going great—and then, she's not ready. You ever have anything like that?"

"No. But then my Baptist momma would've slapped me into tomorrow if I thought about living in sin."

"That's not helpful, Tommy."

Conner shot north on Rio Linda. The flashing blue lights from other patrol units ahead marked the location. As Conner pulled into the church parking lot, he expected a crowd spilling out of the church and into nearby businesses. There had been a rash of daylight attacks on retail establishments in the city, where mobs of thieves grabbed armfuls of whatever they could carry. Hitting a church in the middle of the night was a new direction.

"Where are they? The looters?" Tommy said.

Conner parked near the church entrance, ahead of another Sacramento Police Department SUV, and stepped from his vehicle. He couldn't spot a single person near the church, except for the six police officers who had responded to the call.

"Dispatch, 1-Sam-12, have a callback number on the RP? Looks like a false alarm."

"Negative, 1-Sam-12. Caller didn't give their name."

An officer rounded the corner of the church building and approached Conner. "Nobody's here, Sarge. What gives?"

The hairs on the back of Conner's neck pricked up. He swiveled around and surveyed the darkened windows on the street opposite. They were lured here.

"Got movement across the street—second floor, left side," an officer called out. His brass nameplate read Tucker.

Conner spotted the window and the flare of a cigarette. Someone watching the police respond to this snipe hunt?

"We see any evidence of a break-in? Broken windows, open doors, anything?"

"Nada. Simmons and I walked the perimeter. No sign of entry. No sign of anything," Tucker said.

"Someone wanted all the units in District 1 to respond. A report of a large crowd breaking into businesses would draw us out here."

"They needed a diversion so they could pull off whatever they were into somewhere else," Tucker said.

"Maybe. I haven't heard anything new from dispatch. Why would we get a callout to the edge of Tru Heights territory?"

"Westgate Crips are on the other side of the freeway. I could see them making a false report to push us to roust a couple of their rivals."

"Well, nothing going on here. Why don't you and your partner hit the road. Let dispatch know this was a dry hole," Conner said.

"Got it, Sarge. You need Parker and Cortez in the other unit? They're watching the back of the church."

"Nah, send them on their way, would you?"

"You got it."

"Thanks, Tucker. Be careful out there. I've got an uneasy feeling about someone sending us here."

"I hear you."

Conner started back to his SUV, paused, and turned. "Hey, Tucker, anyone check the front door lock?"

"Yeah, I shook it. Locked up tight."

Tucker and his partner got into their SUV, shut off the lights, and backed out of the church parking lot.

Tommy Robinson wandered to the front entrance and peered through the smoked glass doors. "Place is empty. Nothing going on—hey, what's up with this?"

A metal donation bin sat to the right of the front door. Gang graffiti adorned the side of the four-foot-tall, repainted mailbox.

Conner caught the glint from a thin wire attached to the donation box door. On the concrete below, a cut padlock lay in the shadow.

Tommy reached for the bin.

"Tommy! Wait!"

Conner ran to the young officer as he tugged on the lid.

"Stop," Conner said.

Tommy was focused on the unlocked donation bin and didn't hear Conner.

Conner shoved Tommy as a click echoed in the entry vestibule. A microsecond later, a fireball erupted from the donation bin.

A pressure wave of heat and metal shards exploded. Conner caught the blast in the back as he pushed Tommy away. The force of the explosion picked Conner off his feet and threw him into the brick wall opposite the donation bin.

Conner couldn't hear anything through the ringing in his ears, and his vision was a blurred kaleidoscope of flames and smoke. From where he fell, he could see the parking lot and the window across the street. The glowing ember from the cigarette was gone, but he swore he spotted a flashing red strobe.

Another explosion sounded to his right. A flash of orange shot from the parking lot. Conner squinted through his warped vision and saw a police SUV on fire. Tucker and his partner, Simmons. He couldn't see them anywhere.

He tried reaching for his shoulder-mounted radio microphone and his arm wouldn't move. A quick glance down and Conner saw his broken arm pointing in the wrong direction.

"Tommy. Tommy, you okay?"

Conner couldn't hear anything but the high-pitched ringing in his ears.

He wasn't even supposed to be working tonight. Conner swapped the shift with a buddy so his friend could go spend some time with his kids.

Conner felt cold, and a heavy blanket of exhaustion fell over him. Emily. He wanted to tell Emily how much he loved her one more time. She'd wanted to take it slow, but now he felt regret. He should've told her how he felt when he had the chance.

The sirens in the distance pierced through his muffled hearing. They would not be in time.

"Emily . . ."

CHAPTER TWO

"HUNTER HERE." DETECTIVE Emily Hunter was used to the late-night callouts. As a homicide detective, she knew evil wasn't born from darkness, but the shadows made the cowards who lurked there bold and brave. The darkness gave cover to the worst of us. Emily knew there was plenty to fear in the dark. She knew this call was going to be another reminder of the fact.

"Detective, please hold for the watch commander," a tense voice said over the connection.

"Emily, it's John Watson."

"Hey, Lieutenant, what's up?" She picked up on the stress in his voice.

"There's been an incident."

Emily pulled a notebook and a pen from the end stand.

"Where do you need Javier and me?"

"You need to get to the Med Center, Emily. I've got Detective Medina en route to a crime scene in North Sacramento."

"If the crime scene is—"

"Emily, it's Brian. You need to go to the Med Center," Lieutenant Watson said.

"Brian? What—what happened? Is he okay?"

"The details are sketchy at the moment. Looks like our people responded to a call and were targeted by an explosive device."

"A bomb?"

"Two of them. Brian and three other officers are in the trauma center. Emily, Brian's in serious condition. You need to be there. I'll send an officer over to drive you."

Emily shot up from the bed. "Don't bother. I'm on my way."

"I don't want you driving. You'll have an officer on your doorstep in ten minutes. Chief's orders, Emily."

Emily disconnected the call without responding.

She got dressed on autopilot while images of Brian and their last day together swirled in her mind. They'd arranged time off and spirited off to Napa for the day. She'd found someone she could be herself with. No airs, no pretense, just comfortable with one another. He dared to think about a future . . .

Dreams of the future had a nasty reputation for crushing your soul.

Out of habit more than anything, she grabbed her department identification, badge, and weapon. She slung her jacket over her shoulder, swept her dark brown hair in a quick ponytail, and made for the door where a uniformed officer waited on her doorstep.

"Detective Hunter? I'm to take you to the Med Center." He looked young, so young his Sam Browne leather belt was shiny and stiff. Thinly built, the officer had avoided the "freshman fifteen" new cops tended to pack on after the academy. His bright brass name tag read MILTON.

She locked her door and motioned for Officer Milton to lead the way.

The black-and-white police SUV idled at the curb. Emily climbed in the passenger side and Officer Milton strapped in.

"What do you know?" Emily said.

The young officer turned to Emily, and a cloud settled in his gray eyes. Fear? Apprehension? Emily couldn't tell. There was a lingering scent of smoke on him.

"The watch commander got reports from the units responding to the blast—two of them. The first one was at the door of the church on South Avenue, and the second looked like it was set to take out anyone who responded to the blast."

"They were targeted?"

"Called in a bogus looting complaint to 911 to make sure multiple units responded."

Emily stiffened. This was the first time she'd experienced a direct attack on officers.

"Any word on how Brian—Sergeant Conner—is doing?"

Milton broke eye contact. "No, ma'am. I heard he saved his partner—took the brunt of the first blast."

"Damn him. He wasn't even supposed to work tonight."

Officer Milton shoved the SUV into DRIVE and pulled away. Emily glanced at the darkened windows in the neighborhood as they drove past. Everyone was snug and safe in their beds. A twinge of resentful jealousy swept over her.

Milton pulled the SUV under the covered entrance at the UC Med Center. The waiting room overflowed with officers anxiously awaiting updates on their brothers.

Lieutenant Larry Hall stood off by himself with a cell phone lodged to his ear. He caught Emily's glance as she came through the doors. He motioned her over and put the phone in his pocket.

The big Black man enveloped her in a hug. His worried expression shook her.

"How's—" Her eyes began to well. The more she fought them back, the more the tears tracked down her cheeks.

"He's in surgery right now. The doctors said he broke an arm and had a deep gash on his forehead from either shrapnel or hitting a hard surface when he fell. They are concerned about concussion, and internal injuries from the pressure of the explosive charge."

"What are they saying? Is he going to be okay?"

Before he could answer, a doctor entered the waiting room, and twenty officers fell silent. Afraid to breathe.

"Family of Tommy Robinson?" Emily tried to read the doctor's expression. Professional. Neutral. A trauma surgeon used to giving bad news.

A small Black woman weaved between the uniformed officers. One woman, a police chaplain, kept by her side. The doctor directed them to a set of low couches away from the crowd.

Emily watched as the doctor spoke to the young woman. He bobbed his head as he conveyed his message. The woman sprung up from the couch and threw her arms around the surprised doctor. The chaplain rubbed her back and gave the room a thumbs-up. Officer Robinson was going to be okay.

A few officers nodded or exhaled their relief in response. Still, the condition of the three others was unknown.

"Lieutenant, do we know what happened out there?"

"I spoke with Detective Medina. He's trying to get a full picture and timeline for what happened. It looks like our units were lured to respond to a specific location."

"Anyone claiming responsibility for the bombs?"

"I haven't heard anything. Too early—someone might claim it in the morning. Our bomb squad will sort out what they can find out about the devices."

"Excuse me, are you Detective Hunter?"

Emily turned and found the young woman who had received the update on Officer Robinson.

"How's Tommy? Brian's told me about him."

"The doctors say he's going to be fine—only because of Sergeant Conner. He saved my Tommy's life. He pushed him out of the way. If he hadn't—"

Emily put an arm around her. "I'm glad Tommy will pull through." At the same time, she wished Brian hadn't put himself at risk. She knew he was the kind of man who would always put others first. He was the same in their relationship. Had she thrown it away when she told him she wasn't ready to move in together? The thought of what they had and what she may have done to it made Emily quiver. What if—

She tracked the doctor who'd given the update on Tommy Robinson. He was pushing his way through a set of double doors into the emergency room.

"Excuse me, Mrs. Robinson, Lieutenant," she said as she stepped away, making a course through the waiting room toward the double doors.

She grabbed a slow closing door before it locked. The doctor was reading a file at a counter down the hallway.

"Excuse me, Doctor," she said.

He glanced up. "You shouldn't be in here, miss."

"The man who came in with Officer Robinson—Conner, Brian Conner—can you tell me what's happening?"

"Miss, I'm sorry. I can't talk about a patient's condition. Are you the next of kin?"

Emily paused for a second. What was she, really? He didn't have any family left. "I am, yes."

The doctor nodded to a nurse sitting at a computer terminal behind the counter.

"Patient's name?"

"Conner, Brian Conner."

"Date of birth?"

Emily stiffened. "June . . . 20th."

"Year?"

"Um . . ."

The nurse glared over her glasses. "And your name?"

"Emily Hunter."

"Mr. Conner's emergency contact information says—"

"Listen, Brian doesn't have anyone to—I need to know how he's doing. Those officers out there in the waiting room. We are his family." Brian's parents passed years ago, and no siblings. He told Emily he was an orphan now.

The nurse sighed. "If you'd let me finish. Mr. Conner listed you as his emergency contact. You also hold medical power of attorney." She printed off a document and handed it to Emily.

Emergency contact? Brian listed her as his "next of kin" and she felt a swirl of guilt for second-guessing the direction of their relationship mixed with anxiety over not getting to tell him why.

"What's this?"

"An advance directive."

A chill fell around Emily. She knew what the document meant. She'd worked with her mother's memory care facility to make sure they knew what Connie Hunter's end-of-life wishes were.

"Are you saying . . ." She couldn't finish her thoughts.

"Please come with me, Miss Hunter." The doctor's voice pierced the veil of fear—the shock of the unknown.

Emily followed him to a quiet end of the corridor, walled off by flimsy curtains separating patient bays.

"I'm Doctor O'Rourke. I did the initial trauma workup on Mr. Conner. He's in surgery right now. I'm afraid he's in critical condition."

"Critical? I heard he was serious, but stable. What happened?"

"Outward indications were a fractured arm, lacerations, and head trauma. Once we got him in a CT and ultrasound, we found he had a lacerated kidney, and a ruptured spleen. We had to rush him into surgery to stop the internal hemorrhaging."

"Will—will he be okay?"

"If we're able to stop the bleeding in both locations—two different surgical teams are working on him. I'm concerned about the cerebral edema we're seeing."

Emily shook her head, trying to sort out what she was hearing. Internal bleeding, ruptured spleen, edema.

"Brain swelling?"

"Yes, exactly. It's often the result of traumatic brain injury. The blast he experienced—he got it twice, once from the pressure wave of the blast, and then when his head struck a solid surface."

"What happens next?"

"Once he's out of surgery, the next twelve hours will tell. The edema—the building intracranial pressure—is dangerous and it can be life-threatening."

"You've seen this before, right? You can fix it?"

"I was an army doctor in Afghanistan. We saw too many cases like this with TBI caused from roadside IEDs and mortar rounds. The key is getting his pressure down. I've asked for a neurosurgeon consult the moment he gets out of surgery. If he can't control the pressure, we'll need to do it for him."

"Another surgery?"

"It's possible."

"When can I see him?" Emily gripped the advance directive with whitened knuckles.

"It's going to be a while, a few hours at best. You should go get some rest. I promise to call you the moment he's out. Once he's out of recovery we'll contact you. He may not be conscious—the TBI."

Emily slipped the doctor her card and thanked him. "Please let me know the second he comes out of surgery."

Before she left, the doctor took her by the shoulder.

"Miss Hunter. He is in critical condition with multiple trauma. You should prepare yourself in the event the surgery doesn't go well." He tapped the advance directive in her hand. "You should make sure you know what he wants in the event it comes to that. I'm sorry, but you should be ready to make some hard decisions."

Emily shook and a deep anger formed in her gut. She pulled the advance directive away and ripped it into shreds. "I won't be needing it. He's going to make it."

Emily stormed out the double doors to the waiting room. The officers who waited for updates locked eyes with her. She found Lieutenant Hall and went to him.

"It's not good, Lieutenant. Critical. He's in surgery—will be for a few hours. The doctor told me he'd call the minute he's out."

"We'll find you a quiet place to sit and wait for updates. I think there's a chapel down the hallway—"

"I can't sit around and wait. I'll go stark raving crazy waiting. I need to be doing something."

"You need to rest, Emily. Brian will need you once he starts recovering."

"I'll rest—sometime. Right now, I need to find out why this happened."

"Emily. You're too close to this. You shouldn't be anywhere near this investigation. Javier has it in hand. Let him do his job. He's a solid detective. You trained him."

"I need to be out there."

Hall exhaled. "If I ordered you to stay away, what would you do?"

"I'm going out there. Javi needs all the support we can throw at him."

"I thought as much. Detective Medina is the lead on this. Understand? You follow his lead. If he feels you're too close, or getting in his way, you're benched. Got it?"

"Yes, LT, thank you."

She knew Javier was perfectly capable of leading this investigation. He'd proven himself as a top-notch detective and he knew how to talk with people and get them to open up to him. Especially when he worked with the victims. He could coax repressed details from recently traumatized victims, which often led to the arrest of their assailant. He had a few more years in the department, on patrol, but never groused that Emily was the lead detective because she had more time in grade. All in all, they made a good team.

Emily wheeled around and found Officer Milton. She tapped him on the shoulder.

"Time to drive Miss Daisy. Let's go."

CHAPTER THREE

FIRE ENGINES, POLICE vehicles, and the ever-present news vans encircled the church parking lot, appearing from the mist whenever bad news was born.

"You were there tonight?" Emily said.

Milton's hands tightened on the wheel.

"I can smell the smoke on you."

"Oh, yeah. I was there. It was bad. I'm sorry. I didn't mean to say it like that. Innocent people shouldn't get hurt. At least everyone got to the hospital."

"Milton, you can let me out here. You're relieved of driving duty for the rest of your shift."

"You sure? I don't mind. I can hang around and help."

"I appreciate it, but I think we've probably got . . . let me check with Detective Medina. He might need help with door-to-door."

"Thank you, Detective. I have to be involved in this. The sergeant— Sergeant Conner—shame to see what happened. Everyone says he's one of the good ones. Whoever's responsible for this—I need to help."

"Let's go find Detective Medina and put you to work."

Emily approached the barrier of yellow plastic tape strung between police vehicles. A bored officer leaned against one of the black-and-white

SUVs. He put away his phone and held out a clipboard as Emily drew near.

"We keeping you from something, Officer?" Emily said.

"What? Sign in. I don't care what you do."

Emily went rigid. "Listen, asshole. You have one job here and one job only. You document every movement in and out of this crime scene. You need to be able to testify to every living, breathing thing coming and going—when they arrived and when they left. You screw it up and a defense attorney can make an argument that evidence found was contaminated or could've been placed there after the fact. You got me?"

The officer pushed back from the SUV and blinked.

"I said, you got me?" Emily said, inching closer to the officer.

"Yeah, yeah. I got it. I got it." He handed the clipboard to Emily.

She signed the log, noted the time, and handed the clipboard to Officer Milton, who did the same.

The officer retrieved his clipboard and raised the tape barrier for Emily.

"Where's Detective Medina?"

"The detective was near the front door last time I saw him."

Emily didn't respond and made her way toward the cluster of lights set up near the front of the building. The bright halogen flare highlighted the smoke- and scorch-marked blast near the shattered glass doors.

"I can't stand lazy cops. Don't you ever become one of those, Milton."

"No, ma'am. I can't tolerate anyone who won't do their job."

Emily spotted Javier near the front walkway, talking with a fire department battalion chief based on the firefighter's white helmet. The slight gray at Javier's temple reflected under the bright light. An inch under six feet, Javier looked small next to the taller fire chief.

Javier had an object in his gloved hand, and Emily thought they were having a heated discussion about it.

"Javi . . ."

"Emily. How's Brian?"

She shook her head. "Too soon to tell. He's messed up. Doctors don't know yet."

"Should you be here? I mean, Lieutenant Hall gave me a heads-up, but do you think it's a good idea?"

"I have to, Javi."

"All right. I had to ask. Chief Cummins and I were trying to figure out what this is." Javier palmed a blackened scrap of plastic, wire, and circuit board.

"Where'd you find it?" Emily asked.

The fire chief spoke up. "Next to the burned SUV—where we think the secondary device was placed. To my eye, it looks like the guts of a cell phone."

"It's too big for a phone. Looks more like a timer—you know, like from a kitchen."

"It's a twelve-channel micro servo controller," Officer Milton said, peeking over Emily's shoulder.

"A twelve what?" Javier said.

"A servo controller, or what's left of one."

"Javi, this is Officer Milton, who's about to tell us what a servo-what-chamacallit is."

"Clay. Clay Milton, sir. The servo controller is the link between the servo motor and a high-level programmable logic controller. It adapts the original signal and forwards it to the motor."

"Okay, pretend I don't speak nerd," Emily said.

Milton flushed. "You need one of those to drive a motor, like a radio controlled car, or drone, or a robot. Did you find any other debris with this?"

The fire chief pointed to the curb, where the toasted SUV smoldered. Pressure from the hoses used to douse the flames pushed charred material to the gutter.

"Mind if I go look?" Milton asked.

Javier shrugged. "Why not?"

Milton pulled on a set of nitrile gloves and approached the collected debris in the gutter. Squatting over the small collection of burned bits, Milton gently separated the material with the tip of his pen.

"Detectives, I think I have something."

Emily and Javier joined the officer as he pointed his pen at a melted round plastic lump.

"What am I looking at?" Emily said.

"It's an—and there should be another—yes, here. Wheels. Rubber wheels. This was a radio-controlled vehicle, a car, or a robotics platform."

"You think this delivered a bomb?" Javier asked.

"Very possible. Likely, even. The servo could power the wheels, steering, a camera, and probably trigger a device."

"Someone drove this into our patrol vehicle and detonated it?"

"They'd be pretty close. The signal wouldn't have much range."

"I gotta ask. How do you know so much about this geeky stuff?"

Milton's face reddened again. "I teach robotics at Sunrise Charter High School on the weekends."

"Well, aren't you a regular Professor X," Javier said.

"Now whose geek flag is flying?" Emily said.

"There are a few pieces here, but the parts are basic and easily accessible at hobby stores or online," Milton said.

"Someone purposely targeted our responders with this device," Emily said, scanning the buildings in the area. Apartments, commercial buildings, and the device could've been triggered from any of them.

"Milton, I'm going to put you with our crime scene techs. Grab every single scrap of material from the device," Javier said.

"Yes, sir, on it."

Javier took a step back while the young cop went to work.

"Em, you doing okay?"

"No, I'm not—not even close. Our people are being targeted. How do you think I feel? Brian—" She started to choke up.

"From what I've heard here, Brian saved his partner. The initial blast would've killed the kid if he hadn't pushed him out of the way."

She nodded. "I know." She pointed to the black stain and broken glass at the front of the building. "That where it happened?"

"Yeah. The device was hidden in a donation bin by the front door."

Emily approached the spot, careful not to step on any broken glass or charred blast debris. Someone had turned the metal donation bin into an oversized pipe bomb. Thanks to the generosity of a parishioner, a pile of clothing, heavy winter jackets, and shoes had landed on top of the bomb. They didn't smother the blast, but the heavy material redirected it slightly.

Rather than the explosion coming directly out of the bin's door, the blast directed most of the force down and to the right, away from where Brian had tackled his partner.

It was still a deadly explosion, but it gave Brian a chance. A chance was all she needed right now.

She spotted a silver object in the debris by the front door. Emily sidestepped around a jagged metal shard with the words THANK YOU FOR YOUR DONATION stenciled on the surface.

Crouched over the silver item drawing her attention, Emily recognized it immediately. Her father had one like it. An inexpensive wristwatch. It was at least fifteen, maybe twenty years old. A thumb wiped off the black residue, revealing an inscription on the back of the case: NOVEMBER 2ND.

It wasn't Brian's. Maybe it belonged to Robinson, his partner. Still, she wondered why an older—almost vintage—watch bore a more recent inscription.

"Hey, Javi? Got an evidence bag on you?"

Javier strode over to her location. "What ya got?"

She dangled the watch by the band.

"Oh, you shouldn't have. And here I didn't get you anything."

"A bag, smart-ass."

Javier pulled a small brown paper evidence bag from his jacket pocket and handed it over.

Emily dropped the watch in the container. "The date November 2nd mean anything to you?"

Javier wrinkled his brow. "Nothing—was it the date you waited in line at a K-pop concert? I know it left you breathless."

"I'll K-pop you. Wait, you were the one who got tickets for the show."

"My date was way into the scene—which was one reason it was our one and only date."

"Yeah, I'm sure that was the reason. But this date on the watch—it doesn't ring any bell with you?"

"Nope, not one."

"Excuse me, Detectives," Officer Milton called out.

"Whatchagot?" Javier asked.

"It's a piece of circuit board. Got writing on it."

Emily and Javier returned to the curb where Officer Milton stood. He turned the fragment of green circuit board over in his hand. "Look, right there at the resistor."

"Like I know what a resistor is," Javier said.

"I see it. Numbers. They're really small. You have your flashlight, Officer?"

Milton clicked on his Maglite. "The numbers reflect the light."

Emily squinted and made out *11-2-* before it disappeared in a melted char. "Handwritten, for sure—some kind of reflective paint, maybe?"

"What does this mean?" Javier asked.

"You ever see anything written on these things before? You know, in your robotics classes, Milton?" Emily asked.

"No. You'd take a risk shorting out the board unless you know what you're doing."

Emily stared at the charred board. An edgy sensation crept up her spine. No. It couldn't be . . .

"Javi, the watch. This was the same date—or was before it got toasted. November 2nd. The officers in the unit this thing took out— who were they?"

Javier pulled out his notebook and flipped through pages. "Here it is. Simmons and Tucker."

Emily felt a chill. The bomb. There was a message here, but the targets were random. The first one—the bomb responsible for putting Brian and Robinson in the hospital—was it to lure Tucker responding? Or were the officers in the wrong place when the church was bombed? Was the watch significant, or simply more debris?

CHAPTER FOUR

EMILY LEFT OFFICER Milton to work with the crime scene technicians. She and Javier returned to the hospital where Officer Tucker and his partner, Simmons, were taken after the explosion.

While Javier drove, Emily scrolled through her phone at the photos of the police SUV. The damage from the blast wasn't as bad as she feared. Fire damage occurred after the explosion.

"Javier, did you talk with Tucker or Simmons before they went to the hospital?"

"Already gone by the time I arrived. Why?"

"The bomb. It looks like it took out the front of the unit. Driver's-side wheel and quarter panel. Front bumper and the engine compartment took most of the damage. If it had gone off under the fuel tank . . ."

"Would've been a much bigger bang."

"Does it mean our bomber couldn't see exactly what he was doing? Milton said the thing 'drove' under the SUV. Did he miss the target?"

"He didn't miss. Two of ours are in the hospital."

"Yeah, maybe you're right."

When they arrived at the hospital, the waiting room had thinned out somewhat. There were still eight uniformed officers clustered in one row of the waiting room. Enough of a presence to make a pair of blue-ball-cap-wearing Crip gang members make a turnabout after they'd entered the hospital.

Javier split off to the information desk, and Emily found Lieutenant Hall sitting with a tall Black man.

"Any news, Lieutenant?"

"Not yet. Last update I had was he was still in surgery."

Emily nodded.

"Emily, this is my husband, Mark."

Emily shook his hand.

"It's nice to finally meet you. Larry talks about you all the time," Mark said.

"I do not," Lieutenant Hall said.

"You do and now I know why. She is a force."

"Well, we are lucky to have your husband watching our back. He's one of the good ones, but we try not to let him know. It'll go to his head."

"Don't I know it," Mark said.

Emily knew Lieutenant Hall hadn't gotten to his position without some of the old guard in the department questioning his suitability for the job. After all, he was Black and gay—too much for some hard-liners—the same people who gave her grief for being a woman in a man's job. It wasn't an easy path to a command position for Hall. But from where Emily stood, the man did it with professional pride.

"Emily, what were you and Detective Medina able to find out from the scene?"

"Lieutenant, this one is worrisome."

Hall frowned. "You don't worry easily, Detective."

"This was an attack on our officers. Two explosive devices after a phony callout. They wanted to make sure they targeted first responders. The first one got Brian and Robinson. The second is even more concerning. We think it was driven under one of our units."

"Driven?"

"Like a radio-controlled car or something. It came for our officers."

"Are you serious?"

"Looks like it. Javi and I want to talk to Tucker and Simmons to figure out why someone would target them."

"Any leads on who's behind this?"

"Not so far. I haven't checked social media to see if someone is claiming credit for the attack. It was on the boundary of some gang territory, so that is going to be a consideration."

"Damn. I gotta brief the brass on this one. Make sure you keep me updated on this as you go—my feeling is it's going to be the only priority."

"You got it, Boss. Any word on Tucker and Simmons?"

"I heard a mention about orthopedics. Broken legs from the blast."

Javier joined Emily. "Hi, Boss. Emily get you up to speed on this one?"

"Detective, we need to get a solve on this quickly. If someone's targeting our people, we're one incident away from burning the city down. Tension is already tight between the department and the community. If we have an officer-involved shooting because they mistakenly thought they were being attacked . . ."

"Can you give us someone from the gang unit? They'll know the intel on who's who out there."

"I'll make a call."

"Thanks, Lieutenant."

"Detective Medina has the lead on this, Emily. If you need to take a couple of days to—"

"Not necessary, sir. We'll get it done." Emily couldn't afford to look weak by taking time off because of Brian's injuries. Some of the old-school knuckle draggers would see a woman couldn't handle it when the job got personal.

Lieutenant Hall locked eyes with Emily. "Don't make me regret this, Detective."

Javier tugged on Emily's sleeve. "Let's go find our guys and see if they know why they were singled out."

The orthopedic unit was more crowded than Emily expected on a weekday night.

Reese Tucker and Marlon Simmons were in rooms next to one another in the back of the unit. Emily spotted the uniformed officer posted in the hallway, probably assigned there by the watch commander.

Emily recognized the officer from a crime scene but couldn't recall his name until she got close enough to read his name tag.

"Prescott, how are our boys doing?"

"They got messed up pretty bad. A bomb? That's what these gangs are doin' now? Time for payback."

Emily knew the emotions were going to be running hot.

"We need to find out who's behind this first."

"It's obvious. I'm no detective and all, but this was right on the doorstep of UBN territory."

Emily knew UBN, or the United Blood Network, was a loose alliance of street gangs. They weren't much of a presence in the North Sacramento area. But the Tru Heights Bloods were.

"It's too early to tell who called the shots on this one," Emily said.

"We need to roll up on every single one of them and bust some heads until we get some answers," Prescott said.

Emily ignored the bravado. From experience, she knew officers like Prescott were all bark and no bite—but the line of thinking was infectious. She and Javier needed to find out who was behind the attack before it got out of control.

"Which room is Tucker in?"

Prescott jutted his jaw at the farthest room.

Emily followed Javier into the small treatment room. It was crowded with a doctor, two nurses, Tucker, and a worried woman.

Tucker sprawled back on a bed. Two of the medical staff were finishing up plaster casts on his lower legs.

"How's he doing?" Emily asked.

The woman at his bedside was the first to speak. "He was in a lot of pain. The drugs are starting to work now. Are you the detectives assigned to find out what happened?"

"We are. I'm Detective Medina, and this is Detective Hunter. Are you his . . ."

"Wife. Theresa Tucker. The doctor let me come in while they got him settled."

"Did your husband say anything about what happened?"

"No, not really. He was kind of out of it, maybe in shock. He was babbling about how sorry he was I had to see this. Sorry he let me down. He's never let me down—ever."

Emily took stock of the fresh plaster casts on Tucker's legs. He was lucky. If the bomb came to rest directly under him, or under the fuel tank, it could've been much worse.

"Mrs. Tucker, did your husband ever mention anyone in particular who would do something like this to him?" Emily asked.

She scrunched up her nose. "He didn't talk about the job much. Said he didn't want to bring it home to us—me and our daughter. But someone in particular? No, he's never said anything."

Tucker roused and tipped his head up, which seemed to take all the strength he had.

"Hey, Detectives. Find out what happened?"

"We were hoping you could fill in the blanks for us," Emily said.

"Afraid I got a lotta blanks there too. After the explosion by the church—hey, wait. The sergeant. How is he?"

Emily swallowed hard. "He's still in surgery."

"We were about to clear the location. Someone called in a fake report. Then the explosion by the church. I pulled my unit to the curb—it's the last thing I remember until I woke up in the ambulance. Simmons was in there with me. I think he's okay."

"I'm fine. Maybe next time try not to run over a land mine," Officer Simmons called out from the room next door.

"Is that what happened? Did I trigger another bomb?"

"It doesn't look like it," Javier said. "The bomb was placed under your unit after you parked."

"No shit?"

"That's what we've got. It's like it was designed to hit responding officers."

"Damn. I mean I heard of it when I was doing SWAT training. But to see it actually happen. That's a game changer," Tucker said.

"You know anyone who might be capable of this? Receive any threats recently?" Emily asked.

"Detective, I've been on the job for ten years. Everyone's capable of pulling off a hit on a cop. It's only common sense and fear keeping them from trying. I guess the fear is wearing off. As for threats—every damn day."

"Nothing directly warning of an attack like this?"

"No, but in my patrol district, you got a large portion who don't want us there, want us defunded or abolished. Could have been any of them."

Emily glanced at Javier, who nodded. He knew what she wanted to ask.

"We found unusual stuff in the bomb debris, one with a date on it," she said.

Tucker stared at Emily.

"What date?"

"November the 2nd. We were hoping you could tell us if it means anything."

Tucker leaned back in his hospital bed. Emily's news of the cryptically addressed device was clearly jarring.

"I got no idea. I mean, sure, I've made people angry. Arrested suspects who claimed they were innocent and would promise to get even. It was always idle talk."

"Looks like they're done talking now."

Tucker closed his eyes. "The date. What year? I've been on the job a while. Why?"

"Wondered if it meant anything."

"Sorry. Nothing clicks."

"If you think of anything, let us know," Javier said.

Tucker nodded, and he slid his glance to his wife.

Emily understood. "We'll contact the watch commander to have someone watch you and the family."

"Thank you, Detective."

His wife grew quiet. There was much about the real world her husband kept from her.

A nurse knocked on the doorframe. "Excuse me, is one of you Detective Hunter?"

Emily turned and regarded the thin, scrub-wearing woman. She wore a hairnet and booties. "That's me." She recognized the surgical garb. Brian . . .

"Detective, the doctor wanted me to let you know Mr. Conner is out of surgery and is in recovery."

Emily let out a breath she wasn't even aware she was holding in.

"But there was a complication . . ."

CHAPTER FIVE

EVERY POSSIBLE NEGATIVE outcome swirled through Emily's mind as they made their way into the recovery room. She knew it must be bad because they never let anyone come into recovery.

"Doctor, Miss Hunter is here about Mr. Conner," the nurse said before she disappeared.

The doctor was a woman dressed in surgical scrubs looking at a monitor and an image that, to Emily's eye, looked like abstract art. Without turning around, the doctor called out, "Miss Hunter, come here. I want to show you what I'm looking at."

Emily approached the monitor. The doctor was five inches shorter than she was, with dark chestnut hair pulled back and deep brown eyes. A sense of exhaustion hung over her like a shroud.

Emily swallowed. "What can you tell me? I don't know what I'm looking at."

The doctor turned to face Emily and leaned slightly on the counter. She cast her eyes on the detective for a moment, as if she was assessing how carefully she had to tread.

"The patient—"

"Brian. His name's Brian."

"I understand. Brian suffered a series of traumatic events, any one of which could have proved fatal. A lacerated kidney, ruptured spleen, bruised heart, a collapsed lung we didn't even know about until we got in there. He lost a great deal of blood. He received a transfusion because he was bleeding out internally.

"I removed his spleen. The kidney was damaged beyond repair, so it was removed as well. He tolerated the surgeries like a trooper. I'm impressed, actually."

"Then what's the problem? I heard there were complications," Emily said.

"Here on this image. The patient—Brian—is experiencing edema, swelling, in his brain."

"I heard it was an issue."

"It's getting worse, and if it continues at this rate it is life threatening. He'll begin to suffer irreversible organ failure."

"What can you do?"

"I need your permission to perform a craniotomy. I need to open his skull to relieve the pressure."

"Why do you need my permission? Just do it."

"The advance directive Brian prepared didn't want extraordinary measures taken to continue his life in the event something catastrophic occurred. That is what we are talking about here."

"You can't do anything?"

"There is a provision in his advance directive allowing the person designated as his medical power of attorney to make the decision."

"Then do it."

"I want you to understand, by doing this you are possibly going against his wishes. The procedure to relieve the pressure on his brain comes with risk."

"You're telling me if you don't do this, he'll die?"

"It's very likely if we can't control the pressure."

"Do it," Emily said. She'd deal with any fallout from Brian after the surgery. She'd be happy to have him around to be angry at her.

"Good. I hoped you'd agree because, frankly, I didn't want my good work patching up the rest of him to go to waste."

"When can you do it?"

"I'll get him in right now—a few minutes to prep him, but this one shouldn't take long. I'll be assisting on this one while the neurosurgeon performs the craniotomy."

"Thank you, Dr. . . . I didn't get your name."

"Duffy, Hannah Duffy."

"Thanks, Dr. Duffy."

The doctor swept out of the hallway and slipped away to prep Brian for another surgery. The nibbling of self-doubt started creeping up her spine. Did she make the right decision? What if she was responsible for—

Emily didn't finish the thought because a hospital employee shoved a clipboard at her.

"You need to sign these." The short woman in a flower-print smock had reading glasses dangling from a gold chain around her neck. A hospital ID said Bonnie worked as a patient liaison.

"What are they?"

"Consent forms. You are Brian Conner's next of kin, aren't you?" The statement came across haughty and impatient from someone supposed to work with patient families.

"I am. Is this for the procedure Dr. Duffy told me about?"

Bonnie turned the clipboard toward her and glanced down. "Yeah. Dr. Duffy. You need to sign these."

Bonnie shoved the clipboard at Emily again. She tapped a pen on the bottom of the page. "Here."

Emily took the pen and signed. Bonnie flipped the page. "Here too." Emily scribbled three more times until Bonnie was satisfied. With the liaisoning finished, Bonnie plodded away, no doubt to bring more sunshine to other worried families.

In the surgery waiting room, Javier pointed out the television mounted high on the wall. A local news reporter was telling viewers about a breaking news story.

The television switched to an on-scene reporter and Emily recognized the location as the church where the bombing attacks occurred. From outside the yellow tape barrier, the television camera focused on the damage to the black-and-white police SUV and the church door.

A young, thin man held a finger against his earpiece, listening to the handoff from the studio.

"Thank you, Andrea. We're here live at the scene where sources report an explosion damaged a local church. Police officers responding to the location were caught up in the blast. At least four officers were transported to local area hospitals."

The camera pivoted to the right, bringing two men into the frame.

"We have a witness to the explosion. Tell the viewers exactly what you saw."

The tall, lanky Black man jutted his chin to the smoldering police unit. He wore a red bandanna, a red puffy jacket, and a black T-shirt with an image of hands in chains. "The po-lice rolled up like they do in our neighborhood and this is what happens. We don't need them here. Every time they come here, one of ours dies. This time, it was their turn."

"Are you suggesting the police officers were deliberately attacked?"

"I hope they take it as a warning. We don't need them and don't want them in our community. We'll take care of our own. Stay the hell away from us."

Emily elbowed Javier. "Are you getting this? We need to ID this guy."

"Shouldn't be too hard to run down. He's wearing gang colors in Tru Heights territory. Don't see them acting as community spokespersons though. The gang unit might have this guy on their radar. I'll give them a call."

The camera panned over to another man standing next to the gang-banger who was now throwing gang hand signs to the camera.

"Councilman Davis, what can you tell us about this incident?"

Rob Davis was a city council member and wasn't a friend to the police department. Any chance he had to vote against a budget request, or policy change, Davis was the first in line. He was also tight with the director of the Office of Public Safety Accountability. The office was previously the Office of Police Accountability until Davis and others made allegations that the fire department responded slower to incidents in neighborhoods with predominantly Black and Brown residents.

"Oh, this ought to be rich," Emily said.

Councilman Davis cleared his throat and wrestled the microphone from the reporter.

"Tonight's incident is a result of the city's policing policies. Look at how they came in numbers to invade this community. They claim it was in response to a call about rioting and looting. Do you see any evidence of rioting? No, and neither did they. A quick drive-by would have confirmed as much. Yet they show up armed to the teeth and threaten this community while they sleep in their beds. I'm not surprised it came to this."

"Councilman, are you justifying this attack on police officers?"

Emily leaned toward Javier. "I like this kid. He's not gonna let Davis skate on this."

The politician looked squarely at the camera. "When you push a community to the breaking point, they are going to fight back. At least this time, no innocent civilians were harmed."

"You motherfucker," Emily said. "It isn't even his district."

The reporter wrestled the microphone back and addressed the camera. "There doesn't appear to be any answer to who is behind the bombings here in North Sacramento. Tempers are soaring and rhetoric isn't going to help find out who placed those devices. Not since Ted Kaczynski, the Unabomber, has the city faced targeted attacks. Kaczynski, as you might recall, was strong on rhetoric too. From North Sacramento, Mark Walker reporting."

"I like that kid," Javier said.

"He handled Davis like a pro. The Unabomber thing . . . you think we have another serial bomber on our hands?"

"Don't know what to think yet. I'd like to know why someone went after us," Javier said.

"Right? It seems random. As much as I hate to give the councilman any credence, we gotta make sure there wasn't a targeted hit on any specific officer in retaliation. Means we'll need to dive into personnel files. Complaints, misconduct allegations, you know . . ."

"Won't be popular with the union. Going after a victim looking for dirt," Javier said.

"Which is why I'm glad you're the lead on this case, Detective Medina."

"You're an evil woman, Hunter."

"It serves me well. I'm gonna camp out here until I hear word about

Brian. Why don't you go home and rest. I'll let you know when I have an update."

"You want me to bring you anything? You need me here with you? I don't mind."

"I know you don't, Javi." She gave him a hug. "Go on. I'll be fine."

Javier reluctantly agreed and headed out. Emily found a spot on a sofa and waited. The silence closed in, and the doubt circled back. Had she done the right thing, going against Brian's wishes?

CHAPTER SIX

TWO HOURS FELT like ten. Emily couldn't doze off on the stiff waiting room sofa because she was afraid she'd miss an update on Brian's surgery. Or, if she was asleep, somehow the procedure wouldn't go right. She knew it was foolish to think she had any sway over what happened in the operating room, but for a woman who needed to be in control, this wait was excruciating.

Every time the door to the surgery wing opened, Emily searched for answers. The faces, tight expressions or downcast eyes—she guessed the nature of the messages delivered to those who waited.

She shifted her position on the sofa so she could watch the door. When Dr. Duffy pushed through the doors to the waiting room, her tired eyes searched until she landed on Emily.

She strode over and Emily stood, a hitch in her breath. Waiting.

Dr. Duffy didn't waste any time. "The procedure went well. The edema isn't increasing. He's responding and the fluid is draining."

"Is he conscious?"

"Not yet. It may take some time. And we won't know if there is any long-term damage from the intracranial pressure he experienced. I'm hopeful, and I'm glad we performed this when we did. It saved him immediate organ system failure."

"When can I see him?"

"He's in recovery now. I want to make sure he's stable before we move him to ICU. The next twenty-four hours will be important. It won't be easy, Miss Hunter. Brian has a long recovery ahead. I hope he's a fighter."

Emily nodded and bit her lower lip. "Can I see him?"

"I wouldn't advise it. He's getting the best possible care right now. We installed a drain tube to prevent the fluid from building up. He's still comatose."

"I understand. I need to see him."

Dr. Duffy paused and looked Emily in the eye. "All right. Come with me."

Emily followed the doctor through a series of hallways until they arrived at a door marked RECOVERY.

Dr. Duffy handed Emily a set of surgical scrubs and a mask. "Put these on. We can't risk any contamination. And you smell like smoke."

Emily didn't know she'd picked up debris at the crime scene. She quickly donned the scrubs and mask and followed the doctor inside.

She spotted him immediately. Brian was in an isolated, glass-enclosed space, which she supposed was to keep contaminates from the open wound she imagined in his skull.

She drew close to the glass, surprised only a small drain tube protruded from the back of Brian's head. It was the tube down his throat and the hiss of the respirator taking her attention.

"Can't he breathe on his own?"

"We're giving him a little help. He won't work as hard while he's recovering from his surgeries."

"When will he wake up?"

"It's entirely up to him."

"Can I go in with him?"

Dr. Duffy nodded and pushed the partition aside.

Emily eased to his bedside and found a patch of skin on his arm that wasn't bruised, broken, or poked with IV lines. He looked gray and fragile, and she was afraid her touch would hurt him.

She leaned close to his ear and whispered. "I'm here. I want you to fight, dammit. Come home to me."

She swore the muscle on his arm twitched.

"Can he hear me?"

"I think he does," Dr. Duffy said.

She turned back to Brian and leaned close. "I will find whoever did this. I promise you."

Dr. Duffy tapped Emily on the shoulder. "We should let him rest now."

They left the glass-enclosed room and Emily discarded the scrubs in a hamper by the door.

"What happens now?"

"It's going to take time. After everything his body has endured, there will be rehab and he'll need time to heal."

"Will he be able to go back to work?" Emily knew how much being a cop meant to him. If this injury was life and career threatening, it would be hard on him. He wasn't the kind of man to sit around and watch the world go by.

"Honestly, I don't know. He might, but it's going to be up to him to do the mental work and therapy to get there."

"Mental work?"

"He has a TBI. We won't know the extent until he's out of his coma and able to work with our therapists. He might not be the man you knew. Now, the best thing you can do for him is to go home. You need to rest. We have your contact information. The moment anything changes, we'll call."

Emily knew the doctor was right. She was running on adrenaline and caffeine fumes and due to crash any minute.

After leaving recovery, Emily wandered out to the waiting room. The uniformed officers had disappeared, but Lieutenant Hall remained behind. He spotted Emily and stood. She could tell he was trying to read her emotions.

She came to Hall and surprised him with a hug. "Thank you for being here."

After Emily gave him an update on Brian's condition, the lieutenant gave her a hug in return.

"Let's get you home."

"I need—"

"You're going home, and that's that. End of discussion, Detective."

Lieutenant Hall drove her home and avoided conversation about Brian or the investigation. She tried to talk about Councilman Davis and his attack on the department. He deflected it with "Haters gonna hate."

He pulled to the curb at her home and grabbed her arm before she got out. "He's going to be okay, Emily. You need to be there for him and you need to make sure you take care of yourself too."

"Part of it means getting the bastards who did this."

"It means being smart about it and not reacting to all the Councilman Davis types. We do our job and find out who's behind the attack on our people. Check in with me tomorrow. You decide where you need to be. If your head is with Brian, fine. Be there. But if you're up to it, Detective Medina will need all the help we can give him."

Emily agreed and Hall waited until she unlocked her front door before he pulled away.

A weight pushed against the door as she tried to pull it closed behind her.

A moment of panic surged through her until she recognized the yellow eyes staring back at her.

"You," Emily said, closing the door after the black cat pushed her way inside.

"Why, yes, please come in."

Without a pause in her step, the cat trotted to the kitchen and pawed at a cabinet. The cat was a regular visitor going on two years. An older woman on the next block had given up trying to keep the feline confined to a single domicile.

Emily tossed her keys on a side table and joined the impatient trespasser.

"You don't live here. Does Mrs. Rose know you got out again?"

The cat's wide, yellow eyes looked back at Emily.

"Fine."

Emily opened the cabinet and pulled out a ceramic food dish and poured a cup of dry food from a bag tucked under the counter.

The cat crunched and purred at the same time.

Emily retreated to her bedroom and took off her work clothes. She noticed a bit of a smokey chain-smoker tinge emanating from them as she tossed them in the laundry bin. Same as Officer Milton.

A quick rinse and a fresh change of clothes into a comfy pair of gray sweats and a worn T-shirt from a local band that didn't exist anymore.

She couldn't erase the vision of Brian from her head, with the wires and tubes connected to his broken body. Then there were the injuries she couldn't see. The traumatic brain injury and edema.

Emily fell into her living room sofa and took in the quiet. She'd always enjoyed winding down after a long day and could usually disconnect from the job. This time, the connection wouldn't release. This time, it was personal.

After a fitful few hours of trying to sleep, Emily gave up and threw on her running shoes. She had at least half an hour of predawn light to put in a few miles.

The cat met her at the front door and slipped out when Emily opened it. It shuffled off down the sidewalk, looking for the next house to invade. Where had the cat been all night? One look at the black hair clinging to her leggings gave her the answer.

Her neighborhood was still. A few wispy, orange-tinted clouds hung over the Sierra Nevada range to the east. Emily plodded off and kept to the sidewalk. Usually, a brisk morning run would center and calm her. This morning, with City Councilman Davis's anti-police rhetoric echoing in her head, she grew angry.

How could he blame Brian and the other injured officers for this attack? She picked up her pace, and by the time she made her three-mile loop, one thing Councilman Davis said stuck in her mind. "When you push a community to the breaking point, they are going to fight back."

What happened to the neighborhood?

She reached her front porch as the morning newspaper plopped on the wet lawn behind her.

Emily reached and shook the water from the ever-shrinking daily paper. The headline was lifted from the councilman's interview. "Police Bring Chaos to Community."

Emily tossed the paper on the front porch. She didn't need to read the article. Davis's posturing photo on the front page was all she needed to see.

Inside, Emily snagged her cell phone, figuring Javier would be up by now.

He answered on the second ring. "Emily, everything okay? Brian?"

"Everything's fine. Just peachy. Brian needed more surgery, and he's still in a coma. The doctors say it's up to him now. I hate this wait-and-see game." She shook her head, trying to chase the image out of her mind. "Hey, I called you to see what you thought about what Councilman Davis said last night."

"Lots of thoughts, but none I can share in polite company."

"Is there anything we know about the neighborhood and police activity? Anything our injured officers were involved with?"

"I haven't looked yet. I mean, we're called out for gang activity, drive-bys, and the usual. Tucker, Simmons, and Brian's interactions there—I don't know."

"I'll come in and start pulling it together. Unless you want me out canvassing the neighborhood to see if anyone is willing to say they saw something."

"I don't know if the neighbors are ready for you on their doorstep. An f-bomb in the morning doesn't sit well with your first cup of coffee."

"I promise to be on my best behavior, Javi."

"That's what worries me."

"The lieutenant said you'd need all the help you can get."

"What did the lieutenant say?"

"Don't let your paranoia wrap around the axle here. It's a big case with big complications. It's going to be an all-hands-on-deck kinda deal."

She heard him pause for a moment. Background noise pegged him sitting at his desk in the detective bureau.

"Are you already in the office? Did you get any sleep last night?"

"Did you? Never mind. When can you be here? The chief has a briefing set in an hour. You should be here if you can."

"I'll get cleaned up and be right there."

"I appreciate it—the cleaned-up part."

"Ass. It's for the chief, not you." She disconnected the call.

CHAPTER SEVEN

EMILY ENTERED THE detective bureau forty minutes after she'd hung up with her partner.

She found Javier hunched over his desk sorting through a stack of documents. He glanced up and a shadow of relief coursed through his eyes.

"What you need me to take on?" she asked.

He pushed back from the desk. "Need coffee? Of course you do. Come with me."

"What's up, Javi?" she asked when they rounded the corner out of the detective bureau.

"Something's not adding up here. I got the crime report data for the last year. The reported crime numbers are down and so are the number of reports we submitted. If the councilman is claiming the police are invading the community, wouldn't you expect those numbers to be higher?"

"I'm following. I sense you found more."

"The number of incidents is down, but the citizen complaints are up—way up. In a way that doesn't seem to correlate to the crime in the area."

Emily leaned over the counter and poured a paper cup full of dark coffee for each of them.

"Anyone can file a citizen's complaint about anything. You know that. How do those complaints break down?"

"I hadn't gotten that far yet. There were a little over seven hundred complaints filed. About two hundred sustained—mostly discourtesy, unlawful search, and neglect of duty."

"Doesn't sound like Davis's armed band of killer cops tearing the neighborhood apart. He said, 'You push a community to the breaking point, they're going to fight back.' Anything there about use of force, shooting reviews, or something that would make people think they needed to fight back?"

"Not yet."

Lieutenant Hall strode into the break room with his empty coffee mug. "I didn't see you come in, Emily. You here or just dropping by?"

"I owed you a call, Lieutenant. Thought in person would be best."

He nodded. "Good, good. If anything changes and you need to be away for a while, let me know. No problem."

"Thanks, LT."

Hall dribbled the last of the coffee into his mug and winced at the bitter taste. "Both of you, let's go. The chief wants his briefing."

Javier gathered a stack of files from his desk, handed one to the lieutenant and one to Emily. When Emily cracked hers open, the crime scene photos were clipped to the reports.

Although she'd been there, seeing them in stark relief in her hand felt otherworldly and cold. A chill ran through her when she flipped to the photo where Brian had fallen.

"Em, you coming?" Javier said.

She closed the file and joined Javier and Lieutenant Hall outside of the detective bureau.

"Anything new I need to know?" Hall asked as they made their way to the chief's conference room.

"Nothing," Javier said.

The chief's secretary, Sandy, wasn't her usual chipper, friendly self when the detectives entered the outer office. "Briefing in the conference room. He's already there."

Hall glanced at his watch, confirming they weren't late for the meeting.

The conference room was half filled when they entered. Chief Thomas Clark sat at one end of the long table. Clark was a tall, thin man who looked like he'd fallen off the cover of a western novel. Weathered face, piercing blue eyes, and a take-no-bullshit personality. Emily found him to be an outstanding leader and a cop's cop, having spent thirty years on the job. Above all, he protected his people. The look on his face, if Emily had to label it, was fury.

Next to Chief Clark was the deputy chief, Jillian Swanson, and Captain Billings, less than a month into the job.

Two faces Emily didn't recognize were a man and a woman in dark business suits. The Black woman had her hair pulled back and bore an intense expression. Her male counterpart leaned casually in his chair, his expensively razor-cut hair falling into place when he shook his head at something the chief said.

The pair exuded fed. Smug attitude.

"Detectives, meet Special Agents Collin and Burley, from Alcohol, Tobacco, Firearms, and Explosives," Chief Clark said.

Emily, Javier, and Lieutenant Hall took empty chairs opposite the ATF agents.

"They were telling me we have nothing to worry about," Clark said through a tight jaw.

Man Fed, as Emily thought of him, casually swiveled his chair slightly so he could make sure the new arrivals could listen to him. "We believe this is a one-off. A second event isn't expected."

"Event?" Emily stiffened. "This was an attack on our officers. It was purposeful and deliberate."

"We don't see it. No group or known domestic terror organization has claimed responsibility. The device was crude and the suspect was lucky it even went off."

"Tell the four officers in the hospital they were lucky," Emily said.

Man Fed glanced at his buffed nails. "Listen, we're here because your mayor's office was concerned about a serial bomber loose in the city. Yes, it's regrettable officers were injured. Perhaps they could have been more careful—"

"You're blaming them?" Emily said.

"With more training, they'd be able to recognize threats in the field." Emily shook her head.

"Evidence says the secondary blast was designed to take out responding officers. We're looking into why they might be our bomber's focus," Hall said.

"Which officers were targeted with the secondary?" Chief Clark asked.

"Tucker and Simmons, sir," Hall replied.

"Tucker's a good cop. Simmons too. Both on the job over ten years. Know their way around the community. I can't think why anyone would go after them. Are they out of the hospital?"

"Tucker broke both legs. He should be discharged today. Simmons was released an hour or so ago," Javier said.

"There you have it. Sounds more like the church was the target and your officers got in the line of fire. There's no reason to expect another event," the ATF agent said.

"I'm supposed to take you at your word?" Chief Clark said.

"It's not my word. Listen, serial bombers have an agenda. They want people to know they're responsible for the damage they inflict. In this instance, no one is claiming the bomb, there's been no posting of any manifesto, and the devices were small and caused only minor injuries."

"Minor injuries? I have a sergeant in intensive care after brain surgery. You call that a minor injury?"

The fed started to speak.

"Don't you dare mutter the words *collateral damage*. My sergeant wasn't put in the hospital by mistake. Our officers were lured there and attacked," Chief Clark said.

"I'm sorry. What Agent Collin meant to say was the device was smaller—smaller in scale to what we've seen in cases like Oklahoma City, the Boston Marathon, or the first World Trade Center attacks. They were clearly designed to maximize damage and casualties. This device was more focused. They had a specific target in mind."

Emily had to admit she had a point. An unsettled feeling tightened her chest.

"How do you know there was only one target?" Emily asked.

The woman shifted in her seat. "There's no way to be absolutely certain. In other cases where a serial bomber was at work, they leave a message or an indication another attack was pending. You don't have that, do you?"

Emily shook her head, but the November date inscribed on the back of the watch niggled at the base of her brain.

"We could bring an ATF team in and—"

"Thanks, but I think we have the resources we need to run this down," Chief Clark said.

The chief stood, signaling the meeting was over. To his staff, he said, "Find the person responsible for this." The message was clear. This was a city matter and the federal agencies weren't invited.

As everyone filed out of the office, the chief paused. "Hunter, my office."

"Yes, sir."

"What did you do now?" Javier said.

"Probably wants me to tell him about why you're not one of the city's most eligible bachelors anymore." Emily relished the opportunity to remind Javier his reporter ex-girlfriend placed him on the annual list and summarily pulled him when their relationship ended.

"The reporter was biased."

"Or . . . she came to her senses."

Emily followed the chief and stopped outside his office door. He lowered his voice. "Emily, how's Sergeant Conner? Any update?"

"He's still unresponsive. The doctors were able to repair the physical damage—spleen, kidney, broken arm—it's the brain swelling that has them concerned. They had to open up a hole in his skull to relieve the pressure."

"What are they saying about his prognosis?"

"They aren't saying anything. It's up to Brian."

"I'm sorry to hear it, Emily. He have any family I can reach out to?"

"No, we are his family."

"If he needs anything, I want you to tell me."

"Thank you, Chief."

"Don't thank me yet. You're not going to like this," he said as he pushed into his office.

Emily stopped short when she saw another person in the office.

Councilman Davis.

CHAPTER EIGHT

THE COUNCILMAN STOOD when Emily and the chief entered.

The chief gestured to the chairs opposite his desk and Emily dropped into one, surprised Davis would dare venture into what he considered enemy territory.

"Councilman, I caught your statement on last night's news. Can't say I appreciated the unprovoked attack on the department," the chief said.

"Chief, I've not hidden anything from you. You know what my position is on over-policing the community. This is the price these bad policy decisions come with."

"Then why are you here?"

"Something has to change, Chief. We can't continue the level of violence—"

"On that, we agree, but I think you suffer from a misconception on where this violence is coming from. Take last night, for example. We respond to a call for service from Del Paso Heights. We arrive only to find the call was bogus, but our officers were lured there so they could be attacked."

"In response for years of oppression. It was only a matter of time until this powder keg exploded. Your officers are like an invading force coming into my community. Body armor, guns, pepper spray—my people are only protecting themselves. The police bring crime, guns, and violence into these marginalized neighborhoods."

Emily couldn't sit still and listen to Davis any longer. "Your people, Councilman? You don't represent that district. Why were you even there last night?"

Davis locked eyes with Emily. "I represent the people of this city. I—"

"No, you don't. You were elected by the voters of your district—a district on the other side of the city. My question stands. What were you doing there at my crime scene last night, and how did you know about the attack?"

The chief's brow furrowed, and he nodded subtly, recognizing where Emily was going.

"My responsibility is to this city. We see evidence of police overreach everywhere. Last night is the most recent example."

"How did you even know this occurred?"

"I received a call from a constituent."

"This constituent give a name?"

"He didn't. They said an act of reprisal took place."

"Reprisal? For what, specifically?"

"Listen, Detective, I didn't sit there and interrogate my caller. They said it was reprisal and hung up. It doesn't take too much imagination to figure out why. You need to look at what your officers are doing."

"This call—did it come in on your city-issued cell phone, by chance?"

Davis paused. "Why?"

"Because I'd like to know how the caller knew about the bombing attack."

"They probably witnessed it."

"All the more reason I'd like to talk to them. Did they say they saw what happened out there?"

"I will not allow you to harass good citizens of this city. They saw what they saw and called me."

"When?"

"Excuse me?"

"When did they call you?"

"I don't remember. Around eleven, I suppose."

"How long after the call did you arrive at the church in Del Paso?"

"I didn't time myself. Maybe thirty to forty minutes."

"I caught your news briefing while I was at the hospital with our injured officers—it was, what, eleven thirty?"

"Your point, Detective?"

"My point is you got a call before the bomb went off. And you got it in time to make sure you could put your mug on the evening news."

"Are you saying I had something to do with this?"

"Did you?"

"This is outrageous. You accuse a public official because you are out of touch with the people who live in this city."

"I didn't accuse you of anything, Councilman. You have to admit, the timing of the call, if there was one, and you showing up to grandstand at the scene is suspicious. If I didn't know better, I'd say you were played."

The silence from Davis meant he hadn't considered the call as a ploy to draw him to the crime scene.

"No one plays me, Detective. Watch yourself. The current mayor might support the police industrial complex this city has allowed to fester in our neighborhoods. There's an election looming ahead and there are changes in the wind."

"I think you overestimate our reach in this city," the chief said.

Davis stood, buttoned his jacket, and tugged on the hem. "I came here today to put you on notice to get your house in order, Chief. Last night's events are likely to reoccur as long as your policies restrict the basic freedoms of our people. They've had enough."

"That sounds like a veiled threat, Councilman," the chief said.

"Not a threat. Call it a premonition."

The councilman turned on his heel and left the chief's office. Chief Clark leaned back in his desk chair. A slight twitch in his upper lip gave away his distrust of the politician.

"Emily, tell me what you're thinking."

"That man is being played and he won't even let himself see it. His hard-line anti-cop sentiment is hardly a secret. What a 'tool,' pun intended, to spew his hate."

"He's not taken too seriously in city hall, but he's loud and gets his face on television enough to make some believe his line of bullcrap."

"I want to pull his phone records for the call he claims he got. The call came before our people responded."

"Which means the person who planted the bombs might be our caller."

Emily nodded. "Or there was no caller and he knew the bombs were there."

"You're going to have to be careful here, Emily. You've gone after political types before—you know the undertow is pretty nasty."

"I'm aware. I'll be on my best behavior."

"That should scare me," the chief said with a laugh.

Emily grinned. "What?" She rose from the chair. "I'm going to ask for a warrant for the phone records even though it was a city phone. He's got no right to a privacy claim on a city phone. I anticipate the good councilman will object to our request to hand it over because of some invasion of privacy argument. Still, I want to cover all the bases on this one."

"What do you make of our ATF friends thinking this was a one-off?"

"I'd like to believe it. But this feels more developed, more focused than a one-off church bombing."

"No one has claimed responsibility," the chief said.

"No . . . Chief, does November 2nd mean anything to you?"

"Not offhand. Should it?"

She explained finding the cheap wristwatch at the church bombing. "I don't know if it was something dropped in the donation box, or if it means anything."

"That's a couple of months from now," the chief said.

Emily bit her lower lip. "It's an old watch. I'm not getting a forecasting vibe from this."

The chief settled in his chair. "I think you caught the vibe from the councilman. He's not going to back off his position that we're at fault here."

"I should take a run at citizen complaints, any progressive discipline, that sort of thing. I want to head off the councilman's argument that we brought this on. I know the sergeant, but the others by reputation only."

"Careful, if you go there. We don't need the rank and file thinking we're making this investigation about our people."

"Something the councilman said. Reprisal. If the caller did say it, I want to find out what it's about. I have a plan—it's a bit unorthodox."

"Of course it is."

"Trust me, Chief."

"Always do, Detective. Always do."

CHAPTER NINE

JAVIER WAITED IN the hallway outside of the chief's office. When Emily emerged, he pushed off the wall. Although he tried to hide it, she could tell Javier was worried about being excluded from the meeting.

"Javi, don't give it a second thought. The chief wanted to use me to rattle Davis, I think. It keeps you in the clear to interview him down the line, if we need to."

"I can't imagine why the chief would think you capable of such unprofessional conduct," Javier said with a smirk that brought out the dimple in his cheek.

"Ass." She smacked him on the shoulder.

She tipped her head down the hall toward the detective bureau.

As they made their way back to the office, Javier said, "The chief passed the case off to the feds, didn't he?"

"No, it's still ours. But I think the heat is on." Emily recounted the visit with Councilman Davis and the phone call he claimed he received in the moments before the bombing.

"You think he's targeting our cops? I mean, I wouldn't put it past him. It kind of lines up with his rhetoric."

"Maybe—or one of his followers who buys his anti-police sentiment. We need to run it down. There's something there. I can feel it. The way the councilman talked about reprisal. He made it sound personal, like he had an axe to grind," Emily said.

"I've never heard about any personal run-in—always seemed more of a move to pander to his base."

"Last night's attack wasn't even in his district. And there he was after getting a phone call before the first units responded."

"Who made the call?"

"We can track the number—probably an untraceable burner phone. But I know someone we can ask," she said.

As Emily parked the SUV, Javier caught the sign in the storefront window.

"Are you kidding me? Benjamin Tooker?"

"Tooker is connected with the community."

"Tooker's an ex-felon, remember? Did time at Pelican Bay."

"He also helped us figure out who was behind the murder of Roger Townsend."

"Who are you and what have you done with my partner?" Javier said, opening the passenger door.

The modest storefront sign proclaimed TOOKER INVESTIGATIONS. The building perched square in the middle of Oak Park, one of the oldest communities in the city—and predominantly African American. A score of gentrification efforts tried to redevelop the area, but the community fought off the "improvements," which were thinly veiled efforts to push out long-term residents in favor of new, more lucrative tenants.

"He's a PI now?"

"I don't know," Emily said. "Let's go ask." She pushed inside and found herself in a small waiting room. Four folding chairs lined one wall.

A shuffling sound preceded the scrape of a warped wooden door opening at the back of the waiting room. A thin, older Black woman clutched her handbag, and she shuffled out of the back room.

"Please find her," the older woman pleaded.

Barrel-chested Benjamin Tooker followed her and put a hand on her shoulder.

"I'll do what I can, Miss Tina."

"Thank you."

The older woman cast her eyes down and passed the detectives without a word.

Tooker looked the same as the last time Emily saw him. An imposing Black man, slightly over six feet tall, with a weight lifter's heavily muscled upper body. He'd managed to stay out of prison in a system designed to churn people back into the machine.

"Detectives, it's been a minute."

"It has, Mr. Tooker. Looks like you've been busy." She pointed to the sign in the window. "Tooker Investigations?"

"Yep. It's legitimate. I have my state license and everything."

"You're a licensed PI?" Javier said.

"I know what you're thinking. How could a Black ex-con be a private dick? I have a Certificate of Rehabilitation and the state board gave me their approval."

"No, it's cool and all. I didn't know it was possible," Javier said.

"They review cases like mine on a case-by-case basis. As long as I don't screw up, others like me might have an opportunity."

"What kind of cases do you take?" Emily asked. "The lady who was here a second ago, she mentioned something about 'finding her.'"

Tooker's expression darkened. "Miss Tina's granddaughter is missing. Mom's a drug addict and the girl, she's fifteen, and she's disappeared."

"She call and make a missing persons report?" Emily asked.

Tooker narrowed his eyes. "Ain't no one outside this community going to bust their ass to look for a missing Black girl. Come on, Detective, you know that."

"We can get her name, her photo out there . . ."

"You seen her photo in the newspaper, on television? Miss Tina has tried, but how do you think it feels when you're told your granddaughter isn't newsworthy?" Tooker said.

"Can you help her?"

"I—I hope so. A young girl—I'm worried. She's been gone for over a week. I know a few places to run down where she might hole up. A girl like her could find herself in trouble before she knows what happened."

"Anything we can do to help?" Javier asked.

Tooker handed both detectives a small black-and-white flyer with the girl's photo and basic information. Danika was a fresh-faced girl who looked older than her fifteen years. Something Emily knew could lead to trouble with certain elements in the city who preyed upon vulnerable girls. She was a sophomore at Grant Hight School and attended the Church of Salvation. The same church at the center of last night's bombing attack.

"If you happen to see her . . ."

"Got it. The church—the Church of Salvation. There was an incident there last night. You hear about it?" Emily said.

"Who hasn't?"

"What's the community saying about it?" Emily asked.

Tooker bit his lower lip and exhaled. "The community is tense waiting for the next bomb to drop—literally. They expect the police to come in and push us out like we're squatters in our own homes."

"They're expecting retaliation from us?" Emily asked.

"That's the way it usually happens."

"Who would want to go after police officers?"

"The question you should be asking is why someone would want to do this. The people living here, minding their own, see police and it's never a positive thing. Got me? You got cops up in here who go out of their way to fuck with people. When people get fed up and they snap, what do you think happens? I've seen that setup before," Tooker said.

"But to go to the extent of setting off an explosive?"

"Even those thugs in the Tru Heights know better. They know the payback would be off the chain. They can't risk the cops coming in and putting a kink in the supply chain, if you know what I mean."

"I think I do. Who would want to blow up a bunch of cops?" Javier asked.

"People here are upset, angry, and protest, demonstrate, and complain about over-policing. They don't lob bombs at them. This came from outside the community. Gonna build the wall even higher between the police and the people who live here."

"Any thought on who would want to put this neighborhood in the crosshairs?" Emily asked.

Tooker shook his head. "I don't know. The community leaders are talking about trying to keep the police out of the neighborhoods to avoid overheating the issue. They want to establish our own community safety patrols to deal with our issues—like a missing fifteen-year-old girl."

"That's not going to build trust."

"Did we ever have it? And no, the community safety patrols are a ridiculous idea. It'll give power to the wrong people and we'll be worse off than before. There's no simple answer, Detective."

"Thanks, I appreciate your time. Good luck on the PI business. I hope you find Danika," Emily said.

"Me, too, and soon."

As they left the office, another pair of older ladies entered, carrying a plate of freshly baked cookies.

"They know a way to a man's heart," Javier said.

"Speaking of heart, what's up with you and Jenny? Last I saw, things were getting pretty cozy."

"Jenny's great."

"Why do I hear a *but* coming?"

"She got a job offer and it's a good one. She should take it, but it means she'll move to Portland."

"Ouch."

"Yeah. I'm not thinking a long-distance thing will work. My hours, the demands of her new job. There won't be any free time available to make it work."

"Have you told her how you feel?"

"Use the 'F' word? Are you crazy?"

Emily shook her head at her partner. "You don't get it, do you?"

"Get what?"

"Maybe she's waiting to hear you tell her you want her to stay. Is there a future in this relationship?"

"Thanks, Dr. Phil, but I'm not going to ask her not to go and have her resent me for missing out on a big career opportunity."

"Might be you who'll be missing out," Emily said, as her cell phone chirped.

"Hunter here."

"Miss Hunter, it's Dr. Duffy from the Med Center."

"Doctor, is everything all right? Brian?" Emily's throat tightened.

"You should come—quickly."

CHAPTER TEN

THE HOSPITAL ELEVATOR car stopped at the floor and opened at a glacial pace. "Come on, come on, come on."

Getting to the hospital was a blur. Javier drove her and all she could think about was Brian and what if . . .

She sprung through the gap and hurried down the corridor to the room where she'd last seen Brian. She shouldn't have left.

She burst into the room. Brian wasn't there. The room was empty. Oh my God, she was too late. She needed to lean against the doorjamb to steady herself.

A rattle behind her didn't faze her. What happened? He was supposed to pull through.

"Excuse me," an orderly said from the hall. "I need to get past you."

Emily turned to leave the room when she saw Brian lying on the hospital bed the orderly pushed.

Relief swept through her when Brian's eyes cracked open. "Hey, you," he said in a gravelly voice. His brown hair was rumpled and the shaved patch on the back of his head made her wince.

"You're awake. When . . . ?" Relief swept through her. But she sensed there was more left unsaid.

"Not long," he said. His usual soothing voice was rough, pained.

Dr. Duffy swept into the room, focused on the clipboard in her hands.

"Doctor, what's happening? When you called, I thought—"

Dr. Duffy glanced up. "I'm going over the results here. We took Mr. Conner for a scan. He experienced a seizure. It's not uncommon in patients with a traumatic brain injury. It was a small focal seizure, and I needed a scan to look for any scarring or physical changes in his brain. I don't see anything here and that's a good sign."

"I don't remember having a seizure," Brian said as his bed was locked in place.

"Most don't. Yours was mild—you might have thought you were dizzy. You were waking up and your brain was working overtime to get the connections firing again."

"Will he have another one?" Emily asked. She stepped around the doctor to Brian's bedside and rested her hand, ever so gently, on his uninjured shoulder. Did he shudder when she touched him?

"One in five will experience another episode. Should it happen, it can be controlled with medication. I'm calling this a post-traumatic injury seizure. Not an epileptic event. If there's more than one incident, then we need to consider epilepsy."

"What happens now?" Emily asked.

"Mr. Conner has some rehab ahead and needs some time to heal from his injuries. He'll be with us for a few days. We'll start work with a rehab specialist today."

"So soon?" he asked.

"We've found the sooner we can get TBI patients up and engaged, in therapy and exercise, the outcomes are better."

"You think I'll be able to go back to work?"

The doctor paused, tucked the clipboard under her arm, and pursed her lips. "I don't see any reason you won't be able to do everything you did before—as long as you take the time to heal," she said. "The TBI is one thing, but you suffered other physical injuries, which will take time to mend. Don't minimize the potential for PTSD after what you've been through. It will take time."

Brian seemed to relax under the thin hospital blanket.

"All right, then. I'll let you two catch up. Oh, Mr. Conner, someone from physical therapy will be in to start working with you this afternoon."

Once the doctor left the room, Emily pulled a chair to his bedside. She caressed his cheek. "Dammit, you had me worried."

"I'm sorry. I knew something was off with the donation bin when Robinson opened it. The lock was cut."

"You remember?"

"Yeah, I guess that's good, right? I remember everything until the blast. I felt the heat and the pressure wave—then nothing."

"They told you what you went through? The surgeries? Brian, I needed to make decisions. You made me your emergency contact? I didn't know; I wasn't ready." Her eyes welled. Would he see the surgery as a betrayal? Against his advance directive wishes?

"Hush, it's all right. Dr. Duffy told me about the second surgery to relieve the swelling in my head."

She reached over to hug him gently.

"Your emergency contact?"

Brian looked away for a moment. "Yeah. I don't have anyone else. If you don't want to take that on, I get it. You made it pretty clear you weren't ready for us . . ."

"Brian, that's not fair."

Quick to change the subject, Brian shifted in his hospital bed. "What do you know about the church? Are my guys okay?"

"Robinson is okay. Tucker and Simmons got a little busted up from the second bomb."

"Second? There was another device?"

She nodded. "From what we've been able to put together, the first device, the one you found, was meant to draw in other responders."

"Why would someone want to go after us?"

"No idea. The second device was placed—driven, actually—under the unit Tucker and Simmons were riding. Thankfully, the engine block and wheels took most of the force of the blast. Broke both Tucker's legs, though."

"Tucker and Simmons are good cops. I can't think of any reason they'd be on someone's hit list."

"We found a date written on some of the debris. No one can put together what it means, yet. November 2nd."

"Anyone claiming responsibility for the bomb . . . bombs? They'd have to tell us what that date means."

"Nothing. There's a city councilman making noise about how it's our fault for over-policing the neighborhood and this was some sort of reprisal." She paused. Then, "What can you remember from the time you rolled up on the scene? Anything might help."

Brian closed his eyes for a moment. They were getting heavy. The conversation was wearing him out.

"We expected a crowd. That's what the caller reported. There was no one there. The church. It was the location we received from dispatch. We pulled up and it was quiet. No one was around. Nothing."

"It was what—after eleven? Is it always that quiet out?"

"There's usually people around. Some hanging out on the corners, people sitting on their front steps talking. You know, the usual stuff people do in a neighborhood. There wasn't anything going on—nothing at all. It was—unusual."

"Like they knew something was gonna happen?" Emily said.

"Maybe. The only thing I remember seeing is we were being watched. The building across the street from the church. I think it's an apartment complex. In the second-floor window. There was movement. No lights on in the place. But I thought I saw the red glow from a cigarette."

"After you realized the callout was a bust, what did you do?"

"Once we assured the church was secure, I started releasing units back to their patrol sectors. My first thought was someone lured us out there to divert us from something else. Any reports of significant activity elsewhere in the city?"

"Nothing. It looks like the lure was to pull as many units to the church as possible."

"There are easier ways to ambush officers on the street."

Emily carried the same thought. More importantly, who would know the specific officers who would respond? The officers couldn't say—unless it was for something they wouldn't want out in the open.

CHAPTER ELEVEN

EMILY LEFT BRIAN promising to check back on him later, when his physical therapist came to take him for evaluation. When she came out of the patient room, she found Javier on the phone. He leaned against the nurses' station and a grim expression washed over him.

"I understand. We'll find out what we can and—yes, sir. We will, sir."

Javier pocketed the phone.

"Sounded ominous," Emily said.

"Lieutenant Hall. The chief's office got a call about a bombing."

"Someone finally claimed responsibility for it?"

"The call was a warning about another attack. It's supposed to happen sometime today."

"Any idea who called? I know they didn't set up a trace."

"According to the lieutenant, the guy never gave a name, or a reason for the attack—only that it was coming."

"What are the chances it's bullshit?" Emily said.

"Fifty-fifty, according to the lieutenant."

"Too serious to ignore."

"Seems that way. The chief has an officer safety bulletin coming out within minutes."

An officer safety bulletin would hit the computer displays in all the patrol units and desktop computers throughout the department. They usually warned against specific threats, or persons who posed a credible danger to officers. In this case, Emily wondered what the bulletin could offer.

"The usual be aware of your surroundings?" Emily said.

"The chief is doubling up on patrol units in Del Paso, South Sac, and Oak Park."

"Sounds like the chief. He's not about to let some community activist like Davis dictate where and how we do our job. Chances are, if there is another threat, it's going to come in one of those patrol districts."

"Additional units will give him more eyes on what's happening out there. There will be guidance to avoid community confrontation to keep from fanning the flames."

"The chief got the call. Who else? Let's swing by city hall and see if Councilman Davis is doing another press conference."

"You think he made the anonymous threat? I can't see him going that low," Javier said, as they left the hospital.

The clean, modern lines of city hall plaza were juxtaposed with tents and makeshift cardboard and plastic homeless shelters along the eastern side. The occupants used Cesar Chávez Park across the street to barter and make drug deals to help them coexist with their demons. Emily and Javier navigated around the small encampment, reaching the open plaza in front of the city hall entrance.

Television news crews were wrapping up their broadcasts and stowing their equipment when they arrived. Emily tapped one of the camera operators on the shoulder.

"What'd we miss?" she asked.

"The usual blather from a politician."

"Davis?"

"Yeah. He claimed he received information the city was under attack. No specifics, and no details. Came across as a guy desperate to see his face on the news. I don't know if we got anything we can use tonight. We made a quick decision not to go live—thankfully."

"City under attack? That's a fresh approach."

"Different label, same crap. Blame the current mayor for the problems we've had for years."

"I hear you. Thanks," Emily said.

Emily tugged Javier by the sleeve. "We need an inside source and I think I know who to talk to."

Sitting in the waiting room, Javier fidgeted and leaned toward Emily. "When you mentioned an inside source, I didn't think you meant inside, inside," he whispered.

A voice called out. "The mayor will see you now, Detectives."

Emily opened the heavy wood door and found Mayor Ellen Carsten propped behind her desk. The mayor was in her mid-forties, Emily guessed, and always looked ready for a television spot with her carefully coifed dark blonde hair and piercing blue eyes. The mayor smiled when she spotted Emily. She clicked the television remote and tossed it aside.

"Emily, good to see you. How's your mom doing?"

The mayor and Emily had "bonded" during an investigation involving the mayor's chief of staff. Emily shared her mother's condition during a time when the political winds seemed to shift against the mayor. Emily was able to keep the blowback away from the mayor's office and focus on who was burning the homeless camps in the city.

"Thanks for asking, Mayor. She's doing well in her memory care facility. The River Gardens Project. She has her good days and bad days. Dementia is difficult. The silver lining is most of the time she doesn't realize there is a problem."

"I don't remember if we talked about it before—my father suffered with Alzheimer's in his last years. It's heartbreaking. You've done so much to keep your mother safe. Anyway, what can I help you with, Detectives?"

Emily jutted her chin at the television on the wall to the left. "You catch Councilman Davis's press conference?"

"How could I miss the grandstanding SOB?"

"What's his deal?" Emily asked.

Mayor Carsten rose from her chair and strode to the window looking out on the city. Her pencil skirt hugged her slim frame. "His deal? He's made no secret of it. He wants my job."

"What's he done? He's been a councilman for a hot minute after he ran a hardware store."

"What he has are donors. It takes cash to run for office, and it takes even more to keep it. I used most of mine to win reelection after my chief of staff was caught burning down homeless camps. I don't have much political capital left."

"You're not giving up, are you?"

Mayor Carsten turned from the window. "No. I'm not about to give up. I'm going down fighting. Unless something gives, though, I am going down."

"What's your take on his keeping-police-out-of-the-community bit? He's supporting homegrown security patrols."

"We've worked hard to bring the violent crime rates down. The police department working with local communities made that happen.

To backtrack and blame the police for everything fuels his position. It will tear down any trust between the city and the people."

"Does he have some personal axe to grind with SPD?"

"I don't know. I haven't heard him say anything to make me think he does."

"Are people buying his 'I'm one of the oppressed' act?" Javier asked.

"Look at his FPC filings. He's formed a committee—the Safer Sacramento Streets Committee—and the donations are coming in from all over the city. His campaign war chest is full and he hasn't even declared he's running yet."

"But you think he will?" Emily said.

"You can count on it, Emily. This guy's got a plan."

"What would he gain by supporting the attacks against our officers?"

"If he has his way, we'll see a separate, unregulated police force controlling large swaths of the city. Who benefits? Only the people who want to run their community like an empire where they make the rules and they reap the rewards off the backs of the people who live there. Pay for protections scams, turning a blind eye to gang activity, and controlling who gets access to city services. We can't let the city devolve into chaos."

Emily pondered the future of a city run by warlords. "Don't you have some dirt on this guy? Opposition research, you call it?"

"The guy is careful. No money trail to hookers or social media posts that would trigger an outburst against him. He's a rags-to-riches story. Some humble electronics store owner turned community activist for the people."

"Electronics store?" Emily stiffened.

Javier stepped closer to Emily. "What electronics store?"

"I don't recall. Some store he had in the Pocket Area. He sponsored kids' teams out of the place. That's where he got his start in the community outreach—with those damn radio-controlled planes."

Emily turned to Javier. The look on his face said he got it too. Radio-controlled toy planes weren't far from the device piloted under Officer Tucker's SUV.

CHAPTER TWELVE

FULL CHARGE ELECTRONICS took up a quarter of an aging strip mall in the Pocket Area south of the city. The window displays included radio-controlled planes and cars. Signs boasted hobby enthusiasts could find their electronic parts and equipment here. If you didn't know how to build your project, classes were offered.

A DAVIS FOR CITY COUNCIL poster hung by the front door, and next to it was a small sign: WE DO NOT SERVE POLICE, FIRST RESPONDERS, OR OTHER FASCISTS.

"Welcoming, don't you think?" Emily said as she climbed out of the SUV.

"Pretty much confirms it's Davis's place." Javier joined Emily and leaned on the SUV. "We goin' in or what?"

"Soon. I asked for some help. I wouldn't know what the hell I was looking at in there. Wires, transistor-thingies. I wouldn't know the difference between something a kid would use to make a toy car or a pipe bomb," Emily said.

"You can't use the bomb squad to tear the place apart."

"Give me a little credit, Javi."

"It's only based on your history—you know, the whole bull in a china shop thing you have going for you."

"I do not. I'm . . . focused."

Emily knew her partner meant she tended to go wherever the evidence led, with little regard to who she might piss off. Javier had done more than his share of cleanup in the wake of her "tendencies."

"Here comes our hired help." Emily pointed at an older gray sedan pulling into the lot.

Officer Milton stepped from the driver's side, tossing a cigarette on the ground. Dressed in tan cargo shorts and a purple T-shirt emblazoned with a ROBOTS DO IT WITH PRECISION logo.

"Milton, thanks for coming out," Emily said.

"My pleasure, Detective. Thanks for letting me do this. Like I said, I think I can help. I've been meaning to check this store out for a while, anyway. I live on the other side of town. This one is kinda out of the way."

"Nice of you to dress the part," Javier said.

Milton glanced down at his attire. "What?"

"Never mind."

Emily pointed to the storefront. "We need you to go take a look inside. Let us know what looks off to you. We think there might be a connection to this electronics store and our bomber."

"Okay. What do you need me to do? Photos, or listening to employees? Or want me to try to buy bomb parts?" Milton was eager to start. Emily wrote it off as his eagerness to do some honest-to-God undercover work.

"No—none of that James Bond stuff. I want you to go and look around. You said you teach robotics to high school kids, right? Go see what's going on. If there's anything, make a mental note and come back out."

"No photos, then?"

"No, Milton. No photos. Go in and act like you're shopping and come back out and tell us what you saw. Got it?"

Milton nodded nervously. "Yeah, I understand."

"Okay. Go. Detective Medina and I will be right here. If it doesn't look right, come outside."

Milton tugged on the neck of his T-shirt and strode to the door.

"You think this is a good idea, Emily?" Javier said.

"We can't go in because Davis knows who we are. If he's in there, or told his people about us, we wouldn't be able to look at what he's got in there."

"Think Milton can pull it off?"

"He's got the nerd factor going for him."

Ten minutes later, Milton came out of the store with a black plastic bag in one hand and a smirk on his face.

Milton circled around the SUV and joined Emily and Javier.

"The place has everything. I mean everything you need to put together a robotics project, cars, boats, and airplanes. There was a class going on in the back room for a robotics team from another high school. I listened in and those kids are advanced—I mean they were talking linked robot pairs and using AI—"

"Focus, Milton," Emily said. "Was there anything you saw tying this place to our bombing attacks?"

Milton blinked. "I didn't see explosives. Then again, they probably wouldn't have stuff sitting around out in the open. But I did find these." He handed the black plastic bag to Emily.

She opened the bag and looked at an assortment of electronic gizmos and whizzbangs. "What am I looking at?"

"They are twelve-channel micro servo controllers and circuit boards."

"Like the ones found at the church bombing?" Emily said.

"Exactly like those. I bought two of each so we can compare them against the fragments we found."

Javier peeked in the bag. "How common are these and could our bomber pick them up at any store?"

Milton straightened and put his shoulders back. "These are common in hobby projects."

"Then how does this help us?" Javier asked.

Milton pulled one of the new circuit boards from the plastic bag. The white cardboard box listed the specs and details for the board. Milton opened the end flap and slid out a green-colored circuit board. "See? Right there. Each board has a serial number. If we can find a number on the fragments we collected at the crime scene, we might find out where it came from. If it's close to these serial numbers, it might have come from this store."

Emily grinned and glanced at Javier. "Nice work!"

"Not bad, Milton. Not bad," Javier said.

"You think I'll get reimbursed for this? I spent like two hundred fifty."

"Yeah, I think we can arrange it."

"Cool," Milton said. A relieved look crossed his face.

"You didn't see Councilman Davis in there, did you?" Emily asked.

"Yeah, I did. He was the one teaching the class to the kids."

CHAPTER THIRTEEN

"YOU MEAN, HE knows how to build a bomb?" Lieutenant Hall said, pushing back from his desk.

Emily and Javier returned from the Full Charge Electronics store to brief the lieutenant about the Davis connection.

"He knows his way around components and the hobby craft side of the business. Could he make a car like the one used on our people? Yeah. Does it make him a bomb-maker? Not enough there yet," Emily said.

"If the circuit boards link to the shop, we've got something actionable. We could ask for a warrant based on that and Davis's proficiency with the type of electronics needed to assemble an explosive device," Javier said.

Lieutenant Hall stood and pinched the bridge of his nose. "A city council member, a highly visible community activist . . . If the mayor's office gets wind of any investigation we have involving an elected official . . ."

"Mayor Carsten is on board."

The lieutenant's head shot up. "She's what? She knows about Davis?"

"The mayor knows Davis is a vocal critic of her administration and her support of our department. He's made no effort to hide his opposition to her agenda. I think she expects him to run against her in the next election."

"But as far as Davis being a person of interest in our bombing attack?" Hall asked.

Emily shook her head. "No, she's not aware of that plot twist. I think she'd welcome a very visible investigation into a potential rival."

"This is going to be a mess, isn't it?"

"I'm sorry, sir. Seems like it has potential to break that way."

"Sir, I'd like to assign officers sit on Davis," Javier said.

"And let him complain city resources are being spent watching him? He'd spin that to make it sound like he was a victim because he's opposed anything wearing a badge. No, we need more to tie him to the bombing. You said he teaches classes? Maybe it's one of them?"

"Sir, with the timing of the phone call he claims he got, he's tied into this," Javier said.

Before Hall could respond, an officer burst into the office. "Sir, you gotta pick up line two."

Hall reached to his desk phone, punched a flashing button. "Hall here." He listened intently for a moment, then clutched the phone to his chest. "There's been another one. Go see the watch commander."

Emily and Javier ducked from the office. The nervous energy was already spreading through the building. Another attack on an officer had occurred.

A detective was on the phone at her desk, and Emily asked if she knew what was going on.

"Another bomb. Not sure if there are injuries—Del Paso Heights again."

The watch office was busy taking calls and directing communications. The watch commander, Lieutenant Burrows, was a thirty-year veteran and usually handled the demanding job with the skills of an air traffic controller, keeping units deployed around the city. He looked stressed. One of his had been attacked.

In the corner of the room, an officer slumped against the wall. He bent over, catching his breath. Radio speakers in the room carried the transmission from the field. They were usually switched off. The clipped phrases and edginess in the voices gave Emily a tightness in her chest.

The watch commander noticed Emily and Javier and gestured for them to look at one of the six monitors mounted on the wall.

Lieutenant Burrows studied a video screen. "There. See it?"

The screen flashed bright white. The image Emily saw was a police SUV in flames.

"What do we know?" Emily said.

Burrows hit the button to rewind the footage and played it again. The SUV pulled to a stop at an intersection and, moments later, the flash of the explosion engulfed the vehicle.

"West El Camino and Truxel. Unit responds to a call on a suspicious person hanging out at the appliance store on Truxel. They're a block away at the light when they got hit."

"Injuries?"

Lieutenant Burrows frowned. "It's not good. Our two officers were busted up and burned. Both made it to the burn unit. McKinley and Ryan. But there was a civilian on a motorcycle who pulled up to the red light as the blast hit. He didn't have a chance."

"Oh, man. The motorcycle guy, we know anything about him?"

"Not yet. There are some civilians beginning to gather, and looks like it's not a friendly group. You and Detective Medina should get out there before we lose control of the scene."

"Will do. I know Ryan," Emily said. "I thought he was working out at Cal Expo doing security at the state fair."

"He was. He said he got tired of spending his time dealing with the homeless camped out on the expo grounds. The city won't do anything, so he wanted to pick up the slack in Patrol District 2. He and McKinley would roll out as backup."

"There wasn't any suspicious person there?"

"First unit on scene didn't find anything."

"Another phony call-in," Emily said.

"Crime scene techs are trying to secure the scene and process as much as they can before the crowd pushes them out. A couple of bottles been tossed already."

"Got ugly fast," Javier said.

"Yeah, the word coming from the scene is a Black man was killed because the police were in the neighborhood."

"He the guy on the motorcycle?" Javier asked.

"Indeed. Like our officers had anything to do with it."

"Sounds like the same line Councilman Davis has been throwing around," Emily said.

Javier pulled his cell phone from his pocket and tapped in a text message. It chimed back seconds later.

"Milton is going to drive by the electronics store and see if Davis is still there. Then he'll meet us at the El Camino and Truxel crime scene."

"You have a new friend, Javi?"

"He's managed to keep us moving forward with the tech aspects on this."

Emily glanced at the large map of the city on the wall, tapped on the location. Truxel and West El Camino. She stepped back. "Lieutenant, we getting any intel from the scene on gang activity? Like rival gang friction? El Camino Crips and Tru Heights going at one another? The last bomb was in Tru Heights territory; now this one in Crip land."

"Nothing yet. Could explain why there's a crowd presence already."

Emily and Javier hurried to the parking lot and joined four other units heading to the scene. Emily slid behind the wheel.

"Want me to drive, Em?"

"I'd like to be there before Christmas." She started the SUV.

"What? I'm a good driver."

"Yeah, okay, Rain Man. You drive like an old woman."

"I'm careful."

"You're poky. Now strap in."

Emily pulled the SUV from the lot and the other police vehicles followed her path. She took I-5 North to Interstate 80 and turned off at the Truxel exit within ten minutes of starting the engine. The SUV caravan shot north and the sea of flashing blue and red lights ahead marked the location.

Emily pulled into a shopping center parking lot and weaved her way closer to the location marked by yellow crime scene tape. The center was a community hub with a check cashing establishment, a dollar store, and a shuttered grocery store in one of the city's "food deserts." As they pulled to a stop near the barrier, Emily heard the crowd. They gathered on the opposite side of the street and shouted anti-cop slogans, defund the police, killer cops, and another Black man killed at the hands of dirty cops.

The news camera set up on the opposite sidewalk gave the protesters somewhere to perform. The outlet made them bolder and more aggressive, shoving one another so they could get their face on camera.

Javier pointed to the husk of an SUV and the bent wreckage of a motorcycle next to the police vehicle. There were medical supplies, IV lines, gauze, and gloves strewn on the pavement, a testament to the hurried treatment rendered after the explosion. At the side of the charred

SUV lay the crumpled form of a motorcycle rider, based on the helmet sitting next to him.

Emily could tell the EMTs had tried to render aid, and once they found him too far gone, they left the saline IV, intubation pathway, and defibrillator pads in place.

"Why didn't they put up a screen?" Emily asked as she got out of the SUV.

"I'll tell you why," a gruff voice called out from another black-and-white SUV. The officer held a gauze pad to his forehead. The block chin and bloated frame made him easy to spot. Stark. An officer hovering around past retirement age not for the commitment to the job, but where else could a narrow-minded bigot push his considerable weight around? Stark was quick to complain about Emily's rise to a detective slot. It wasn't the place for a woman. He'd been vocal about "the weaker sex" wearing a badge. Stark bemoaned women couldn't do the job and would be useless as backup when a situation escalated. The thing was, Stark was the one who failed to show up when Emily needed backup.

"Stark, you okay?"

"What does it look like to you? I guess you must be a detective."

"What happened?" Emily said.

"What happened was I got clocked by a beer bottle when we're trying to keep the mob back from the crime scene. They don't want the body covered up. They want to cry and moan to the camera about how one of theirs lies in the street. Screw them. That asshole can rot where he lies."

"You should get checked for a concussion, Stark. You sound like your feelings got bruised." Emily strode past to the tape barrier.

"Yeah, well screw you, too, Hunter."

"Yep, definitely a concussion," she said.

Javier suppressed a grin and signed both himself and Emily in with an officer posted at the tape.

"Medical examiner on the way?" she asked.

"Yes, ma'am. The watch commander said they are about five minutes out."

Emily nodded and approached the firebombed SUV. She caught the strobe of a camera near the SUV and was ready to chase someone away from her crime scene when she realized it was Officer Milton.

"Milton got here quick," Emily said. "He give you an update on Davis? He spot him?"

"Haven't heard. I guess he hightailed it out here," Javier said.

Emily scanned the opposite intersection, half-expecting the councilman to pose for the camera.

The doors on the smoldering SUV were flung wide open. The dash had melted, dripping down to the floorboard. Emily hoped they got the officers out before the flames overtook the passenger compartment. Lieutenant Hall mentioned they were taken to the burn unit.

"Excuse me, Detective," a crime scene technician said. He held a camera to her, the screen illuminated on the back of the bulky black Nikon.

She squinted and stared at the image on the small LED screen.

"What am I looking at?"

"I found this. Officer Milton said I should show you," the tech said.

The technician led her and Javier around the front end of the SUV. The passenger side took more damage than she first thought. The front tire was gone and the quarter panel sheared off, torn like a thin sheet of rice paper.

"Looks like a bigger explosive this time around," Emily said.

Javier elbowed Emily. "There's the missing piece of the fender." He jutted his jaw toward the motorcycle.

The ripped section of sheet metal was embedded in the rider's chest. He'd stopped at the light next to the police SUV when the blast took him.

"Damn. You shoot photos of our victim here?" Emily said.

"I did. But this is what I want to show you." He squatted near the torn front end. He placed his camera on the ground and shone his flashlight under the remains of the SUV.

"Is that . . . ?" Emily said.

"Yep, the front wheels of a radio-controlled car. Isn't that what you found at the church bombing?"

"This one was driven under the SUV, like it was with Tucker and Simmons?" Javier said.

"How far away could someone control this thing?" Emily asked. She looked for Milton, but he must have been cataloging evidence.

"We didn't find camera parts last time and I don't see any in the debris here. Means they had to watch this thing. The operator was in the line of sight," the technician said.

Emily stood and turned in a circle. The gas station across the street was set back from the street. In the shopping center where she stood, the main building was a squat one-story structure, set a distance from the road. There was only one building tall enough to watch this intersection. A bank sat on the corner of the parking lot, so close that it blocked visibility at the light. She craned her neck up at the top of the tall bank building. A red glow flickered briefly from the roof. The red light Brian mentioned before the church bombing.

"Javi, run!"

She pulled Javier and the crime scene technician away from the downed SUV and up to the parking lot.

An electronic whine sounded and a police SUV in the parking lot exploded, knocking them to the pavement.

CHAPTER FOURTEEN

A HIGH-PITCHED RINGING in her ears muffled everything. Smoke. Heat. Flames. She had a sense of people rushing around her.

"Javi!" Emily shouted, but his name echoed in her skull.

She oriented herself and leaned against a lamppost in the bank parking lot. A touch to her elbow.

Javier was trying to say something, but she couldn't hear anything over the loud ringing in her ears.

She spotted Milton running to her. He called out, but his words sounded like they were muffled through cotton.

"Glad you had the time to change into something a bit more professional." Javier pointed out the white Tyvek protective suit the officer wore.

Milton's face flushed. "To be honest, I needed to change in the bank parking lot because the officer didn't believe I was one of us." He unzipped the front of the disposable suit, and the purple robot shirt peered out from underneath.

Emily shook her head at the young officer's admission. She let Milton and Javier pull her to her feet.

Emily spotted an odd green rectangle jutting from the wet rubble. Donning a purple nitrile glove, she gently tugged it out of the debris flow headed for the storm drain.

An electronic circuit board. She knew it hadn't come from the charred police SUV because the one in her hand bore a message from the bomber. *They all must pay.*

The words chilled her. Was this guy announcing a war against cops?

The sudden blast sent the protesters scurrying from their posts across the street. Cardboard protest signs dropped as they ran. ACAB—All Cops Are Bad—Killer Kops, and Defund the Oppressors were the theme and Emily had to wonder, when did they print and prepare these props? Props for a planned political statement. The timing was too coincidental. Emily had barely made it here, and yet these protesters were already in full throat.

Who told them?

"Anyone hurt?" Emily called out.

An officer to her left said, "Other than my unit, we're good. I'm looking at six months of paperwork here to explain why I'm not driving this back to the shop."

Emily scanned the parking lot and suddenly recalled the red light on the roof of the bank building.

"Hey, Javi. Did you see anything up there before this?" She pointed to the bank.

He glanced at the roofline. "No, can't say I did. You spot something?"

Emily glanced from the bank to the intersection where the first bomb had detonated. A clear line of sight from the bank roof. Someone there could watch the police SUV approach and time their strike with the traffic. The second one was closer, between the intersection and the bank.

"Brian mentioned seeing a red light, or a glow from a window before the first church bomb. I saw something up there."

"Milton, was Davis in his store?" she asked.

"I didn't see him. The class was over when I drove up."

Emily started toward the bank, and Javier took her by the elbow. "Where do you think you're going?"

She glanced up at the bank roofline.

"The bomber isn't there anymore. He used this second blast as a diversion so he could climb down from there and split."

"Detective Medina has a point, ma'am," Milton said. "SWAT should clear the building, to be sure."

Javier glanced up at the bank's roofline. "The bomb squad ought to clear it first. They're already here. Procedure is they're called out whenever there is an injury caused by an explosion."

"Yeah, good point, Javi." She reached for her radio at her belt and clicked the button to transmit.

"That ain't gonna work," Javier said.

She turned the compact radio in her hand and noticed the black case now bore a jagged hole.

"Must've happened when I fell."

Javi used his radio and called for the bomb squad supervisor.

"He'll be right here. His team is on the other end of the parking lot," Javier said.

"Hey, Javi. Before the bomb squad pokes around, let's ask Air-1 to make a pass over the building."

"Good idea. Don't need any surprises waiting, especially if your guy is hiding up there."

Air-1 was the department's helicopter and Emily had noticed it orbiting to the north, monitoring the protest as she and Javier had arrived.

"The message—*they all must pay*—it's the kind of thing someone who didn't care who they hurt would say. We need to make sure it's clear before the squad goes up there."

"Shouldn't this be a SWAT thing?" Milton asked.

Javier made the call as two officers in dark utility uniforms strode in their direction.

"You the detectives who called for us to check out a device?" the taller of the two said. Lieutenant Vega, according to the embroidered tag on his uniform.

Emily introduced themselves. "I don't know if there's a device or not. But our bomber used the roof as a place to observe his targets. I saw a light up there before this second blast."

The police helicopter made a close pass over the bank and hovered over the flat roof. Javier's radio clattered with a response from the airship saying the roof was clear—no one waited up there to ambush other officers.

"Your idea to call for Air-1 to clear?" Vega said.

"Yeah. Didn't want to risk you guys walking into a trap," Emily said.

"Thanks for that," Vega said.

"You bet, Lieutenant."

Vega took in the square box of a building. "If there's an access it's going to be inside, or maybe something I can't see from here in the rear. We've already had two devices. Wouldn't put it past this guy to drop another where we don't expect one."

He wheeled around and ordered the officer with him to ask the fire department to bring their ladder truck around.

"We'll access the roof using their ladder. I'll let you know what we find."

The bomb squad supervisor strode to the building and waited for the ladder truck to pull into position.

The red-and-white Sacramento Metro Fire Department truck cruised to the spot Vega wanted and the massive ladder truck whooshed to a stop with a hiss of air brakes. The truck idled, and a firefighter took control of the ladder mechanism.

The silver extension ladder lifted from the bed, pivoted to the left, and extended so the topmost rungs kissed the edge of the roof.

Vega and his squad climbed the ladder, and from this distance Emily could tell they were on edge, looking for someone, or something, waiting for them.

A minute passed without a signal from the squad. Javier's radio crackled to life. "Detectives, you'll want to see this."

"Wonder what they found?" Emily asked.

"You tell me about it."

"What?"

Javier glanced at the ladder truck.

"You're afraid of heights? You big baby."

"I'm not afraid of heights. I am afraid of falling. There's this thing called gravity . . ." Javier said.

"Oh my God. Gimme your radio."

"What'd you find, Lieutenant?" Emily called out using Javier's radio.

"You were right. Our guy was here. By the looks of it he camped here, and he had a present waiting for us."

"Another device?"

"Sure enough." Vega was calm about the discovery. Emily felt a surge of anger, knowing another bomb was waiting to take out responding officers

"We've disarmed the device. Come on up."

Javier shook his head. "Not happening."

"It's only two stories tall."

"Have a nice time. Send me a postcard or something."

She rolled her eyes and headed for the ladder truck. A firefighter showed her where to climb, attached a safety harness, and Emily stepped up onto the truck.

The first few steps up the ladder were easy, but halfway up she looked down through the metal rungs and a queasy feeling rolled in her gut.

"It's only two stories, Emily," she told herself.

At the top, she paused for a moment as she tried to think through how to leap from the ladder to the roof. One bomb squad officer on the roof took her hand, helped her unclip her harness, and step onto the flat roof.

The first thing she did was waive down at Javier. The view from the rooftop, even though it wasn't a skyscraper, gave a panoramic overview of the intersection and the streets in both directions.

Vega called to Emily. "Detective, over here."

Emily joined the lieutenant with an uncomfortable sensation of her foot flexing the roof panels as she stepped. The surface was a fine granite pebble finish.

Vega and two of his team circled around a small pipe bomb.

"It was attached to the roof access panel. There was a battery-powered actuator to charge the blasting cap in the pipe bomb. If we came up the hatch from inside the building—well, it wouldn't have been pretty. Simple, but kind of elegant if you think about it. We'll take photos of this thing before we take it down and dispose of the device."

"Can we pull prints from the pipe itself?"

"I don't want to risk a techie getting their hand blown off."

"But if we can pull a print—"

"I got something better for you." He handed a small brown paper evidence bag to her. "It's got the actuator we found attached to the access panel. And you'll want your CSI types to document this."

He led her to the corner of the roof closest to the intersection. A pile of cigarette butts and a message written in chalk.

Two down—many more to come.

CHAPTER FIFTEEN

EMILY WAITED ON the rooftop until the bomb squad had carefully lowered the pipe bomb from the side of the building using a rope and a padded sling.

Waiting squad members secured the device into a heavy-gauge steel vault. It was too volatile to risk on-scene detonation in a crowded public location.

The CSI team climbed up the ladder and the first one was a tech Emily recognized.

"Hey, Detective. You always bring me to the nicest places. At least this one has a view."

Terri Trujillo was a pert redhead with five years under her belt as a crime scene tech. Emily was happy to see her here. Terri was meticulous and took her time documenting a crime scene.

"It's just me up here. I've got Jack down there with Detective Medina working up the intersection."

"Was Jack the one who was down there when that thing went *boom*?"

"That's him. He's fine. He'll be dining out on this war story for weeks."

"Works for me. Say, you hear anything yet on your application for the academy?"

"Not yet. The HR rep said it could be up to another month before they announce."

"You'd be a good cop, Terri."

"I've been following you around for a few years. I might've picked up a thing or two. What you got for me?"

Emily described the bomb and how it had been attached to the roof access panel. Then she showed Terri the cigarette butts and the handwritten chalk image.

Terri dropped a black nylon bag and pulled a bulky black camera and yellow tented evidence markers—the type with bold numbers and small ruler marks on the bottom edge to provide a reference.

She dropped the number 1 marker next to the cigarette butts, backed off, and snapped a series of photos at varying angles.

"Got us a nervous chain-smoker here. None of them burned all the way down. Camel filters."

"I'd love to pull some DNA from those."

Terri snapped photos of the roof and structures as she made her way over to the roof access panel. She stopped and photographed what Emily thought was a smudge on the roof surface. Emily looked over Terri's shoulder and saw it was a footprint—a large one.

"We had the squad up here. Might be one of theirs," Emily said.

"Doesn't look like a Vibram boot print. I'll run to see if we can look at comparisons." She dropped an evidence marker and returned to her nylon bag.

When she returned, Terri unrolled a thin sheet of material over the footprint. She connected a small battery pack to the wire lead coming from the sheet.

"It's an electrostatic print lifter. It uses static electricity to pull the print to the pad. It's kinda cool and saves us from the old fashioned pouring a mold stuff. And it's more detailed. Check it."

Terri lifted the pad, turned it over, and there was a clear outline of a footprint, the tread, and even a wear spot at the heel. "I'll see if I can find the tread manufacturer for you."

"Nice."

There wasn't any way to take the chalk message with her, but Emily snapped a few shots of it with her phone while Terri finished up.

Emily carefully climbed back down the ladder and joined Javier.

She spotted Milton working with Jack, the CSI tech at the burned SUV in the intersection.

Emily handed her phone to Javier with the photo of the message on the screen.

"*Two down—many more to come*. Which two is he talking about? The two officers in this SUV?"

"I don't know but it's the message more are to come that has me a bit twisted up. Whatever this is, it's personal to this guy."

The protest crowds had scattered when the second bomb exploded. When they realized the explosion was across the street from their position, a few hardcore demonstrators recaptured their positions on the street corner opposite the downed motorcyclist and charred SUV.

While Emily was on the roof, the medical examiner's van had arrived and partially blocked the view of the onlookers. Screens were in place to give the dead a small measure of privacy.

"Finally. Who did the ME send out?" Emily asked.

"Dr. White. Said she'd work as fast as possible to get the cyclist taken care of. She noticed the public attention."

Elizabeth White was a forensic pathologist, and Emily considered her one of the best. Meticulous, smart, with a dry wit.

"I was going to check in with her," Javier said.

The detectives met Dr. White at the rear of the medical examiner's van where she snapped off her gloves and dropped them in a biowaste container.

"Hey, Doc," Emily said as they reached the van.

Dr. White grabbed a tablet and tapped in her notes. "Hey back, Detectives. This one shouldn't be much of a mystery. Wrong place, wrong time. Poor bugger. I did find an ID on him."

She put the tablet down and pulled a small plastic bag from her backpack.

Emily took the bag and examined the driver's license. "Oh, this won't be good." She handed the ID to Javier.

"Malcolm Davis?"

"Yeah, Rockhead Davis, the El Camino Crip shot caller. You heard the crowd over there earlier. They blame this on us."

"First the Tru Heights Bloods, now the Crips—if we can say the skinheads are involved, we'll have a gang trifecta. This is ugly."

Dr. White unwrapped herself from the white Tyvek protective gear, tossing it in the waste container. "I'm certain cause of death will prove to be pulmonary barotrauma. The body evidenced secondary blast trauma with a dozen metal fragments shot into him from the force of the explosion. The burns came last."

"Barotrauma?" Emily asked.

"It's the initial injury you'd expect. A pressure wave from a blast. It's basically an overpressure of the lungs, heart, and bowel. They blow out."

Emily thought about the pressure wave Brian had experienced.

"There's no treating that kind of injury, is there?" Emily said.

"Not usually."

"What about TBI?"

Dr. White bit her bottom lip. "I'm sure he suffered TBI, but the barotrauma was the likely culprit here."

"I mean . . . if someone experiences a blast pressure wave from something like this and experiences TBI, what kind of treatment should they expect?"

"Are you okay, Emily? Headache, dizziness, did you lose consciousness?"

"No, no, not me."

Emily noticed Dr. White relax slightly. "Good. Because I don't normally work with live patients. But for you I'd make an exception," she said.

The doctor leaned on her van. "Recovering from TBI takes time. The human brain is resilient and finds ways to heal itself. Depending on the severity, someone could be looking at a long rehabilitation to allow the neural pathways to rewire themselves—walking, talking, and motor functions can be impaired. Mood and personality changes are common. Someone with TBI might experience emotional outbursts, anxiety, or depression. It takes time."

Emily's mind spun with images of Brian in ICU, with the tubes and wires. The stark black-and-white photos of the bombing scene. Now this. It was becoming all too much. It was as the chief had warned. It was personal.

Emily blinked back tears. "A lot to take in."

"Someone you know caught up in one of these bombings?"

Emily couldn't respond. The words couldn't find purchase on her lips. She put up a hand to Dr. White—a pause—before she retreated to the bank parking lot. She couldn't hear more of the raw, unfiltered truth. Would Brian recover? Would she?

Her thoughts swirled and formed a dark whirlpool. Would their relationship survive? At some level she blamed herself for his injuries. Was he distracted because of her? She barely moved when Javier leaned on the unit alongside her. He didn't say anything.

After a moment, Emily broke the silence. "I'm sorry about—"

"You have nothing to apologize for."

"I don't want to let you down."

"You couldn't."

She let out a deep sigh.

"I'm worried about Brian. What if these things Dr. White mentioned—what if Brian—"

"Hope—it's about hope," Javier said.

Emily chuckled. "What, is that some Robert Frost motivational shit or something?"

"Nick Fury from the Avengers."

"Did you just quote a cartoon on me?"

"First of all, it's a graphic novel. Secondly, it's underrated as social commentary."

"Unbelievable."

"Brian will face a long road ahead. He's already showing improvement. It's going to be one step at a time, but it is a step."

"Is that some comic book pablum too?"

"No, that one's from me."

Emily leaned her shoulder into his. "Thanks, partner."

"Of course."

She appreciated Javier's strength and reassurance. But she had to wonder, where would she and Brian be a month from now, six months? Would they have anything left to rebuild? She couldn't help but obsess that her uncertainty about moving in together had distracted him to the point where he didn't spot the explosive device.

Emily turned and glanced over her shoulder at a new arrival at the crime scene. "I should have known it wouldn't take long. What a vulture."

Councilman Davis stood among the regathering protesters, cheering them on.

CHAPTER SIXTEEN

"AT LEAST HE was late for the cameras," Emily said.

"Or was he? Milton said he couldn't find him."

"It was starting to calm down over there," Emily said, jutting her chin at the intersection.

Davis grabbed a sign from a protester and held it aloft. It read, STAY OUT OF MY NEIGHBORHOOD, OR ELSE.

"Man, I'd love to cuff him and drag his ass downtown," Emily said.

"He's hoping you do."

"I know he'd pretend to be a martyr for this bullshit anti-cop crusade if we did."

Emily pushed off the SUV and stared at the protest from the bank parking lot across the street. What did Davis gain by inciting this kind of reaction? What was it the mayor said? Davis wanted her job. This was orchestrated to move the community to back him. The question burning into her mind was: Did Davis orchestrate the bombings to make his push?

"Come on, Javi. Something we need to check out."

Emily got behind the wheel and started the engine.

"Where we going?"

"Full Charge Electronics."

"Davis's place?"

"We need to flush his alibi before he has a chance. I want to know when he left. Even if it wasn't him, someone knows how to make his little toys. I want to shake the bushes and see what comes slithering out," Emily said.

"You sure that's smart? Coming at him head-on?"

"It's the only thing he'll understand."

Emily piloted the SUV to the electronics store in the Pocket Area and pulled to the front door. Not hiding their approach.

A bell sounded when they entered. A thin, acne-scarred man in an off-white hoodie was parked on a stool at the counter. He put down a magazine as the detectives approached.

"Yeah?" the counterman said.

"I understand you hold classes here about building robots and radio-controlled cars and shit," Emily said.

"Yeah."

"You had one today, right?"

"Yeah."

"You're a talkative one, aren't you? How many people come to those things?"

"Classes? Yeah, man, they're a draw."

"People pay for them?"

"Yeah."

"Good. I need a list of everyone who attended a class in the last—oh—make it two months."

"Wait, are you guys cops or something?"

Emily pulled her jacket aside, displaying her badge.

"Don't you need, like, a warrant?"

"Not really," Emily said. If the counterman gave her the material, then she really wouldn't need a warrant.

"I don't know, man. Seems like some government oppression right there. Our right to assemble and stuff."

"No one's saying you can't assemble and play with your toys."

"These aren't toys. Our class today was advanced robotics and taught people how to make some next-level devices."

"Like devices that could carry a package—let's say a bomb—and detonate it under a police vehicle?"

"Wait. What? Now wait, we don't do that here."

"Then show me a list of the people who came to class."

"I don't know, man. I gotta call the boss."

Emily stepped back from the counter while hoodie-boy made his phone call. The walls in the store were a weird mix of photos from Ukrainian drones dropping explosives on Russian troops and posters of thrash-metal bands.

The counterman slipped into the back room while he was on the phone. Emily overheard a few words—*police, wants student information, hard-ass woman cop.*

The bell chimed again and in strode Councilman Davis, his cell phone in hand. He stabbed the DISCONNECT button when he spotted the detectives.

"I understand you're infringing on our constitutional rights, Detective." It wasn't a question.

"Only if there's some provision of the Constitution allowing you to attack police officers."

"There's none of that happening here, Detective."

"Then show me the list of students."

"So you can go harass them? I think not. Come back with a warrant."

"You really want to go that way? I could draw this out and block your little indoctrination clinic here," Emily said, pointing to a poster of Che Guevara on the wall in the back room.

"I could ask you the same thing, Detective. You really want to be the cop who loses her badge because she trampled on my First Amendment right to free speech?"

"Free speech isn't the issue. Killing innocent civilians and maiming police officers is the issue. Or do you somehow justify that?"

Emily felt herself tense up, and Javier must have noticed it too. He bumped her elbow. "We got a call," he said.

It was enough to break Emily's glare off the councilman.

"I'll be filing a complaint with the Office of Public Safety Accountability, Detective. You are exactly the reason other officers are being targeted. Your badge doesn't give you the right to push into my business, or trample on my rights. You, and the others, cause this community unrest. And there's more to come."

Emily froze at the words echoing those found etched in chalk at the bank building.

"What did you say?"

Javier tugged at her elbow. "We gotta go—now."

Emily caught the concerned expression on her partner's face. It wasn't the usual save-Emily-from-herself look she was used to seeing.

She followed Javier from the electronics store and heard the shop door lock after they stepped outside.

"Javi, what is it?" She glanced at the cell phone in his hand.

Please don't let it be Brian. The flood of emotion was unexpected, and she felt her knees wobble.

"We got us a connection on the circuit boards. Milton found it."

"What? How did he manage to pull it off?" Emily also felt a rush of relief that the news didn't come from the hospital.

"I said the kid missed his calling."

Emily unlocked the SUV. "What did he find?"

"The components from the church bombing came from this place." Javier tipped his head toward the plate glass doors of the Full Charge Electronics store.

Emily glanced at the storefront and caught Davis's profile watching them. He held his cell phone to his ear. Probably following through with his threat to call the Office of Public Safety Accountability.

"Time to get us a warrant," she said.

CHAPTER SEVENTEEN

MILTON WAITED FOR them in the detective bureau. He had laid out the circuit boards he purchased from the Full Charge Electronics store. The young officer looked determined when the detectives arrived.

Emily noticed Milton had found the time to change into his uniform, but she figured he still wore the purple robot T-shirt underneath.

Javier glanced at the two rectangular components on his desktop. "These are the ones you bought at the councilman's store?"

"Yes, they are." He took a pen from his uniform pocket and pointed to a spot in the lower corner of the board. "These are metal core polycarbonate circuit boards. They are more expensive and are designed to hold up under extreme conditions like heat and vibration. There is a serial number printed here. Not all manufacturers do this, but since this is a high-end product, they inspect and give each a serial number."

"Okay, I'm following so far."

"These were part of an order Full Charge made a month ago. Ten boards. I bought the last two."

"Eight more out there unaccounted for?" Javier said.

"Six," Emily said. "At least two were used in each of our bombings. Maybe three."

"Exactly, Detective. These serial numbers were in sequence. Check out the last two digits."

Emily leaned over the boards and squinted.

"Oh, here." Milton handed her a large magnifying glass.

"You always carry one of these?" she asked.

He blushed and pointed to the numbers again, his excitement building. "The numbers on these two boards end with sixty-seven and sixty-nine."

"Okay . . ." Emily said.

Milton picked up a tablet and touched the screen, bringing the device to life. He scrolled through a line of photos.

"Here, this one." He handed the tablet to Emily.

It was a charred fragment of green circuit board. Black soot and ash covered most of the piece of electronic debris. The bottom corner still held a sharp ninety-degree edge with a partial serial number with the last two digits of sixty-eight.

"Puts it in sequence with the board I bought at the store," Milton said.

Javier glanced at the tablet. "Looks like it could be the same kind of board. How sure are we it came from Full Charge?"

"The manufacturer sent ten boards." Milton took the tablet from Javier and pulled up an email. "This is the invoice from the manufacturer for ten PX twelve-channel micro servo controllers, with sequential serial numbers from sixty-six to seventy-five. The fragment found at the church came from Full Charge Electronics."

Emily stood back from the desk and regarded the young officer. He was clearly proud of his discovery.

"Not bad, Milton. Not bad at all. Any chance we can find pieces of these servo-whats-its from the other devices?"

"I'm working through it. There's a lot of debris to sift through. Mike

Black in the crime lab is letting me set up down there. I mean, as long as you want me to do this."

"I'll make a call to the watch commander and see about assigning you on a special detail," Javier said.

"Thanks, Detective. Anything else you need me to do before I go back to the lab?"

"Yeah, if you could write me a paragraph about what these things are—the servo controllers—and how you tracked the manufacturer down. I'm gonna need the detail in our affidavit for a search warrant."

"Will do."

Milton found an empty desk and began writing.

Emily leaned toward Javier. "Did boy wonder just crack this case?"

"He might have found a crack, but we don't know if it's *the* crack."

"I can't wait to search Davis's store."

Javier rubbed the back of his neck. "This is getting really ugly, you know, right?"

"Davis is in the middle of this."

"Maybe. Even if we nail down that these bomb parts came from his store, we don't have enough to prove he's the one making them, or that he was at the locations when they were set off. We know he wasn't at the last one."

"Which is why I want the list of people taking his Anarchy 101 class. If he's not the bomber, he knows who is, and he's probably training them to do it."

Javier glanced at his watch. "We need to brief the lieutenant before we pull these search warrant affidavits together."

"Yeah, once we have the thumbs-up for a warrant, Davis will go ballistic."

Emily and Javier knocked on Lieutenant Hall's doorframe. He was on the phone and gestured for the two of them to come in and sit.

"That's not necessary," Hall said to the person on the other side of the connection. "No, let me make myself clear. I'm not doing it. You want to push it up the chain, feel free. But this isn't the time." Hall hung up, slamming the receiver down.

"Lieutenant? Everything okay?" Emily said.

"You must be making new friends out there, Emily. That was Lieutenant Marsh from Internal Affairs. He wants me to put both of you on ATO while they consider opening an investigation on you. Administrative Time Off was always the knee-jerk response to a complaint. Seems they are getting pressure from the OPSA."

"Councilman Davis made good on his threat to call the Office of Public Safety Accountability," Emily said.

"Apparently," Hall said. "You want to get me up to speed?"

Emily and Javier filled him in on the Full Charge Electronics shop, the matching circuit boards, the councilman's appearance at the crime scenes, and the veiled threat of more to come.

Hall sat back in his chair and rocked slowly, turning over the bits and pieces his detectives offered.

"I see where you're going on this. Davis is a self-righteous pain in the ass. You're onto something with the bomb components coming from his store. What we don't have is the link between Davis and the bomb. He'd argue someone came into the store and bought the parts. He'll claim he had nothing to do with it. There's nothing tying him directly to the devices."

"Yet," Emily said.

"If Davis is half as smart as he thinks he is, you'll need to find more than a paper trail leading back to him."

"If we can get the search warrant—"

"I'm going to stop you right there. You don't have enough to ask for a search warrant. You'd be asking to search a city official's personal business to find what? Electronics in an electronics store. You know full well he wouldn't keep bomb-making materials in a public location."

"Then we reach for his house, other properties, and—"

"There's nothing to tie his home, or cars, to your investigation. If you go down that path, you're playing right into his hands—and the OPSA."

"What are we supposed to do, Lieutenant? Sit on our hands until the next officer gets targeted?"

"You'll figure out a way to find what you need. You can't run at Davis head-on."

Emily huffed and crossed her arms. She knew there were holes in her theory naming Davis as the bomber. He was such a snide little man. What was in it for him?

"It comes down to the why," she said.

"What do you mean?" Hall asked.

"The why. Why would Davis be involved? What's in it for him? He wants city hall. He wants the mayor's office. The part I can't connect with him yet is—why attack cops? Why Brian, Tucker, and Simmons? Why the two on West El Camino this afternoon? The why. What's their connection to him?"

"What do we know about McKinley and Ryan, the two officers in the last attack? How are they doing?" Javier asked.

"I haven't gotten an update from the hospital. Initial reports were serious but stable. Don't know the nature of their injuries. Ryan I don't know. McKinley's been around a while—good cop from what I know," Hall said.

"Any connection between Tucker, Ryan, and McKinley?"

The lieutenant leaned forward. "Good question. I don't know. But I'll pull the personnel records."

Emily stood. "Thanks. Javier and I will head over to the hospital and see what Ryan and McKinley can tell us. Besides, I'd like to drop in on Brian and make sure he's not conning a nurse into sponge baths."

CHAPTER EIGHTEEN

THE TRAUMA CENTER waiting room was becoming too familiar. Officers from the northern patrol district were there, supporting the two officers and their families.

Emily felt the anxiety in the lobby the moment she stepped through the doors. The faces waiting were new, but they all shared the same concern, anger, and fear. It was thick in the air, and Emily sensed it seep into her pores. When would it stop? Uniformed officers gathered on one side of the lobby area encircling and guarding the family members who arrived and waited for word from behind the double doors leading to the trauma center.

The other side of the waiting room held the usual assortment of the walking wounded. Non-life-threatening stabbing victims and domestic violence survivors waited their turn to explain their conditions to attending medical staff. Some couldn't make eye contact with the nursing staff who triaged new arrivals, while others treated it like just another evening in the city.

Her thoughts shifted to Brian and guilt swept through her. Guilt over where she'd left their relationship—in the rubble along with the bomb fragments. Intellectually, she knew she hadn't caused his injuries, but deep down in that soft core where she didn't let many people in,

Emily grieved for what might have been. Could it be rebuilt?

Emily shook herself free from the downward spiral when she felt the gaze from a sergeant across the room. She told Javier she'd check in with the senior officer while he got an update from the information desk.

Sergeant Earl Berney was Emily's Field Training Officer when she was fresh from the academy. Berney had thirty years behind the badge and wasn't easily impressed with the young female officer assigned to him. He was firm but fair, an ideal not universally adopted when training rookie officers for real life on the streets.

"Sergeant? Any news on our guys?" Emily asked.

Berney rose from the uncomfortable waiting room chair, a stiffness in his knees taking a toll.

"Detective. It's good to see you. Not here, but good, nonetheless. Ryan got the worst of it, passenger side. Busted arm and leg, a few cuts and scrapes. Damn lucky. McKinley skated with some bruising, and a concussion."

"I heard burns. Considering what could have happened . . ."

He shook his head and waited until a pair of officers passed. "Lucky don't seem to cut it, if that's where you were going. The troops are getting restless. These attacks. Some are itching for a little payback."

"I get it. We don't even know who to get payback from. I'm working on it. You know Ryan and McKinley well?"

"Well enough. Ryan came to the district six months ago, and McKinley was there when I drove up. Both solid cops. Nothing to single them out for a hit like this. Of all the cops in my district, these two were the ones I could count on to play it straight. Good in the community. These two men didn't deserve to get dragged into some gang war against the police."

"What are you hearing on the street?"

Berney glanced at a knot of officers sipping at tepid coffee near the nurses' station. Their conversation was hushed, but the cadence and tight posture spoke of the coiled spring tension they shared. The sergeant tipped his head to a corner of the lobby away from the officers.

He and Emily gathered near the window at the edge of the waiting room. He gestured to the world outside. "The gangs control the streets if we let 'em. They want to expand their hold on these neighborhoods. They're counting on the city getting weak in the knees and telling us we can't do our jobs. It's bad enough we book a guy, and he's back out on the streets without posting bail before we can finish our reports."

"That bad?"

"You know it is, Detective."

"You ever run across Councilman Davis?"

Berney grunted. "Waste of space politician. He's always out getting the locals riled up over some slight he blames us for. Defund the police, he says. He'd be the first to call 911 if his precious little McMansion got vandalized."

"He's been making noise like these attacks were our fault."

"Yeah, I've heard it. It's more of the same. He's been trolling that line for the better part of a year. Looks like someone bought into his particular brand of crazy."

Emily listened and was taken by Berney believing it was a follower, not so much the actions of the councilman himself.

"If you hear anything about these attacks, would you let me know?"

"Of course. You watch your back out there, Detective. I don't have time to retrain another one to replace you." A smirk spread on his weathered face.

"Let's hope it doesn't come to that, Sarge."

Javier joined them and held a note with the rooms where they could find Ryan and McKinley.

"Medina, you can learn from this one," Berney said, hooking a thumb toward Hunter.

"Oh, I have. I can swear now much more fluently, can talk with my mouth full, and hold a grudge for years," Javier said.

"Ass," Emily said.

"See what I mean?"

Emily started for the elevator. "Come on, Javi, or I'll show you what a grudge really looks like."

Before Emily was out of earshot, Sergeant Berney pulled Javier by the arm. "You watch her back. You hear me? She has a tendency to—"

"Jump first and look second?"

"You're familiar?"

"On the regular."

"Medina, today," Emily called from across the waiting room.

Javier rolled his eyes. "I got her," he said to Berney. Then, to Emily: "Coming, dear."

She snatched the room assignment list from him. "They're both in the ER still?"

"Apparently. The information desk mentioned they had a rush of admissions from a multi-vehicle accident on 99, south of town."

The emergency room in the trauma center was arranged in a large horseshoe, with patient bays separated by thin curtains. A whiteboard at the nurses' station listed the patients' last names and more personal information than patient privacy typically allowed. It was all about cutting through the administrative red tape to get the patient the treatment they needed as soon as possible.

There were gurneys in the hallway as overflow. Emily saw the bumps, cuts, and scrapes she associated with a freeway pileup

Javier pointed at the board. "Ryan and McKinley are in bays 8 and 9."

Emily felt an uncomfortable déjà vu sensation going to meet another officer victimized by the bomber.

The curtain was open at Ryan's bed. He was awake and sitting up. The smell of fresh plaster from the casts on his arm and leg hung in the air.

Blake Ryan was tall, and his legs stuck out from the end of the bed. His head was shaved to hide the creeping hair loss. Ryan had a reputation as a joker, but his expression was anything but jovial.

"Ryan, how you holding up?" Emily asked.

"We've had better nights. Ain't that right, Mac," Ryan called through the curtain to his partner.

"You gonna hold this against me, aren't you? I run over one land mine and you'll never let me forget it."

Emily pulled the curtain back and McKinley was similarly propped up on his bed, squinting in the harsh overhead light. He had a butterfly bandage on his forehead and a small line of sutures on his temple next to his right ear.

Ryan glanced at his partner. "Damn, you look like the Elephant Man. Close the curtain."

"Oh, eff off. Like you're a male model, baldy. Maybe it was a streetlight reflecting off your dome that distracted me."

The banter, Emily knew, was a way to blow off stress and also said their injuries weren't life threatening.

"You didn't run over a land mine, McKinley. Someone singled out your unit. They used a remote-control car and drove it under the vehicle."

"They used a remote?"

"And hit you while you were stopped at the red light."

"I didn't see anyone—where were they standing?" Ryan asked.

"We think they were on top of the bank building. Waiting."

"Anyone else hurt?" McKinley asked.

"There was a motorcyclist next to you. He didn't make it."

"Dammit. Was it Rockhead?"

"Yeah, it was. You guys knew him?"

"We do. We'd left a meeting with him at a chicken place down West El Camino."

"You met with him?"

"Ryan and I check in with Rockhead from time to time. This one was because he wanted to try and broker a peace between his Crip set and some newer rival gangs pressing into the area. Thought he could pull it off. He could be pretty convincing," McKinley said.

"Who knew about the meeting? I mean, someone was waiting for you to drive by. Would they have any reason to go after you and Rockhead?"

"Rockhead called us less than fifteen minutes before he wanted to meet. We didn't broadcast the fact we were setting up a meeting."

"Other than the usual disgruntled criminal justice consumers, who'd want to come after you two?"

"There's no shortage of possibilities there. But it's been relatively peaceful in our patrol district. Much more calm than, say, five years ago. The wild, wild west El Camino back then."

A nurse came in and checked Ryan's vitals, the usual pulse, blood pressure, and oxygen levels. She told him they'd start getting the discharge paperwork going.

Emily glanced at McKinley as he squinted and turned away from the harsh light.

"You okay there, McKinley? Concussion, I hear?" Emily asked.

"Yeah, the light is killing me."

"You know an officer named Tucker?"

"Reese Tucker? Yeah. We used to work together. Good dude."

"You know he was the target of an attack yesterday?"

"I heard. I understood he was responding to the bomb that Sergeant Conner got caught up in."

Of course, McKinley would know Brian. He was in North Sacramento too. Adjoining patrol districts would back up one another on calls.

"Brian—Sergeant Conner—is upstairs. He's recovering. Know of any reason someone would want to get even with him?" Emily said. A dark sensation crept in. She felt Brian had a connection to the bombings but couldn't lock it down.

"No. Not at all. The sergeant is a by-the-book kinda guy. He's not badge heavy, doesn't involve himself in street drama. He's the kind of guy I'd want for a partner if I wasn't saddled with dead weight like Ryan."

Me too, she thought. Then why was she reluctant to move forward in their relationship?

"Hey now. I'd come over there and beat you with my cast, but they'd claim it was elder abuse," Ryan said.

"I'm forty. And, speaking of dead weight, was weight the reason you got the boot from SWAT?" McKinley said.

"Oh, funny. Talk about weight? You haven't run a mile since the academy. And you're gonna use the boo-boo on your noggin as an excuse for a year."

"No one's chasing me—why run?" McKinley said.

"You were assigned to SWAT?" Emily asked, interrupting the partners.

"Yeah, a while back. The hours made it tough on the family, so I left.

That's where I met Tucker and Sergeant Conner," McKinley said.

"Tucker was a SWAT guy? I hadn't heard," Emily said.

"For a minute."

Emily felt a puzzle piece drop into place. A connection between the injured officers. Brian, Tucker, and McKinley, and their assignment to the department's tactical unit.

CHAPTER NINETEEN

EMILY AND JAVIER left the two officers as they were getting ready for discharge from the emergency room. As they left, Emily let Sergeant Berney know Ryan and McKinley would be released as soon as the paperwork was completed.

The sergeant tried to hide his relief behind a tough facade, but Emily knew from experience the man cared about the people he worked with.

"Sarge, McKinley told me he used to work SWAT."

"He did. Got out of it a while back to spend more time with family. Had the seniority to land a shift with weekends off, so he took it. Can't blame him for making it a priority. He was a good operator from what I hear. The SWAT commander was sorry to lose him."

"McKinley mentioned Tucker was a SWAT guy too."

"He might have been. I don't remember. I didn't get calls from the SWAT commander trying to get him back like I did McKinley. Why you ask?"

"The SWAT assignment is the first common thread between the officers," Emily said.

"If you ask me, the common thread is working in the North area. Gangs, ghost guns, fentanyl—the forgotten city up there."

"How is Rockhead getting offed gonna play up there?"

"Rockhead? Was he the guy on the motorbike? Oh man, it's not gonna go without reprisal. Rockhead was kind of a known element there. Kept the balance. If he's out of the game now, it's gonna be a bloodbath for the throne."

"Keep your head down, Sergeant."

"Always, Hunter. Always."

Berney crossed the crowded waiting room and bent to speak with a woman. Emily figured she was the wife of one of the officers. The relief gushed from the woman when Berney gave her the update.

"Where now?" Javier asked.

Normally, she would power through the exhaustion. The tumble she took after the bombing near the bank was more than she thought.

"Javi, since we're here, I want to check in on Brian. You mind?"

She kept the blooming headache to herself.

He glanced at his watch. "Tell you what. Jenny's about to get off work. I'll call and meet up with her for a quick dinner."

"You two need to figure out what the long-distance relationship might look like, I suppose?"

Javier shrugged and let out a deep breath. "Maybe. We'll see where this goes. She's got a hell of an opportunity up in Portland."

"Yours is thinking about moving and mine is in a hospital bed. Hope this doesn't say anything about our prospects for long-term relationships."

"It's complicated. Isn't that what the kids say?"

"Go. Get some time with Jenny. We'll catch up later—maybe in the morning," Emily said as she massaged her temples.

Emily tracked back to Brian's room in the post-surgical wing. A nurse at the desk pointed out his room, third down on the right.

She peered into the darkened room. Brian was sitting up, staring straight ahead. His eyes shifted to the door when she appeared in the threshold.

"Hey," Brian whispered.

"What you doing sitting here in the dark?" Her hand reached for the light switch.

"Don't!"

She jerked her hand back from the wall panel. His harsh words cut deeply.

"I'm—I'm sorry. I didn't mean it to come out like that," he said.

"The light?"

"Yeah, it hurts."

"From the concussion."

"I suppose. It's the least of my problems, it seems."

Emily bit her lip. She wasn't used to Brian complaining about anything. He was always the kind to take whatever came his way and move on. Was this the mood changes she'd been warned about? She couldn't help but feel his anger or frustration personally. She knew it wasn't her fault. But did he?

"How did physical therapy go?" She thought a change of topic might pull him out of the funk.

"Shitty. I couldn't make it to the door."

"Brian," she said as she came to his bedside. "You've been through hell. It takes time. The surgeries—all the anesthesia they pumped in you. Don't expect—"

"Stop. Just stop. Don't tell me what I've been through. I'm sitting here with a drain in my head, stitches across my gut. I'm pissing in a bag. I know what I've been through."

"Brian, I'm trying to—" Her eyes welled.

"Trying to what? Make yourself feel better?"

"That's not fair."

"Fair. What's fair about me being here? What did I do to deserve this?"

Emily's tears streaked down her cheeks. She knew this wasn't the man she loved talking. It was the pain, concussion, and drugs. That didn't cushion the blow, though.

"What happened out there? It's kinda one big blur. Robinson? He make it?" Brian asked while clamping his eyes shut.

"Robinson's good. You saved him."

She saw Brian's shoulders relax.

"There was another bomb—a few hours ago. Caught Ryan and McKinley out on the street."

"Oh no. Are they . . . ?"

"They're gonna be okay. Got busted up a bit, but nothing serious. You know them, I hear."

He nodded. "Mac, back from my time on SWAT. Good dudes."

"We're trying to figure out why these officers were hit." He seemed to be coming back to his old balanced self. She dared taking a breath before she kept pressing on.

"Like someone went at them specifically?" he said.

"Yeah."

"Dammit. I should be out there. Now I'm useless."

"It's not your fault. I know it's hard but be patient with yourself. You'll snap back to where you were. It takes time and I'll be with you."

His jaw tightened, and Emily saw he was fighting back a response. Instead, his left hand flicked out and his thumb hit the button for his pain medication. Seconds later, his eyes closed and his face relaxed.

The muzzled response hurt as much as any razor-edged comment.

She took a chair next to him and whispered, "I love you, Brian."

He didn't respond, and Emily took the back of his hand and gently kissed it.

Rest. He needed the rest to heal. Emily wished him to wake and be the man he was before—kind, loving, warm, and good-natured. She knew it was going to be a long haul. The tears started again and streamed down her cheeks. Had she lost him?

She wiped the tears away with the back of her hand and composed herself. She tucked Brian's hand under the thin sheet and kissed his forehead.

As she pushed away from his bedside, Brian groaned.

"I'll check on you again later," she whispered.

When she reached the door, she heard a muffled reply.

"Love you, Em."

She closed her eyes and took his drug-induced admission as a sign things were going to be okay.

The feeling lasted for about a minute when her cell phone vibrated in her pocket. The number displayed on the caller ID was River Gardens Memory Care, her mother's facility.

"This is Emily," she said.

"Emily. We have an issue. An issue with Connie. Could you possibly come over? It might help if she sees you."

CHAPTER TWENTY

THE EXTERIOR OF the River Gardens Memory Care was placid and serene, belying the confused and troubled minds of the residents who resided within the locked facility.

Connie Hunter needed more day-to-day assistance than a traditional assisted living facility could offer—and a horrible experience with a poorly run facility with uncaring staff put her in the emergency room.

Emily couldn't care for her any longer. God knows she tried moving Mom in with her, but her deteriorating dementia made it dangerous, even with a live-in caregiver. Confusion, forgetfulness, wandering out alone at night, and leaving the stove on were more than Emily could manage.

It killed her to "put her mother in a home," as Connie called it, but in one of the fleeting moments of clarity, Connie agreed she wasn't able to care for herself and didn't want to be a burden to her daughter.

No sooner than she'd entered the facility, Emily heard Connie scream, "I need to go!"

Emily peeked in the room and found a red-faced Connie sitting in her recliner. A young Black doctor kneeling next to her and one of Connie's favorite caregivers, Tina, stood next to her recliner, rubbing the seventy-four-year-old's shoulder.

"Mom, what's going on?"

Connie's red-rimmed eyes shot to her daughter. "Finally. You need to take me home."

Emily's heart broke for the second time tonight.

Emily got on her knees in front of her mom, took both of her withered hands in hers, and said, "Mom, you are home."

The old woman scanned the room. "This isn't my home. If I'm not back in time to make dinner for your father, there will be hell to pay."

Emily's father had died over a decade ago, and as far as she remembered, he was never a stickler about having dinner on the table when he came home from work.

Filling in the gaps. That's what Emily called it. People with dementia, like her mom, filled in the holes in their lace-like memory with fantasy.

She'd had these breaks with reality before, but they'd been less frequent, and the last time she had a serious episode was at the old facility when staff didn't make sure she kept up on her medications.

"Mom? Have you been good about taking your prescriptions?"

"All my prescriptions are at home."

Emily glanced at Tina.

"She received her regular dose this morning. I came with her evening dose and Connie was a little confused."

"I am not confused. And don't talk about me like I'm not here," Connie said.

"Miss Hunter, may I have a word?" Dr. Washington swept his hand to the door.

Emily joined him out in the hallway. A tall, handsome man with dark, expressive eyes.

The doctor pulled his glasses off and wiped them with a cloth from his jacket.

"Miss Hunter, I don't think we've met. I'm Gregory Washington. I believe Connie has experienced a panic attack. She's still aggravated—rapid breathing and pulse rate. It's too high for my liking. With your permission, I'd like to give her a light sedative to break this panic attack. We do need to figure out which of her other meds we can adjust to prevent episodes like this from reoccurring."

"She's been confused like this before. It's always been an issue with missing meds."

"I'll take a blood draw and see if there is anything else going on, an infection, or something brewing. You've seen it before, I'm sure. It doesn't take much for patients like Connie to take a turn."

Emily liked this guy. A doctor who didn't treat her like an idiot and seemed to care about his patients.

"Is a sedative necessary? I hate the thought of pumping more chemicals into her."

"I understand. This is a very light, short-acting sedative. I think the trade-off here is a sedative versus the risk prolonged blood pressure and rapid heart rate could pose."

This was the second time a doctor had asked her to consent to a medical procedure. If this kept up, she was the one who would need the sedative.

She rolled it around in her mind for a moment. She couldn't leave her mother to worry and panic herself into a stroke. Emily nodded.

"Good. We'll make her comfortable."

Emily and the doctor came back into the room and Connie reached for her purse, readying to leave.

"Mrs. Hunter, while I'm here, let's give you a flu shot. Your records show you're overdue."

"I really should be going. But I suppose since you're here," Connie said.

Emily watched as Dr. Washington prepared two narrow-gauge syringes. Emily glanced over his shoulder. He hadn't lied to Connie. She was getting a flu shot—and a little something extra.

He stood slightly behind Connie, rolled up her sleeve, and wiped the area with an alcohol wipe.

"Ohhh, that's cold," Connie said.

"I'm sorry," Dr. Washington said as he slipped the narrow-gauge needle into the soft flesh of her arm. He followed with the second syringe. Both administered back-to-back, seconds apart.

"Now, Mrs. Hunter. I want you to rest here for at least fifteen minutes. Sometimes there is a reaction to these flu vaccines."

The doctor caught Emily's eye.

"I'll stay with her, Doctor."

Dr. Washington packed away his equipment and prepared to leave. "I'll check back with you in a bit."

"Let's get you comfy, Mom."

Emily took her mother's purse, the empty one Connie carried like a thin connection to her past, and placed it on the coffee table. When it dropped on the surface, an old magazine shifted, revealing a small collection of white pills underneath.

Emily got Tina's attention and pointed at the pills her mother had stuffed away.

Tina led Connie to her bed. She was already getting drowsy.

"Her pulse is dropping back to where we like to see it," Tina said.

"I'll make a note of this and make sure staff watch her take her meds. This does happen from time to time. Her electronic profile will display a blue banner on the bottom alerting staff to monitor while they administer her meds."

"Thanks, Tina."

"Thank you for coming and getting her to calm down a bit."

"Dr. Washington is great."

"I'd like to see more of him around here, if you know what I mean."

Emily chuckled. "Yeah, he's not too hard on the eyes."

She glanced over at her mom and her face muscles were already relaxing. The tension, fear, and anxiety floating away.

"Mind if I hang out here with her for a while, Tina?"

"For as long as you want."

Emily settled on her mother's sofa and tucked a pillow under her head so she could watch her mom. The sofa was more of a love seat and Emily had to curl up or hang her legs off one end while she sprawled out.

She twisted and found a comfortable position watching her mother's breathing—slow, deep, and steady. At least one of them was able to relax tonight.

Emily ruminated over what could happen next in her mother's memory issues. So far, Connie remembered and recognized her—sometimes out of place and back in time, but she knew who her daughter was.

Doctors warned her there may come a time when her window of recognition would slowly close. She'd seen it happen to other residents in her mother's facility. Family members were demoted to a familiar face.

Emily closed her eyes, listening to her mother breathe. When she woke, would she remember her daughter?

CHAPTER TWENTY-ONE

"EMILY," A VOICE said, followed by a soft shake. "There's someone here to see you."

Emily opened her heavy eyelids, blinking, taking a moment to realize where she was. She hadn't meant to fall asleep on Mom's sofa. She shot awake. Was something wrong?

The day staff had come on and Rhonda sensed Emily's concern. "Connie's fine. She's still resting. The doctor came in a few hours ago and said she needed the extra nap time."

Emily hoped she wasn't a snoring, drooling mess when Dr. Washington dropped in.

"There's someone here to see you. Out at reception."

Emily checked her watch—7:00 a.m. She had surrendered to the exhaustion last night.

"Who is it?" Emily said, stifling a yawn.

"I don't know—he's another police officer. He said it's important. I didn't want to let him back here—you both needed your sleep."

Emily swung her legs off the sofa and she was stiff from the cramped position. She must not have moved.

"I'll be right there. Tell Javier I'll be out in a minute." She stretched the kinks from her neck.

"It's not Detective Medina. It's another officer, in uniform."

Emily stiffened. Her first thoughts were of Brian. Something had happened.

She ran her fingers through her hair and adjusted her blouse. She tossed her jacket on as she shot out from her mother's door.

Emily spotted the blue police uniform leaning on the reception desk. The officer was someone she'd seen before but couldn't recall his name.

"Detective, I—"

"What is it?"

"You weren't answering your phone. The watch commander was trying to reach you. Detective Medina said you might be here."

Emily pulled her phone from her pocket and the battery was dead.

"What's going on?"

"The watch commander wanted you to respond to a reported crime scene."

"Why didn't Detective—never mind. Where is it? It's not another one of ours, is it?"

"No, ma'am. But the watch commander wanted me to warn you about news media at the scene. We've set up a perimeter to keep them back."

"When did this happen? How long ago did we respond?"

"About two hours."

"Shit. Let me get my act together and I'll be right there. Give me the address, would you?"

The officer pulled a folded note from his shirt pocket and handed it to her.

"This is a pricey neighborhood. Pocket Area, right?"

"Yes, ma'am. Oh, you should know. The chief is on scene."

"Crap on a cracker. That's burying the lede, Officer. I'm on my way."

Emily retreated to her mother's room, where Rhonda was getting Connie ready for the day. Dressed and fresh looking, her mother smiled when Emily entered.

"Hello, dear. This is a nice surprise."

She didn't seem to remember her panic episode last night. One of the small silver linings from dementia—short-term unpleasant memories evaporate quickly.

"Good morning, Mom. I thought I'd pop in and say good morning before breakfast."

"Well, I'm glad you did. It's always good to see you."

It wasn't so good last night, Emily thought.

"You should do something with your hair, Emily. It's unkempt and a little wild. A touch of makeup might help too."

"Help, Mom? And what am I looking to help?"

"My dear girl, you aren't getting any younger."

"Thanks for the reminder, Mother."

Rhonda helped Connie to her feet, and the woman showed no grogginess from the sedative the evening before. Emily gave her mom a hug and a kiss on the forehead before Rhonda whisked her off to breakfast.

Emily ducked into her mother's bathroom and tamed the bedhead she saw in the mirror. She washed her face and, despite Mom's direction, didn't see the point of wearing makeup to a crime scene. Not that she was one to trowel it on to begin with. She tugged on her jacket lapels. Presentable. For a murder investigation.

Emily left the facility, warmed up her SUV, and glanced at the address the officer had given her. She knew the general area, and she'd pull up directions from her . . . dead phone.

Once in the Pocket neighborhood, Emily started looking for street signs. She passed the Full Charge Electronics store and thought about dropping in to see what Councilman Davis was teaching in his Bomb-Making 101 class. The sign on the storefront said CLOSED. Nerds must run later hours. They hadn't emerged from their cocoons in mommy's basement yet. Everything else in the strip mall was open.

Two blocks past the electronics store, Emily caught a break. She caught the street she was looking for: Monte Vista. She turned right and into a sea of red flashing lights. Fire trucks, hose lines crossing the street to a Tudor-styled home.

She was one block away, and between her and the home were three news vans, each with a camera crew filming and reporting from the scene. Emily tucked her SUV into a space between a fire engine and a news van and followed the fire hoses to the gated house ahead.

At the curb, Emily ducked around the media circus and found the crime scene tape. An officer lifted it for her and logged her into the scene on his clipboard.

The home was more imposing the closer she got—flagstone pathways, iron gates, four-car garage. No wonder the media frenzy. This was one of the city's elite—a home invasion?

The fire crews were poking and prodding the front of the home where flames had charred the exterior surface. The source of the blaze was a vehicle in front of one of the garage bays. A Tesla, and not the cheap one. Battery fire? She wondered—until she spotted the bomb squad commander.

"Emily," Javier called from the front steps of the residence.

She strode up to join him.

"Our case took a strange left turn."

"Another bomb, I take it? Whose place is this?"

"Councilman Davis."

"What? Davis screwed up and blew himself up?" Emily said.

Javier pointed to the now charcoal-colored Tesla. "Same as the other attacks. A device ended up under his car and took him out."

"Did he make a mistake and set off his own bomb?"

"Doesn't look that way. We didn't find any evidence of bomb materials in what was left of the vehicle, or in the home. He wasn't making the devices here."

Emily rubbed the back of her neck. "We find any pieces of the device, the radio controller gizmos, like we had at the other scenes?"

"Everything's burned to a cinder. The fire was hot—the electric car's battery caught and made a mess of it. Anything we might've found there is gone."

"And Davis?"

"We think he was getting in the vehicle and hadn't even shut his door yet. The blast blew him out of the driver's seat and tossed him twenty feet away." Javier pointed to a charred spot on the lawn.

"Medical examiner come and gone?"

"Left about five minutes ago."

Emily kicked a pebble with the toe of her boot. "My phone died."

"Next you'll tell me the dog ate your homework," Javier said with a grin, which dissolved when he caught the furrowed brow and dark circles under Emily's eyes.

"You okay? Brian?"

Where should she begin? Brian's sudden aggressive posture? Her mom lost in time and place, again? Her own feelings of helplessness from all of it crashing down on her?

"No, no, Brian's fine. No, he isn't but I had an issue with Mom last night."

"Connie? Don't tell me the new facility neglected her or forgot about her medications. I remember the hoops you jumped through to find

River Gardens."

"They were on top of it. Mom had a panic attack—another one of those episodes of sundowner's syndrome where she thinks she needs to escape and find her way home. The doctor gave her a sedative and it was enough to break the cycle and let her rest. I stayed with her last night."

"Oh, man, I'm sorry. I'd ask Mom to come over and sit with her, but she's visiting family in Escondido."

"I know she would. Lucinda has always been a lifesaver. She seemed better this morning. Anyways, sorry I'm late."

Javier shot a glance at the home. "A fancy place for a city servant, huh?"

"No kidding. The electronics store must be doing pretty good because he couldn't afford this on a city salary." Emily nodded to the massive double door entry. "I heard the chief was here . . ."

"He is. Inside with Mrs. Davis."

"Didn't know there was a better half—and she obviously must have been. No disrespect to the dead," Emily said.

"Hold that thought. Follow me."

Emily followed Javier up the marble steps into the home's entry foyer, which was as big as her entire living room. A world apart from the old-world Tudor exterior, the spaces she could see were modernist, blond wood, glass, and metal. Cold.

Emily leaned in and whispered, "It looks like some hipster museum without the cool stuff."

To the left, a large living room, formal, and a design Emily felt was stiff and uninviting. Voices ahead. Emily recognized the deep, resonant voice of Chief Clark.

When they turned into a custom-designed chef's kitchen, Chief Clark stood next to an ebony dining table. A man dressed in an expensive suit and a raven-haired woman were seated at the dark table. Untouched coffee in front of them.

Clark nodded to Emily while the suited man spoke to the woman.

"It's up to you. If you don't want to talk to them, you aren't compelled to."

Emily had come in mid-conversation. The councilman's wife wasn't making eye contact with the man seated next to her. She stared at the table, tight jawed. Emily thought there was more anger than grief.

"They killed my husband," the woman said.

Chief Clark tipped his head to the table and Emily knew he wanted her to talk to the newly minted widow, woman-to-woman.

Emily pulled a chair from the table and sat next to Mrs. Davis. She had experience dealing with people in crisis, after the loss of a family member. Mrs. Davis wasn't the one out in front of the cameras. That was her husband.

"My name's Emily Hunter and I'm a detective. We want to find out what happened to your husband. We want to find out who's responsible for this. Can I ask you a few questions about tonight?"

Mrs. Davis remained stoic.

"I'm Tad Hawkins. I represent the councilman and Mrs. Davis on legal matters." He spoke in a stiff, aloof manner. His posture said he was full of himself from his Savile Row suit to his buffed and manicured nails.

"That's nice, Tad," Emily said. Then, in a softer tone to Mrs. Davis: "You said something about 'they' killed your husband. Who wanted to harm him?"

Mrs. Davis stiffened and turned to Emily. "You have the gall to ask? Okay, I'll play your little game, Detective. You did. You people killed my husband because he knew what you did. What you always do and cover it up."

"I'm not here to talk about politics. Whoever killed the councilman is targeting police officers too. We both want the same thing—to find out who did this."

Mrs. Davis was silent for a moment. She shifted the coffee mug in her hands. Emily noticed a burn, and soot and ash, on her left hand. She'd tried to reach her husband as he burned on the front lawn.

"Mrs. Davis, can I have someone come and take a look at your hand? Your burn."

She released the coffee mug with her left hand and held it in front of her, examining it as if it were a foreign object.

"He was gone when I got there. I—I couldn't do anything to help him. The last time I touched my husband . . ."

"You were here, in the home, when it happened?"

"Is this necessary now, Detective?" the attorney said.

"Yes, Tad, it is." Then, to Javier: "Could you ask one of the EMTs to come in and take a look at Mrs. Davis?"

Emily redirected her gaze to Mrs. Davis. "You were here, then?"

She nodded. "We were here in the kitchen getting ready for a quick bite. Robby said he had to go out. He got a phone call, then said he needed to run off to this meeting."

Emily noticed plates on the counter. They were about to sit down for a meal together.

"Did he mention who called?"

She shook her head.

"How about where he was going?"

"He didn't say. Only that he'd be back within the hour."

"I take it you heard the explosion. Did you see anyone or hear anything when you went to find out what happened?"

She closed her eyes and a slight twitching motion came over her as she recalled the event.

"I went to the door to see him off. He had a file folder with him. I didn't recognize it—it was one of his personal files he kept in our office here. I thought I heard something when he reached the car."

"What was that?"

"The Tesla is very quiet when it starts—nearly silent. There was this hum. The best way to describe it was a high-pitched buzz. I thought we needed to service the Tesla again. Then . . ."

"This buzzing sound. Would you describe it as an electric whine, like a zipping noise?"

Mrs. Davis looked at Emily for the first time.

"Yes, how did you know?"

"I heard the same thing last night—right before a vehicle exploded next to us," Emily said.

Chief Clark stiffened.

"I wasn't imagining it? It wasn't coming from our car?"

Emily nodded and touched Mrs. Davis's trembling hand. "I don't think so. Someone purposely hit the councilman. Who'd have a grudge?"

"Other than the police and this waste of a mayor we have?"

"Other than those . . ."

"Robby would listen to everyone. It was what made him effective as a community activist. But some of them were only in it for themselves. Gang leaders—he actually tried starting a council where they could air their grievances. He thought it would de-escalate the tensions and prevent violence."

"Let me guess. It didn't turn out as he planned?"

"Not hardly. They damn near had a shoot-out in the middle of his attempt at a peace conference."

Emily thought back to her talk with Sergeant Berney. "Ever hear him mention a gang member with the name Rockhead?"

"Yes—yes, he did. This Rockhead person was his biggest ally in trying to bring the gang violence down in North Sacramento."

"Rockhead was killed last night. The same way your husband was."

Mrs. Davis looked shocked. "Someone killed them because of what they believed in?"

"We're looking into every plausible explanation. That's definitely one we need to follow up."

"Why? Why would someone do this?" The widow cradled her face in her hands and sobbed. The reality was finally sinking in.

Javier returned with the EMT, who knelt next to Mrs. Davis and started by checking her blood pressure.

Emily joined the chief by the white marble counter. "She say anything before I got here?"

"You got the gist of it. Her weasel of an attorney has her convinced we bombed his car."

"Because of the whole anti-cop and defund-the-police business?"

The chief nodded and turned his back to Mrs. Davis. "Like we have time to track down everyone who hates on us. It's smoke to cover up everything else going on in the community. Guns, drugs, no employment opportunities, businesses shuttered after the lockdowns. They're frustrated. They're lashing out at anything or anyone they can."

"You heard her say something about some files?"

"Yeah, what are you thinking?"

"Someone lured him outside. It was urgent enough for him to stop the meal he and his wife were about to sit down to, and he needed to make sure he brought a file with him. The file is probably toast, but I'd sure like to know what was in it."

"Something worth killing for?" Chief Clark said.

"Especially with the connection between the councilman and Rockhead," Emily said.

"Where does that leave us with the officers in last night's bombing?"

"I'm working on it. Not sure—yet."

Emily stepped back to the table. "Mrs. Davis, there's going to be a lot happening. Is there anyone who can come and be with you?"

"I have . . . my sister. She lives in Roseville."

"Would you like me to call her?"

"I can do that. What happens next?"

"The medical examiner will take care of him. When she's finished with the legal necessities, they'll call you. That's when you can arrange for a local funeral director to take over."

"What do I do? We . . . we never talked about what he wanted."

"The funeral director at the mortuary you choose will help walk you through the options. I can ask someone to come from victim services to help."

"No. This is something I should do."

"I understand. Part of what I need to do now is figure out who is responsible and why they did this."

Mrs. Davis scowled. "You know who's responsible. You people did this."

Back to this again, Emily thought. *Change the line of questioning here.*

"The phone call—the one the councilman got before he left. Did you hear any of the conversation? It could be important."

"No. It came through on his cell phone."

"Did he seem upset with the call?"

Mrs. Davis paused for a moment. "Upset? No. He seemed anxious, in a hurry to go meet with this person."

"And he never said a name?"

She shook her head.

"But he grabbed a file to take with him?"

"Yes."

"But you don't know what was in the file?"

"No."

"Would you show me where the file came from? You said there was a home office?"

Tad cleared his throat. "I don't think that's going to happen, Detective."

"Mrs. Davis? What about it? Could you show us where the file came from? Maybe you can tell which one he took?"

"When you're holding a warrant, Detective," Tad said.

"We can. But I didn't think this would be the best time to have a bunch of cops and evidence techs swarming all over the house. And, of course, Mrs. Davis would need to leave the premises while we conduct a search and remove every shred of paperwork in the house. That's not what she needs right now. I have no interest in confiscating anything from his office. But, if you insist . . ."

"Fine. I'll show you. The sooner you're out of my home, the better." Mrs. Davis pushed off the EMT who was coating her hand with burn ointment and stood.

"I'd advise you not to consent to a search by government officials."

"Shut up, Tad. You and Robby's conspiracy theories . . ."

Mrs. Davis led Emily and Javier to a room on the opposite end of the home, past a wine storage room, with sleek steel and black glass refrigerators, an expensively furnished home gym, and another sitting room with library shelves packed with what looked to be aging first editions.

Mrs. Davis paused at a set of double mahogany doors and pulled them open.

Emily took a step inside and scanned the glass and stainless-steel desk, where a large computer monitor took up most of the surface.

"You can see how much of a hurry he was in. He left the file drawer open," Mrs. Davis said, gesturing to the black lacquered cabinet behind the desk.

The man was organized. Emily had to give him his due. Row upon row of files, all tabbed and labeled. One file was missing from the tightly packed drawer—most likely the one Davis was in a hurry to grab.

Emily leaned closer and saw the label for the missing file. The small block letters sent a shiver through her. "Conner, Tucker, Miller, Cortez, Black, McKinley, Whitman."

Emily snapped a photo of the file label and showed it to Javier.

"Thank you, Mrs. Davis. If you need anything, here's a card with my contact number. If you can recall anything, no matter how insignificant you think it might be about what the councilman was doing when he left, please call me."

Mrs. Davis took the card and nodded. She slammed the file drawer, harder than she needed to. The anger and frustration at not knowing what got her husband killed spilled through.

Emily and Javier backtracked to the kitchen, where Chief Clark spoke on his cell phone.

"Yes, I understand how it looks—"

He listened to the person on the other end of the connection. His eyes locked on Emily.

"Yes, we'll be there." The chief disconnected the call, pocketed the phone.

"That was Mayor Carsten. She's heard about the BBQ out front. We need to go brief her. She's apparently getting pressure to respond, and her staffers want to drop the hammer on the police department."

"But she's not going to?" Emily said.

"I don't know, yet. At least she's giving us a chance to say our piece."

Mrs. Davis and her attorney started down the hall. Emily wiggled her phone. She leaned toward the chief. "I need to show you something—outside."

She led the way out of the opulent home to the front yard, where the smell of the charred Tesla made her nose itch. At least she hoped it was only the charred electric car she was smelling and not bits of its owner.

"It looks like a hit list," Javier said as Emily held it out for him and the chief.

"We should track down these other officers and warn them," Emily said.

"The watch commander can handle it while we head to the mayor's office."

"The mayor?" Emily asked.

"A storm's brewing," the chief said.

Emily agreed to meet the chief at city hall. She knew with the councilman's death there would be mounting political pressure to solve these attacks. When politics got involved, common sense often got left in the dust.

"Something about this doesn't sit well with me," Emily said as the chief left the Davis compound. Someone going after cops, as unhinged as it was, could be explained. Someone with an axe to grind, a personal grudge. The councilman's death and his list of officers was harder to fathom. What did one have to do with the other?

"Like why did he end up blown to bits in his front yard?" Javier said.

"There's that. We can't rule out he accidentally blew his own ass up. But I think we're looking for a link between the two."

Javier glanced at the blackened husk of the car. "The electric car battery burned so hot, there won't be much evidence to sort through. From what we do have, it looks like the same kind of device used in the other attacks. You heard what Mrs. Davis said—the sound before the explosion. It's possible he was targeted too."

"Wanna ride together?" Emily asked.

"Sure. Let me have an officer drive my ride back to the office when they're done here."

Javier strode off and handed his keys to an officer at the perimeter.

He jogged back and jumped into the passenger seat. Emily backed away from the curb and for a moment she swore she saw a dark figure with a hoodie pulled up tight watching the councilman's home from a thick hedge a few houses down. When she stopped and peered into the hedgerow, there was nothing there.

"Thought I saw someone hanging out," she said.

"Probably a curious neighbor afraid their property value might take hit."

"Maybe."

Emily took another glance into the thick hedge and headed down the street, back toward downtown.

"You recognize any of those names on the file label?"

"Other than Brian, McKinley, and Tucker? No."

"We'll need to search personnel records. The watch commander's office will confirm current patrol assignments."

"I still can't wrap my head around why a city councilman would keep a list of officers."

"Davis was anti-cop from the gate. I wouldn't put it past him to keep dirt he'd uncovered, or a file of complaints against officers."

"You didn't happen to see your file in there, did you? It would be the big thick one."

"The complaints would have been from you."

"Doesn't take away from their validity."

"Yeah, it kinda does."

CHAPTER TWENTY-TWO

EMILY FOUND A broken parking meter marked with a heavy canvas hood locked over the post. The spot was on the eastern edge of Cesar Chávez Park, where a single protest sign marked an upcoming gathering of concerned fans over the local basketball team, calling for a coaching change after another disappointing season.

City hall was across the street and it appeared calm. But looks were often deceiving in this place with a history of backroom deals and dirty politics.

Emily was right. Inside the city council chambers, two television news crews were setting up their equipment for a segment, likely taped for the evening prime-time news.

The mayor's office was buzzing with frantic energy when the detectives arrived.

A receptionist with a phone tucked to her ear spotted Emily and pointed to the mayor's office. Emily pulled the heavy wooden door open and Mayor Carsten stood behind her desk pointing a finger at Chief Clark.

"How the hell do you think it looks when you can't even protect an elected city leader?" Mayor Carsten fumed behind her desk.

Emily had seen the politician angry before, but this was white hot.

"Mayor, Councilman Davis was killed at home. There was nothing the police department could have done to prevent this attack. And based on the councilman's very public disdain for the police, do you think he would have let us?"

"Emily, the public perception is reeling out of control. A vocal opponent of my office—of the police department—is murdered after he blames us for mismanagement. How do you think that's going to play?"

"Frankly, I don't care," Emily said.

Chief Clark closed his eyes.

"Excuse me?" the mayor said.

"I don't care how his death is going to be spun in the local media. What I do care about is why Davis was attacked. You and I both know his death had nothing whatsoever to do with you or his pipe dream to run against you in the next election."

The mayor pointed out the window overlooking the park. "The people out there—they believe there's a connection. You complain about the city and you get killed. They are already making a martyr of this guy."

"Listen, no one will believe Davis was a saint. He spent his time inflaming the community and I think everyone knows it. These attacks have to be linked. The bombs—the way they were delivered—are connected. There's no link to the mayor's office," Emily said.

"Small mercies," the mayor said. "The public will make up their own story unless we can get out in front of it. The chief was telling me he doesn't have a suspect to run down."

"The attacks have been directed at our officers, until tonight. I believe Davis still holds a connection to the other attacks," Emily said.

The mayor returned to her desk and collapsed heavily in her chair. "Davis wasn't exactly on the same page with your fellow officers, Emily,"

Carsten said.

"No, that's a given. But the connection is there. He was lured out. Someone waited outside with a bomb."

"Who was he going to meet?" the mayor said.

"The wife didn't know. We'll start to put the warrant together to search phone records. The councilman's cell phone was destroyed in the blast, as was the file he was carrying with him."

"Any takers on whether it was a burner phone?" the chief asked. "We'll have a hard time figuring out what the meeting was about." The chief crossed his arms over his chest, something Emily noticed him do when he was anxious, usually about something he couldn't control.

Emily pulled her phone out, scrolled to the photo of the file label, and handed it to the chief.

"This was the file name—the one he took with him." He held the phone to Mayor Carsten.

"Who are these people?"

The chief pointed at the image on Emily's phone. "These are officers—or former officers with our department."

"Was Davis keeping book on staff complaints? Might have been OPSA reports, or notes on complaints submitted by his constituents," the mayor said.

The mayor handed back the phone.

The chief shook his head. "These officers, I recognize the names. All of them are solid cops. I even pinned a couple of awards for meritorious conduct on a few of them. Whatever this was, it wasn't misconduct we investigated."

"Maybe complaints that didn't go anywhere—exonerated or unfounded," Emily said.

"I have no recollection of these officers being investigated on any violation. I sign off on those investigations. I would know if they were. There's something else going on here."

"What are you saying, Chief?" the mayor asked.

"I'm not sure, but I think Detective Hunter is onto something here. These officers weren't under investigation for misconduct, like Davis would usually spout off about. They were, each of them, outstanding officers. They had to be or I wouldn't have approved their assignment to our SWAT operations."

Emily knew the SWAT connection existed between Brian, McKinley, and Tucker. But all the officers on Davis's list? Not a chance it was a random connection.

"All of them? Assigned to SWAT?" Javier said.

"They were. This goes back a few years. I was still a captain, if I remember correctly. But they were on the team at the same time."

"If Tucker, McKinley, and Brian were targeted, the rest of these officers are at risk," Emily said.

"Some of them don't work with the department any longer. Retired, transferred to another agency. There're a couple here who quit."

"Why would Davis keep a list of former SWAT cops?" Emily asked.

"Good question."

Javier stepped next to Emily and tapped at the image on her phone. "What if Davis found some dirt and was going to file a complaint against these officers?"

"I don't like where that leads," Emily said.

"For what? And even if he did, the statute of limitations, and most collective bargaining agreement terms, wouldn't let us do anything about policy violations from when these officers were on the SWAT roster—three years or more for some of them."

"What if it's criminal?" Emily said.

"Even then—well, except if it's murder. Which it can't be because we'd sure as hell know by now. All the jailhouse gossip would have grabbed onto something like that," Chief Clark said.

"Who called Davis out of his home?" the mayor asked.

"Did someone on this list get wind of what he was trying to do and go after Davis?" Javier said.

"Emily, can you ask Sergeant Conner what he remembers about his time on the team with these officers?" the chief asked.

Emily flipped back to the last encounter with Brian in the hospital. He wasn't much in the mood for answering questions. She wasn't even sure he would talk to her.

"I can try, sir." She bit her lower lip after the response.

The mayor pressed her palms on the desk. "Where does it leave us with the public? What can we tell them? Certainly none of this?"

The chief paced across the room and stopped in front of a photo hung on the wall. He stared at the framed image.

Emily noticed his shoulders stiffen. "Chief?"

"When was this taken?" Chief Clark asked, tapping a finger on the glass.

Emily joined Chief Clark and took in the photo of a city council meeting. Three council members looked like they were being sworn in—Councilman Robby Davis among them.

"At the January council meeting when Davis, Maldonado, and Jefferson came onto the council. Little did I know he would become such a pain in my political ass. If I recall, he brought supporters from a crime victims' group, or something," the mayor said.

"He wasn't always this antagonistic?" Emily said.

"Davis campaigned on a platform of cooperation and building a better Sacramento together. A few months into his term, something changed."

"I don't remember him being anything but an ass," Emily said.

"Because you only see the best in people," Javier said.

The chief tapped the glass. "This guy. This one—recognize him?"

Emily peered at the man in the background. One of thirty supporters in the council chambers while the new members were being sworn in.

"No, should I? I mean, he looks like the others. A smile plastered on his face during the swearing-in ceremony."

Emily looked again. The man looked to be in his late thirties, short, cropped hair, seemed to be serious about the swearing-in ceremony. Hard to tell from the photo, but he appeared athletic, arms and shoulders filling out the polo shirt. "I don't recognize him. Should I?"

"His face. I know that from somewhere—can't place it," the chief said, tapping a finger on the glass.

"I don't remember Davis having much support from crime victims' groups—even before his anti-cop sentiment began to leak out. The change in position would have alienated the tough-on-crime lobby."

"He didn't," the mayor said. "He ran on this 'clean money' platform. He didn't take campaign cash from lobbyists, businesses, or unions. Small donations from individuals only."

"What made him flip his switch? Why the change in his public persona?" Emily asked.

"I couldn't put a finger on it. The first time I saw it come up was at a council session. A routine budget request from the chief to add something to the department's budget. Wasn't long after this photo—six, eight months, maybe. Davis came out of his chair and started bad-mouthing the department, claiming excessive force complaints were off the hook, and wanted to start dismantling the department," Mayor Carsten said.

"I remember the session," the chief said. "Totally out of the blue.

I don't remember what the request was for but Councilman Davis attacked the department, questioned what our role in the community should be, and wanted to replace us with community patrols and social workers to respond to calls instead of 'an armed militia,' as he called it. Really bizarre."

"No one expected it from him. I know a couple of other council members called him on it, but he refused to back down."

The mayor glanced at her watch. "Chief. They're eating us for lunch. We should be on the same page here before our press conference. Safe to say the usual—can't comment on an ongoing investigation line?"

The chief nodded.

The mayor stood and straightened her jacket hem. Her chief of staff stood ready and Chief Clark looked like he was being led to the firing squad. Emily knew how much he loathed press conferences. He wasn't the type of man who liked to boast about his accomplishments, unlike the newly departed councilman.

"Chief, Mayor Carsten, hold up a sec. What if we approach this differently?"

Emily huddled with them and whispered her idea. The chief shook his head no, but Emily tugged on his jacket sleeve and dug in on her approach.

"It could work, but it's risky, Emily," Clark said.

"Life is a risk."

Chief Clark didn't respond.

"Chief, we need to go now," the mayor said.

"All right. We'll do this your way—for now." The chief left with the mayor and her entourage.

Javier stood next to Emily as the city power brokers left the office. "I don't like this idea, Emily."

"We don't have a choice."

"There's always a choice, Em. Putting yourself out there as bait? What were you thinking?"

"Let's go see how it plays out."

CHAPTER TWENTY-THREE

THE MAYOR AND the chief stood at the rostrum and waited until the news crews were ready. Red lights on the camera told they were recording.

Mayor Carsten approached the microphone. A slight pause and a glance around at the news crews to ensure she had their attention. "It's with great sadness I report that City Councilman Robby Davis was killed at his home a few hours ago. We are piecing together the last few hours of his life. He was steadfast in his commitment to this city. We may not have always agreed on the approach, but Councilman Davis always did what he believed to be in the best interest of his constituency. I have complete confidence in our police department to investigate—but make no mistake. Robby Davis was murdered and we will leave no stone unturned in the search for the person responsible.

"Chief Clark, can you update us on the investigation?" the mayor asked as she stepped away from the microphone.

The chief appeared solemn and his sharp features gave him a no-nonsense vibe. "Thank you for your confidence in the men and women of our department. Councilman Davis was a vocal critic of me and my department. His policy leanings will have no bearing on the rigor of this investigation. We cannot allow citizens of this city to fall prey to violence in their own homes. We cannot discuss the specifics of this investigation, but we can tell you the councilman was murdered using what we believe were the same methods as the attacks at the church on Del Paso Heights, and yesterday's bombing on West El Camino."

The chief found Emily in the audience and paused. She nodded, and the chief continued.

"These attacks are the act of a coward. We now know there was a connection between the bombings and Councilman Davis."

A murmur spread through the council chamber.

The chief raised his hands to silence them.

"I'm not saying the councilman had a hand in the attacks. He is a central figure in our investigation and we believe he may have known who was responsible. My best detective is on this case and has developed several leads to bring this case to closure. Detective Emily Hunter has a proven track record of bringing the toughest criminals down. I can tell you Detective Hunter will bring the councilman's killer to justice and there is no stopping her."

Javier leaned to Emily. "Damn—they put you right out there on front street."

"That's the idea. This guy showed his hand. He was desperate in his hit on Davis. It's where we dig in."

The press conference concluded without answering further questions from the media.

A reporter who knew Emily stepped over to her.

"Detective, can I have a word on the record?"

Emily knew the reporter, Kari Hardison, from the last remaining newspaper in the city, and she'd always been fair in her coverage.

"Sure, Kari. I have time for a quick one," Emily said.

The reporter pulled a small recorder from her purse and held it discreetly in front of her. Making sure no one else was in range of her discussion, she flicked the button on the device, recited the time and place, and began.

"Detective Hunter, the bombing attack on Councilman Davis marks the third such attack in the city. The chief of police claimed there was a connection between them. Does this mean the bombings weren't random?"

"We believe each attack has been deliberate. There have been five bombings, actually. Two at the church in Del Paso, and we saw something similar last night on West El Camino. In each case, we have reason to believe the attacks were not random."

"The councilman was a vocal opponent of the police department. How is he connected to the other attacks?"

"In the councilman's crusade against the department, we believe he stumbled upon the person responsible for the bombings."

"Anything you can share with us?"

"The bomber thought he could eliminate the evidence when he attacked the councilman—he didn't and we're coming for him."

Kari clicked off the recorder and shoved it back into her bag.

"Thanks, Detective. Off the record—you have a specific individual in mind?"

"I can't comment on specifics of the investigation, Kari. But we have our direction mapped out."

"Is there any caution, or guidance, you can offer to the public?"

Emily thought for a moment. The bomber had carefully targeted their victims. Except for the gang member who pulled his motorcycle next to the police cruiser . . .

"Kari, this terrorist is a coward. He's afraid to get up close and personal. We know he watches like a Peeping Tom. He probably gets off on it. But when it all boils down, he's a coward. People should keep an eye out and if they see something—say something. Above all, if they find a suspicious device, don't go near it. Call 911."

"Thanks for this, Detective. And please watch yourself. I thought it was unusual for the chief to out you like that. This bomber's a nutjob and he could come after you. Davis believed the bomber was unhinged."

"We'll be ready."

Emily hoped she would be.

Javier closed in after the reporter left the council chambers. "I hope you know what you're doing. I don't like the idea of the chief dangling you out there like bait."

"Why, Javi, do I detect 'feelings'?"

"Not so much feelings as much as a smidgen of concern."

She faced her partner and leaned in. "Something came to me while I was talking to the reporter—the connection to Davis."

They headed for the main exit from city hall. Emily couldn't shake the feeling that her chat with Kari Hardison shook something loose.

"The chief said Davis might know who the bomber was," Javier said.

"He did. I'm sure of it now. He was killed because of it. Kari just said something. She's been talking with Davis. He was going to out the bomber to the reporter, Kari."

"What? Her?"

"She said Davis called the bomber unhinged. The only way she'd know, or believe that, would be if he told her. I'm betting Davis was on his way to meet her," Emily said.

"She called and lured him out?"

"No. Not lured. I think Kari got ahold of something that she needed David to confirm. We'll have to pull the cell records, but I don't think she lured him. He was being watched."

"And the reporter was being used. But destroying the files. How would our guy know Davis would grab them before meeting with the reporter, if that's where he was headed?"

"Maybe he got lucky on that point, but I'm certain Davis was killed to shut him up," Emily said.

"And you as much as told the reporter you know too. That's asking for trouble."

They followed the stragglers from the city council chambers and waited at the crosswalk for the light to change.

Emily was jostled in the scrum of pedestrians crossing the busy street. She wheeled around and looked for the person who gave her a shoulder as they passed. Emily couldn't be sure who it was.

A woman waiting to the right of Emily let out a startled "Oh" as she sidestepped.

Emily stubbed her toe on a black lump at her feet. It took her a moment to recognize a large rubber wheel like those used in the bombing. Instead of an explosion, the tire bore a handwritten note.

Back off. Don't make me add you to my list.

Emily bent to pick up the rubber wheel.

"Looks like we got his attention," she said.

Emily pivoted on her heel, trying to find the person who bumped her in the crowd. Javier scanned the sidewalks around Cesar Chávez Park. Dozens of people strolling through the park. Any of them could have delivered the strange message.

Emily turned the wheel over in her hand. Her attention shot to a partial message scrawled on the rubber. The words *Remember Them* were visible.

Emily grabbed an evidence bag from the rear of the SUV and

carefully secured the rubber wheel.

"Remember them . . ." Emily said.

"Remember who?" Javier said.

The messages were starting to add up. *Don't make me add you to my list* and *Remember them* gave Emily pause. List? Was it Davis's list of officers' names? Remember who?

"Let's take this back to the office." She held the evidence bag.

"I hate puzzles," Javier said.

Halfway back to police headquarters on Freeport, Emily's cell vibrated. Her first thought was her mom was having issues again. It was amazing how a small vibration from a cell phone could create an anxious shock to her system.

The caller ID wasn't a familiar number. Maybe it was Dr. Washington.

She stabbed the CALL button. "Hunter here."

"Hey, it's me." Brian's voice came through her phone.

A wave of relief swept through her. The call wasn't to tell her about some fresh problem with her mother. But a new anxious tension grew when the last interaction with Brian played in her memory. He was talking—but where would this conversation lead?

"Everything okay?" she asked, gritting her teeth for the response.

"Just peachy. I—I wanted to say I'm sorry for being an ass."

"What was that? You're breaking up there. It sounded like you were saying you were sorry . . ." There was a playful lilt in Emily's voice.

"You aren't going to make this easy, are you?"

"Why, Brian, whatever do you mean?"

"You're impossible, you know that?"

"So I've heard. How are you?"

"I'm bored."

"Well, I'm flattered that I'm a distraction for you."

"It's not like that. I—I feel bad about how I acted and wanted to say I'm sorry. Hey, can you tell me if Tommy made it?"

Emily's forehead wrinkled from a nagging sensation she sometimes had with her mother—and her failing memory. She'd had talked with him about the bombing and that his partner was okay. He didn't remember.

Rather than tell Brian they'd already talked about it, Emily took a different course.

"I'll come by and fill you in. A thread came up and you might help connect some of the dots for us. You see the news today?"

"I can't watch television. The screen hurts my eyes."

Just as well, Emily thought. She wasn't sure what reaction he'd have with the account of additional attacks.

"They're coming to drag me to physical therapy in about fifteen minutes. My social calendar is free after."

"Great. I'll come over. Need me to bring you anything?"

"I would kill for some red licorice—you know, those long twisty ones."

"Really? I've never seen you eat those." As long as she'd known him, Brian was into organic, unprocessed, natural foods.

"What happened to 'my body is a temple'?" Emily said with a playful lilt.

"For what good it did, I think the temple is closed for the season."

There was more than a hint of self-pity in his response. What harm could a little sugar do? Still, it seemed out of character.

"I'll grab some on my way over."

"I can't wait."

"For me or the red licorice?"

"Yes . . ."

"All right. I asked for that. See you soon. Work hard at PT. Love you."

"Okay."

Brian disconnected the call.

The lingering "okay" bit at her more than she was willing to admit. He wasn't drug induced this time . . .

Javier roused her from her thoughts.

"Everything all right?" he said.

"I'm not sure. He didn't remember talking about the bombing before. I know it could've been the pain meds, or the post-surgical fog. But . . ."

"You're worried about him."

"I am."

Javier pulled into the police department parking lot and stopped near the entrance.

"Tell you what. Give me the rubber wheel and the message, and you go see what's up with Brian. I'll have Milton sort out if this is the same wheel we found at our church bombing."

"You don't mind?" Emily asked.

"Do it. I don't need my partner to go all sad puppy over what's happening to her boy toy."

She smacked him with a backhand to his shoulder.

"I'm not some hormonal teenager."

"Really? It's hard to tell sometimes. Go."

"Ass."

She got out and took the keys from Javi while he started to the office door. "Let me know if you come up with anything on those. And thanks."

He told her to go, and he ducked inside. Emily pulled the SUV out of the lot, and it was a bit early for the hospital. She didn't want to interrupt Brian's physical therapy session.

There was a stop on the way she thought might help pull things into focus.

CHAPTER TWENTY-FOUR

EMILY PULLED THE SUV into the small lot in front of Benjamin Tooker's office. The former felon turned-private-investigator stood in the doorway seeing off another lady caller based on the empty serving tray tucked under her arm.

Tooker smiled at the woman, and Emily swore she saw the lady swoon. Tooker's eyes flicked over to Emily as she got out of the SUV.

Tooker whispered to the woman, and she glanced at Emily with a jealous sneer.

Emily approached the office, and the woman turned to leave, giving Emily an eyeful of cleavage as she strode past.

"Benjamin, I have concerns about your investigative abilities if you think that woman is bringing you cookies out of the goodness of her heart—which you can almost see from the sundress she had on."

Tooker laughed. "Come on in, Detective."

Emily followed Tooker inside and followed him to his office. It looked more organized than some of the PI offices she'd visited in the past. Typically, they had files strewn about, empty take-out containers filling overflowing trash cans, and cameras with telephoto lenses on their desk to follow cheating spouses.

Tooker's office was sparse, tidy, and his desk surface was squared away. A single manila file folder on a red blotter took up the center of the workspace.

He gestured Emily to one of the mismatched chairs facing his desk.

"What can I help you with, Detective?"

Behind his desk were four serving platters of cookies, zucchini bread, and the odd Bundt cake. He caught Emily eyeing the collection.

A slight grin crossed Tooker's face.

"Any word on your missing girl, Danika?"

The big man's shoulder's slumped. "No. Not yet. Family seems to think she's run off. I'm worried about what she'll find out there. Anyways, you didn't come out here to ask about a missing Black girl, did you?"

Emily shook her head. "No. I want to pick your brain on what's behind these bombing attacks. You know about the most recent one? Councilman Davis?"

"I heard. Do I need to give you my alibi, or somethin'?"

"I could use a quick solve on these cases. But no. I want your take on Davis. I'm having trouble pinning him down. He came into office as a middle-of-the-road type, then took a hard left into defunding the police and community agitation. What was his deal?"

"What does it matter now? Dude's dead."

"What explains his sudden shift in his political leanings? I think he was killed for something he knew—something he was going to expose. Ever hear anything like that?"

Emily could see him working to consider what or, more accurately, how much to say.

"Listen, I know there are issues between the community and the police," Emily said.

"You think?"

"I wonder if Davis didn't use them to advance whatever his personal agenda was?"

"Hell yeah, he did. You ever notice his habit of showing up at protests, memorials, or places where someone got themselves shot?" Tooker said.

"As a matter of fact, I have."

"He's not even our councilman—I mean he wasn't—but he'd float in like he was our savior. Rubbed a lot of folks the wrong way—him doing that."

"Because it isn't his district?" Emily asked.

"Not only the district thing. He came off like another White liberal carpetbagger who would come in and save us from evil. I mean, these communities need assistance; everyone knows it. But Davis would talk and talk and absolutely nothing would ever happen. No after-school programs to keep the young ones off the street, no increases in the school funding, no connection with the churches, food pantries, and no job training programs to give folks a hand up."

"Davis came across as the spokesman for these neighborhoods. Are you saying he wasn't?"

"He had no clue what was going on in our streets. We ignored him for the most part. A few young fools would show up at his events and mug for the camera. He never brought anything to our community other than negative attention."

"He was up front about his distrust of the police. Any idea why this was personal for him?" she asked

Tooker rubbed his chin and took to the chair at his desk.

"I mean, you said it. There is a long-standing history of bullshit—issues involving the over-policing of certain neighborhoods. But you might be onto something here with Davis having a personal grudge. I never heard what it was, but there was a time, maybe six to eight months ago, when he was actually following officers on patrol."

"Following them?"

"Yeah, like he had a death wish or some shit."

"What can you tell me about a Crip shot caller who goes by the name of Rockhead?" Emily asked.

"Yeah, I heard about him too. In his youth, Rockhead was a brawler. Would instigate showdowns between rival sets for fun. It's how he earned his name—dude could take a punch. Shame about him, though. He was a big stabilizing factor out there. He kept the peace and made sure no one got out of line. Rumor is he was brokering a treaty to bring the violence down across the North area."

"I heard. Anyone who'd want to go after him?"

Tooker nodded. "Not everyone saw it the same way he did. Turf's a funny thing. When Rockhead talked about a treaty, it meant the grip some of these thugs had on their community was threatened. Davis wouldn't be left with anything to bitch about either."

"I felt Davis fed on the unrest."

"Having Rockhead taken out would serve his narrative."

"I don't think Davis put a hit out on Rockhead," Emily said.

"Maybe not, but he wouldn't lose any sleep over it either."

Emily paused and thought about how much to share with the ex-con. "You know of any reason someone would go after specific cops?"

"You mean the bombs? They weren't random attacks?"

"What if they weren't?"

"Someone's got a bone to pick with a cop who busted them, or who set them up on a bogus beef."

"Any chatter about payback out there? Someone who has an axe to grind?"

"Nothing I've heard. I'm not gonna be your snitch, Detective. Besides, a bomb is more of a White boy thing, ain't it? Oklahoma City and all? My people would be more up close and personal. They'd want the man to know where it was coming from, you get me?"

"Yeah, I do. There's more than a few people who want to put the blame for these attacks square on the community."

A soft knock sounded at the door. Emily turned to find another young woman in a very short dress holding a tray with a cover over what Emily thought must be another zucchini bread based on the smell.

"Mr. Tooker, might you spare a moment?" the woman said.

Emily rose from her chair with a smirk. "Mr. Tooker is all yours." Then, to Tooker: "Thanks for your time. And you might want to keep an eye on your waistline. Lots of carbs in here . . ."

"Thanks for your concern, Detective," Tooker said.

Emily slipped past the young woman in the doorway.

"Miss Tanya, what can I do for you?"

Emily smiled and shook her head. The PI business was being good to Benjamin Tooker.

She strapped into her SUV and pulled out heading to the hospital where Brian should be done with his PT by now.

Something Tooker said stuck in her mind. *Someone's got a bone to pick with a cop who busted them, or who set them up on a bogus beef.*

She'd start by asking Brian about the officers on the list and who might want payback.

CHAPTER TWENTY-FIVE

EMILY FOUND BRIAN in his room, grimacing as the physical therapist lowered him from a walker to his hospital bed. A sheen of sweat shone on his forehead. He glanced up at the door when Emily entered. He cast his eyes down and looked embarrassed.

"How'd it go?" she asked.

"Just missed the show," Brian said. "She's trying to kill me."

The physical therapist cracked a smile. "He's being dramatic."

"Just honest." Brian scooted back, trying to use the unbroken arm to prop him up.

"We're gonna do this again later." The therapist folded the walker and leaned it in a corner of the room.

"That sounds like a threat," Brian said.

She didn't respond but smiled and bounced out of the room.

Emily leaned over and gave him a quick kiss on the cheek. "How'd it go?"

"Made it two laps around the nurses' station. It feels weird, like it's not even my body. I'm stumbling around and my balance is off. You try to use a walker with one good arm."

She gestured to the disconnected IV machines next to his bed. "At least you're not tethered to those things." Emily noticed the pain medication pump was gone. It had to be a good sign, she hoped.

He leaned in his hospital bed and tried to find a comfortable position. "I can't wait to bust out of this place."

"What are they telling you?" Emily said as she pulled a chair next to his bedside.

"In case you haven't noticed, I have this drain thing in my fricken head. There's still fluid draining. They want to get it under control. Oh, and apparently, I had a small seizure in recovery. The doctors want to watch for those too."

"What do the doctors think? Do they expect it to happen again?"

He shrugged and looked away. Emily could sense the frustration and a hint of depression settling in. It was understandable, considering everything Brian had been through. But it was such a shift from his outgoing, positive demeanor. Was this part of a personality change? She was probably overthinking everything. The man had been blown up . . .

A change of subject seemed like a good idea.

"I don't know if you remember when I asked you before—the bombs?"

"I have brain damage. Is that what you're asking?"

Emily ignored the jab.

"Tommy is okay. You saved him. Who would want to go after Tucker?"

"Tucker? Why would he be someone's target? The guy is solid. He's dependable and he's the kind of guy who'll have your back . . ."

Brian's forehead creased as he turned it over in his mind.

Emily could tell he didn't remember having this part of the conversation before.

"Since then, we've had another attack and we think there is a connection to the department's SWAT team members."

"What? Tucker's not SWAT. I mean he used to be but he's not now. Who else was attacked?"

"McKinley and Ryan had their unit hit while they were stopped at a red light on West El Camino. They got lucky and got away with minor injuries. They're gonna be okay."

"They were my guys too. My patrol district. What makes you think whoever did this is going after my team?"

"McKinley and Ryan were SWAT, too, right?"

"McKinley was. Where is the connection? Tucker and Mac are by-the-book officers. They are good out there in the community. Who'd want to take them out?"

She pulled a chair close to his bedside. "That's what Javi and I are trying to piece together. The officers who were targeted were former SWAT cops. The same time you were. But we found a list of names."

"Like a hit list?"

Emily shrugged. "The list was from a file Councilman Davis had—"

"The city councilman is behind this? I mean, I know he hates cops, but a mad bomber?"

"He was killed a few hours ago with another bomb. Here's the odd thing—he owned an electronics store and had the knowledge and materials to build the devices."

"He blew himself up?"

"It doesn't look like it. The wife says he got a phone call and ran out of the house to leave for a meeting. The bomb under his car made sure he never made the meeting—oh, he grabbed a file to take with him. We'll never know what was in the file because it got incinerated along with him. But we do know the file label was a list of officer names—yours, Tucker's, McKinley's, and other officers."

"A file? What would he be doing with a list of our people?"

"More importantly, what was in his file? If someone wanted to keep the file under wraps, they found a way to do it. Kill the councilman and burn the file."

Brian grimaced when he adjusted himself on the bed.

A nurse wearing light blue scrubs entered the room with a pill cart. She checked Brian's chart, then his wristband, and told him it was time for his meds.

He took the small white paper cup, tossed back the pills, and swallowed them with a gulp of water from his tray.

"What were those?" Emily asked.

"They told me I'd need my pain meds after PT. I'm pretty sore. There's some stuff to prevent blood clots and the anti-seizure meds."

The nurse pushed her cart from the room.

"What did you, Tucker, Mac, and the rest of these guys have in common?" Emily handed Brian her phone with the photo image of the file label.

He squinted. "It's hard to read—the glare." He held it at an angle and read the names. Another wrinkle appeared on his brow. There was more brewing behind his eyes—anxiety, perhaps.

"What is it?" she asked.

"These guys—we were on the SWAT team at the same time—five or six years back."

"Why would someone want to go after all of you?"

"I—I can't think of anything. I mean we responded to dozens of incidents, barricaded suspects, high risk warrant service. Nothing stands out that would make someone want to come after us."

Brian started nodding off.

The pain meds were already taking effect.

"What are they giving you for the pain?"

He shrugged. "Whatever it is does the job. My face feels fuzzy, and my pain level dropped from an eight to a two."

"Can you remember any one incident where it went off the rails? Did the team shoot someone a family made noise about? Lawsuits? Claims of excessive force?"

Brian laid his head back on the pillow. "What are you trying to say? We brought this on ourselves?"

"No. Not at all. I'm trying to understand if there is any reason someone would do this—to the officers on this list." Emily pocketed the phone and was unsure how far to push. He was getting angry, but the pain meds were dulling his senses.

"We didn't do anything wring—I mean wrong. We all did what we were told." Brian slurred his words and worked his mouth like it was full of cotton.

"Who was the team commander back then?"

Brian's breathing became slow, and his facial muscles relaxed.

"Brian? Who was the SWAT commander back then?"

"Lieutenant Whitman. He retired."

Emily called up the photo of the file folder again and saw Richard Whitman listed without the rank designation. He was the one Sergeant Berney said had retired.

Brian was out and gave a slight snore. He had to heal, and it would take time. The external injuries, broken bones, cuts, and bruises were mending. The unseen injuries were another matter. Emily was afraid he might never fully recover from the effects of the TBI.

Emily pushed out of the chair. "I'll check on you later." She bent and gave him a kiss on the forehead. And he didn't respond. The pain meds had put him out.

Brian hadn't given her much to go on. There wasn't a catastrophic incident where officers on the SWAT team shot an unarmed man or breached the wrong home—he'd remember and it would be all over the department. High school gossip had nothing on cops telling stories. She'd have heard about an incident in all of the violent, gory detail.

Emily couldn't recall any television accounts of tactical operations gone wrong either.

There was one place she could go to find out if any of the names on the list crossed a line and put a target on their back. She didn't want to go there, but Emily didn't see another way out.

CHAPTER TWENTY-SIX

INTERNAL AFFAIRS WAS a place no one found willingly. Emily had darkened these doors a handful of times—usually in response to a complaint filed by a "citizen" who felt arresting them was unconstitutional, or an example of government overreach. She'd even been summoned to the IA offices to provide statements about other officers.

There was a stigma about hunting other cops that gave the officers assigned to Internal Affairs a reputation. The Rubber Gun Squad, or worse. Emily had run across a few detectives who targeted other cops as sport, looking for scalps to hang out. They usually burned out quick or were caught dirty themselves—thinking they could get away with their misdeeds.

John Mason was not of that mold. He took the assignment so he could manage school and daycare arrangements for his two kids. The job rarely required overtime and usually left the weekends free.

Emily had gone to the academy with Mason and remembered the burly Black man as one of the brightest cadets in the class. He worked patrol and landed in Internal Affairs five years ago, about the same time Emily made detective.

She rapped a knuckle on Mason's door.

"I was surprised by your call, Emily," Mason said in a deep baritone.

"How are the kids?" Emily asked, slipping into a chair at Mason's desk.

"Like weeds—growing right before my eyes. Kyle is going into third grade and Cynthia is in fifth and acts like she's in high school. It's giving me these gray hairs."

"I do notice a bit of 'frosting' up there."

"Can it, Hunter. I don't have time to go sit in a salon for three hours for a perfect cut and color for my 'season' like you do."

"Neither do I. I've been known to cut my own hair."

"I can tell. What brings you by? Here to unburden your soul, Detective?"

"Does that line actually work? On anyone?"

Mason shrugged. "You'd be surprised."

"I need your help." She passed her cell phone over to Mason. She filled him in on the attacks and how she found the list with the officers' names displayed on her phone.

"You can't be investigating other cops, Emily."

"That's why I'm here."

"What do you expect me to do? I can't open an IA investigation on these officers. It has to come from command. Even then, you know the law. We only release information to the public if the complaint was sustained. If it was unfounded, or not sustained, there wouldn't be anything to report."

"I'm looking for an incident where the SWAT team got blamed—excessive force, a shooting, a case big enough to make someone come after them. There has to be some record of that, wouldn't there?"

"I understand. But I can't dig through old records on a witch hunt."

Emily knew the request would be sensitive. Mason was following protocol, and case files were protected at the highest level.

Emily tapped a number on her cell's SPEED DIAL. She locked eyes with Mason while the phone rang on the other end.

"Yes, sir. I could use your assistance in Internal Affairs—"

She turned in her chair away from Mason. "No. Why does everyone think I did something?" she said into her cell phone.

"Yes. It does. There's a SWAT connection," Emily said to the person on the other end of the phone.

"Thank you."

She held the phone to Mason.

"Your lieutenant didn't jump on board with your fishing expedition?" Mason said as he took the phone from Emily.

"It's not Lieutenant Hall," she said.

"Then who do you think is going to go your bail on this?'

"The chief."

"You called Chief Clark to authorize this investigation?" Mason smiled and shook his head in disbelief.

"I keep telling you it's not an investigation. I'm not saying the team did anything, but someone believed they did when they took down a cousin's meth lab or something."

"Okay, I'll call your bluff."

Mason took her phone. "Okay, Medina, give me your best Chief Clark imitation—and make sure you use his urban cowboy drawl."

Emily closed her eyes and shook her head.

Mason's eyes widened, and he stiffened.

"Sir. Yes, sir. I'm sorry, sir."

Emily could hear the tone of the chief's direction to Mason.

"Yes, sir. I will, sir."

Mason handed the phone back to Emily. His breathing and heart rate came back to normal.

"Thanks, Chief. Yes, I'll be right there."

She disconnected the call and shoved the phone in her pocket.

"When can you have the complaints for me?" Emily asked.

"Unless I want to be assigned to a kiosk in the Arden Fair Mall shopping center, I'll have to move heaven and earth to give you what you want."

"I didn't know we had a mall security cop station."

"We don't—yet. It'll take a minute. Give me those names again."

"Thanks, Mason."

"Don't mention it. I mean, don't mention it—to anyone. This is the kind of information that gets careers torpedoed if the wrong people find out."

Emily pulled up the names from her phone and Mason typed each one into his desktop computer. He peered into the screen as the search results appeared.

"You're looking for something where they were all present?" Mason said.

"Yes." Emily stiffened waiting for the connection.

"Nothing. McKinley has a three-year-old discourtesy allegation, which was sustained. The others, nothing. Oh, Whitman had an open investigation when he retired. Don't have the details on the case listed. But the group thing you were looking for—nothing there, Emily. Sorry."

"Thanks. I appreciate the look. Hopefully, it's nothing. Councilman Davis made it seem like there was something we were hiding."

Emily left the Rubber Gun Squad offices to meet with Chief Clark, who, if she was honest with herself, didn't enjoy getting used as leverage in her investigation. Time to take her medicine.

She entered the chief's outer office and Sandy, his secretary, pointed to the chief's door. "He said for you to go in the minute you got here."

Emily tried to read the expression on Sandy's face. She'd learned over the years the chief's secretary was like a mood ring of what was to happen on the other side of the door. If true to form, the pink blush on Sandy's neck meant Emily was in for a stormy time with the top cop.

Emily drew a deep breath and opened the chief's door.

Chief Clark was standing behind his desk. He had a file in his hand and, without so much as a greeting, he held it out to her.

"You're gonna want to see this."

She took the folder and inside was a city council agenda for tomorrow's session. The first agenda item was a vote of no confidence in the police department and Chief Clark.

"This is bullshit. Did Councilman Davis put this on the agenda before he died?"

"I don't know who put this together, but the document underneath spells it all out. Claims we've abandoned our public safety mission, let gangs, guns, and criminals run free all over the city. And we can't even protect our own, let alone the community."

"Ouch. Who put the message together?"

"I had a drop-in from the union rep saying there is some rumbling about officer safety. Coupled with your call from Internal Affairs saying you're looking into our officers and it paints a picture even Bob Ross and his happy trees couldn't fix."

Emily smirked. "I didn't peg you as a Bob Ross painting kind of guy."

"What can I say, Emily, I'm a complex guy." He motioned for Emily to sit.

She imagined what it would be like to be in his chair. Every decision an officer made, a bad arrest, or an excessive force complaint, rested on his shoulders. Now he'd got a series of attacks with a SWAT officer connection. "I don't think it's because of our people—like a bad shoot. But this connection is too strong to discount."

"How do you want to handle it?" the chief asked. He took a deep breath and rocked back in his chair.

"IA was a dry hole. They couldn't find any complaint where our people were listed. The way I see it, there are two possible origin stories for our bomb attacks. The first is someone is holding a grudge for a SWAT action resulting in their arrest, or the arrest of a family member. Seems the most likely path. The IA results notwithstanding."

"And the second?"

"Someone didn't want the information Councilman Davis had to get out in the open. They wanted it hidden. If one of the SWAT officers covered it up . . ."

"I don't like where this leads," the chief said.

"Me either. We've got to run that option down. One officer on the list—the SWAT commander, actually—he's retired now. Lieutenant Whitman. Mason told me there was an investigation open when he left. What can you tell me about him?"

"Whitman. I can tell you everything you need to know about Rich in one word—troublemaker."

CHAPTER TWENTY-SEVEN

EMILY PULLED INTO the gravel drive of the place personnel records gave as Richard Whitman's address in the rural enclave of Rescue, a small community in the western portion of El Dorado County.

Although it was less than an hour's drive from the city, it seemed a world apart.

Javier pointed at a yellow and blue flag on the roadside. "That's the fourth State of Jefferson flag we've passed. Tells you we're not in Kansas anymore."

The State of Jefferson movement was a small, but vocal, group who believed the existing California government failed to represent all of its citizens, especially those in rural and, as it happened, predominantly White communities.

"The chief said Whitman retired after Martin Cruz got the captain's job over him. Made accusations about Martin getting the job because he was Mexican—you can imagine how that went," Emily said.

"Cruz is Puerto Rican. He was a good captain too. Sorry to see him take a medical for his heart condition."

"Here's the address," Emily said, pointing at a wooden post with metal numbers nailed to it.

Emily turned in and the road was wash-boarded and barely graveled. When she was about to turn around, the road circled to a clearing in the thick brush and scrub oak. A farmhouse-style building perched in the center of the open space.

"It looks like one of those log cabin kit homes—they aren't cheap," Emily said.

"Leave it to you to make this a home improvement show. Someone's home. We got smoke coming from the chimney."

Emily piloted the SUV to a spot in front of a similarly designed log building with three garage doors. She spotted a six-wheeled ATV parked alongside the outbuilding. The rifle rack attached to the all terrain vehicle was disconcerting.

Emily got out from the driver's seat and waited by the front bumper of the vehicle.

"You change your mind about a knock and talk?" Javier asked.

Emily jutted her chin at a black dome covering a camera at the corner of the home. She turned and spotted another on the garage behind her.

A flutter of movement from a window near the front door told her Whitman knew they were there.

"He'll come out, even if it's to tell us to get off his property."

Seconds later, the sound of a dead bolt turning in the heavy wooden front door preceded a barrel-chested White man with long gray hair and a beard to match. A pair of silver beads had been woven into the tips of his beard.

"Lieutenant Whitman?" Emily asked.

"Just Whitman now. Who are you?"

"Detectives Hunter and Medina, Sac PD."

"The department's really gone down the woke road, I see."

Emily ignored the jab. "You got a minute? We need to talk to you about your time on the SWAT team."

"Those were the good times. We knew what our mission was and the brass had our back."

"You heard about the attacks on our cops, right?"

"I heard some. Sounds like we aren't doing anything about it either. What do you expect from people who don't hold respect for society? They want to bleed all the benefits they can shove into their stolen purses and are the first to cry and pull the race card when someone calls them on their shit."

Javier took a step away from the SUV. "The cops who've been attacked. It wasn't random street violence. They were SWAT officers—ones you worked with when you were the unit commander."

"My team? Why?"

"That's what we were hoping you could help us with," Emily said.

Whitman ran a hand through his beard. "Don't know how I can give you anything. I've been away from the job for a couple years. You think this involves my SWAT operators?"

"Pretty sure. I found a list at one of the crime scenes. All officers who were assigned to SWAT at one time or another. Three of them went to the hospital. You're on the list too . . ."

"Well, shit. You best come in, then," Whitman said and turned into his home.

Emily followed, and Javier was on her heels as they entered. Whitman closed the three-inch-thick door and locked it. There was a Ruger rifle next to the front door with a thirty-round magazine. Emily guessed the ex-cop had his own stash of weaponry in the home.

The side table by the door had three spare magazines for the rifle and a stack of newsletters from a local militia group, known to direct their bile at anyone not like them.

"Come, we can talk in here." He led them to the kitchen and Emily was surprised to find it well-appointed and furnished with high-end appliances.

"Nice kitchen. I looked at getting that range for my place. It was more than I could afford. I'm impressed."

"I cashed in some accrued vacation when I retired and fixed this place up. You can't judge a book by its cover, Hunter."

She smiled.

"Now what's this list about?" Whitman asked.

Emily slid her phone across the butcher block kitchen table. Whitman picked it up and studied the list.

"These were my guys, all right. Good team there. Never gave me a lick of trouble—not a one of them. Which ones were attacked?"

"Conner, Tucker, Ryan, and McKinley."

"You don't have a line on who's doing this? The word I've been hearing is some gangs were trying to pull off a Seattle-like neighborhood takeover. You know, a place where they ran the show and the police weren't allowed to enter. Some of the lefty politicians seem to support them."

Emily was a little surprised at how connected Whitman was. His off-the-grid image in his well-appointed compound in the foothills didn't gel with his political awareness, or the twelve-thousand-dollar Wolf Range in his kitchen.

"There was some noise out there, mostly from a city councilman— Davis. He's not going to be spreading the word anymore. He was killed a few hours ago by one of the bombs. He was the one with this list."

"Huh. Curious. Davis made no secret about his disdain for us. Had his people threatening lawsuits, depositions, and now he gets offed. You're the detective, but don't you find that a bit odd?"

"We do. Like someone didn't want him to reveal who was on his list."

"Your list—the SWAT operators we had—man, they were a tight group. Do anything for one another. Still do, actually. One of the guys did the gas line work for my kitchen. What I'm saying is, if you're thinking one of them had anything to do with this—you're flat wrong. I'd be more interested in why such a list existed in the first place."

Emily thought it interesting that Whitman's paranoia went right to one of the team members. Protective of his men? Or did he have something to be paranoid about?

Whitman poured a cup of coffee for himself. He didn't offer one to Emily or Javier.

"We know the team is at the center of this. What comes to your mind when you think about callouts ending in a shooting, or complaints against your officers?"

"The nature of what we did—the tactical operations—put us in high-risk situations. The likelihood of deadly force is higher, and on a few occasions we needed to do that to prevent harm to an innocent civilian. As far as the complaints—they go with the job. I'd be more worried if my people didn't get any complaints. It would mean they weren't doing what needed to be done. None of them—not a one while I was in command—none of the complaints were sustained."

Emily was taken by Whitman's use of the phrase *none of the complaints were sustained.*

"No one incident stands out? I understand you had an IA complaint pending when you left."

Whitman took a sip from his mug. "You know why I retired?"

"No. Why?"

"Because of this bullshit right here. You people always trying to second-guess what we do on the streets. Someone panics and calls 911 because their husband threatens them with a knife. We get shit on because we arrest the dirtbag. Or better yet, we respond to a barricaded armed suspect and he kills himself rather than surrender to us—like that becomes our fault."

"No one's blaming you or the team. We're trying to find who's behind these attacks so we can stop the next attack. Don't you want to prevent another of your guys getting sent to the hospital, or worse?"

"This wouldn't have happened if the politicians didn't coddle these thugs. All the releases without bail, letting violent criminals out of prison early, and reducing penalties for crimes—it emboldened these dirtbags. I mean, damn, they got their own city hotline to call when some cop looks at them cross-eyed. Of course they don't want a police presence in their neighborhood. It would disrupt their game of ripping off affluent parts of the city and bringing it back to the projects. All these people understand is carrot and stick. They stole the carrot and it's high time they get the stick."

Javier stiffened. "You're blaming an entire community for the actions of a few? Not to mention that bombings are more of a White boy thing."

"Don't seem like a few with the protests and marches sanctioned by the city. Then they push police reform when all it really means is don't arrest their people. When they claim a right to dictate what I think—"

"Those people being Black and Brown?" Javier said.

"Well, you don't see White folk taking to the streets."

"Charlottesville ring a bell with you?" Javier asked.

"I think we're done here," Whitman said, downing the last of his coffee.

Emily laid one of her cards on the butcher block. "Call if you remember anything that would make someone want to come after you and your team. You might not give a shit, but I don't want to see another cop in the hospital."

Whitman escorted them to the front door and closed it behind them.

"Well, isn't he a little ray of racist sunshine?" Javier said.

"No kidding. But he did say something that got me to thinking," Emily said as they strode back to the SUV.

"What? His progressive take on police reform?"

"Focus, Javi. Whitman is a Neanderthal. Everyone knows it. But when he said the team was placed in high-risk situations and sometimes the 911 callers regretted reporting . . ."

"I don't remember him saying those words, exactly."

"Think about those high-risk warrant operations, or the barricaded suspects he mentioned. The DV cases where the battered spouse changes her mind—any of them could have a grudge against the officers involved in the arrest if the team arrested, or even used deadly force on, someone they called 911 over."

"Could be hundreds . . ."

"I think I know a way to narrow it down—what if the watch inscription was a message to us? November 2nd."

CHAPTER TWENTY-EIGHT

BACK AT THE detective bureau, Emily and Javier took to a quiet interview room. Emily suggested the space out of earshot of the rest of the detectives because what she proposed was risky.

"You sure you want to do this? Once people find out what we're looking at—it could get a bit spicy around here," Javier said.

"Mason couldn't give us anything on the officers on the list. But Whitman confirmed something for me. There were no sustained complaints. He knew IA wouldn't have a record to disclose. That doesn't mean a public complaint wasn't made. Remember Whitman mentioned the 'hotline' for complaints against cops?"

"It's bad enough having IA trying to unearth complaints against these officers, but you're thinking about taking it to the Office of Public Safety and Accountability? Whitman's hotline, you called it. If it gets out, we'll be seen as collaborating with the enemy. It's career suicide," Javier said and he leaned back in the chair usually reserved for interrogating suspects. It looked like he felt that way right now.

"That's why I want to make sure you're on board with this before I let the lieutenant know what we want to do."

"You think he'll let us reach out to OPSA?"

"He'll think it's a great idea."

———

"This is a terrible idea, Emily," Lieutenant Hall said.

"Boss, listen. IA was a bust. We won't have the full picture until we look at citizen filings with OPSA. There might be a link to our bomber."

"Emily, find another pathway. This has too much potential to backfire on us."

Emily leaned back in the chair and fumed for a moment. She knew it was an uphill battle, but still she hoped the lieutenant would understand.

Javier gestured out the lieutenant's door at an anxious Officer Milton.

"Your boy wonder need you?" Emily asked.

"Tell him to come in," Lieutenant Hall said.

Javier motioned for Milton. Emily took it as another sign her request for outside help was done.

Milton sheepishly entered. "Lieutenant. Detectives."

"You need something?" Javier asked.

"Yes. No—I mean I don't need anything."

"Okay, then."

"The bomb fragments from Davis's place."

"Spill it," Emily said.

"Oh, yeah, sorry. There was a piece of PCB in the debris collected on scene and—"

"PCB?" Emily asked. "Speak to me like I'm not a nerd."

"PCB is the printed circuit board. Remember those boards I bought at Full Charge Electronics? Those were PCBs. There was a fragment collected at the bombing at the councilman's home that had a portion of a serial number."

"I didn't think we had anything after that electric car fire," Emily said.

"You said the board from the church bombing had a number in sequence with the ones you bought at Davis's store," Javier said.

Milton pulled a photograph from a notebook and handed it to the detectives. "And so does this one."

Emily and Javier huddled over it and examined the three images in the photo. The serial numbers were in sequence, one after another—sixty-eight, sixty-nine, and seventy.

"Davis was done in with one of his own devices?" Emily asked.

"Or the components for the bomb delivery systems came from his electronics store," Milton said.

Emily handed the photo back to the officer. "Not bad, Clay. Not bad at all. You ever work up an affidavit for a search warrant?"

Milton's eyes widened. "No."

"Well, you're going to learn how."

"Detective Medina, would you and Officer Milton start on the search warrant affidavit? I need a word with Detective Hunter," Lieutenant Hall said.

Javier glanced at Emily and he paused. Emily nodded and let him know she could handle whatever the lieutenant had in store for her. She couldn't read the expression of the lieutenant's face. She'd seen it before—the look of frustration of working within a system that was more interested in bureaucracy, status quo, and placating special interest groups.

"Close the door, would you?" Hall asked.

Emily shut the door after Javier and Milton left the lieutenant's office.

"Emily, do I need to pull you off this case?"

"No. Why would you think you had to?"

Hall rubbed his temples, then tipped back in his chair. "Listen, I know you want to bulldog this investigation and march into OPSA with a demand for every complaint filed since George Washington chopped down his daddy's tree. I'm telling you, it's a minefield. When word gets out you're 'collaborating' with OPSA, and it will, it's not going to be received well."

"I can handle it."

Hall let out a deep breath.

"Emily, you and I walk a very narrow ledge. There are those who are waiting for us to step out of line and use it as proof we don't belong here, because we're not like them. I can't let you self-destruct. You're the best detective I've got and if you're charging off with blinders on because you're too close to this—"

"We *are* too close to this, Lieutenant. Our people are being targeted, and every corner I turn, there's another stonewalling attempt. Like Whitman. He knows more than he's telling us. Whitman immediately clammed up when we mentioned his old SWAT team. They are being taken out and he's hiding something."

"I mean you and Brian. Are his injuries clouding your judgment?"

"No."

"You were pretty quick to answer, Emily."

She knew Brian's injuries and the long-term implications for his recovery were lodged in the back of her mind. The future of their relationship seemed suspended by a thread too.

"I'm sure. I mean, am I pissed Brian is sitting in a hospital bed with a drain tube coming out of his head and he's gonna be dealing with the aftereffects of traumatic brain injury? Damn right, I'm pissed. It's not clouding my judgment, Lieutenant. It's motivating me to find out who's responsible. I know our SWAT team is drawing fire. Let me go find out why."

"You cannot ask the Office of Public Safety Accountability for copies of complaints filed against your fellow officers. It would end your career."

"But—"

"No *buts* on this one, Emily. It's a direct order. *You* are not to contact them. Period. There are other ways to find the information you need. Incident reports, news accounts. Get another way to find what you're looking for. Hell, have someone outside the department ask. You've already pushed the envelope asking Mason in Internal Affairs to get involved. I need you to tread carefully."

"When have you known me not to?"

Lieutenant Hall couldn't keep a straight face. "Detective . . ."

"I hear you. I'll color within the lines on this one. There's too much at stake if I screw this up."

"All right, then."

"I will not contact the Office of Public Safety Accountability."

Lieutenant Hall narrowed his eyes. There were some things a supervisor couldn't say out in the open. "Find another way."

Emily stood. "I understand. I will follow your instructions to the letter."

"Emily, don't make me regret not putting you on the bench for this one."

"Thanks, LT."

Emily left his office and checked in with Javier. He was halfway through the search warrant affidavit with Officer Milton.

"Hey, Javi, I need to run something down. Be back in thirty."

Where she was going, she couldn't risk Javier getting pulled into the current.

Emily grabbed her jacket and headed out.

She would honor the lieutenant's order and not personally contact the Office of Public Safety Accountability. She would find another way. And she knew who could make that connection.

194

CHAPTER TWENTY-NINE

EMILY WAITED IN the mayor's office while Carsten finished up with a budget meeting. Emily couldn't imagine anything duller and more sleep-inducing than an hour of spreadsheets, cost reports, and spending projections.

Although, she thought the mayor probably had better hours than she did as a detective. There were perks to the job, like a driver to shuttle her wherever she needed to go and VIP tickets for any sporting event in the city. But there was the whole getting elected thing. Emily doubted she could bite her tongue long enough to survive an election.

As far as politicians go, Emily found Mayor Carsten genuine— almost like a real person. Emily nabbing her former chief of staff for extortion and murder had had a humbling effect on the mayor.

The mayor swept into the room while Emily was in mid-daydream.

"Detective. Any progress on our bomber?"

Mayor Carsten dropped a stack of files on her desk, kicked off her shoes, sat on the sofa, and rubbed the ball of her foot.

"Some." Emily laid out the SWAT connection and the list of officers' names Davis kept. "My gut tells me it comes down to a single SWAT call out where these officers were present."

"What kind of callout are we talking about? A hostage-taking? A search warrant?"

"Kinda what I wanted to come and talk to you about."

"Me? What can I possibly do?"

"There are certain things I can't ask for—or, more accurately, can't be seen asking for."

"I don't think I'm following."

Emily huffed and dove right in. "I think we'll find the connection to the SWAT incident in a citizens complaint filed with the Office of Public Safety Accountability."

"A complaint? Like a citizen who felt the SWAT officers overstepped?"

"Hear me out. My thought is whoever is behind these bombings wants to go after these officers specifically. They probably tried to go through the official channels and were shut down. Told their complaint was without merit. Could be enough to make you mad, right?"

"Okay, I'm following."

"You've tried to handle it the official way and you're told to go pound sand. If they couldn't make OPSA listen, they might feel they had no other option. The complaint might have never made it to IA. Or, if it did, it might have been papered over—covered up."

"I don't like the thought of that. How does Davis figure in?"

"There are two possibilities as I see them. The first is he listened to a complaint and didn't act before they turned rogue—but he knew who was behind the bombing."

"They didn't want him to expose them?"

Emily nodded.

"And the second is Davis was going to release the names of the SWAT officers and the person behind the bombings to the media."

"Either way, Davis had information the bomber didn't want released.

He knew and could have stopped this from happening," the mayor said.

Emily leaned back on the sofa. Davis wasn't the altruistic type. He had to have an angle that would make him come out on top. More than exposing a few bad cops. The thought of bad cops, cover-ups, and where Brian fit in the picture was unsettling. "Maybe he thought the action against the officers—I don't know. He was going to be the one to blow it open in the press, painting the neighborhoods as out of control, and he'd be the only one to make them safe again."

"Son of a bitch. He played right into this guy's hands," the mayor said. "What do you need from me?"

"Would you be able to ask for OPSA complaints where these officers were listed?" Emily handed the mayor her phone again.

"And you can't ask them directly because?"

"I don't think they'd release it to me. But more to the point, if the cops on the list learn I'm looking into complaints filed against them— well, it wouldn't be good."

Mayor Carsten rocked back and rubbed the bridge of her nose. "If I ask, won't they know what I'm up to?" The mayor glanced at her desk.

"I have a thought." Mayor Carsten rose from the sofa, padded over to her desk, and flipped open one of the files she left there.

She tapped her finger on a file and Emily joined her, peering over her shoulder. The document in the file folder was a budget request from the Sacramento Police Department. To Emily's non-accountant eye, it looked like a list of replacement equipment. A couple of lines stood out. Acquisition of an armored personnel carrier for high-risk SWAT operations was the first entry to draw her eye.

The mayor called out to her assistant. "Carrie."

The young woman stood in the doorway, notepad in hand.

"Would you get Jackson Azzi from Public Safety Accountability on the line for me, please?"

"Yes, ma'am."

"What are you going to ask him? Azzi likes his press releases, especially when he believes he has some dirt to expose," Emily said.

"Then we'll give him a nudge."

Emily wasn't sure where the mayor was going. Azzi was a hothead and a firebrand, selected by the city council in a close vote to lead the accountability office. He'd been vocal in his disdain for first responders, and his biggest backer was Councilman Davis.

"He's going to feel a little vulnerable now without Davis in his pocket," Emily said.

The mayor smiled. "You're starting to understand how things work in city hall, Detective."

The mayor's intercom buzzed, and she hit a speaker button. It was her assistant's voice. "Mr. Azzi on line three."

"Thanks, Carrie."

Mayor Carsten punched the blinking red button.

"Jackson, thanks for taking my call. I need to run something by you."

"How can I help, Mayor?" The deep baritone sounded through the speaker.

"I'm reviewing a budget request from the chief of police—"

"Deny it."

"Don't you even want to pretend to be objective, Jackson?"

"It's already a bloated department. You need to gut their funding and send it into the community who need help, not more of the same warrior mentality these people bring."

Carsten didn't engage with Azzi and continued. "The department is asking for funding to purchase an armored vehicle of some sort to assist with hostage rescue and SWAT operations."

"More weapons of war to be used against the people of this city. We need to demilitarize the police force, not add to the problem."

"Here's what I need from you, Jackson. I want to see if there are instances where equipment like this helped or hindered when used in response to a call. I need to be able to articulate the specific details where a crime, or a call for assistance, was met with SWAT-level response and how it ended badly."

"When the big guns come out, it always ends badly, Mayor."

"Okay, then. Give me the data I need to question this budget item. Can you provide a list of complaints your office received where SWAT resources were used—in, say—the last—"

Emily held up five fingers.

"Five years?"

"What are you going to do with them—the complaints?"

"Like I said, I need concrete examples to cite where the type of equipment used in the police department's response got in the way of a good outcome." The mayor rolled her eyes at her own words.

A pause on the other end of the line meant Azzi was considering the request.

"All right. I can dig up what you need. We keep four and a half years of data. That will show a pattern of excessive force used against innocent civilians."

"When can you send it? The council is pressing for a decision on outstanding budget requests."

"Give me a couple of hours and I'll have it for you. Mayor, a word of warning?"

"Yes, Jackson?"

"If I find the people who filed these complaints against the police are harassed, or retaliated against—"

"That's not going to happen, Jackson. You have my word."

Azzi hung up, and the mayor silenced her phone as well.

Emily arched her eyebrow. "You got him to give you what you wanted without directly asking. If the SWAT response went off the rails, we can look at that incident to see if our officers were involved. Nicely done."

"I've learned you often need to approach things indirectly. Something the chief tells me isn't your go-to move."

"I can't think you guys spend too much time talking about me," Emily said.

"More than you'd think. The information Azzi finds should get you started, Detective."

"Thank you, Mayor."

"I gave Azzi my word. This cannot result in citizens who used the process to file a legitimate complaint against the police being targeted for payback."

"I understand and we're keeping the circle tight on this one."

Carrie, the mayor's assistant, knocked on the door. "Mayor, the Planning Commission is ready for you."

Mayor Carsten rose from her desk, tucked into her shoes, and took the file Carrie held out for her.

"Duty calls, Detective. As soon as the complaint file comes in, I'll let you know."

Emily thanked the mayor and left with her, the mayor turning to the conference room and Emily out of the offices.

She hoped she'd made the right decision. Azzi's complaint files could be the break she was waiting for—or it could blow up in her face.

Only time would tell, and Emily had the feeling time wasn't on her side.

CHAPTER THIRTY

BY THE TIME Emily got to her SUV, Javier had texted her and said the search warrant affidavit was completed and a deputy district attorney on call would personally walk it to a judge for approval.

"Wow, Javi, that's great."

"Milton, turns out, was able to lay out a compelling list of facts about the PCBs, their use, the connection to the store, and the fragments recovered from the bombing scenes. He put it together. We couldn't make a case to search the Davis home, but I think we'll have a lock on the business."

Emily hung up and agreed to meet Javier at the electronics store when the warrant was approved and issued. She wanted to drive by her mother's place and check in. She had a nagging suspicion her condition was deteriorating.

It was a slow, gradual decline, and there was little medical science could do to intervene. The inevitable end left people like Connie Hunter hollow shells of their former selves. As an added bonus, Emily found many of the people who suffered like her mother were in generally good health otherwise, which meant they lived long enough to make sure the ending was a miserable existence in their last years.

Emily entered the River Gardens Memory Care facility, and she immediately noticed she'd arrived in the midday slump as she called it. The time of the day where the activities took on a slower pace. Music, or quiet reading, or one-on-one with a therapist, were common, and the place took on a library-like feel with a subdued atmosphere.

She found Connie in the dayroom listening to a staff member playing the piano. Emily couldn't pick out the tune, but the five residents who gathered to listen were enjoying themselves.

Dr. Washington passed and paused when he spotted Emily standing at the back of the room.

"Your mom is doing much better," he said.

"She looks good."

"Once we got her calm, and staff put her on medication monitoring, everything seems to have settled down for her."

"Thanks for everything you did the other night. You were good with her."

"Connie is showing signs of some additional deterioration in her cognitive ability. It's subtle, but there have been some increasing issues of confusion and her connection with time and place."

"From the missed medications?" Emily asked, but a prickly sensation at the back of her neck told her there was more lurking in the shadows.

"I suggest we work with her primary care doctors and order a CT scan workup. We need to make sure we're dealing with Alzheimer's here and not something else."

A cold ball formed in Emily's gut. There it was. The "A" word. Alzheimer's. Doctors had mentioned it before and warned it might be coming, but Emily thought they had more time. The sand on the simple dementia hourglass had run out.

"Are you—are we dealing with Alzheimer's disease now, for certain?" Emily asked.

Dr. Washington's shoulders drooped, and he leaned closer to Emily. In a low voice, he said, "Yes, we are into Alzheimer's territory now. The deterioration of her cognitive functions and her panic attack the other night tell us what we're facing. The CT scan will pinpoint how far along we are and help us adjust medications to make sure she's as happy and comfortable as possible."

Emily glanced at her mother, gently swaying with the music, and wondered how long she could enjoy these simple pleasures.

"I'll call her doctor—can I tell her to coordinate with you?"

"Yes. Yes, of course."

"I'll be there when they do the scan. She gets confused about things like that."

Dr. Washington placed his hand on Emily's arm. "I know. We'll make it as easy for her as possible. I don't want to sedate her for the scan, but if she's agitated we can give her help—a little propofol and Versed. Light sedation and she should be able to tolerate it well."

"I could use a little of that right about now," Emily said.

Dr. Washington grinned. "You know, even though she's not living with you now, there's still a significant weight on you as a caregiver. Your primary care doctor can give you a prescription for something to deal with this new anxiety in your life. There's a new group for caregivers— you know, others going through the same thing. Sometimes it helps to know you're not alone in this."

Alone. She hadn't been alone. Brian had been there with her and his experience with his mother's Alzheimer's journey. Now he was suffering with his own brain trauma. She felt her breath catch. There was no family to help. Javier's mother had pitched in more times than she could count to sit with Connie and make sure she didn't wander off. Emily wasn't sure where to turn when her mother's condition worsened. When would she forget who Emily was?

"Thanks, Doc. I need to pass on the meds. Can't take anything that would dull my senses to the point where I was a danger to my partner. Although, sometimes, I think he's the cause of my anxiety." Emily grinned.

"I understand." He handed her a card with a woman's name—Millie Clark. "Millie is the contact for the support group I mentioned, if you want to check it out. They meet here on Wednesday evenings."

"Thanks, Doc. I don't know about sitting around with a bunch of people feeling sorry for themselves."

Emily couldn't imagine sitting in a little circle taking turns "sharing" the day's troubles with their aging parents. It seemed too much like an Alcoholics Anonymous meeting—without the cookies and coffee. She'd never been into a group thing anyway. Besides, if it got back to some officers, it would prove their point that a woman is too weak to do the job.

"Think about it," Dr. Washington said.

Emily shoved the card in her pocket and told the doctor she'd consider it. A little white lie.

Dr. Washington excused himself while Emily watched her mother for another moment. She didn't want to disturb her because, in this moment, she looked content and unburdened with a troubled mind.

Emily turned and, as she headed for the entrance, she heard an older, wheelchair-bound woman coo over something at her feet. As she drew close, Emily found the source of the woman's excitement.

Two Welsh corgis took turns getting pets behind the ears. The woman's gnarled hands couldn't scratch the red-and-white fur but gave soft pats instead. The two corgis didn't seem to mind.

Emily stopped and watched the interaction between dog and resident, and she swore she saw the woman's stress float away.

"You want to say hi to Emma? She's a therapy dog," the man said, holding her leash.

"Sure, I guess."

The dog had the softest fur Emily had ever felt. The dog's brown eyes looked up at Emily, and Emma pushed in closer and rested her head against her leg.

Emily got down on her knees and gave the dog a two-handed scratch on her shoulders.

"You have someone living here? Visiting?"

"No. Emma's a therapy dog and we come here to let folks love on her for a while. Take their minds off their troubles. It helps unlock childhood memories when they had a pet of their own. Staff tell me they'll talk about these therapy dog visits for days after."

"That's pretty good, considering . . ."

"Sure is."

The woman in the wheelchair edged closer.

"Looks like someone's a little jealous."

The corgi trotted back to the wheelchair and stood on the man's foot to stretch taller, enabling the woman to pat her head without leaning.

Emily watched the smile on the woman's face. The power of unconditional love. Emma glanced back at Emily and gave a smile.

Maybe she should get a dog. What would the trespassing cat think of that?

Emily left the facility and headed to the electronics store. She felt a double dose of guilt for leaving her mother and for abandoning Javier to handle the search warrant prep. She'd make it up to him. She knew she was lucky to have a partner like Javi—but she wouldn't want him to know that. He'd be insufferable.

Emily pulled into the store's lot and was surprised to find a CSI crew on hand to help catalog and secure any evidence they retrieved from the store.

Everyone was waiting outside.

Emily parked and approached Javier.

"Didn't need to wait for me."

"Thank you, your royal highness. But we aren't waiting for you to grace us with your appearance. The store is locked up tight. No one's inside. We called Davis's widow to come and unlock the store. Should be here any minute."

"That was thoughtful. Could've busted in."

"Figured we didn't want to feed the councilman's narrative of the police running wild. Gave her a chance to come and unlock the place."

Emily nodded. "Where's Milton?"

"I think he's with the CSI crew briefing them on what we're looking for. Nerd-to-nerd."

Emily leaned on the fender of the CSI van, looking through the darkened window of the electronics store.

"What's up, Em? You seem a little distracted," Javier said.

"I guess I am. Sorry. It's mom stuff."

"She okay?"

"As well as she can, I suppose. Gotta get her in for some tests. See if her brain is shrinking, or some shit. I don't know."

"She seem any different?"

"It's hard to tell. Everything is gradual until you step back and look, then it hits you in the face. It happens right under your nose. If I got her into memory care earlier . . ."

"There is nothing you could have done to change the outcome. You know that, Emily."

"I don't know—hey." Emily stiffened. "I thought you said no one was inside."

Through the dingy glass, a shadow moved inside the electronics store.

"What the hell?" Javier said. "Who—"

A flash burst from deep inside the store. Emily grabbed Javier and threw him on the ground next to her.

A ball of orange flame erupted through the front windows, spewing shards of glass raining out into the parking lot. A sliver of glass stuck into the back of Emily's left hand.

She got to one knee. "Javi, you good?"

"Yeah. Who the hell got in there?"

"Someone who didn't want us to find what Davis had going on."

CHAPTER THIRTY-ONE

THE BLAST BLEW out the windows in the building's front, but the damage from the explosion focused on the racks of electronic components in the main showroom.

Fire Station 54 was a few blocks away and quickly doused the flames, which fed on the combustibles inside. The firefighters directed streams of water from their hoses through the broken window glass. They didn't enter the storefront once they learned the fire had started from an explosive device.

"The more water they pour in there, the less evidence we'll have left. An officer said there was a back door, and it was open when he checked after the blast," Emily said.

A firefighter in a dripping wet turnout coat emerged from the front of the building. Emily hadn't even noticed him enter. His white-colored helmet identified him as the battalion chief.

He shook off some of the water like a Labrador retriever and signaled his team to shut off their hoses.

Fire engine pumps whined as they stopped feeding hundreds of gallons of water into the structure.

"Detectives, we're all clear in there," the chief said.

"No secondary devices?" Emily asked.

"I had a walk-through with our arson investigators. Lots of suspicious material, but no devices or substances that would be harmful to your team."

"Any human remains?" Javier said.

"None. They probably set this off remotely, or hightailed it outta there through the back door—the same way they came in. Not much damage to the rear of the building."

"Thanks, Chief," Emily said.

While the fire commander strode to the nearest engine, Emily stared into the blast-damaged retail space. "It wasn't remotely detonated, right? I mean we saw someone inside."

A bustle from behind the fire engines. "Let me through."

Emily peered around the fire personnel where the councilman's widow stood with her hands on her hips.

"I'll get this," Emily said as she navigated around the fire hoses snaking through to the barrier.

"Mrs. Davis—"

"You people couldn't wait, could you? I told the other detective I was on my way."

A pinprick of a thought poked Emily's mind. "Detective Medina called you quite a while ago. What took you so long?" Emily knew the home wasn't far from the store.

"I needed the key from our business manager. And I called our attorney, who should be here by now."

"Your attorney and business manager. Who else did you tell that the police were about to search the store?"

"Not that it's any of your business—but I didn't have time to tell anyone else."

"You retrieved your key from your business manager. What's his name?"

"Frank Turpin. He keeps backup copies of keys to our properties."

"Turpin ask why you needed a key?"

"Of course not. It's his job. Robby had our keys with him when . . ."

"Turpin wanna know what the search was about?"

"We know what the search is about. You're trying to ruin the reputation of a good man. You do this to his business, try to drag his name through the mud. It won't work, Detective. We're onto you."

"Mrs. Davis, we have no interest at all in your husband's reputation. It is what it is. What I am concerned with is why someone would want to burn the business down. Just a heads-up—the arson investigators will be contacting you."

"They can speak with my attorney." She turned on her heel and strode off.

Emily rejoined Javier, and a Tyvek-clad Officer Milton exited the storefront, black smudges adorning the white protective suit.

"He looks smug," Emily said.

"He's in his element."

Milton approached Emily and Javier with a huge smile plastered on his face.

"Detectives. The place is a mess. The racks of component parts we were looking for—the servo controllers and PCBs—all gone. Completely and thoroughly."

"Why the happy face, Milton?" Emily asked.

"Because of this." He thrust a handful of documents toward her.

Emily and Javier huddled together and studied the documents. The top sheets were lists of customers who attended Davis's recent class sessions. Attached to them were copies of receipts for supplies offered at a discount to the class participants.

"Okay, how did these not get trashed in the fire?" Javier asked.

"They were in a filing cabinet in the back room. The fire never got there. And check this out."

Milton took the stack of documents and turned to a page. He tapped his finger on a purchase receipt.

"It's a receipt for a PCB with the exact serial number of the one we received on West El Camino."

Emily searched through the serial numbers, parts specifications, until she found the name of the person who bought the component.

"You sure about this? This matches the serial number of the piece you found at our bombing scene?"

"Absolutely," Milton said, with a hint of pride in his voice.

The document claimed the part was purchased by Frank Turpin, the late councilman's business manager.

CHAPTER THIRTY-TWO

JAVIER CAME BACK to Emily and had the documents sealed in an evidence bag. "We have a BOLO out for Frank Turpin. What are the chances he's holed up at his place? He has an address out on Marconi."

Emily took stock of what was left of the business. The fire crews were departing from the scene. The arson investigator was poking around inside again to complete his assessment of the cause and origin of the fire.

"Milton, hang with the arson investigator and see if you can find anything that pins Turpin to this fire, or the murder of Councilman Davis." She handed the evidence bag of documents back to the officer.

"Mind the chain of custody," she reminded.

"Yes, ma'am."

"Javi, let's go find us a business manager."

Emily and Javier drove separately to the Marconi Avenue address, giving her time to sort, process, and file away her fears about her mom's deteriorating condition. There wasn't anything worrying about it would fix. But a foreboding sense of the next shoe about to drop lingered. Maybe the doctor had a point about the support group. Someone to share this with—Brian had his own worries and needed to focus on recovering.

Emily tried to picture sitting in a group of soccer moms sharing her feelings—yeah, right.

An incoming text sounded from her phone. Javier found the address and pulled to a stop at a gated home on the eastern edge of the city, well past the rows of apartments dotting the central section of Marconi Avenue.

Emily pulled in after Javier. The wrought-iron gates were open and the thick eucalyptus tree barrier at the road gave way to reveal a sprawling ranch-style home. The wing to the right was two stories and a slate gray color with white trim. It reminded Emily of the homes she saw on the coast near Bodega Bay.

Straight ahead was a three-bay garage with rooms above it for a caretaker or a studio.

"Some place," Javier said as they got out of their vehicles.

"The business manager gig must be doing pretty good."

Javier started for the front entrance and Emily grabbed him by the arm.

"Door," she said, tapping the textured grip of the Glock on her hip.

The wide red door was ajar. Open doorways often concealed bad intentions.

The open door and Turpin's connection to a bombing gave Emily some sense of exigent circumstances to enter the home and ensure no one was injured. Unlike television cop dramas, it took a few minutes to go through each room, open closets, look under beds, and make certain no one was there before yelling "clear." It also meant extra care to avoid any explosive devices Turpin might have planted.

"I'll go left—there's a sidelight window next to the door."

Javier nodded, and they approached the open front door with caution. Once at the threshold, Javier positioned himself to watch their backs for threats coming from the garage. With her back to the solid surface, Emily peeked over her left shoulder through the sidelight window.

The interior of the home was neat and orderly, no sign of a break-in. It didn't mean there weren't threats looming deep within the residence.

Emily shook her head and told her partner she couldn't see anything lurking behind the door.

She pressed the door open wider, staying in concealment. "Police department. Mr. Turpin, are you there?"

Emily stepped through the open door, her weapon in a low ready position, and cut right. Javier followed from his position and went left.

The entry opened to a large formal living room, appointed with rich wood fixtures, leather chairs, and a fireplace that looked like it had never been used.

A deeper search for bomb components, or documents connecting Turpin to the explosive devices, would require a search warrant. Once they found there was no one in imminent danger inside the residence.

Emily gathered with Javier near the front door. "You feel any sense of who lives here? I mean, not a single photograph, loose mail, or monogrammed towels—it strikes me as weird for someone with expensive taste like this."

Javier brushed a ceramic pot with an orchid blooming. The dirt was damp to the touch. "It doesn't feel right."

A woman in her mid-forties, dressed in business attire, strode to the doorway. She looked surprised to see Emily and Javier standing inside.

"Excuse me. What do you think you're doing?" The woman huffed.

Emily pulled her jacket aside to show her badge. "Detectives Hunter and Medina. And you are?"

"Detectives? Police? What are you doing in my home?"

Emily and Javier shared a glance.

"Your home? The door was open—"

"Open? Didn't I set the alarm before I left?" The woman craned her neck to look at the alarm panel on the wall inside.

"Are you Mrs. Turpin?"

"Turpin? Please. Victoria Galvin. Was anything damaged? Stolen?"

"Not that we could see. You should come and make certain for yourself."

Victoria stepped inside and cautiously assessed the front room from where she stood.

"We understood this was Frank Turpin's place," Emily said.

"Humph. He gets his mail here. This is my residence. Frank rents an apartment above the garage. When he remembers to pay rent, that is."

Emily stole a glance out to the windows above the garage.

"Have you seen him?"

"I try to avoid him, if I'm being honest. He's an unpleasant sort."

"How so?"

"Sullen, stays to himself most of the time, and keeps odd hours. When I'm forced to speak with him, it's usually to ask him to work on something for me."

"He's your business manager?"

Victoria laughed. "Business manager? Good Lord. The man can barely manage himself. No, Frank Turpin is my handyman. I should say he was my late husband's handyman. I haven't had the heart to let him go."

"A handyman?"

"Quite. Mind if I check the rest of the home? I can't rest until I'm sure everything is accounted for."

"Certainly. May we take a look at the rooms above the garage?"

"Of course—they are part of my house, and if this will help me finally jettison Frank from the premises, feel free."

"We'll check back with you when we're done. Make a list of anything out of place or missing, would you?" Emily said.

They started out the door toward the garage and Javier asked, "How do we access Frank's place?"

"Oh, yeah, that." Victoria picked up a remote and clicked a button, sending the left-hand garage door up on its tracks. "A staircase in the back will take you up to the apartment. No other key needed. Oh, his car's gone."

"What does he drive?"

"A red Toyota pickup. I don't know what year. I'm bad at those things. But it's got one of those metal racks for tools and things in the back. I've never seen him put anything on the racks, though."

"Thanks, Mrs. Galvin. We'll check back in with you."

Emily and Javier approached the now open garage bay. An emerald green vintage 1969 convertible Jaguar XKE was parked in the center stall, and a white 1965 Mustang, which looked to be partially restored, took another space.

"Wonder if these were the late Mr. Galvin's hobby cars?" Javier said.

"Some hobby. The red one is worth over a hundred grand."

"The red one. Really? Even I know that's a Jaguar."

"We found one in a chop shop off of Florin. They were getting ready to ship it to China. The insurance adjuster was crying when we told her we'd recovered the car."

"A hundred grand? It's still just a car, right?"

"Says the guy who drives a Geo Metro."

"It's almost classic and it gets me where I need to go," Javier said.

"Your heap will never be a classic."

"It's reliable transportation and I'm not making any car payments."

"Do you borrow mommy's car when you and Jenny go on a date? 'Cause nothing says cheap-ass like the broken-down beater you drive."

"There's the staircase," Javier said, changing the subject of conversation. "What's the chance Turpin's up there?"

"According to Mrs. Galvin, he isn't around. If he's our bomber, we need to watch our step. Wait," Emily said, sliding her arm out to block her partner.

A thin length of monofilament fishing line stretched across the third step of the stairs.

"He's booby-trapped the staircase. We need to call the bomb squad out here to clear the place before we go tromping around up there."

"I'll make the call—oh, and for the record, I don't tromp," Javier said.

Javier backed into the garage bay and made the call while Emily studied the staircase and the workbench near the Mustang.

Small scraps of copper wire lay against the four-barrel carburetor Mr. Galvin must have been working on before he died. A pair of wire cutters lay on a rubberized work mat.

Emily wasn't an auto mechanic, but she recognized the wire scraps didn't come from the mechanical carburetor. Turpin worked here. He assembled his devices in Galvin's workspace. He must have been sure Mrs. Galvin wasn't going to bother him there. She was too sentimental and grief-stricken to root around in her late husband's space.

Emily pulled a drawer open at the counter beneath the haphazardly discarded wire scraps. The pullout held a collection of wrenches and screwdrivers. Not the PCBs Emily hoped would be there to confirm Turpin's involvement in the bombing attacks.

"The bomb squad is on the way." Javier pocketed his cell phone and caught Emily looking through the drawer. "What'd you find?"

Emily tapped the work surface and pointed at the copper wire fragments. She looked behind the car parts on the counter and noticed a soldering iron. The tip glowed red hot.

"This is still plugged in. We missed this guy, but I'm certain he worked on another device right here."

As she spoke, a chill worked up her spine. The booby-trapped staircase, the cut wires.

A high-pitched whine sounded from the driveway outside the garage.

Emily caught the sudden movement out of the corner of her eye. A four-wheeled radio-controlled car sped into the garage bay.

"Javi, run!"

CHAPTER THIRTY-THREE

EMILY SHOVED JAVIER out the garage door and smacked the button to lower the door behind them.

The whine stopped, stuttered, and started again as the device turned around in the garage. A glint off of a lens mounted on the front of the car meant this one wasn't blind. It followed them.

Emily and Javier ran toward the main house and bounded up the steps where the car couldn't follow.

From within the garage, the car's whine intensified and the garage door descended. It was going to be close.

Emily ducked behind a pillar on the front porch and peeked around, watching the car speed forward against the glacially slow fall of the massive garage door.

The thin design of the wheeled machine let it squeeze partway through before the garage door caught the antenna on the back end of the car. The door continued down and crushed the rear wheels of the device in a shower of sparks.

Emily braced for an explosion, but it didn't come. She poked her head out from behind the pillar and saw the front end of the device protruding from under the heavy steel garage door.

"The bomb squad will have a little extra to work with," Emily said.

"Turpin?" Javier said.

"Sure looks that way. He's getting more sophisticated using a camera on the front of the car so he won't need to watch from a rooftop like he did on the bank building on West El Camino."

"Still, though, Milton thinks he'd be close by to keep the signal connected."

"How close?" Emily asked.

Javier shrugged. "Maybe a hundred yards."

Emily stiffened and stepped off the front porch for a view of the street.

A gray Ford Taurus peeled away from the curb. Javier got on his portable radio and called in the suspicious vehicle.

Emily asked dispatch to make a quick DMV search on vehicles registered to Frank Turpin. No gray Ford Taurus came back from the motor vehicle registry.

"Car wasn't registered to Turpin. Still coulda been him." Emily shoved her phone in her pocket and strode to within ten feet of the door, which was closer than she wanted to be. The crushed device was identical to the pieces recovered from the other devices. The green circuit board and the oversized black tires were a match. This one had an oil-stained, paper-wrapped bundle attached to the front near the axle. Emily guessed it was the explosive charge.

"The squad's here," Javier said.

The grind of a heavy armored truck with a short trailer pulled into the Galvin property. The trailer was a flatbed with what looked like a heavy steel trash can secured to the surface.

"Detectives, we need to stop meeting like this," the bomb squad commander said.

"Lieutenant, we don't pick the locations, but we have a prize for you under door number one."

Emily briefed him on the robotic vehicle and the trip wire she'd spotted on the stairs inside the garage.

The lieutenant asked Emily to go ask anyone who might be in the home to evacuate until they got a handle on exactly what they were dealing with.

Emily didn't need to knock on the front door as Mrs. Galvin had come out to see what the ruckus was in her yard.

"Oh my," she said. "What's this about?"

"Mrs. Galvin, why don't you grab your things and let's you, Javier, and I go grab a cup of coffee while these officers make sure everything is safe for you."

"Safe from what?"

"We found a bomb—actually the bomb found us, so we need to let these men take care of it."

"Goodness. Let me get my purse." Mrs. Galvin slipped back into the house and came out with her purse and a sweater over her shoulders.

"Anyone else inside?"

Mrs. Galvin shook her head.

The detectives escorted the woman away from the house and Emily nodded to the bomb squad lieutenant as they passed.

"Is there a coffee shop nearby?" Emily asked.

"Two blocks up. Nice little place—a local woman runs it." After a pause: "Does this have to do with Frank?"

"What do you know about Frank Turpin?" Emily asked.

A glance over her shoulder gave Emily a view of an officer putting on the heavy protective suit, the one that reminded her of a deep-sea diver.

The local coffee place was tucked into the front of what was once a residence. The front of the building was now a commercial space with a coffee shop with a sign advertising coffee, lattes, and something called an Apple-chino, which Emily thought sounded downright disgusting.

They pushed inside and Emily was a bit surprised the place could hold a business license. The rear door of the coffee shop opened into the residence living room. Four small tables with two chairs each crowded the cramped space, and no one was in the business.

A gray-haired woman greeted them from the doorway of the home.

"Hello, Louise," Mrs. Galvin said. "I brought some friends."

The older woman tottered to the counter, which was more of a bedroom dresser turned backwards. She tied an apron around her thin frame. "What can I get started for you?"

"I think three black coffees would be good." Mrs. Galvin looked to Emily and Javier with a nod.

The woman turned to an old Mr. Coffee machine on the counter behind her and poured three cups with a trembling hand. She placed them on the repurposed dresser, one at a time, in mismatched porcelain cups.

"Thank you," Emily said, getting a sly smile from the older woman.

Mrs. Galvin took her cup to a table and dragged a third chair to accommodate their little party.

Once Emily took her seat, she leaned in and whispered, "What's going on here?"

Mrs. Galvin smiled. "Louise is alone now after her husband died four years ago. She started to isolate and shut herself off from the outside world until she decided to open her home up to us."

"A coffee shop," Emily said.

"Sort of. It's really only friends and neighbors dropping in and sharing a cup. We try to make her feel like she's still connected."

"That's really nice of you. It means a lot to keep her interacting with other people."

Javier scooted his chair in and pointed at the sign in the window. "What's an Apple-chino?"

"Shhh," Mrs. Galvin said.

Louise appeared at the table. "Can I offer you a sample of my Apple-chino?"

"Oh, no, that's fine. I'm good with this." Javier hefted his cup of black coffee.

"Nonsense, dear. I'll be right back. It's on the house."

"Oh, you've done it now," Mrs. Galvin said.

"What?"

"The Apple-chino is the most noxious substance known to man . . . as you're about to find out."

The older woman placed a steaming cup, fresh from the microwave, in front of Javier.

"Tell me what you think?" she asked. It was clear she wasn't going to leave until Javier sampled her offering.

Mrs. Galvin bit her lip.

"Go on, Javi. Tell us what you think," Emily said.

Javier kicked her under the table.

He raised the fresh cup and crinkled his nose when the steamed milk, hot apple cider, and instant espresso mix wafted up.

He took a tight-jawed sip and closed his eyes before swallowing.

"Well?" the old woman asked.

Javier cleared his throat. "Have you tried this?"

"Oh my, heaven's no. I don't like apple cider."

"Then why—never mind. It's . . . unusual. Thank you."

The old woman beamed and shuffled back to her counter.

"How you doing there, partner?" Emily said.

He shoved the cup to the center of the table. "Oh my God. I think I'm going to be sick. If we gave this to the suspects we interrogated, Amnesty International would swarm us."

Mrs. Galvin snickered. "I tried to warn you."

Emily couldn't hold back a laugh at her partner's pained expression.

"Anyway, Mrs. Galvin, back to Frank Turpin. What can you tell us about him?"

"Frank was my husband's acquaintance. Goes back several years. He offered Frank a job as our handyman and he's been there, living above the garage, ever since."

"What kind of handyman work would there be for him around your place? I mean the grounds are immaculate."

"Well, thank you. My late husband and I used to discuss this at length. I didn't see the need to keep a full-time handyman on board. There isn't enough work to justify it. We have gardeners to care for the landscaping, but I never saw a reason. My husband mentioned how he felt sorry for him, that Frank had no one left in his life."

"No family you know of?"

"None I'm aware of. I tried to make him feel comfortable at first, invited him to our holiday gatherings. His reaction was—well—odd."

"How's that?"

"When I invited him to Thanksgiving dinner, he said something like, 'I've had my last Thanksgiving dinner.'"

"What did he mean by that?"

"I have no idea. When I asked my husband about it, he said he lost someone and the holidays were tough on him."

"I understand."

"I did, too, but there was more to it. Frank turned dark. Comments like, 'Enjoy this while you have it,' or 'They're going to take it away from you too.' During the protests a year ago, Frank started antagonizing the police—the people he got involved with, and the threats and instigation. It got him arrested for assault."

"Frank got arrested?"

"He did. All the charges were dropped—against everyone who protested. It made him even more angry—like he was being ignored. He made a comment about making them listen."

"Listen?"

"I had no idea what he was talking about. This was after my husband died—I was focused elsewhere. He always kept the garage locked up and got angry if I needed to find something. In my own garage."

"It's a good thing you didn't. We found a trip wire on the stairs, which looked like a trigger for a bomb. We need to talk to Frank about his connection to some other bombs in the city."

Mrs. Galvin put a hand to her chest. "Goodness. I'm glad he's gone, then."

"Any idea where he would go? Someplace he mentioned?"

She shook her head. "No. I don't have any idea where he might be. I heard him mention visiting family, but my husband said he didn't have anyone. Frank mentioned North Wind—I don't know where that is. He wasn't gone long—maybe two hours."

The name tickled a memory Emily couldn't quite place.

Javier's cell chimed with Pat Benatar's "Hit Me with Your Best Shot" as his ringtone.

He listened for a moment, then hung up.

"The garage has been cleared. It's safe to go back home."

They left their table and the old woman thanked them for dropping by. Javier was the first out the door to make sure he would not be forced to finish the Apple-chino.

Emily's mind kept turning over the name North Wind. She couldn't recall any town or neighborhood with the peculiar name. The only North Wind she knew of was the North Wind Memorial Park . . .

CHAPTER THIRTY-FOUR

THE GARAGE DOORS were up on their tracks and Emily noted the vintage Jaguar remained unscathed. With Mrs. Galvin safely tucked back into her home, the bomb squad was securing their equipment.

"What did you find?" Emily asked.

"Homemade. ANFO. Ammonium nitrate and fuel oil," the squad commander said.

"Explains the smell—the gasoline odor."

"Always a telltale sign. This guy is an amateur. Probably got the idea from reading *The Anarchist Cookbook*, or some militia propaganda. The mixture was a little rich on the fuel oil, and what ANFO needs is compression. You know, like the pressure cooker bombs the Boston Marathon bombers used, or a pipe bomb. The paper-wrapped package you had—it wasn't going to do a lot of damage."

"Is that why we've been lucky none of our people have been killed in these attacks? He doesn't know what he's doing?" Emily said.

The lieutenant tilted his head. "Could be. But he had enough explosive here to ruin your day. The trip wire led to a coffee can full of the stuff. Two other trip wires. Five gallons were upstairs in the loft. We let the windows open up there to air it out. I think he was using diesel fuel—man, the fumes . . ."

"Safe for Javi and me to go up?"

"It's all yours, Detective."

Even though the squad had cleared the garage and loft of incendiary devices, Emily watched where she stepped. At the top of the staircase, there was a strong lingering odor of gasoline.

The loft was open at one end, with a small kitchenette and dining area. A bed was tucked against a wall, and there was a bathroom on the other side of the stairs. It was a nice cozy apartment, if not for the fuel oil stains on the wood floors, and the yellowed sheets on the unmade bed.

"I guess maid service hasn't come today," Javier said.

"Or ever . . ."

Emily strode to the cluttered table where spools of wire and tools were strewn about. There wasn't any sense of organization. Turpin set the bomb and left everything in a rush. The question was—a rush to do what? He knew Emily and Javier were onto him once the widow Davis fingered him as the councilman's business manager.

Frank Turpin was clearly not a manager of any sort, living in an apartment above a garage.

"Who is this guy?" Emily said.

The crime scene team trudged up the stairs. Emily told them where to start.

Two techs began shooting video of the apartment and taking an inventory of the electronics and tools on the table.

"Javi? What's over there, pinned on the wall?"

Emily circled around the table and pulled a photograph from the wall. A family photo, one of those posed numbers, where the two kids dressed alike—matching Christmas sweaters in this case.

"Frank Turpin has a family," Emily said.

"Well, they certainly aren't living here."

"Mrs. Galvin said he didn't have anyone. That was her husband's impression too."

"Divorce?"

"Maybe. I think there's more here. This guy is a loner. He's squirreled away in a garage where he lives in exchange for work as a handyman."

"Why did Mr. Galvin take an interest in him? Charity case? Can't see it. There has to be some connection to the guy to let him live under your roof, right?" Javier said.

"You'd let me live with you if I needed a place to crash, wouldn't you?"

He paused.

"Javi? Wouldn't you?"

"My place is too small for all your baggage."

"Ass."

"My point is—who the hell is Frank Turpin?"

Emily shook the photo in her hand. "I have an idea. It was the place Frank mentioned to Mrs. Galvin. North Wind."

"You think that's where his family moved?"

"If this is what I think it is . . ."

To the techs, Emily asked them to connect with Officer Milton when they wrapped up and to email her the photos when they got a chance.

"Let's go pay our respects to the Turpin family," Emily said.

CHAPTER THIRTY-FIVE

"THIS WASN'T WHAT I expected," Javier said.

Emily and Javier stood on a grassy patch of well-maintained lawn. In front of them, small marble headstones, one for each of the Turpin family. Monica, Taft, and Milly. To the right was a marker with Frank Turpin engraved on the stone. The park's landscaper was able to direct them to the family plot.

North Wind Memorial Park was one of the largest private cemeteries in the county. Acres of headstones, crypts, and niches dotted the landscape. Emily recalled the name of the cemetery because one of her mother's friends was buried here last year.

"That's kinda creepy. Frank's headstone is there, without a date of death. It's like he's waiting."

Emily glanced at the empty date on Frank Turpin's headstone. His wife, Monica, had died on November 2, 2020. An electric jolt hit Emily in the chest. She pulled her cell and scrolled back to the first photos taken at the church where Brian was injured.

The wristwatch. The back of the watch case bore an inscription with the same date. November 2nd.

Emily looked back at the headstones. All of them, the entire Turpin family, had died on the same day.

"Holy shit, Javi. This is the connection. Turpin's family—they died on November 2, 2020." She showed him the photo of the watch.

"And Frank blames the police for their deaths."

"SWAT officers. He blames them for killing his family."

On the way out of the memorial park, they stopped at the office. A subdued man in a black suit greeted them, and once Emily badged him, his mood changed, realizing they weren't there to arrange for an eternal resting place for a loved one.

Emily showed the funeral director the Turpin family photo. "This guy? You ever see him around here?"

"Mr. Turpin. Yes. He comes to visit often."

"He ever say anything about how his family died?"

The man shook his head. "He's never mentioned it. In fact, he doesn't say much. I always assumed it was some sort of car accident with them going at the same time. Comes in, pays his respects, and leaves. Twenty to thirty minutes, tops. Doesn't interact with anyone while he's here."

"You said often. How often does he come here?"

"Usually once a week, not sure what day of the week. We don't have a sign-in book or anything . . ." The funeral director glanced away.

Emily followed his gaze and immediately spotted a man getting up from his knees. He was at the grave markers she and Javi had found a few minutes earlier.

"Javi, you seeing this? Is it him?"

"Could be. Looks like Mr. Turpin," the funeral director said. "I didn't see him arrive."

"He's got a backpack on the ground at his feet. Knowing what he's been up to . . ." Javier said.

Emily knew what Javier meant. His backpack could contain another explosive device. "Sir, we're going to need you to go back in the office and lock yourself inside."

"Has he noticed us yet?" Javier said.

"He looked over this way, saw us standing with the director, and thought it was business as usual."

They both casually got in a maintenance golf cart. Emily tapped the electric cart's accelerator and piloted toward Turpin's location.

The rumble of the cart's tires over the gravel caught Turpin's attention.

"I think our element of surprise ran out," Emily said.

Turpin turned his back, pulled a blue ball cap down, and stooped to grab his backpack.

"He's not walking in our direction. Must be another way out. That's why we didn't see him come in," Javier said.

Emily pressed on the accelerator, but the cart held its slow pace.

"You have your radio?"

Javier held it in his left hand.

"Call it in. Get us a unit behind the memorial park."

Javier got on the radio and Turpin stopped to duck under a section of chain link that had been pulled aside.

Emily drove on and spotted Turpin dropping his backpack, removing a black object, and standing once more, facing Emily, with his face obscured in the shadows by the fence.

A blur formed at his feet and Emily recognized it before the high-pitch whine was heard.

"Javi! Incoming!"

The radio-controlled car bounced slightly as it sped in their direction. It had covered half the distance between them in seconds.

"We gotta bail!"

They both shot from the golf cart, which crawled to a stop in the center of the road. Javier sprinted right and found a small tree. Emily turned left, down a decline and over several rows of brass plaques.

The car had a choice to make and Turpin veered the car off the main path and into the deep grass after Emily.

Emily heard the high-pitched whine behind her and knew the device was closing in. She saw her opportunity ahead in the thicker grass. If the car had a low-mounted camera like the one used at Galvin's home, it would have trouble seeing the terrain in this thick growth.

She found the place to make her stand and waited. The machine picked up speed and shot in her direction.

The car cleared a dense patch of grass and shot into an open trench—a grave waiting to be backfilled. Six urns lay in the bottom of the earthen trench Emily spotted when she jumped over the opening.

The car's momentum couldn't clear the gap and it stalled in the dirt bank on the opposite side.

Emily ducked, and the car exploded. The blast directed into the dirt and clay walls of the trench. A cloud of white ash plumed over the opening, the explosion shattering a pair of urns.

When she stood up, Turpin was gone.

Javier jogged to her position, worry in his eyes.

"You all right, Em?"

"You see where Turpin went?"

He pointed to the gap in the fence line. "By the time I hit the fence, I spotted a gray Ford Taurus make a sharp left turn. Closest unit is five minutes out."

"Dammit. We lost him," Emily said.

They backtracked through the hole in the fence and Emily returned to the Turpin family grave site.

"Frank was here to see his family," Emily said.

"The girl—she was five years old."

"His son, Taft, was twelve. Man, had to be tough, losing your entire family."

"Enough to make him break bad."

Emily scanned the plain brass markers for the Turpin family.

She spotted a white object stuffed next to his wife's marker. Emily pulled a folded index card out from the dirt space next to the brass plaque. A handwritten message in red. "I'm sorry, my love. I let you down. They let you down—and they will pay for it." The message ended with a list of names—the same officers' names Councilman Davis had. Some were crossed out—Brian Conner, among them—and Emily found her name had been added.

CHAPTER THIRTY-SIX

WHEN EMILY AND Javier arrived at the detective bureau, they split up, with Javier going to the records room to pull any reports near the date the Turpin family died.

Emily knocked on the lieutenant's door and found him on the phone. He pinched the bridge of his nose as he listened. "I understand. We'll have a statement for you shortly. I have your number." Lieutenant Hall hung up and locked eyes with Emily.

"Seems your reporter friend picked up Frank Turpin's name as our suspect and wants to run with it."

"It was only a matter of time until it leaked. Kari Hardison? She's the reporter?" Emily said.

"She's not gonna give up on this. She's like a bulldog with a bone, but she is fair, I'll give her that," Hall said. "We need to get to the bottom of the Turpin connection before she does."

Emily briefed him on the Turpin family graves and the updated list of names on his hit list.

"Dammit. I knew putting you out there at the mayor's press conference was a bad idea. We need to get you out of town for a while."

"Not happening, Lieutenant. I need to see this through. There are three more names on this list and we need to make sure Turpin can't get to any of them."

"Emily, Turpin tried to take you out at the North Wind Memorial Park. He's going to make sure he doesn't miss next time."

"Let me worry about that. Javier and I took down his workshop at the Galvin residence. The bomb he used in the cemetery came from his backpack and I think he's running low on his hobby car explosives. We got an inventory of the electronic parts he bought from Davis's store."

"It's my job to worry."

"Javier is digging up the incident reports for the date the Turpin family died. I don't remember a SWAT response where we were responsible for the deaths. Do you?"

Hall bit his lower lip and shook his head. "I'd remember if we accidentally shot a citizen. A whole family? Not a chance I'd have missed it."

"I don't know what's behind this. Brian—Sergeant Conner—couldn't recall any incident where everything went off the rails. Lieutenant Whitman didn't give me much to go on there either."

"Whitman's an odd one, but I can't see him killing a family."

"We'll see what we pull from these reports. Let me reach out to Kari Hardison and see what she knows. I might have to give her a little taste in return. I'll try to convince her to lie low for a day or two so Turpin won't add her to his list. Speaking of lists, I want to connect with the other names that aren't yet crossed off."

"You want me to talk to them?"

"I got it, Lieutenant. One of them is Whitman. And two cops—Tom Black and J. T. Cortez, who I've never heard of."

"I'll tell the watch commander you want to see Black and Cortez."

"Thanks, Lieutenant. I'll keep you posted."

Emily left the lieutenant's office, surprised Javier hadn't already returned with the incident reports from the day Turpin's wife and children died.

Emily placed the handwritten index card in a plastic evidence bag and laid it on her desk. Whitman's name stood out to her. If anyone would know what happened on a SWAT call, the commander would.

She flipped through her notes and found Whitman's phone number. Emily dialed and waited. It kept ringing. No answering machine, no hanging up. The phone kept ringing. She hung up and tried again with the same result. Whitman probably recognized the police department's office number on his caller ID.

She switched from her desk landline to her cell phone and called again. The call kept ringing. Whitman wasn't going to take her call.

Javier came in carrying a heavy cardboard box and plopped it on the center of his desk.

"I thought you got lost," Emily said.

"These files needed the captain's sign-off to pull. He wasn't happy about it."

"What's the deal with needing the captain's approval to pull an incident report?"

"All he said was this was by the book and dredging this up now wasn't going to be good for anyone."

"What a weird thing to say. He mention anything about Frank Turpin's connection?"

"I asked and all he did was shake his head and say it was a damn shame."

"A shame? That's all he said?" Emily said.

"Yeah, it felt off, but he wouldn't say anything more."

Javier flipped the top off the box and it was full of file folders and loose papers shoved into the container.

"This is gonna take a while," Javier said as he plucked a single random sheet from an incident report jammed in the box.

Emily grabbed the first file and opened it on the table. She expected a sudden revelation—a name—a location that would spark a memory.

Critical events have a life of their own in law enforcement circles. There's always a body count, and not the literal bodies of victims caught up in violence on the street. But an administrative body count. In many agencies, when an operation goes off the rails or gets negative press coverage, there's a tendency to find a scapegoat.

The prior chief of police didn't look for someone to blame, meaning the incident didn't bubble up in media or political circles.

She scanned the first few pages of the aging paper document. "Thomas Michael McCracken—ring a bell with you?" Emily asked.

"Doesn't sound familiar. He another officer?"

"No—he was the shooter. He barricaded himself in a mom-and-pop market. He killed the Turpin family."

CHAPTER THIRTY-SEVEN

EMILY READ FROM the file.

"McCracken entered the Capitol City Market on 10th at nine in the morning and got into an argument with the owner—a Mr. Randu Singh—over not selling him a bottle of whiskey. McCracken forced his way behind the counter and grabbed a bottle off the shelf and Mr. Singh tried to stop him."

"Looking for a shot of Jack at nine in the a.m. Says a lot about the guy," Javier said.

Emily ran a finger down the report. "McCracken threw the bottle of booze at Singh and started yelling racial slurs at the shop owner."

"Where does the Turpin family come into the picture?" Javier asked.

Emily scanned the next two pages. "This is about McCracken and his beef with Singh." She grabbed the next file. "This must be the one," she said, pointing at the TURPIN label on the tab.

She opened the report. "Okay, mom and the kids were in the back of the store when McCracken came in. Once the altercation began, Monica Turpin grabbed Taft and Milly and shoved them in a back room to hide while McCracken started beating on Singh."

Javier's brow creased. "Who's reporting this? We know mom and the kids died. They have a witness. Mr. Singh?"

Emily flipped through the pages. Her shoulders sank. "They had a witness—Frank Turpin."

"Oh, man. He watched his family die? That's enough to twist anyone."

"Makes sense now why his life fell apart and he was living in the Galvins' garage apartment. Here—the report says when McCracken knocked the shop owner to the floor, Frank Turpin tackled him and forced him off of the injured man."

"While his wife and kids hid in the back of the store?"

"Looks like it. Says Turpin fought McCracken off while Singh reached for a handgun he kept under the cash register. McCracken took the handgun from the seventy-two-year-old man and pistol-whipped him. He wheeled around and shot Turpin."

"Turpin? Damn. The guy went after his family then?"

Emily skipped ahead with a tinge of dread because she knew how this story ended.

"No. He barricaded himself in the store after he shot Turpin. He thought he killed Turpin and Singh."

"Ah, the barricaded suspect—that's why there was a SWAT callout."

"Exactly. A customer entered, and McCracken pointed the gun at him while he wrapped a chain around the front doors."

Emily closed the file. Trying to imagine what Frank Turpin went through—bleeding out on the store's floor while his family was alone with a gunman. Enough to make anyone crack. It didn't explain— why now? After all these years, why did he start the bombing attacks now?

Javier pulled the next file from the box, a thick folder with a label in bold black letters—INCIDENT COMMANDER.

The first page in the file was a roster of officers who were on scene. "The incident commander was Lieutenant Whitman, which we knew. And his roster is identical to the list Councilman Davis had."

Emily grabbed the card she'd found at the North Wind Memorial Park and held it up alongside the official roster prepared by the incident commander.

"It's identical. Name by name. It's not alphabetical—Whitman logged them in as they arrived on scene." Her breath hitched when she noticed Brian Conner's name.

Javier flipped the page to the incident log. It was a chronological report of events as they unfolded. "First contact with McCracken was by a responding officer, T. Sutton. Suspect McCracken fired off a shot through the front windows and warned the officer to stay back. Officer Sutton saw Turpin and Singh on the floor with obvious injuries."

"We've got an unstable armed suspect with two victims down," Emily said.

"Next contact was to try to initiate communication with McCracken. He hid in the back of the store. He found Mrs. Turpin and the two kids. Then claimed them as hostages."

"I can't imagine Monica Turpin and her two kids . . ."

"It says McCracken refused to give proof of life when contacted. Whitman said he doubted there were any hostages in the store. They waited him out, cut power to the store, and set a perimeter."

"Something had to give." Emily glanced at the chronology and noted the standoff lasted for four hours before McCracken allowed Singh to leave in exchange for a pizza.

"Here it is—four hours after the first contact, McCracken used Monica Turpin as a shield and made a demand for a ride out of the city. Oh, and wanted his medication delivered."

"Let me guess. He was on psych meds for—"

"Antisocial personality disorder, Bipolar Type 1, schizoaffective disorder . . ."

"And he's armed with hostages," Emily said.

"Right? What could possibly go wrong? What I don't see in the log is any indication they tried to negotiate his surrender. Why not give him his meds in exchange for the hostages?"

"Who was the primary negotiator?" Emily flipped open the file again and glanced at the roster of personnel on the scene. "I only see the tactical guys here—all SWAT. The negotiator's report must be in here."

Emily flipped through the labels on the file folders. "We've got reports from the EMTs, crime scene photos, autopsy reports from the medical examiner. Nothing marked as hostage negotiation. Wait, here's one—Frank Turpin."

She yanked the file open and found the interview Frank Turpin gave from his hospital bed after the siege ended. "Javi, listen to this. Turpin said he tried playing dead after McCracken shot him."

"With his wife and kids in the store?"

"Some point after McCracken used Monica as a human shield, Frank was able to grab the phone off the counter and dialed 911. McCracken was in the back room with his family."

Javier glanced at the chronological report and found an entry. "Phone call from store to 911, redirected to incident commander."

Javier tapped on a report page. "Listen, Turpin claims he gave the officers a description of the suspect, noted he was armed with a single revolver, and begged for his family's release.

"The incident commander's log downplays the contact. Get this—'caller's identity unconfirmed. Believed to be suspect impersonating a hostage.' I mean, wow. They could see Turpin from the front door.

"Turpin's interview says he spoke with a lieutenant—he must mean Whitman—and they weren't doing anything to rescue his family. About two hours into the standoff, McCracken caught him on the phone and told Turpin to tell the cops to back away or he'd start killing people," Javier said.

"This is interesting," Javier continued, pointing at an entry on the commander's log. "Blue Team positioned at front doors, Green Team at rear door. Hold position. Looks like Brian was on Blue Team."

Emily swallowed hard. She knew it was part of the job, but facing off with a mentally ill gunman with hostages must've been terrifying. Brian claimed he didn't remember a specific assault or hostage rescue with a November date.

"Turpin was on the phone with Whitman when a sound against the metal back door drew McCracken's attention. He told the lieutenant the suspect was distracted at the back door. Come in the front now. He begged for the officers to enter."

"When did they breach?" Javier said.

Emily shook her head.

Javier ran a finger down the log to an entry near the bottom. "Shots fired inside. Turpin said McCracken panicked when he thought someone was coming in the back door. He grabbed Monica, shoved her on the floor near the refrigerators, and shot her once in the head. The two kids started to scream and McCracken yelled for them to stop. He shot them to shut them up."

"Oh God. McCracken killed them in front of Frank." Emily glanced back to Frank Turpin's interview. The kids were still alive, badly hurt, but alive, and he begged for McCracken to let them go—to get medical treatment. McCracken didn't respond. He paced around, talking to himself.

"He got back on the phone to Lieutenant Whitman and told him his wife and kids had been shot and needed help."

Javier shook his head. "An hour later, another gunshot heard from inside. Caller reports gunman shot himself. Green Team enters from rear and reports an adult female and two children dead. Suspect down."

Emily wondered why Whitman didn't act. He froze. Turpin asked for answers in his post-incident interview. He blamed SPD and the SWAT officers for what happened to his family.

CHAPTER THIRTY-EIGHT

EMILY'S CELL BUZZED, breaking her away from the grim details of the family annihilation. She didn't recognize the caller ID.

"Hunter here."

"Emily, it's Brian. You near a television?" He was calling from his hospital room based on the beeps, chirps, and medical chatter in the background.

"I can be. What's up?"

"That reporter—the one you kinda like—the blonde."

"Kari Hardison?"

"Yeah, her. She's on Channel 9 right now."

"Kari's a print reporter. What's she doing on television?"

"She's talking about SPD, the bombings, and Frank Turpin."

Emily held the phone down, strode across the office, and flipped on the television, tuning it to the local channel. Kari Hardison was on-screen with a red banner underneath reading, "Bombing Suspect Outed as Former Cop."

Emily lifted the phone back to her ear. "What's she talking about? Frank Turpin wasn't a cop. Where did she hear that?"

"She's not wrong, Em. At least not totally," Brian said.

"What are you saying?"

Brian let out a heavy sigh over the connection. "He wasn't SPD. Turpin was with Placer County Sheriff. I think he worked in the jail. Or was going to. I don't remember."

The revelation didn't sit well with Emily. "How would you know this, Brian?"

"Everyone knew. He got on the phone in the store and called out, identifying himself as a peace officer."

"There wasn't any mention of it in the incident reports or the commander's log," Emily said.

"I know there wasn't. We were told to leave it out. At the time it didn't seem like it mattered. It didn't change the outcome. Shooter was dead by his own hand."

"After he took out a mother and her kids." Emily had an edge to her voice. "Who told you to leave it out?"

"Emily, it doesn't matter now. It's old news." His voice took on a harder tone.

Emily felt his anxiety through the connection. "Not according to what I'm seeing on the television right now. It was Lieutenant Whitman, wasn't it?"

"Em, you can't go at him now. He's retired. I kinda think this incident is what made him leave. He's never talked about what happened that night. We wanted to make entry. We had an ops plan worked out. Green Team would distract, and Blue would toss a flash bang, make entry, and take down the shooter. Green would rescue the hostages."

"Why didn't it happen?"

"I couldn't tell you, Em. But what I can say is they are talking about kicking me out of here."

"You ready to come home?" Emily felt a little tickle in the back of her brain. He was quick to change the subject away from that deadly night. "Are you sure it's not too soon?"

"What? You don't want me to leave the hospital because I might be a burden to you?" The sharp response caught Emily off guard.

There it was again. The abrupt mood swing. It wasn't Brian's fault. The traumatic brain injury was doing the talking.

"No, that's not what I meant," she said.

"Really? It seemed that way. I earn a gate pass to get out of this place and your first response is that it's too soon. I mean, you made it pretty damn clear you weren't ready to move in together."

Emily took a deep breath. "I meant, are you well enough to leave?"

"As ready as I'm ever going to be."

"You can come and stay with me," she said.

"I don't need a nursemaid." His response was abrupt and cutting.

Emily tried to tell herself again this wasn't Brian talking. But it still hurt.

"I'm not your nurse, Brian. I thought you could stay with me while you recovered. I'd be there if you needed anything. I—I miss you . . ."

"Yeah, Em. I miss you too. This is hard."

She felt his anger begin to fall.

"I'm too much of a burden for anyone right now. I'll be better on my own."

A pang of heartbreak swept through her when he mentioned being better on his own.

"I don't mind helping you—if you want it." She needed to change the subject and make him think about something else.

"Brian, this whole thing with Frank Turpin stinks." She glanced up at the television and the news had moved on to the next story about the mayor's new initiative to improve high school graduation rates. Emily powered the television off and leaned on her desk.

"The lieutenant was always a stand-up guy. At least he was until this. That family—this one got to him."

"I can see why. Pretty brutal stuff."

"I still see those dead kids in my nightmares."

Emily held the phone to her chest for a moment imagining what Brian must have felt walking into that market. "Why haven't you ever said anything to me about this?"

"And give you another reason to—"

Emily cut him off rather than let him finish something she might not be able to forgive. His moods were volatile.

"You said Whitman seemed changed by what happened in that store."

"Yeah, we had a chance and Whitman froze. We should have gone in. We had a chance to save them. We would've changed the outcome."

"It's easy to armchair quarterback an incident like this. It's only natural to think about how it could've ended differently."

"We always did a post-incident debrief and reviewed actions and outcomes. The lieutenant always led these sessions. He wasn't listening to anything we had to say on the ops plan. Or why he held us back from taking down McCracken when we had our chance."

"How did he justify it?" Emily asked.

A shuffling noise and a small groan from Brian's side of the connection sounded. "Sorry. They're getting me ready for PT. Gotta take my pain meds." A gulping noise followed by, "Where were we?"

"How did Whitman justify not taking down the shooter?"

"He didn't. He told us it was his call and that was the end of it. I can't put my finger on it, but it was like the lieutenant wanted the outcome."

Emily reflected on the interaction with Whitman at his rural compound. Eccentric, for sure. A right-wing Second Amendment proponent, definitely. What could the SWAT commander hope to gain from letting a barricaded suspect kill a mother and her kids?

"Hey, Em, I gotta go. The head pain bringer from PT is here. Oh, and I'm sorry if I got a little hot. I'm working on it."

"I'll try and stop by later."

"That'd be nice. I can spring for some hospital Jell-O."

They disconnected the call, and Emily rejoined Javier. "That was Brian. He caught Kari Hardison on Channel 9 naming Frank Turpin."

"It was bound to leak."

"She said he was a former cop."

Javier pushed back from the table. "A cop? There is no mention of it in the file, not a single word. Where'd that come from?"

Emily shrugged. "I don't know. Brian sounded like he knew. Placer County—not SPD."

"Was he?"

"I gotta run it down. But if he was, why was it never mentioned in these reports?"

CHAPTER THIRTY-NINE

EMILY ENTERED ENEMY territory. Curious eyes and furtive glances followed her. Police detectives weren't known to prowl the corridors of the *Sacramento Tribune*.

"Kari, we need to talk," Emily said from the opening in the reporter's cubicle.

Kari Hardison swiveled her chair around and her eyes widened when she recognized who it was calling her.

"Emily? What are you doing here?"

"I caught your performance over on Channel 9."

A flush crept up Kari's throat.

"I told you I wasn't sure how long I could keep Frank Turpin's identity under wraps. It was out. Channel 9 was about to go live with it and our editor managed to convince them to work the story together."

Emily doubted it was a journalistic decision. More likely, Kari wanted to explore a move from print to television.

"Tell me about Turpin's background."

"What do you mean? You know Turpin is the bomber who's been targeting your people."

"Your on-air report. You mentioned Turpin was a former cop."

"Yes. And?"

"Where'd you find out that little nugget?"

Kari grinned. "Now, Detective, I'm not at liberty to reveal my sources."

"Turpin's background in law enforcement isn't widely known."

"Then I guess that means I'm pretty good at what I do."

"Kari, stop playing coy. Turpin is a fugitive at large and his former employment might be important."

"Which is why we thought it should be aired."

"Listen, Kari. This guy isn't playing around. He's gone after anyone involved in—he's gone after anyone who he thinks has crossed him. You made it sound like he wore an SPD badge."

Kari smiled and leaned in. "All right. I'll give you as much as I can. I've verified the information. Frank Turpin attended the local police academy and was to report to the Placer County Sheriff's Office." She plucked a sheet of paper off of a pile on her desk. "Here."

Emily glanced at the photocopy. It was issued by the Sacramento Regional Public Safety Training Center, but the scant details on the Peace Officer Standards and Training memorandum offered little detail.

"He wasn't actually working as a peace officer on the street," Emily said.

"He had an offer of employment from a law enforcement agency."

"You made it sound like he was a cop who turned against his brothers."

"Well, didn't he?"

"Kari, it's kind of misleading."

"What's important is what happened. His motivation seems pretty clear-cut."

Emily straightened and crossed her arms. Turpin believed he was a cop. Felt betrayed by the law enforcement response to the attack against his family. And targeted those who he believed were responsible for the outcome. There was only one way Kari could have known.

"Turpin is your source, isn't he?"

A glimmer shone in the reporter's eye. "I can neither confirm, nor deny . . ."

"You just did. Kari, be careful with this guy. Did he give you any indication what he's planning next?"

Kari pursed her mouth, considering how much to reveal to the detective. "No. He didn't say specifically. We both know Turpin is damaged goods, right? Anything he says I take with a pound of salt. He is fixated on the people who he blames for letting him down. Said it was about a cover-up. Can you give me a little insight there? I could—"

"I can't comment on an ongoing investigation," Emily said.

Emily knew what Turpin meant. He blamed the SWAT response for the murder of his wife and children.

"Touché."

"Kari, please be careful with this guy. Don't get caught up in his madness. He's dangerous. Keep your distance."

"I have a job to do, too, Emily. But I won't do anything foolish."

"You've been doing this awhile. You know to stay safe. If he does contact you again, please give me a call. I want to find him before more people get hurt."

Kari nodded and Emily left her as the reporter's phone rang. Emily was certain Turpin wasn't done with his attacks. There were untargeted names on his list—including hers.

Leaving the newspaper offices, Emily figured Frank Turpin would reach out to the reporter again. He'd gotten her attention, and he wanted the public to know how he was wronged. All the attacks at the church, the intersection, even the city councilman's place, had two things in common—go after the ones he held responsible, and target his attacks in open, public places. Places where his attacks garnered attention.

Attention. It occurred to Emily that Frank Turpin wanted people to listen to his story—as he believed it. The official reports were sanitized according to Brian's comments. There was the official story, and the version Turpin was acting against. Emily knew the truth fell somewhere in between.

Kari Hardison's information about Turpin attending the regional police academy was interesting, but how did the academy merge with Whitman and his outright refusal to render aid?

Emily glanced at her watch and called Javier.

He recognized her number and answered. "Are you now an inside source for your reporter friend?"

"I didn't have anything she could use. Kari knew more about Turpin than we do. He supposedly attended the regional public safety academy and received a job offer with Placer County."

"He was a peace officer like he identified himself to the 911 operator?"

"Yes, maybe. There's something really murky here. Brian told what he remembered about that incident."

"How is he?"

"I'm—I'm not sure. He's struggling with PT and the pain. He wants to go home. I'm not sure he's ready."

"I get his point. No one can find rest in a hospital."

"I suppose. Anyway, he told me Whitman made the call. He ordered the team to stand down and not try to rescue the hostages after they found out Turpin was inside."

"Curious. What's that about?"

"I don't know. I have a little time before the Regional Public Safety Center closes. I want to go out there and see if they kept any records or if there's someone who remembers Turpin. Might help us understand what's going on."

"You need me to come with?"

"I think I've got this, Javi. You might need to go spend a little time with Jenny and figure out where she's going to land on this out-of-town job offer."

"You sound like my mother."

She hung up as she pulled into the Regional Public Safety Center on the grounds of the former McClellan Air Force Base, off of Watt Avenue. The North Sacramento neighborhood, which had catered to military families and base operations, now found life with social service centers, low-income housing, and had become a favorite hangout for the biker gangs who fought for control of the city's meth trade.

Traffic out of the city was thick on Interstate 80 and backed up on the Watt Avenue exit. Emily thought about skipping the visit to the regional police academy offices, but she had to know more about Frank Turpin in the months before his family was murdered in front of him.

Emily found the squat, tan-colored building and parked in the half-empty lot. The lack of cars struck her until she realized the cadets at this public safety academy didn't live on the grounds like other law enforcement academy campuses. Cadets went about their day jobs and attended classes in the evenings and weekends.

She hoped she wasn't too late to find someone from administration to allow her access to the records—then there was the whole no war-rant thing. Sure, she could request one and a judge wouldn't hesitate to sign. But Emily planned to press the academy staff using the agreements cadets signed to allow law enforcement agencies access to their personal information. Usually, it was to make hiring decisions, but Emily knew the Public Safety Center wouldn't want it widely known one of their "graduates" was the mad bomber of Sacramento.

Emily pushed in through the glass doors and the reception desk was empty. She followed the corridor to the left and found the administration office.

A woman was tending to a copy machine, and by the smell of copy toner in the air, she'd been at it for a while.

"Excuse me," Emily said. "I'm looking for the academy commander."

The woman turned and smiled. "Emily Hunter?"

"Yes."

"You don't remember me, do you? Kris Johnson. We were in Professor Landis's class at Sac State."

Emily flashed back ten years to a sociology class from one of the brightest professors she ever had. Kris was on the fast track to one of the police academies, but Emily couldn't remember which one.

"It's been a minute, Kris. You haven't been here at the regional academy the whole time."

"I went to the highway patrol and blew my knee out during my first year. That was the end of my story."

"Oh, man, I'm sorry. I never heard."

"Turns out the knee was the best thing that ever happened to me. After the surgery, I had to kind of reset with lots of rehab. I met a guy during one of my rehab sessions—and, well, long story short—we got married, and five years later we have two kids."

"Wow. Fantastic." Emily didn't know if she felt jealous Kris had found a stable relationship, or relief that Emily had dodged the rush to have kids.

"Been working here at the Public Safety Center for about three years. It's about as close to law enforcement as I'm getting. I do keep up on your press, though."

Before Kris could ask about her husband and how many kids she had, Emily preempted and said, "I'm here because of an academy cadet a few years back—his family was murdered."

Kris leaned against the copy machine. "Frank Turpin."

"You remember him?"

"The murders happened before I got here. But it was all anyone talked about. Pretty tragic stuff."

"I need to look at any information the academy collected on Turpin. I want to understand who he was before his wife and kids were killed."

Kris collected the printed copies from the machine and placed them on a desk.

"We keep training records for proof of POST certification. We digitized our files so it should make it easy to find them." Kris slipped behind a keyboard and tapped the mouse to wake the system. "Okay, Turpin, comma, Frank." Kris tapped ENTER.

An hourglass in the center of the screen tumbled as the system searched for the files.

"Anyone here who might've taught while Turpin attended?" Emily asked.

"I don't know. It's possible, I guess. His transcripts should list his academy instructors. There are a few still teaching from back then. Howell, Coyle, Whitman—"

"Whitman? Richard Whitman from Sac PD?"

"Yeah, I think so. He was lead firearms instructor and range master. Pitches in from time to time now."

An itch nibbled at the base of Emily's brain. Whitman knew who Turpin was well before the tragic encounter in a convenience store. He knew and ignored Turpin's plea from inside. Why?

"Huh, interesting."

"What'd you find?" Emily asked as she stepped around to look over Kris's shoulder.

"Here's Turpin's records. He didn't graduate."

"I understood he did and had a job offer from Placer County."

"No. Oh—he was in his last cycle, or module. Had about three months to go when *it* happened. He went out on medical."

"Makes perfect sense. He was injured   shot during the incident."

"Here we go. He came back six months later. Says Turpin was discharged shortly thereafter because he got into a physical altercation with staff."

"Let me venture a wild guess here—Whitman?"

"It doesn't say. It's sealed. Can't say I've seen that before. The next entry is a referral for a psychological evaluation."

"He wasn't cleared by a shrink post-shooting?"

"Turpin wasn't injured in conjunction with his academy training. There wouldn't be an automatic evaluation."

Emily stared at the computer screen. She wasn't surprised Turpin wasn't the same man after his family was executed. It would change anyone. Getting physical with an academy instructor would guarantee a cadet would get the boot. While she didn't have the sealed file, Emily was certain Turpin confronted Whitman—the man he blamed for what happened to his family.

"You have the results of the psych eval?"

"Looks like he refused. He never returned and the academy dropped him."

"Any indication of problems with staff or complaints from Turpin before his family was killed?"

"Now you're talking my wheelhouse. I manage the complaints here at the academy." Kris logged off the cadet files program and brought up another database.

"Are there many complaints filed?" Emily said.

"You'd be surprised. Most of them are about hurt feelings, and 'not feeling safe' because another cadet said a harsh word."

"Wait until he lands out on the streets."

"We've got a generation with challenges in social skills. All of their personal interaction has been online, on social media, where they never really interact with anyone. This is new for them. Some freak out when another person talks to them."

Kris scrolled the mouse to open the menu.

"They figure out pretty quickly this isn't the line of work for them. But we see some serious complaints—sexual harassment is still a big one."

"Go figure."

"Yeah, we weed out a couple of knuckle draggers every class."

She clicked the mouse.

"Turpin is here. He did file a complaint. Three of them, in fact, in the month before he went out on medical leave—before the shooting."

"What does it say?" Emily leaned over and squinted at the screen.

"The details of the complaint aren't in this tracking file. But I can tell you all three were filed against Whitman."

CHAPTER FORTY

EMILY ARRANGED FOR Kris to email her the complaint files once she pulled them out of storage. The academy's tracking log recorded no disposition on the complaints, and Kris couldn't recall any investigations underway when Frank Turpin returned to the academy.

Turpin had a beef—multiple disagreements, apparently—with Whitman. Were they serious enough to cause the SWAT commander to withhold a rescue once he found out who was in the store? The thought sent a shiver up Emily's spine. Would he be capable of such a heartless act? Did some psychic switch in Turpin's brain trigger his path of destruction?

No matter how many times Emily pulled up to her house, it gave her a sense of peace. When everything in her life threatened to spin out of control, the restored Victorian home was her safe space away from the madness.

Emily parked her SUV in her drive. She unlocked the dead bolt, and as her hand reached for the doorknob and the second lock, she felt she was being watched.

She swung around and peered into the twilight. There. A glimmer in the street in front of her home. It moved and turned up the street. A dark-colored pickup truck drove away with its headlights off

Emily swung back to the door and fumbled with the key. Turpin drove a truck, according to Mrs. Galvin. She turned the key, grabbed the knob, and forced the door open, slamming it closed after she stepped inside.

The door was two inches of solid wood, but Emily didn't think it would be enough to shield her from one of Turpin's bombs. She'd seen what his improvised bombs could do to a vehicle.

She ran deeper into the house and ducked behind her kitchen cabinets.

Nothing.

She exited her back door and took a step away from her safe spot at the corner of the house. Emily crept against her neighbor's garage and kept an eye out for a bomb-laden device. When she reached the bottom stair at her front porch, she spotted a thick, round tube to the side of her front door. She must have stepped right past the object as she raced inside her home.

She called 911 and reported a possible explosive device at her front door.

Minutes later, Emily caught the flash of blue lights strobing up the street as two Sacramento Police SUVs approached. Emily trotted to the curb as the closest police vehicle arrived.

She described the dark-toned pickup truck and pointed in the direction the vehicle took. The officer pulled away and sped off to find Turpin.

The officer from the second patrol vehicle stood with Emily. "Can I get you anything, Detective?" He was tall with piercing blue eyes. His hands tugged on his ballistic vest. "Hold on a sec."

He trotted to his SUV and grabbed his police "Tuffy" jacket and handed it to Emily. "You look cold and probably shouldn't go back inside until the squad clears that thing." He jutted a strong jaw at the cylinder at her door.

"Thanks," she said, draping the jacket over her shoulders. There was a woodsy masculine cologne clinging to the jacket collar.

"Tim Jensen," he said extending his hand.

"Emily."

"Anything new with Brian? We worked together before he got promoted."

"It's looking like he's getting released from the hospital in the next couple of days."

"That's good news. Any idea how long until he's back on the job?"

"I—I don't know. He's looking at some rehab before he'll be ready for the street."

"We miss him."

Me too, Emily thought to herself. She missed who Brian used to be and hoped the TBI aftereffects would diminish soon.

"Is this one a dud?" Jensen asked.

"Hard to tell. The last couple haven't been."

Emily started toward the front steps and the porch light illuminated a long cylinder shape that, to Emily's eye, looked like a pipe bomb. The tube didn't have the usual metallic sheen, though.

Officer Jensen tugged on Emily's arm. "We should wait for the bomb squad to render it safe."

Emily had seen enough of the squad's work. They were thorough, professional, and cautious. They had to be. Their lives depended on it. Caution often meant the device was rendered safe by blowing it up. Somewhat ironic, Emily thought—exploding the explosive.

She thought about approaching closer and the rumble from a vehicle drew her attention away. The bomb squad had arrived with their heavily armored vehicle.

"Detective, we need to stop meeting like this," the squad lieutenant said as he strode over to where she and Officer Jensen waited.

"Wasn't my idea, Lieutenant. This thing showed up at my doorstep. I think Turpin took off after he left it."

"I heard the radio traffic. They're still looking for the vehicle."

"Turpin's been sending high-tech presents. This one is different. I'd like to see what this is."

"Be safer to throw a ballistic blanket over it and take it away."

"It might be a link to getting Turpin off the street," Emily said.

The lieutenant worked his jaw for a moment. "If this one packs the punch the last two had, you might risk the front of your house."

"Can you at least check it out before you make it go boom?"

"The whole idea is to not make it go boom, Detective. Let me see what we can do."

He returned to his squad vehicle and circled his team. Two of the officers disappeared into the back of the armored vehicle. A heavy metallic clang reverberated in the street as a ramp dropped from the rear of the truck.

Emily tensed when a metallic whine sounded from the vehicle. Then she spotted a small-tracked robot inching down the ramp. She'd seen the bomb squad's robot in action before. The SWAT team could use the robot to enter a scene and use the machine's video feed to assess the space before their members risked entering. It could also be equipped with an arm to deploy a twelve-gauge shotgun.

This time, the robot came toward them with the metal claw arm extended forward. Next to the lieutenant, an officer stood holding a controller for the machine. He worked a joystick, moving the robot onto Emily's front walk.

The lieutenant waved Emily and Officer Jensen over to a safe position on the street with them.

Emily tucked in behind the lieutenant and followed the robot's approach to the device at her front stairs.

"Okay, moment of truth here," the officer with the controller said. He jiggled the control stick forward and used another joystick to manipulate the extendable arm.

A small screen on the control box provided a view from the extended arm.

The video feed followed the camera as it circled above the cylinder.

"What the hell is that?" the lieutenant said.

"Sir, it looks like a cardboard tube. Doesn't appear to have any visible explosive device attached. Still, to be safe, I'd recommend we dispose of it," the officer said while manipulating the robot.

"I need whatever it is," Emily said.

"There's no way to know if he has a secondary device wired in sequence," the lieutenant said.

"Wired in what?"

"Booby-trapped."

"I'm getting a closer look." Emily stepped forward and the lieutenant grabbed her by the arm.

"Don't. This might be to lure you out."

If he wanted to explode this device, he had the opportunity when she unlocked her front door. He left and didn't stick around to watch.

Emily shook off the lieutenant's hand and stepped closer to her front door. Under the porch light, she could make out the foot-and-a-half-long cardboard tube, with both ends open.

The officer operating the robot stuck the arm through the opening in the tube and lifted it up from the pathway. The robot tracked in reverse away from the front of the home and the tube fell away from the robot arm with a hollow clatter when it hit the hard walkway surface.

"So much for a booby trap," the lieutenant called out.

Emily stepped around the tube, which now lay on her walkway. She pulled on a pair of gloves borrowed from another officer and gently pulled a roll of paper documents from the cardboard sleeve.

Slipping off the rubber band, Emily unrolled the pages and found copies of the complaint file from the academy, along with a handwritten note.

It's not what it looks like.

CHAPTER FORTY-ONE

THE HANDWRITTEN NOTE looked like it was scribed by the same hand as the warning she received when talking with the reporter.

Emily couldn't balance the warnings versus the bombings targeting the other officers on the list. Even Turpin added her to the list he kept at his wife's graveside. Yet when he had the opportunity—twice—he didn't take her out.

She took the rolled-up documents to the hood of the nearest police SUV and laid them out. They weren't copies of the complaint files. These were the original documents.

The cover sheet categorized the complaint as misconduct. Emily figured Turpin made a complaint Whitman had done something to him. As she turned the page, Emily found more.

"Huh."

"You pick up your mail, Detective?" the squad lieutenant said.

"Yeah—sorry about the false alarm, sort of. Hey, you ever work with Lieutenant Whitman?"

"Do yourself a favor. If he's your pen pal, don't write back."

"Not my pen pal—besides, I'm not sure Whitman could string words together to write a complete sentence."

"He probably could if he was writing to his redneck friends."

"Javier and I saw the flags and anti-government propaganda at his place."

The lieutenant stiffened. "You mean militia HQ? You're lucky you two got outta there in one piece."

"What's his deal?"

"His deal is he's a conspiracy theory whack job. The department was good to send his ass packing."

"I thought he retired. That's what I heard."

"He might be collecting a pension—that's the system. But believe me—his exit wasn't his decision."

"What can you tell me about why he got the boot? I heard he left after a hostage situation went belly-up."

"Might've been the final straw, but what I understand, he was already under investigation."

"What's IA have on him?"

The lieutenant shrugged. "No clue—they had someone from the DA's office in there for a while who was working on Whitman's case."

"The district attorney was involved? Criminal?"

"Sounded like it. The brass were keeping the circle close on this one."

Emily glanced back at the file. Turpin didn't file a complaint. He was a witness.

"Hey, Detective, I gotta run these guys back to the house. You need anything from me before I split?"

"Thanks for getting here and sorry for the false alarm."

"Easy enough and you did the right thing to call."

"I appreciate you guys getting here so fast."

"It's what we do, Detective."

As the squad packed the robot back into their armored car, Emily gathered the file and stooped to pick up the empty cardboard tube, bringing both inside.

She placed the tube and the documents on the kitchen counter. The handwritten message was puzzling. *It's not what it looks like.* What was Turpin telling her?

Her doorbell rang and she figured it was Mrs. Rose from down the street, curious about the activity on the block.

The view through the peephole made her relax a bit.

She opened the door and Javier stepped inside.

"You're supposed to call me when things like this happen, partner."

Javier was holding a large black cat.

"I found this on your front steps." He held the cat to her with stiff, outstretched arms.

"Not my cat," she said.

"I think it has a different opinion." He put the cat down and it trot-waddled into the kitchen and pawed at a cabinet.

Emily took a silver bowl and a bag of dry food from the cabinet. She poured a small amount into the bowl and placed it on the floor.

While the cat munched, Emily gestured to the kitchen where Turpin's message and file took up the center of the table.

"Where'd you find this?" Javier said.

"Followed me home, like that cat."

Emily stepped around the cat and grabbed the folder from the table. "This showed up on my doorstep. A file from the Public Safety Training Center. Turpin was listed as a witness against Whitman."

"Witness to what?" Javier said.

"I was about to find out. The bomb squad commander mentioned some drama around Whitman before he pulled the plug and retired. I didn't remember hearing anything, did you?"

Javier shook his head. "Nothing I can recall. I mean, he had a reputation for being a racist shithead—but back when I started, it wasn't unusual."

Emily pressed a hand across the file.

"This was an investigation following a complaint at the Public Safety Training Center. I thought it was going to be a complaint filed by Frank Turpin with some allegation about Whitman being mean. This is—check this out."

Emily pointed at a report summary. "Whitman, in the course of his duties as the academy range master and armorer, defrauded the training center."

"Fraud? I didn't peg Whitman for a thief. I would have bet his temper got the best of him and he popped someone."

"Turpin was the primary witness. Turpin went to academy administration and reported he witnessed Whitman take six Glock 19 handguns from the academy armory and sell them to private individuals."

"Now that, I can see. Probably arming his militia buddies."

Emily glanced at her partner. "You're the second person to mention Whitman and the militia."

"You sound surprised. You've been to his home—his compound. All the Second Amendment propaganda, the separatist flags. The only thing missing was a bunch of Duck Dynasty–looking rednecks with assault weapons."

"Whitman's a fringe guy. I see it. I don't get the militia vibe from him. More of a loner dude."

"Well, Whitman was selling his stolen weapons somewhere. If not a militia group, then where did they go?"

Emily flipped through the report. "It doesn't say. Turpin saw him take the weapons from the armory—oh, and get this—he followed Whitman and witnessed him sell the handguns in a church parking lot in North Sacramento."

"Let me guess, the same church he tried to blow up a couple of nights ago?"

"The very same. Can't be by chance. What I don't understand is the connection between Whitman selling guns and Turpin bombing Brian and the other SWAT team members."

"Who bought the weapons from Whitman?"

Emily flipped the page. "That's where this report ends. The last couple of pages are missing. Says only referred to Sacramento Police Department Internal Affairs."

"Fits with what you said about some drama going on before he left the job."

"Why would Turpin want us to know this?"

"Whitman was responsible for what happened in the market the night his family died."

CHAPTER FORTY-TWO

EMILY GATHERED UP the file and centered it on the table. "Turpin's been targeting SWAT members the entire time."

Javier agreed. His cell phone buzzed and he glanced at the screen. "Jenny—"

"Javi, what did you do?"

"What do you mean, what did I do? Why is it always me? Jen said she needed time to figure out what she was going to do."

"When did she say that?"

"Well, she didn't exactly say it—in those words."

"Then what did she say—exactly?"

"I don't know."

"Yes, you do. What did Jenny say?"

"She told me she needed to make a decision soon."

"Jenny wants you to give her a reason, Sparky. Didn't we have this conversation?"

"I can't be the reason she gives up a job—a dream job. She'd resent me for it and I couldn't live with that."

"Tell her how you feel, you big dummy."

"Yeah, yeah, there you go flinging that F word again. I'll catch you in the morning."

Javier let himself out, and she locked the door behind him. Emily hoped Jenny remained in Sacramento. She didn't want to threaten Jenny with bodily harm because she didn't want to deal with a lovesick partner. They were great together and Javi was happy.

When she turned around, the black cat had finished her snack and was cleaning herself on Emily's living room couch.

"No you don't. Off."

The cat flicked its yellow eyes in her direction and didn't break stride in her licking and stretching. A small pile of black cat hair now adorned Emily's upholstery.

Emily picked the cat up and it yowled as she placed it on the floor.

"Stay off."

Emily padded down the hall to her bedroom and changed into dark blue sweats and a well-worn Magnolia Thunderfinger T-shirt. The shirt was a reminder she hadn't been to a live music event in a long time. She found it difficult to enjoy herself when she was always scanning the crowd.

She passed the table and grabbed the academy investigation file. Emily plopped on her sofa and read through it again. There had to be a message here. Turpin went to great lengths to find this file and deliver it to her.

What was he trying to say?

She read through the entire case file again. Turpin was a witness who reported Whitman for what looked like selling guns from the academy armory. The investigative report was unusually sparse of detail. Were the guns legally his, and he was storing them at the armory? Who he sold them to seemed sketchy.

Emily made a mental note to check with Kris at the academy to review the firearms inventory. Certainly, someone would uncover a batch of missing weapons.

"What were you up to, Whitman?"

She glanced at the antique wooden clock mounted in the living room. It was too late to call IA. The Rubber Gun Squad would be done for the day.

She hit SPEED DIAL and waited.

"Emily, you okay?" Lieutenant Hall's voice sounded in her ear.

"Hey, Lieutenant. Yeah, I'm fine."

"You don't sound fine."

"What I sound like is pissed and confused."

"The pissed off, I'm used to. What's got you confused?"

"The Whitman and Turpin connection."

"Lieutenant Whitman?" The tone in Hall's voice changed.

"What can you tell me about him retiring? I understand he was under investigation—possibly criminal—for something to do with weapons sales."

"It was pretty much common knowledge IA was coming for him. He even bragged about it. I don't recall anything related to firearm sales, though. I thought his mouth finally caught up to him. No one was sorry to see him leave."

"What about the connection between him and Frank Turpin?"

"The only link you've uncovered between them is the hostage stand-off at the convenience store where Turpin's family was killed. I think we know he holds Whitman accountable for what happened."

"I think there's more to it. Turpin was a witness in whatever this gun deal was."

"When was this?"

Emily flipped to the pages in the investigative report. "About two months before Turpin's family died."

"You're thinking—"

"He let the gunman take out his family hoping he took out Turpin too."

"Damn, Emily. That's cold. You think Whitman set the store hostage thing up?"

"Too many moving pieces for Whitman to manage. I believe once he realized it was Turpin inside, he decided to let things play out."

"To get rid of the witness against him."

"That's what I'm thinking. There was a district attorney called in to assist on the IA case. I need to reach out to the DA."

"Not a bad idea. You might find resistance there. IA won't release information on an investigation that wasn't substantiated. There won't be anything in his personnel file if the allegation wasn't sustained."

"Whitman received a Lybarger warning, which means he couldn't refuse to answer questions in his administrative hearing," Emily said. "If it related to criminal conduct, his statements would be on the record."

"But could keep his right to remain silent on a criminal investigation."

"If IA called in the district attorney to sit in on the administrative inquiry . . ."

"You're thinking they got what they needed on the criminal side?"

Emily sighed. "Maybe. But they didn't arrest him or charge him with anything."

"Not that we know of . . ."

A thought germinated in Emily's mind. She'd witnessed other cases where a suspect was caught red-handed and wasn't thrown into the churn of the criminal justice system.

"Whitman was an informant."

After the phone call with the lieutenant, Emily couldn't sleep. She was wired and couldn't shut off her mind with the possibilities.

Whitman was a snitch. But who was he informing on? Did he testify in open court? Was he still on the line?

It explained his lifestyle, off the grid and holed up in an armed compound. It wasn't a militia group; it was a front. He was hiding.

Emily's mind began to sort out who Whitman was afraid of enough to hide in his foothill compound.

A mental list included the militia types he probably sold the weapons to at an inflated price. Then there was Frank Turpin. Whitman's inaction sealed the Turpin family's fate. Watching the man at his family's graveside, Emily was convinced he wasn't about to let their deaths go unanswered. The index card she found stuffed in the crack between his wife's marker and the grass left a road map of the pain he felt.

Brian, Councilman Davis, and the SWAT officers were punished, and there were more names on the list, including hers and Whitman.

Turpin was working with the prosecutors on the gun dealing charges Whitman faced. The disgraced lieutenant wanted revenge, and once he found out it was Turpin who'd been shot and held hostage, he let him bleed out. Emily wondered when the lieutenant realized the man's wife and children were inside. Did Whitman even care?

The pieces fit, sort of. There was a hole Emily couldn't put her finger on.

Emily closed her eyes and tried to imagine the scenario. Brian told her how the team wanted to breach and take down the gunman. Whitman balked. He froze. The more Emily pondered it, the more she concluded the lieutenant purposely held the team back.

Her chest felt heavy. A vibration swept through her core. She shot awake and a pair of yellow eyes stared back at her. The cat perched on Emily's chest and purred.

"You're heavy."

Emily pushed the bulky creature from her chest and the cat responded by swatting Emily's hand away. No claws were involved—a warning. The cat was comfortable so don't mess with her.

"Really? That's how you're gonna be? You might find the neighborhood snack options drying up."

The cat yawned and broke eye contact before it stretched and plodded off of Emily's chest.

Emily's neck was stiff from dozing on the sofa. A peek at her watch told her she'd slept until after five. The uneasy sleep didn't fill in the blanks.

After a quick shower and a change of clothes, she found the cat waiting at the back door.

"On to the next sucker?"

The cat squeezed through the opening into the dim morning light.

CHAPTER FORTY-THREE

EMILY GATHERED THE file and the cardboard tube and opened her front door. Cautiously, she scanned the yard, looking for another present from Turpin.

Nothing was delivered overnight, so Emily made her way to her SUV and hurried inside, locking the door. "Dammit, Em, get ahold of yourself. You can't let this guy live in the shadows."

She pulled away and headed toward the office. The file slid on the seat next to her when she made a turn. The address of the market was visible at the bottom of one of the exposed pages.

Emily hung a hard left and, ten minutes later, she pulled into the empty parking lot of the convenience store. Brightly lit inside, Emily could see some modifications since the November standoff. There was a large glass enclosure for the clerk, separating them from the street customers who wandered in from the night.

The neighborhood had taken a bit of a tailspin since. In the predawn hours, five young kids dressed in red T-shirts and red tennis shoes hung out trying to look tough. Emily pegged them as fourteen to sixteen.

Inside, Emily spotted a lone clerk rearranging cartons of cigarettes behind the glass. He was an older Sikh man wearing an orange head covering.

On a hunch, Emily entered, and the door chimed drawing the clerk's attention. His face relaxed when he registered it was a lone female customer. His hand retreated from under the counter, where Emily assumed there was a weapon stashed.

She placed her badge on the glass. "Detective Hunter. You wouldn't be Mr. Singh, would you?"

"I am. Is there a problem, Officer?"

"No. No. No problem. Were you here in November a few years back?"

His eyes were hooded under a heavy brow. "Why do you ask?"

"I'm working on a case that started here on that night."

"I was. A night I can never forget."

"Can you tell me how it began?"

"How will it help? The man is dead—by his own hand."

"There were others here when it started."

The man's chest heaved and his eyes closed. "Those beautiful children. They did nothing to deserve what happened to them."

"Did you know them?"

"They would come in maybe once a week. The parents—the Turpins—dropped by to get the kids an ice cream cone from the machine. It was a special treat."

Emily looked around, trying to visualize the scene.

"I got rid of the machine. It didn't seem right to keep it after . . ."

"I understand. The father, what can you tell me about him?"

"He was always polite and seemed to care about his kids. When that man McCracken attacked me, he jumped in to try and stop him. He never saw the man's gun. McCracken shot him and kicked him, stomped on his head, then he turned to me."

"I thought it was your gun," Emily said.

"No. I didn't have one—then."

"When the police got here, do you remember what happened?"

"After Turpin was shot, he managed to knock the phone from the counter and was talking to a man outside—a man in charge. He begged for someone to come and stop McCracken from hurting his family."

"What happened?"

"Nothing. The man kept hanging up on Turpin. He said something odd."

"What was that?"

"He should have kept his mouth shut."

"Turpin said that?"

The old man nodded. "I never understood. He tried to stop the man from robbing me. I never got to ask what he meant."

"I'm sorry this happened to you."

"I'm only lucky he beat me again and I was unconscious when he killed those children."

"Small mercies."

Emily glanced across the street at the young thugs. "They give you any trouble?" Emily shot her jaw in their direction.

"There are more of them lately. Once in a while they come in and one or two of them will try and sneak off with a six-pack of beer or something."

Emily knew it was a matter of time before they graduated to more aggressive action.

"I'll see what I can do. Get a patrol unit to swing by once in a while."

"Thank you. Was I able to give you anything that could help?"

"Another piece of the puzzle, Mr. Singh. Another piece of the puzzle."

Emily left the store and strode directly across the street where one of the young men looked out from under a red hoodie sweatshirt and whispered to his cohorts, who stiffened and turned to face the angry-looking woman striding toward them.

"I know you guys aren't going to bother the old man in there," Emily said.

She was close enough to confirm her earlier suspicion. These were pimple-faced kids trying to act the part of their harder older brothers and uncles. A stint in juvenile hall wasn't likely for the petty street crime they were into, and they knew it.

A compact figure in the back of the pack peeked around the others. Dark eyes took Emily in. There was wariness there in a thin frame. They looked ready to bolt if Emily drew closer.

An oversized red sweatshirt swallowed the small one up. The sleeves bunched up and hung below their hands.

Furtive; scared, maybe. Then it hit her. The small dark eyes were familiar. She'd seen the face before—at least a photo of her.

"Danika? Is that you?"

The girl Benjamin Tooker was looking for.

Danika's eyes widened, and she ducked behind the boys.

That was the answer Emily needed. One of the taller boys took a step toward Emily. "Whachu want with Dee?"

"I need a word with her."

"She don't need to talk to nobody."

"Why don't you let me hear it from her?"

"I done said it."

Emily parted her jacket, exposing her badge. "And who are you?"

The young tough tried to act like he didn't care, but a twitch in his lip gave him away. He tipped his chin a little higher so he could look down on Emily.

"I'm Red Dog. I run this crew. I speak for us."

"I need to hear from Danika, Lil Pup, or whatever you call yourself. You need me to call some patrol units out here and roust you off your little corner of the world? Maybe pat you down, see if you've got anything you shouldn't."

"I'd like to see you try."

"I'll talk to her, Red." Danika came out from behind her protectors. Emily saw relief in Red's face that he wouldn't need to back up his bluff.

Danika stepped off the curb and stood inches from Emily's reach. Careful and wary of strangers.

"Danika, your people are worried about you."

"They shouldn't be."

"Why don't you come tell them. Hanging out here isn't the smartest decision."

"I'm fine here."

"She fine. You hear? So get on up outta here," Red Dog said.

Emily ignored him and pulled her cell phone out, handing it to the girl. "Call your mom. Let her know you're okay."

"She don't care."

"If she didn't, how did I know you'd be out here?"

"Fine." The girl huffed and put her hand out for the phone.

Danika dialed a number and waited. "Mom, it's me." The girl's voice cracked a little, and she turned away from Emily and her street crew.

Emily gave Danika a little privacy and whispered to Red Dog. "Thanks for looking out for her."

He nodded. "She a good kid. She really got family looking for her?"

"That and half her community in Oak Park."

"Told us she didn't have no one."

"Sometimes it feels that way."

"True that."

Danika wiped tears away with her free hand. "I'm sorry, Mama." She handed the phone to Emily. "Mama wants to talk to you."

Emily took the phone back. "Hello, this is Detective Hunter."

"Detective, thank you for finding my baby. Are you the same lady detective I saw with Benjamin?"

"Yes, ma'am."

"Is—is my baby all right? Did you arrest her?"

"She seems fine and she's not in any trouble—yet." Emily held Danika's stare with her own.

"Can you bring her home to me?"

"Can you tell me why she needed to leave?"

There was a pause on the other end. "She and my boyfriend didn't get along."

"How's it going to be when she comes back home?"

"We'll work it out."

"She's your daughter. You need to make sure she feels safe in her own home."

"She's safe. Ain't nobody saying she being abused or such."

Emily cradled the phone to her chest. "Danika, can you go home?"

She shrugged. "Depends on Tommy Lee, Mama's boyfriend."

"He hurt you, do anything to you?"

"No. Nothing like that. He's acting like he has a say in everything I do. He's not my daddy."

Emily lifted the phone back. "I'm bringing her back and I'll meet you at Benjamin's office."

The call finished; Emily told Danika to say goodbye to her friends.

While she did, Emily called Benjamin Tooker.

When he answered, she gave him an update on the girl and the family situation.

"I got you. I'll have Reverend Lewis and his little birds here when you bring her."

"Birds?"

"That's what he calls his family council. Longtime church members who do family outreach. They're like busy little birds."

"Think they can help smooth this one out?"

"They'll keep an eye on them."

"All right, then. See you in twenty minutes."

Emily pocketed her phone and gestured Danika toward the SUV she had parked in the store lot.

Before she left, she squared up to Red Dog. "I appreciate what you did for her, but I still want you to leave old man Singh alone. He's been through enough and he doesn't need putting you in the hospital on his conscience."

"He don't have the stones."

"After what he's seen? Ask around."

Emily felt Dog's posture soften.

"Whatever."

He and his posse moved off.

"Let's bring you back where you belong," Emily said to Danika.

"I don't know where that is anymore."

"Me either, Danika. Me either."

CHAPTER FORTY-FOUR

EMILY DROPPED THE girl back at Benjamin Tooker's office, and the church ladies—the reverend's little birds—were hovering around. Tooker broke away and leaned in Emily's car window.

"Thanks for finding our lost sheep, Detective."

"She seems like a good kid who didn't know how to handle the changes going on at home."

"These ladies, as meddling as they may be, will keep an eye on the situation. I'm glad you found her before something bad happened. We don't need another child lost around here. It happens too often."

From behind them, a voice called out. "Bless you, brother Tooker for bringing our girl home."

"Of course, sister, of course."

"What did you do? I found her," Emily said.

"Technicalities, Detective. Technicalities," Tooker said with a grin. "Thanks for letting me have this one. I owe you."

"I will collect."

"I know you will, Detective."

He returned to his office door to a round of applause from the reverend and his flock.

Emily smiled and shifted the SUV into DRIVE.

When she arrived at her desk in the unit, a three-inch-thick file was on the center of her desk with a red ribbon tied around it.

Javier returned from the unit's coffee urn and the half-burnt aroma reached Emily before he did.

"Someone from the mayor's office dropped by. You know what that might be about?"

"I might."

Emily took one of the coffee cups from her partner and drew a sip of the potent brew.

She put the cup down and pulled the end of the ribbon. The cover sheet of an OPSA file, the names Whitman and Turpin in bolded letters.

At first, she thought it was a rehash of the incident reports she and Javier had reviewed because it began with a statement signed by Turpin against Whitman. However, in the section marked Disposition, Emily found this investigation was technically still open. It said, deferred pending district attorney review.

"DA review? I get that on a use of deadly force, but didn't the hostage-taker kill himself?" Emily said. "Mason needed approval to release this file—check out who had to sign the authorization."

Javier glanced down at the page. "Chief Clark?"

"Himself."

"Why didn't he say anything about Whitman when his name first came up?"

"I don't know. Didn't think it was going to relate back to an IA case, maybe?"

"You don't think he was trying to withhold it from us?" Javier asked.

Emily paused for a moment. Would Chief Clark try to cover for Whitman?

"I don't think so. No. He wouldn't. That's not in his DNA. You've seen him with bent cops. He doesn't tolerate that in his house."

Emily opened the file. The first three pages were a retelling of the store shoot-out. The same narrative Turpin had provided. Nothing new here. She flipped to the next section.

"What the hell is this?" Dark black bars filled the document, blacking out entire paragraphs. "It's been redacted."

"Who's responsible for that bullshit?"

Before Emily had a chance to respond, a deep voice answered. "I am."

Emily and Javier turned to find Chief Clark behind them.

"Chief?"

"Grab the file and let's go to the lieutenant's office."

Emily gathered the file contents and followed the top cop to Lieutenant Hall's office. Emily tried to assess the chief's mood—which translated to how much deep water they were about to dive into.

Hall pulled his reading glasses from his nose as the chief entered his office. A pair of detectives prairie-dogged over their desk partitions to witness the trouble Hunter and Medina had found.

"Chief. What can we do for you?" Hall said. There was a tightness in his voice.

"Close the door, Emily," the chief said.

She slipped in and closed the door behind her.

Emily handed the file to Chief Clark. "Why is our file on Whitman redacted?"

"It was sealed by court order." He turned to the back of the file and tapped a finger on a Sacramento Superior Court order to redact information requested by the Sacramento district attorney to protect the integrity of an investigation in progress.

"It's dated a month after the hostage situation at the convenience store."

"That's when it came to a head. The DA had been using Whitman after they caught him stealing weapons from the public safety academy armory."

"Turpin was a witness in the theft."

Clark looked surprised. "I hadn't heard, but it makes perfect sense now. In the aftermath of the shooting, the criminal investigation against Whitman dried up and the case they were going to file against him went away."

"Because the primary witness against him was shot. Whitman knew it and let it happen. And let the man's family die."

"That's one hell of a leap, Detective. Got anything to back that up?"

"I think the answer is in these redacted pages. You know why the DA had them sealed?" Emily asked.

"It was before my time as chief. But what I know is the criminal case was dropped against Whitman when he turned and became an informant."

"Giving up who he sold the guns to—like his militia buddies," Emily said.

"Who was running the investigation? It wasn't us," Lieutenant Hall said.

"The DA ran it with their investigators. It's unusual—they don't do it often. But they couldn't exactly ask us to investigate him when he'd been stealing weapons under our noses—sort of."

"I get it. They don't have the staffing to do a full-time investigation. What's the status?"

"I have no idea. Whitman's not on our dime anymore—part of the condition of the deal he got. The DA didn't feel we earned any follow-up."

Emily leaned in to examine the affidavit attached to a court order. She tapped a finger on the deputy district attorney's signature. Tami Simpson-Lewis.

"Tami would know. She's not Simpson-Lewis anymore, but she owes me a favor."

"Go cash it in, Detective," Chief Clark said.

CHAPTER FORTY-FIVE

JAVIER AND EMILY reached out to Tami Lewis at the DA's office. The speakerphone rang and reached her assistant.

"Ms. Lewis is in court and we expect her back when they recess in a few hours."

"Which department?" Emily asked.

"Department 7."

Emily hung up without replying. "Come on, partner. We're going to court."

Emily drove them to the court parking lot on 10th Street.

The detectives passed through the metal detectors at the court entrance by flashing their badges.

"Isn't Department 7 criminal arraignments? She'll be swamped."

They pushed into the packed courtroom. A plexiglass barrier surrounded what was once a jury box where twelve angry men sat—except they were dressed in jailhouse orange. In custody arraignments.

Emily spotted Tami Lewis in one of the back rows of the courtroom. She took an open spot next to Tami and leaned in close.

"Checking out the new deputy DAs?" Emily asked.

"This batch is so young."

"You were once too. They'll be fine."

"I'm not so sure. The blonde over there in the second chair—last week the judge had to tell her to put her cell phone away. The guy next to her—I had to instruct him he couldn't object to what the judge says. They are giving me gray hair."

Emily glanced at Tami's carefully coiffed honey blonde hair. Tami caught her looking. "I pay a lot to cover it up."

"Speaking of cover-ups—I need to talk to you about an old case."

"Which one?"

"Richard Whitman."

Tami locked eyes with Emily. "Hallway."

Tami got up and pushed out through the heavy wooden doors into the crowded hallway, where attorneys conferenced with their clients before their cases were called.

Tami found a space along the wall.

"Tami, this is my partner, Detective Medina."

The attorney shifted her eyes to Javier, then back to Emily. "What's this about Whitman?"

"You remember the criminal case you were handling back a few years, when he was still working with our department?"

"Yes." Answered like a careful attorney.

"It's come up again."

"What has?"

Emily got close to Tami and whispered. "Come on, Tami. You know what I'm talking about. Whitman stole weapons from the police academy armory and you were using him as your CI. He couldn't sell more guns because he wasn't working there anymore. What was he doing? Ratting out his militia buddies for you?"

Tami's eyes lit up. Emily knew she'd hit a nerve. "We had an agreement with your department. This is off limits."

"It wasn't our business until the guy who witnessed Whitman stealing the guns gets shot and watches his family die. Now Frank Turpin is out for any officer who was involved in not rescuing his family."

"The bombs? That's Turpin?"

"Yes."

"Dammit. I thought we were done dealing with Whitman's bullshit."

"He's not currently a CI for you?"

"No. Not for years."

"When's the last time you had any contact with him?"

"That's hard to say. Once he gave up his gun contacts, he didn't have anything more he could give us."

"You didn't have him feed you inside information on the militia groups in the area?"

Tami tightened her jaw and scowled. "You're off target there, Detective. Whitman never told us about any militia groups—and it wouldn't surprise me if he was running with those fools. Whitman was telling us who he sold the weapons to in the city. Not the militia—he sold guns to the street gangs in North Sacramento."

"Gangs? Whitman was arming street gangs?"

"He was, and we mined the intel for what we could get. He sold three dozen guns and told us who bought, and who used them in a crime, letting us recover over two dozen firearms and get them off the street."

"There's still a couple dozen unaccounted for. Isn't that something we should know?"

She shrugged. "It was the elected-one's call. I think she wanted to use it as leverage against your former chief. Since it never went anywhere, it was dropped."

"Any of the gangs know he snitched on him?"

"There were one or two who figured it out. Both of them died—one just the other day."

Emily stiffened. Gang members go toes-up every day. It was part of the risk they assumed when they donned the gang's colors. But the timing bothered Emily.

"The one who died recently—was it a banger who goes by Rockhead?"

"Sounds familiar."

Emily's gut churned with the new information. Guns for gangs. One of the gang members who bought them was killed by a bomb.

"Will you let me have the unredacted file on where the guns went?"

"I'll have to get a court order to release them."

"How hard will that be?"

"It'll go to the DA himself. He was closely aligned with the old DA. I'll need something bulletproof to talk him into it."

"I'll get you an affidavit within the hour."

Tami glanced at her phone. "I'll let my team know to look for it. In the meantime, the clerk of the court just messaged me. One of mine is starting to melt down."

"Thanks, Tami."

"We need to catch up."

"We do. I'll call you and Becca from the crime lab."

"Sounds good." She cast her eyes once more to Javier. "Nice to meet you, Detective. Keep this one on the right side of the tracks now, would you?"

"It's my daily goal. Some days I do better."

She smiled. "Don't we all."

Tami strode back into the courtroom, where voices were shouting over one another as the doors opened.

Javier turned to Emily. "What am I missing here? Whitman sells guns to gangs. Turpin's taking out cops. Are these two related, or am I trying to force-fit the evidence to make sense? I have an idea, but I need your adopted nerd's help to figure it out."

CHAPTER FORTY-SIX

OFFICER MILTON STOOD near a table, examining heaps of burned debris. Bits and pieces of charred car parts, circuit boards, and rubber wheels lay in organized piles on the work surface. There was a slight tang of smoke and melted plastic in the air.

The officer looked up from his work when the detectives entered, and Emily swore he looked like a ten-year-old kid caught with his hand in the cookie jar.

Emily bent over the table and tried to assemble a puzzle in her mind. Which pieces went with which device and which one of these took the Brian she knew away from her?

"Tell us what you got," Javier said.

Milton straightened the front of his Tyvek suit, which crinkled every time he moved. "These vehicles were constructed from the same component parts as the others. Same circuit boards, servo controllers, engine, right down to the wheels."

"Okay, but how does that help us? We already know they were made by the same guy—Frank Turpin, right?"

"They were kit projects. I mean, projects made from a parts list from the councilman's electronics store."

"Turpin took classes at the store. He made a fleet of bomb-laden cars," Javier said.

"I can prove they are his handiwork."

Emily looked at the two piles of disassembled parts. "From this mess?"

"Yes, Detective. I think I can."

"I need you to be a little more definitive here. Tell my non-nerd self what makes you certain Frank Turpin made these devices."

Milton's forehead scrunched up, and he started spouting technical details, the heat of the soldering on the circuit board, the precise placement of the servo controllers, and the frequency of the receivers. Emily stopped him.

"Give me something specific I can take to a jury and tell them Turpin is our guy."

Javier bit his bottom lip, as if the thought of Turpin slipping away was going to be muddled in toasted electronic bits and technical jargon.

"Em, we know he built these things. We saw them in the cemetery. We *saw* him."

"We saw him with those devices. A jury is going to need more than that to convict him on multiple attempted murder charges."

Milton reached for a binder behind him. "The squad turned over residue samples to the lab—here it is. The first two bombs—the church and the North Sacramento intersection—both were consistent with chemical signatures from ammonium phosphate and fuel oil."

"Like Oklahoma City?" Emily said.

"Yes, but much smaller. The circuit board chassis couldn't carry a heavy load."

"Okay, what about the other one?" Javier asked.

"The device that chased you and me in the cemetery?"

"It didn't chase us," Javier said.

"I beg to differ," Emily said.

"Never mind. What about the cemetery device?" Javier said.

"It was black powder. It was a big noisemaker. No shrapnel, nothing."

"It was to cover for his escape. Turpin wasn't trying to take us out. He was buying time to sneak out the gap in the fence and escape."

"But the device at Galvin's place was loaded with ANFO too. The squad told us," Javier said.

"It was, and because we got to look at it closely, I can confirm it was him. The solders are messy, bleed off to the left. The one you brought me, the remnants from the cemetery, the device you saw him deliver, had the same—and I mean identical—sloppy soldering work. It's like a fingerprint. I see it all the time with the kids I teach. Is Turpin right- or left-handed?"

Emily thought back to Turpin at his family's graveside. He bent and placed what turned out to be the index card next to his wife's marker.

"He's right-handed."

"That fits. He made these—all of them."

"You're certain?" Emily asked.

"I am. I could testify based on my experience working with the high school's robotics program."

"Good. I want one of our criminalists to confirm your findings." Emily noticed Milton's shoulders slump. "It's not that this isn't great work. We need to be loaded for bear when we take this to the DA. The criminalist has the credentials and has already been certified as an expert witness in these cases."

"I understand. I'm sorry."

"Don't be sorry. You might have given us what we need to unravel this mess."

"We have Frank Turpin on the list of people who attended classes at the councilman's store. All these boards came from there. It's him. I know," Milton said.

"That's where we start," Emily said.

She thanked Milton again. He looked like he was still stinging from being told his findings needed to be verified by someone else. Or was it more like uncertainty?

On the way out of the conference room, Javier leaned toward Emily. "Did you actually use the phrase 'loaded for bear' in there? Who are you, Grizzly Adams?"

"Who's that? Some old-timey movie star?"

"It was a book first—never mind."

Emily mulled over the idea of their suspect coming into focus. Turpin was the man behind them, yet why did he risk sending the warning message and the academy files? Her gut churned with another possibility.

CHAPTER FORTY-SEVEN

"LIEUTENANT WHITMAN? ARE you crazy, Emily?"

Emily looked down the hallway and waited until a pair of sergeants passed them.

"I realize how it sounds. But we know he's bent. Selling guns to gangbangers who could turn around and use them on us. He was a snitch for the DA, and let's not forget he let the hostage situation unfold the way it did on purpose. Yeah, he's capable of doing this."

"But why? And why now? After all these years, why did Whitman pick now for the time to melt down? And why target his old team?"

Emily nibbled on a thumbnail. "I don't know—yet."

"Listen, you heard Tami at the courthouse. She said one of the gun buyers was Rockhead. What if Whitman wasn't going for the cops but was targeting Rockhead instead?"

"That's a bold theory."

"We know Officer McKinley said he was meeting with Rockhead before the bombing. Who would lose if Rockhead was really trying to broker a peace deal between the gangs on the north side?"

"I can think of lots of people who wouldn't want to see a deal. Gangs who didn't think they got enough territory, for one."

"If Whitman is still selling guns, he wouldn't want his buyers to disappear."

"There's nothing to support the idea he's still in the game. He's been cut off from his primary gun supply at the police academy."

"I know he's in the middle of this," Emily said.

"Knowing it and proving it—"

Emily paced in a small circle. "Turpin was the witness to the gun theft, and Whitman let him bleed out during the hostage standoff hoping he'd die—"

"So he couldn't testify against him," Javier said.

"But Turpin didn't die. He didn't go after Whitman until now. Something triggered him."

Javier mulled it over and Emily saw his eyes flicker as he tried to put the pieces together. "Grief, maybe? He was in the hospital for his gunshot wound too . . ."

"Why did the prosecutors decide to drop the gun charges on Whitman?"

"Your friend Tami didn't mention anything about that, did she?"

"Only that he couldn't provide them with any new intel. She made it sound like the case decisions were going on above her level."

"We aren't going to barge into the district attorney's office and demand answers."

"We can't. But I know who can. And it might help us figure out why Whitman would want to go after his old team. Was Turpin working with Whitman to take revenge on the SWAT team?"

———

"No," Chief Clark said from behind his desk.

Emily stood before him. "Chief, we're not asking for him to reverse any decision a prior DA made. All we're looking for is why the case against Whitman fell apart. It's got to be more than they didn't need him as a CI anymore."

"Emily, I can't ask the sitting DA about old case filing decisions. Once I open that door and start asking why they acted on one case and not another, it changes everything. We're no longer impartial and—"

"Chief, our officers are being attacked, and that case—the case with Whitman and Turpin—is at the heart. We need to know what happened. Officers are in the hospital, a city councilman in the morgue, and the public is at risk with these bombing attacks in the city. You wouldn't be asking them to change any charging decision. We're only asking for background—why didn't they pursue the case against Whitman?"

The chief worked his jaw and leaned back in his chair. "I'll make a call."

"That's all I can ask, Chief. It's up to them how much they give a shit about the public."

"Mind if I phrase it a little differently?" the chief asked.

"You can church it up all you like."

The chief shook his head. "I'll do my best, Detective. I'm sure you and Detective Medina can find another thread to pull on while I make this call."

"Yes, sir."

Javier was waiting back in the detective bureau and was on the phone when she strode back to her desk. He waved a hand, getting her attention, and pointed to the phone extension on her desk.

She picked it up and covered the mouthpiece so whoever Javier was talking with didn't know she'd come on the line.

"Let me run this back to make sure I have it correctly," Javier said. "The academy armory lost track of one hundred and fifty-two firearms from 2015 to 2022? Is that right? An average of twenty a year?"

"That's what the audit found," the voice on the other side said.

"Lieutenant Whitman was the armorer during this period?"

"Yes, he was."

"How did your audit discover the missing weapons?"

"Like I said, the armorer at the time had control over ordering and disposing of the academy weapon assets. Whitman ordered the new-generation Glock handguns to replace the older models we had in stock. The records show purchase orders for one hundred and fifty-two new handguns coming in."

"To replace the older models?" Javier said.

"Yes, and to replace broken ones."

"Does that mean a matching number of older, broken guns were taken offline and disposed of?" Javier said.

"It did. The inventory numbers matched up. The old weapons were listed as destroyed."

"Sounds like the standard policy," Javier said.

"That's where the audit caught the discrepancy."

"Walk me through what the audit uncovered," Javier said.

"Like I said before. The serial numbers for the handguns taken offline at the academy never showed up on the police department's weapons destruction inventory. Every time a weapon is crushed, or melted down, the serial number is recorded. These never appeared on any list of destroyed weapons."

"They weren't destroyed? And Whitman was the person who was supposed to make sure they were turned over for destruction?"

"That's right."

"Thanks, Brad. I appreciate it."

Javier hung up the phone. "Your DA contact, Tami, said Whitman had stolen a couple dozen guns. This is much bigger. Did Turpin know?"

She shrugged.

"Who would know?" Javier said.

CHAPTER FORTY-EIGHT

"YOU NEED TO go to confession," Javier said from the passenger seat of the SUV.

Emily had parked the police SUV in the church parking lot where the first bomb struck. The place Brian's life had nearly ended. The church window was still boarded over, and the dark ash burned into the red brick exterior near the door was a reminder of what had happened there.

A sturdy new drop-off box now stood next to the entrance. It looked like a cross between a mailbox and a heavy-duty storage container.

"They got a new donation box back up quick," Emily said.

"No shortage of families in need around here."

Emily pointed to a young woman towing a child by the hand walking to the church doors. The woman's thin, threadbare jacket hung limp on her shoulders. The child wore mismatched shoes and stained sweatpants. She didn't press into the church. Instead, she stopped at the donation box, removed a small object from her jacket pocket, and looked over her shoulder before dropping it into the locked container.

The woman scurried off with her child and disappeared around the building next door.

"That seem a little odd to you? The woman didn't look like she could spare anything, yet she put something in the donation box."

"What are you thinking?"

"This is where it began. There's more to this donation box. Come on. Let's check it out."

Emily got out from behind the wheel and paused on the pavement before continuing.

"You want to talk to the one who dropped something in?"

"No. I don't want to jam her up. She looked like she was afraid to be seen. I think there's someone who can tell us what's going on."

Emily and Javier followed the path to the side door of the church. Emily tugged on Javier's shoulder, urging him to stay by the building as the door flung open.

Two women, in their mid-thirties, Emily guessed, came out of the building and they didn't notice the detectives as they talked.

Emily overheard a few words, including *food pantry*, *voucher*, and *exchange*.

As they wandered off, Emily stepped in behind them and entered the church.

This side entrance opened to the business side of the soul-saving operation. Less praise be and more praise me based on the portrait of the Reverend Clarence T. White greeting visitors to this part of the church. Slicked-back gray hair, ruddy complexion. The effect made him more of a carnival barker than a man of God.

The behind-the-curtain view of the sanctuary was richly appointed, with polished wood, gleaming leather chairs in the waiting area, and flickering candles to give off a somber aura.

Emily stopped a harried-looking woman rushing from a hallway. She held a clipboard and a stack of file folders tight to her chest.

"We're looking for Reverend White," Emily said.

"Follow me. I'm headed to his office. Word of warning—he's in a mood."

She quick-stepped down the hall to a set of dark wood double doors. The woman took a deep breath, rapped a knuckle on the door, and waited for a deep, gruff voice from within.

"Come in."

"Excuse me, Reverend. You have visitors."

The reverend perched behind a massive ebony wood desk with task lighting purposefully arranged to make the man look like he was onstage. And perhaps he was.

His burgundy suit and purple shirt let Emily know the reverend was a showman.

Reverend White removed his reading glasses and narrowed his eyes at the two visitors. "Do they have an appointment?" He addressed his assistant and didn't glance at Emily or Javier. "Then tell them to make an appointment."

Emily flashed her badge. "Consider an appointment made. Reverend, we need a minute of your time."

"This is a house of worship. I cannot condone the forces of violence banging down my door."

"Nobody's banging anything. But we are talking about violence here at the church. The bombing the other night . . ."

"It's fortunate no innocent souls were harmed. Your people brought that to my doorstep. My community cannot accept the occupation of my streets by a racist military police force."

Emily recognized the reverend was trying to bait her into an argument.

"The officers who came here were lured and attacked. They were told the church was in danger. They were injured trying to protect you."

"I didn't ask them to come here. I didn't ask you to come here, either. Yet there you stand searching for a reason to arrest someone."

Emily needed to cut through his anti-police rhetoric.

"This church has served this community for years. It's become a safe place for those who live here," Emily said.

The man nodded. "We've worked long and sacrificed to make this a sanctuary."

"I know the gangs consider this off-limits."

"They do. We do everything we can to make the neighborhood a safer place to raise a family. A place where kids can walk to school without fear of getting caught in a gang shoot-out."

The church employee slipped out of the room. The look on her face said it wasn't the time to bother the reverend. Javier tipped his jaw to the door, and he followed her into the hallway.

"Admirable goals, Reverend White. Does that include turning in guns off the street? I saw a woman drop one in your donation bin out front when we got here." Emily stretched the truth, but she was more convinced the church was collecting guns and getting them off the street.

"Now, Officer—"

Emily put up a hand to stop him from responding.

"Reverend, I'm not interested in who's dropping off what. I don't care where they come from, and any weapons we can get off the street is a good thing. Don't bother denying what I witnessed out there at your donation bin."

Reverend White paused, tented his large hands together, and stared at Emily. "What do you want, Detective?"

"I think we both want the same thing. What do you do with the weapons turned in by members of the congregation?"

He paused for a moment. "We cannot trust the police to dispose of them. They're more interested in arresting someone who was trying to do the right thing by turning in a deadly weapon."

"Where do they go?"

"I'm not going to say. You'll only persecute them."

Emily thought for a moment. "Do you make a record of the weapons turned in? Photos, serial numbers, anything like that?"

"I'm not comfortable discussing this with you, Detective."

"You and I want the same thing. Guns off the street."

"But our means differ. You want to punish and blame. We don't ask who brought them, or where they came from."

"I believe there's at least one in your donation bin."

"Do you have a warrant?"

"We can go in that direction. I'll post a uniformed officer next to the donation bin. How will it look to your congregation?"

Reverend White's jaw tightened. He placed a hand on a desk phone. "One call from me and every preacher and minister in the city will be in the mayor's office voicing concern over the gestapo policies of this police department."

The church leader's words echoed the sentiment of the late Councilman Davis. Gestapo policies. He'd spouted a similar position over a television broadcast hours before he was murdered.

"You know Councilman Davis?" Emily asked.

"Are you threatening me with the same fate?"

Emily shrugged. "Take it any way you like. You seem to share the same views—I mean shared, with him being dead and all."

A crack of concern broke through the good reverend's hard exterior.

"The councilman was an upright, Christian man who cared about his community. He recognized what this community could be and what was preventing it from becoming a safe haven for everyone."

"That involved guns, didn't it?"

"That was a part of it. But he advocated for much more than that. A peace between these warring gang factions. Laying down of arms. Open communication and dialogue to stop this cycle of violence among our own people."

"Part of the plan was getting guns off the street."

"And more. He was going to announce a gun buyback program to give people more of an incentive to give up these weapons of destruction."

"And you started by collecting them in the donation bin. How many people knew they could drop off a gun at the church?"

"The entire congregation. We announced the program in the sermon a month ago."

A spark ignited in Emily's brain. The donation bin was collecting weapons and someone didn't want them found. Brian and his partner weren't the target—the guns were.

CHAPTER FORTY-NINE

AS REVEREND WHITE continued to drone on about making the community safer from the inside out, Emily turned on her heel and left.

A gun buyback would usually involve multiple agencies and a strict chain of custody to make certain every firearm was documented from the donation to the point it was fed into the crusher or melted into slag. If the councilman was moving in this direction, he would put the connections in place, take the weapons into custody, and pay the donors for each gun surrendered.

She heard Javier's voice in the hallway. He leaned casually on a doorjamb, and he caught Emily approaching when he gave a subtle gesture with his hand holding her back.

Emily posted up against the wall and listened. The assistant's voice was anxious, high-pitched, and rapid. Javier's demeanor and soothing speech were trying to calm her.

"I understand," he said. "You don't want anyone else getting hurt from these weapons. You're doing the right thing here," Javier said.

"Reverend White takes care of these . . . things."

"Do you keep any kind of records on the weapons you find in the donation box?"

"I'm—I'm not supposed to."

"But you do . . ."

"Yes. The reverend will fire me if he finds out."

"We'll try not to let that happen. Why did you think it necessary to keep a record? I think it was smart on your part."

"I have a bad feeling about where these things go. I can't say for sure—but I don't think they ever get destroyed."

"What do you think happens to them?"

"I—I think he sells them."

"Sells them? To whom?"

"I don't know."

"Would you be willing to show me whatever records you kept?"

Emily heard a filing cabinet open and close with a metallic clank.

Javier stepped away from the doorjamb and pulled his cell phone from his jacket. Emily imagined him holding it out to her as he asked her to look at a photo. "This guy look familiar? How about him? This one?"

In the last photo, she stopped him. "Yes, that one. I've seen him here with Reverend White. They were arguing with each other."

"You able to hear what they were talking about?"

"No. They both got pretty heated and said things that shouldn't be uttered in a house of God."

"You're certain this is the man you saw arguing with the reverend?"

"I'm sure. About a month ago."

"Okay, thanks. I appreciate—"

From the direction of the reverend's office, the sound of broken glass echoed out into the hall. Emily pivoted from the wall and took a step toward the reverend's office when an explosion ripped the door off its hinges.

Emily felt a heat wave rush from the open doorway. She put her arm up to shield her eyes when orange flames started to climb the walls inside the office, feeding off the drapery and elaborate wall art. The tendrils parted, and the reverend stumbled through the opening. His clothing aflame, he tried to swat the flames away, but his movement fanned the flames and made them spread up his chest.

Emily spotted a fire extinguisher on the wall near the office Javier had ducked into. She snagged the red canister and ran back to where the clergyman now lay face down in the corridor.

She sprayed the foam over Reverend White and doused the flames.

Javier shot down from the office with another extinguisher and sprayed inside the office seconds before the sprinkler system turned on and shot a steady stream of fetid water down on them.

Emily bent over Reverend White and put a hand to a patch of unburned skin on his neck, feeling for a pulse.

"Is he . . . ?" His assistant crept next to Javier and grabbed his arm to prop her up.

"He's alive. We need to call for help."

"I called 911 like Detective Medina said. What else can I do to help? I'll get oxygen . . ."

The assistant ran off before Emily could respond.

"You okay, Em?" Javier asked.

"Yeah. I swore I heard glass break seconds before the explosion."

"I'll go take a look in his office." Javier trotted through the sprinkler spray to the smoldering room where they had met with the church official. The sprinkler system did its job and tamped down the flames.

A rattle from behind Emily sounded at the assistant's return with an oxygen bottle on a rolling cart. She connected a mask and a rubber line, handing it to Emily as she cranked the knob on the top of the cylinder.

Emily didn't hear the sirens from the fire engines, but three turn-out-clad firefighters plodded down the hall to their location.

"We've got him," one firefighter said, dropping a medical bag next to the reverend.

Emily rose from the floor and followed Javier's path into the office. She found Javier bent over, examining the broken glass near the shattered window.

"What did you find?"

Javier stood and carefully tread around the broken shards.

"Check this out." He pointed at a common red brick on the floor behind the preacher's desk.

"That didn't cause any fire."

"No, but this did." He gestured to the bottom of a broken bottle.

"An old-fashioned Molotov cocktail?"

"Looks that way. The brick through the window made sure this could hit the target."

"Turpin? Changing up his MO?"

"Yeah, 'bout that. Cindy, the reverend's assistant, identified a guy having an argument with the good reverend—"

"I overheard—about a month ago."

Javier handed her his phone. "This is who Reverend White was jawing with."

Emily focused on the familiar image.

"Whitman? Now what business would he have with the Right Reverend White?"

"Cindy didn't come out and say it, but it was around the time the gun donation drop-offs started."

"I could see Whitman as a church bomber. Add a hate crime to his résumé," Emily said.

"If we can make a connection—"

From behind them: "Excuse me, Detective Medina. I have what we talked about," Cindy, the assistant, said. She looked sheepish and reluctant to turn over the information she kept on the weapon drop-offs.

Javier approached the doorway where the woman stood with her wide eyes, taking in the fire damage. She put a hand over her nose to ward off the smoke stench lingering inside.

"In my office." She ducked out of sight and Javier told Emily he'd go with Cindy to gather the records.

Emily took a last look at the charred office. The remaining windows were slicked with soot from the fast-burning flames.

She rubbed a thumb against an unbroken pane. Tinted. The southern exposure would beat directly into the window and the church tinted them a dark gray.

Whoever threw the firebomb into the church couldn't see their target. Was it luck they caught Reverend White sitting at his desk? Or was it Emily's luck she walked out of the meeting?

CHAPTER FIFTY

EMILY FOUND JAVIER in the assistant's office. Her gaze fell upon a pair of cardboard boxes, one of which had two sawed-off shotgun barrels sticking out.

"I want these out of here," Cindy said as she placed a third box on the tabletop.

"How long have you kept these here? There's enough to arm a small army," Javier said.

"About a month—around the same time I spotted the reverend arguing with that man."

Emily peeked in the box she'd placed on the work surface. She recognized the blue fabric in the box as the one she'd witnessed being deposited in the donation bin earlier. She poked it with a pencil and unraveled the material revealing a Glock handgun. A blue steel revolver and an Astra .380 semiautomatic pistol were in the box with a handful of knives, including illegal switchblades and butterfly knives.

"What you got, Javi?"

"Looks like eight handguns and a pair of sawed-off twelve-gauges. Six boxes of ammo, 9mm and .45 caliber."

"All of these collected in the last month?" Emily asked.

"Yes. I don't like the thought of them sitting out in the collection box, so I check every couple of hours and bring them inside."

"The night of the bombing here at the church, did you clear it out before you left?"

"I ran out of time. If someone dropped anything in after hours, I wouldn't know."

Emily didn't recall any mention from the crime scene team on weapons parts in the debris, but she made a mental note to check with the evidence techs because they were more focused on the radio-controlled cars.

Cindy handed a piece of paper to Javier. "This is the log I mentioned. The first entry is a little over two months ago."

Javier took the list and whistled. "There must be fifty guns listed here."

"Fifty-two. Including these ten here."

"Where did the other forty-some guns go?" Emily asked.

She shrugged. "The reverend said he was taking care of them."

"Thank you, Cindy," Javier said. "I know this was a tough decision."

"We can't risk these awful things getting back out on the street. If a child was hurt and I had a chance to prevent it . . . I could never forgive myself."

"You're a good person—that's why," Javier said.

Cindy blushed and tried to straighten her waterlogged sweater. "I should find out where they're taking the reverend and notify the church elders."

She ducked out of the room and stepped outside where the firefighters were getting White ready for transport.

"Well, didn't you pull out the charm today," Emily said.

"What?"

Emily rolled her eyes. "I bet you anything she put her phone number on the bottom of the document she gave you."

"Oh, she did not. You're—oh, she did."

"See? Once again, you're oblivious when it comes to the opposite sex."

"Should you say 'sex' in a church?" he asked.

Emily grabbed a slightly wet cardboard box. "I'm telling your mom you were hitting on a woman in a church."

"As long as you don't tell her it wasn't a Catholic church."

They toted the cardboard boxes to their SUV and loaded them into the rear hatch. As Emily lowered the door, she glanced back at the smoke-scarred front of the building. It struck her then. It looked like Brian wasn't targeted for the attack and he was in the wrong place at the wrong time. The list? Was it a cover for the actual reason for the bombing?

As they buckled up, Javier glanced at the brick church building and the firefighters dragging smoldering furniture from the reverend's office out into the parking lot, where they were doused with water from a fire hose.

"You can't see through those tinted windows," Javier said.

As she started the engine, Emily glanced back at the corner of the building where the broken window stood out amongst the three other heavily tinted glass panes.

"I noticed. If the reverend was a creature of habit, he'd be in his office—Whitman would know," she said.

"Yeah, if it was him. He'd been here before. He'd know the layout. But he couldn't be sure White was at his desk."

Emily clinched her jaw and backed out of the parking slot. "It's got to be Whitman, right? Your new church lady friend ID'd him arguing with Reverend White. We've been saying Turpin's our bomber. This was a brute force move and seems more up Whitman's alley. They can't be working together . . ."

"Good point. Remember when Milton told us what he found going through the blast debris?"

"He was talking nerd about the circuit boards and how they came from Davis's store, so no," Emily said as she swung the SUV onto the main road heading south.

"The soldering on the circuit boards. He swears it was Turpin."

"Turpin was in a class at the councilman's place. He could've used one of those kids to make the boards without knowing where they'd end up."

Javier paused for a moment, then pulled his cell phone from his jacket. He tapped in a number from memory.

"Milton, it's Medina. Can you put your hands on the list of people who were taking classes at the electronics store?" A pause. Then: "You can? Good. Look for Whitman, Richard. See if he was working on some electronics project at the store when—

"What? You're sure? Thanks, and set it aside for us. We're on our way back to you now." He pocketed the phone.

"What did he come up with? Nothing?"

"Milton is dead certain Turpin is the bomber. Whitman wasn't among the people signed up for classes at the councilman's electronics store. The parts came from there too. But get this, Whitman *was* one of the students in Milton's adult education classes on robotics. You know the one he told us he taught?"

"Whitman knew how to make those car thingies?"

"According to Milton, he does. And he was pretty good at it."

"Then why doesn't he think Whitman built these things?"

"I can't answer that. Other than he kept saying it was Turpin."

Emily ground her jaw while she piloted the car back toward police headquarters. "Turpin? Whitman? Which one of these assholes would gain from a hit on Reverend White?"

"If it was White he was after," Javier reminded.

"It has to be. If one of them was going after me, or you, Javi, there are easier ways to do that," she said as she swung the SUV into the police department parking lot.

"R/C car!"

"Exactly."

"No! R/C car straight ahead."

Emily caught the small dark car zipping toward them. The low-slung car slammed into the oil pan under their feet.

CHAPTER FIFTY-ONE

"BAIL!" EMILY YELLED as they both shot from the SUV and put some distance between them and the bomb-laden device.

Emily circled behind the SUV at a distance and waved off another police vehicle entering the lot. She had the officer use his vehicle to block the entrance to the public safety complex.

She joined Javier on the far side of the SUV.

"Why hasn't it gone off?" he said.

"How did he know to wait for us here?"

Emily heard a car speeding away on the street in front of the department. She caught a gray blur as it whipped around a corner.

"Looked like the same car we saw when Turpin was visiting his family."

"Turpin . . . Whitman? Why would one of them want to take us out?"

"I don't think it's us. I think it's what's inside."

"What? The guns we recovered from the church?"

"What else?"

Within twenty minutes, the bomb squad had retrieved the car from under the SUV and it was laden with enough crude explosive to render the SUV and everyone in it to cinders. The car had struck the low-hanging oil pan and broke off the antenna it needed to receive signals from the operator. A slight error saved Emily and Javier.

Officer Milton rushed to the parking lot, fastening the top two uniform buttons as he ran. He was out of breath when he reached the detectives.

Emily spied the cigarette pack in his front shirt pocket. Not exactly regulation and probably explained his breathing struggle.

"What can you tell us?" Emily asked.

Milton bent over the device. "This one was made recently. An updated circuit board and brand-new servo controller. I can track the manufacturer for sales information. But this is what I was telling you about. The builder left his mark on this one. Almost the same right-to-left drift on the solders."

"Made by Turpin?" Javier asked.

"I'd swear to it. He's not going to quit," Milton said. He responded in a stiff and uncomfortable fashion. Furtive, perhaps. He bit his bottom lip.

"I thought I saw Turpin's car—the gray one tearing away when this thing hit us," Javier said.

"Why would Turpin want to destroy these weapons? Why would he care?" Emily said.

"Maybe because his family was killed with weapons like these," Milton said without looking away from the device.

Emily thought the response out of character, but he doubled down on Turpin as the bomber.

"Whitman's the one who wouldn't want these guns out in the open. Are they both in this together?" Javier asked.

"Doesn't seem likely. Not with their history,"

Javier stole a glance at the car chassis, then to Milton. "The only thing keeping this from going boom was this broken antenna?"

Milton nodded. "Any remote ability to control this stopped like he flipped a switch. No signal to detonate the explosive package."

"We have anyone who can respond to Whitman's compound see if we can put eyes on?" Emily asked Javier.

He snagged his cell phone and stepped away.

Emily stared at her SUV with the doors wide open after she and Javier jumped from the vehicle. If the damn thing hadn't broken—she wheeled around. "Javi. We gotta go."

Javier held the phone to his head, doing more listening than talking. He caught her looking in his direction and he waved her over.

"Whitman—"

"Is on the phone right now," Javier said.

"What?"

"He called 911. The dispatcher said it's a cell phone—probably a burner so she doesn't have a location. She's patching it through."

He tapped the SPEAKER button. The phone was on mute and the 911 dispatcher's voice sounded over the line.

"Can you speak to me without him hearing? Just say yes or no."

"Uh-huh."

"That's Whitman. Is he turning himself in?" Emily said.

"He called."

A rustle sounded in the background. Another voice was in the room with Whitman. A man's voice.

"Is that Turpin?" Emily asked.

Javier shrugged. "Can't say I've ever talked to the guy. Has to be him, right?"

Emily nudged Javier. "Unmute the phone."

Javier hit the button on his phone.

"Lieutenant Whitman. This is Detective Hunter. Is Turpin there with you?"

"Damn right," Whitman replied.

"He armed?"

"What do you think?"

"He making threats against you?"

"You're quite the detective, aren't you?"

"What I think is you tried to blow up my partner and me. Why shouldn't I hang up and let this unfold? Isn't it exactly what you did to him in that store?"

"What do you expect me to say?" Whitman said. The anxiety was in his voice and it told Emily she'd hit the nail on the head.

"Let me talk to him."

"I don't think it's going to happen."

"Why don't you let him tell me," Emily said.

She heard Whitman rustle on the other end of the call. "Someone wants to talk to you."

"What do they want?" The voice was some distance from the phone. Emily tried to picture the room from her visit to Whitman's home. There was a slight echo. The vast living room gave her an open vibe to be sure, but she couldn't recall the echo within the rustic log cabin building.

"That woman detective wants to talk to you."

"Gimme the phone—slowly."

Emily heard a grunt as Whitman moved.

The next words Emily heard turned her blood to ice.

"Now it's his turn to know what it's like to feel helpless."

CHAPTER FIFTY-TWO

THE CALL ABRUPTLY ended. Emily envisioned Turpin dropping the phone on the floor and crushing it under his heel.

Javier hit the REDIAL button, and the call went unanswered.

"We have a response going to Whitman's place yet?"

"Don't know yet. I can check with the watch commander."

"No time. We can call on the way."

They jogged to the SUV and shot out of the parking lot.

"Turpin is making Whitman go through the same thing he experienced in the market. And we know how that ended."

"Turpin gonna make a murder suicide deal here?" Javier said.

"He could. Makes sense with his message to his dead wife. The whole 'I'll make it right' thing."

Javier had his phone to his head. "I'm waiting for the watch commander."

"Call Lieutenant Hall."

Javier disconnected the call as Emily took the corner fast and threw him against the door. He hit SPEED DIAL for the lieutenant's number.

"Lieutenant, it's Medina. You up to speed on the Whitman situation?"

Javier hit the SPEAKER button.

"I am. We have a SWAT team en route and coordinating with El Dorado County since Whitman is in their backyard."

"Anyone on-site yet?"

"First units are ten minutes out."

"Emily and I are en route."

"How'd he get back there so fast?" Emily asked.

"We've got enough resources out there. You guys need to come back and work this case so when we take these guys into custody, we'll have everything tied up for the bombing attacks and the murder of Councilman Davis and church burning with the Good Reverend White."

"I know the place—Whitman's compound. Javier and I have been there. Whitman knows us."

"Is knowing you a good thing? I mean, you are on his list."

"Turpin is reenacting the events as they happened the night his family was murdered. He blames Whitman—and from what Javi and I found, he's not totally wrong."

"I get it. Hold on a sec."

There was muffled chatter in the background until the lieutenant came back on the line.

"First El Dorado County units are at the Whitman place. There's no one there."

"Are they positive? Turpin could be keeping out of sight. Whitman built it like a fortress."

"The deputies made entry. The home is empty."

Emily pulled to the side of the road. She looked to Javier. "If Turpin is replaying the events from the night his family was killed . . ."

"The mini-mart. He'd take Whitman to the location where they died," Javier said.

Emily swung a U-turn and headed back into the city.

Javier took the phone off speaker and filled the lieutenant in on where they were headed. He disconnected the call and shoved the phone under his leg.

"The lieutenant said they'd have a patrol unit at the market in ten minutes."

"A long response time for a call like this."

"Yeah, apparently the units in the patrol district were diverted to bogus 911 calls."

Emily stepped on the accelerator and flipped on the switch for the blue strobe emergency lights.

They pulled near the store and skidded to a stop across the street from the market. She couldn't see anyone inside the premises from this vantage point. The proprietor, Mr. Singh, wasn't in his glass-enclosed bubble.

Emily shut off the lights and drew up from the driver's seat. On the corner ahead, she spotted four of the street thugs she'd encountered when she found Danika.

"Javi, let me have a word with the town council up here. Keep an eye on any movement inside."

Javier nodded and opened the rear of the SUV. He pulled on a ballistic vest and tossed one to Emily before she made her way to the kids hanging on the corner.

She carried the vest with her as she made her way to the small group. She recognized the leader.

"Hey, Red Dog. What you see going on over there tonight?" Emily gestured to the store.

"We ain't done nothing. We've been givin' the old dude some space, like you said."

"See anyone go in there?"

"It's a store."

"In the last couple hours, you see two White guys go inside—like maybe one didn't want to?"

Red Dog jutted his scraggly bearded chin at the market. "Yeah, we seen 'em. A couple White dudes kickin' it. The bigger one looked like he was already drunk—ya know? Kinda swerving and stumblin' around. Dude didn't need another six-pack—if ya know what I'm sayin'."

"Where did they go? They still inside?"

Red Dog shrugged. "I dunno."

"They inside," one of the others said. "They car still there." He pointed to the side of the market.

Emily glanced over into the lot and in the far corner against the market wall was Turpin's red pickup.

"You guys probably need to split. It's about to get busy around here."

"How's Danika? You get her hooked up with her people?"

"She's back home. I think things are going to work out for her."

"Good. Good. She better than this."

Emily caught a patrol car closing on the market from the opposite direction. The flashing lights got Red Dog's attention, along with the rest of his crew.

"This what you talking about?"

"There's gonna be more—a whole lot more. You probably don't want to be seen here."

"We got a right to be here. But all right. We'll split. Don't need to get caught up in whatever you got going on in there."

Red Dog motioned to his posse, and they ambled away from the market moments before the black armored personnel carrier drove up to the storefront.

Six black-clad SWAT team operators stepped from the rear doors and took positions behind the heavily armored vehicle. She noticed two other team members talking with Javier back at their SUV.

The long rifle barrel marked one man as the team's sniper. He and his spotter were let out earlier to find a suitable position to watch the front of the market.

Emily joined her partner and the two SWAT team members.

"The kids said two White guys entered the store and haven't come back out. Sounds like Turpin was forcing Whitman inside."

The sniper pulled up a photo on his phone and handed it to Emily. "This one? He the hostage-taker?"

Emily craned her head and took in the image on the phone—an old driver's license photo of Turpin.

"That's Frank Turpin. We believe he's holding Richard Whitman. There's history here. Turpin's family was killed in this store. He blames Whitman for their deaths."

"I don't care who he blames. I need to confirm this is my target."

He shoved the phone in a pocket on his load-bearing vest. And pointed to the abandoned laundromat across from the store. He trotted toward the darkened building, where his spotter waited.

"This isn't going to end well for anyone."

A shot rang out from inside the market. The sudden gunfire froze the SWAT operators in place for a moment as they tried to assess where the shot came from.

Emily couldn't see any movement through the front windows. Turpin and Whitman must be in the back room—the spot where Turpin's wife and children were found.

Emily and Javier crept to the armored SWAT vehicle, where she recognized the team's commander.

"Any contact from inside?" she asked.

"Nothing yet. No one's picking up the phone. Turpin took Whitman?"

"That's what it looks like. You know the history of what played out here. Turpin is repeating the scene over again with Whitman in the victim's role this time."

"Whitman might be a shit, but I can't stand by and let it play out. I'm going to end this one way or another."

"Let me try."

Emily tightened the straps on her vest and started walking toward the storefront.

CHAPTER FIFTY-THREE

"EMILY. WHAT ARE you doing?" Javier said.

"Turpin's after Whitman, not us."

"We don't know for sure. They could be in this together and luring us in—like the first church bombing," Javier said.

"I need you to trust me on this. I'll call you on my cell and leave the connection open so you can hear everything."

Emily grabbed a bullhorn from the back of the SWAT truck and strode past the yellow tape barrier step-by-step toward the glass front of the mini-mart. She saw no movement inside the store.

Had Turpin already killed Whitman? Was that the gunshot she heard?

When she drew near the door, Emily saw a chain wrapped around the door handles on the inside. Another repeat of the original assault on the store by McCracken. Turpin was following the script from that fateful day, which meant he didn't plan on coming out of this alive.

"Frank Turpin. Can you hear me?" Emily spoke through the bullhorn and she was certain anyone in the store could hear her—if they were alive.

"Frank. Talk to me."

She spotted a door cracked open—one in the rear of the store. She stepped to the left so she had a line of sight into the far end of the place and caught the sliver of Turpin's face leering through the opening.

"Frank, tell me what's going on."

Turpin closed the door.

Dammit.

Emily's cell chirped with a text message. Javier provided a telephone number for the market.

Emily hit the link and called.

The number rang four times and someone picked it up on the fifth ring without speaking a word.

"Hello?" Emily said.

There was silence on the other end of the connection. An arriving patrol unit's siren squelched briefly as it pulled to the middle of the frontage road to block traffic. Emily heard the echo of the siren's call on her cell phone.

"Frank, it's Detective Hunter. You don't have to do this."

"Detective. He doesn't want to talk to you. Go away," Whitman said.

"You know I can't."

"You don't know what he took from me." Frank's voice in the background came through.

"I do know. He needs to—"

"He needs to die like Monica and my kids. He killed them."

"McCracken killed them."

"Whitman should have stopped him. He let them die. Do you know what those last minutes of their lives were like?"

"No. I can't imagine," Emily said. Truth was, she didn't need to imagine how the murderous rampage unfolded. The coroner's reports from the night revealed point-blank gunshot wounds to the boy. Turpin's daughter was shot in her mother's arms. His wife was made to witness their deaths and was pistol whipped before she was shot. Reverse order from the official SWAT team reports.

"I don't have to imagine it. I lived it. I still live it every day. McCracken was a monster. But Whitman created him."

Created him? Emily thought that was a strange turn of phrase. Enabled, maybe, but Whitman didn't send the man into the store to annihilate an entire family.

Emily knew to keep Turpin talking. She changed up the subject to de-escalate the tension she could hear in Turpin's voice.

"Is Mr. Singh in there with you?"

"He's all right. As long as everyone stays where they are, he'll stay that way," Turpin said.

"Frank, let Mr. Singh go. He has nothing to do with this. You know that. He tried to help you and your wife, remember?"

"What good that did!"

"You're not like Whitman. Let Mr. Singh out. It'll keep the SWAT team from busting down the doors."

"Why didn't they do that when my family was in here?"

"I think you know the answer. What do you say? I know you're not like Whitman. Talk to me."

"Time for talking is done. Nobody listens. Why didn't Davis listen?"

"We know Whitman is responsible for what happened to your family. You gave me the files proving he stole guns from the academy. He's going away. He deserves to be locked up, don't you think?"

"He deserves to die."

"That won't change anything. You know that, right?"

"He's responsible for my family—for what happened to them. For dozens of others . . ."

"What others? Frank, we know about your family and the role he played in that. What others are you talking about?"

"You're the detective. Go figure it out."

Turpin disconnected the call.

Emily redialed the number, and he didn't pick up.

She backtracked from the store and found Javier and the SWAT commander near the armored vehicle.

"You got him talking. That's a good sign," the SWAT lieutenant said.

"Until he hung up on me."

"Keep trying to get him to communicate with you. When he's doing that, he's not harming the hostage."

"Hostages. Two. He has the storekeeper in there too. An older man, Mr. Singh. I asked him to let him out."

"I'll pass it on to the team. Keep trying to—wait, we have movement."

The SWAT operators tensed and Emily noticed a team of three at the left corner of the building. She hadn't noticed them stack up there while she was talking with Turpin.

Peering around the armored vehicle, Emily watched the back door open and a figure appear in the backroom doorway. If Turpin revealed himself, she didn't think the sniper team would waste a moment before they ended the standoff.

The fluorescent lights inside the market caught a flash of orange. The same orange Emily had noticed before.

She grabbed the SWAT commander's elbow. "That's the hostage. Mr. Singh." The orange was from the head covering he wore.

The commander signaled his team over the radio as Mr. Singh ambled to the front door of the store. He unwrapped the chain from the handles and stepped outside where the SWAT team operators at the corner of the building swept toward him. Two officers grabbed him, propelling him away, while one followed, facing back and providing cover from the rear with his rifle.

When the hostage was safely behind the cover of the armored truck, Emily pulled him to the side.

"Are you all right, Mr. Singh?"

The old man's eyes didn't show any sign of relief after he'd been let go.

"He's going to kill him."

CHAPTER FIFTY-FOUR

THE ELDERLY STOREKEEPER'S knees gave way and he collapsed to the asphalt behind the armored car. He drew a deep breath and held his hands clasped together to keep them from trembling.

"Mr. Singh, are you all right? I'd like to ask the EMTs over there to check you out. Tell me what you saw."

"Yes—the man with the gun. He's going to kill the other man."

"Do you remember what either of them said?" Emily asked.

The SWAT commander showed Mr. Singh two photos, and he nodded nervously. "Yes. It is them. This one." He pointed at Frank Turpin's photo. "He is the man with the gun."

"What does the gunman want from him?" Emily asked.

"He said it was to make sure he knew he was going to die—that he deserved it for what happened."

"Turpin's family," Emily said.

"I didn't recognize the man until he said that. He watched his wife and children die. I don't remember the other man."

"He was a police officer. He was there that night."

"I remember the officers who were there. The men who got me out of there alive."

Emily's mind turned the old man's response over in her mind. It had been a few years, the trauma of that night. Lieutenant Whitman was on the phone with Turpin and the killer. Mr. Singh's memory might be fading. She opened the photos on her phone and swiped until she found the one she wanted.

"Was this man there that night?"

He peered at the image, and within seconds responded. "Yes. He was the officer who came in to get me."

It was a shot of Brian Conner. She knew Brian was there. Where was Whitman? If he stayed near the command truck, Mr. Singh never noticed him.

"Wait. Let me see the photograph again."

Emily held the phone out once more.

"No, not that one. The photo of the man inside."

The lieutenant handed the photo of Whitman to the storekeeper once more. The old man covered Whitman's face with his thumb. He focused on the image and his eyes narrowed.

"He was there. I remember after. He didn't come in with the men who rescued me. When I was outside getting medical treatment, he entered the store and bent over the gunman—Mr. McCracken. He picked up the weapon—the handgun. I swear he put it in his pocket, and then put it back on the ground near the dead man. I don't know why he did it. It seemed . . . strange. I didn't think about it because I was grateful to be out of there alive."

Emily knew. She knew exactly why Whitman had picked up the weapon.

"Are you sure it was him?"

He nodded. "Oh yes. He had a slight limp. And his right ear—at the top, it has this scar. Like this photo."

Emily looked at Whitman's image. At the top of his right ear, the helix was malformed, flattened. Not like a boxer's cauliflower ear, but damaged somehow.

"Let's have the EMTs check you out."

Emily helped the man to his feet and guided him to the ambulance on the main road.

Once he was settled, she rejoined Javier.

"The lieutenant moved us back here because they picked up a struggle inside. Not sure what's happening."

"Whitman getting a beat-down?" she said. "SWAT will be getting ready to enter."

Emily leaned on one of the emergency vehicles at the scene. There were pieces of this puzzle that didn't mesh.

Unless.

"Javi. I need you to go back to the office. Pull the files on the original market shootings."

"Turpin's family?"

"Yes. McCracken shot them. We don't dispute that. Find the ballistics from those shootings with the weapon recovered at the scene."

"What are you thinking?"

"Something Mr. Singh said. Let me know what you find. I don't want to tell you what to look for. I need you to tell me if the dots connect."

Javier grimaced. He was used to Emily's way of doing things. She was making him a better detective, but he didn't like it when Emily didn't tell him everything.

"All right. I'll play. We'll talk after this. I'm your partner. It wouldn't hurt to tell me what you're thinking."

She took Javier by the shoulder so she could look directly into his eyes.

"Listen. I need you to do this. You need to be able to testify what you did to follow the evidence. Turpin's mental state—I'm no shrink but that man's spring is wound up so tight he's gonna snap. Unless we can give him what he's looking for."

"What's that? He's not telling us anything," Javier said.

"Yes, he is. Whitman set this in motion. His gun deals, attacking our officers, not rescuing Turpin and his family—all of it. Turpin is telling us exactly what he wants. Go find it."

Javier reluctantly trotted to their SUV and tore out of the parking lot. Emily needed him safe if Turpin went off the deep end. She needed Turpin to engage with her. The SWAT team would not wait to minimize the threat. Releasing the storekeeper worked to Turpin's advantage. Breaching a building wasn't an action taken without planning, and Turpin knew it—and waited.

CHAPTER FIFTY-FIVE

EMILY FOUND THE SWAT commander on the phone and, by the bit of the conversation she overheard, he was getting a report from the sniper team across the street from the mini-mart.

On reflex, she turned and located the two men on top of the building. They were picking up their spotting scope and moving. There was no line of sight on what was going on inside the store.

The lieutenant hung up. He turned to Emily. "You know this guy, Turpin. How far is he gonna take this?"

Emily wanted a solution where Turpin came out on his own. He wanted Whitman to suffer. There was more than one way to make a man like Whitman feel the pain.

"Unless we can keep Turpin engaged, I could see him taking Whitman out and then committing suicide by cop. He blames Whitman for every bad thing that happened to him. He's armed—I could see him using it if we try to breach."

"The storekeeper said Whitman looked scared."

"Whitman's been keeping secrets. Turpin's gone out of his way to make sure we knew Whitman had been stealing guns from the academy and selling them on the streets. He wanted us to know. He wouldn't do that if his only plan was to blow the guy away."

"He's stalling? How long can he expect us to wait?"

"Let me try to find out. I have some connection with him."

As soon as she said that, her mind snapped to being chased by a robot car in the cemetery. Could she trust he hadn't intended something more deadly?

"Try to contact. But you do it from here." He pointed at the armored command vehicle.

"I need face-to-face. I think I can get him to bend."

"If we have a shot at the guy, we're taking him down. We can't have you in the way."

Emily glanced at the store. "Then move the truck up there by the door. I need to show him I'm here and talking—"

"Let's cross that bridge when we reach it. Start from here, if you're gonna try to communicate with him."

Emily huffed. She understood the SWAT lieutenant's role. Keep the scene contained, minimize collateral damage, and Emily knew he would not let her risk herself. Killing Turpin would end the standoff and Whitman would become a folk hero and shift the blame away from himself. He could pull it off too. Anyone who could say differently was dead or not talking—the city councilman, the dead gang member, and Reverend White weren't in a position to talk. And a dead Turpin made for an easy scapegoat.

Whitman once had the support of the rank-and-file street cops. Brian and those around him believed he retired after the mini-mart standoff ended with the tragic deaths of the Turpin family. No one knew about the gun thefts and his role as a snitch for the district attorney selling guns to gang members.

Why Turpin chose this moment to go after the officers who witnessed his family's murders with targeted bombing attacks was still troubling.

The answers lay inside that market.

She tapped REDIAL into her cell and allowed it to ring. No one picked up. She discontinued the call.

The storekeeper, Mr. Singh, stood nearby after being cleared by the EMTs. He remained behind the barrier, and she could read the concern on his face. What would happen to his store? The family's sole source of income? How much violence could one man witness?

Witness. It struck her.

Turpin was a witness. Whitman was still dealing arms. Turpin threatened that operation.

They had it wrong. Turpin hadn't dragged Whitman here. It was the other way around. Whitman wanted to finish what he started years ago.

CHAPTER FIFTY-SIX

"LIEUTENANT, CAN WE get eyes inside the store?"

"I've got my sniper team moving to another location. There's a window. Mr. Singh tells me it's in the storeroom they're holed up in. It's a narrow window high on the wall, but it's the best we've got at a shot to end this."

Emily explained her conversation with Singh and that Whitman might be the actual hostage-taker.

The lieutenant rubbed his chin. "How can we be sure Turpin isn't the one we need to take down?"

"If I have this right, Whitman is setting this up and forcing you to take action against Turpin. He wants his hands clean, but he needs Turpin eliminated because he is the trail back to the illegal gun sales."

"I don't know, Emily. That's a big stretch."

"Can we get eyes in there? You have all these toys." She gestured to a rack full of drones and surveillance equipment in the truck.

"If it's like you say, I can't use a throw phone." The lieutenant pointed out a heavy-duty plastic case. "Whitman would know the case has an open cell signal even if the case isn't unlocked. We hear everything."

"We need to know who the actual hostage is here. Whitman is playing this so we'll take Turpin out," Emily said.

The lieutenant keyed his radio. "Bravo-3, are you in position?"

"Affirmative, Bravo-1. Still no visual."

"Is there a window?"

"Affirmative—too small for entry."

The lieutenant grabbed a small case from the rack and placed it on the seat.

"Standby, Bravo-3. Be advised, Detective Hunter will be in your line of sight."

"I will what?"

He shoved the case in her direction. "It's your theory, Detective."

"What's this supposed to do?" She popped open the case and a bulky black object lay in a bed of packing foam. To Emily, it looked like a vintage VCR camera. She noticed the label on the box: LM-I LASER MICROPHONE.

"It's an acoustic surveillance microphone. It will pick up vibrations on the window and transmit them back. You'll hear them through this headset. I'll get a feed patched in here as well."

The lieutenant gave Emily a quick run-through on the operation of the laser mic. "The important thing is to keep it trained on the windowpane. If they are talking inside, or moving around, it will pick it up."

"That's it? Aim it at the glass?"

"We'll have you covered, and I'll put an operator with you."

Emily gathered the microphone and headset and stepped down from the command truck.

"Happy hunting," the lieutenant said.

Emily wondered if Whitman would take the bait in this hunting scenario.

A SWAT operator in full black tactical gear joined her. Body armor, helmet, and an MP-5 rifle on a sling. The patch on his jumpsuit read MacIntyre.

She recognized the officer's face, but she couldn't recall where she met him.

"Detective, Sergeant Conner says I'm not to leave your side."

"He does, does he?"

When did Brian talk to this guy? Why didn't he have time to call me?

"Yes, ma'am, he did."

"Can the *ma'am*, MacIntyre."

"Yes, ma—call me Mac."

Emily hefted the laser microphone case and circled behind the armored truck making a path to the back of the mini-mart. The rear edifice was festooned with colorful graffiti. Emily made out a couple of gang names and the name RED DOG stood out in a colorful maroon script.

"Where should I do this?" Emily said in a soft voice.

Mac pointed to a dumpster parked near the back fence of the property. "You can use the container for cover and the microphone works best when you keep it stable."

They worked their way to the garbage dumpster and Emily was careful to avoid stepping on broken beer bottles and empty spray paint cans. Even though she was separated by a concrete block wall, Emily didn't want a sudden sound getting the attention of the men inside the store.

The side of the dumpster reeked of urine, and Emily did her best to hold her breath while she placed the case on the top of the dumpster.

Mac took a position at the opposite end and radioed his status to the rest of the team. Emily heard a microphone click in response.

She rested the boxy laser device on the lid of the dumpster and donned the headphones. Emily flicked the power switch and trained the device on the glass windowpanes mounted high on the back wall. They were grease-stained and nearly opaque. She hoped the technology would cut through the film and pick up any sounds from inside.

There was nothing at first. Then a slight shuffling sound. Emily was rewarded with Whitman's graveled voice in her headphones.

"This must seem like déjà vu to you. They ain't gonna come to the rescue."

"Shut up," an anxious-sounding Turpin responded.

"This is gonna end the way it was supposed to years ago."

"You killed my family. They were innocent and had nothing to do with this."

Emily figured the "this" Turpin was talking about was the gun thefts he discovered at the academy.

"I don't have their blood on my hands. What happened to them is on you," Whitman said.

"Don't talk about my family. No one will ever believe your lies."

"They did. And now here we are because you wouldn't let it go," Whitman said.

"Let it go? I'm supposed to let the fact you killed my family go—like they didn't matter?"

"You'll join them soon enough."

Emily could put the pieces together, but Whitman wasn't saying enough to put him in the driver's seat on this hostage standoff. Everything she'd heard so far could be explained away as Whitman trying to put his hostage-taker off balance or distract him while he tried to make a run for it.

She put the laser microphone down on the case, picked up a small chunk of asphalt, and hurled it at the window.

The jagged shard shattered on the window without breaking the glass but made a lot of noise as it exploded against the surface.

She grabbed the laser microphone and trained it on the window once more.

"They're coming," Turpin said.

"When you're dead, no one's going to tell them any different. Get up. Now."

Emily heard a shuffling sound and the squeal of a door opening. They were moving from the back storage room.

"Time to play this out," Whitman said.

CHAPTER FIFTY-SEVEN

"THEY'RE MOVING TO the front of the store," Emily said to Mac.

He relayed the update to the team on his radio.

Emily left the laser microphone and headset on the dumpster and ran to the armored command center.

The SWAT lieutenant was preparing the teams to breach as she arrived.

"You heard?"

"We did. Whitman wants it to appear he's the hostage."

"He wants us to take out Turpin. Turpin knows about Whitman's gun running."

"Looks like you called it. Now we can end this."

"I need Whitman to admit what he's done. The bombings, arming street gangs. What we have now—any decent defense attorney will sow the seeds of doubt to a jury."

"What are you suggesting, Emily?"

"Let me go in—alone."

"I'm not sure that's the best way to—"

She grabbed a shotgun from the rack in the command truck, one with a green-colored stock. Emily slid twelve-gauge shells in the magazine into the belly of the weapon.

"Whitman will fess up—he can't help himself."

The lieutenant shook his head. "I'm not gonna be able to talk you out of this, am I?"

"Nope." She shouldered the shotgun and stepped from the command truck.

"I'm gonna put a team on your tail. If it starts going south, I'm sending them in."

Emily approached the front of the store. Since Mr. Singh fled the establishment, the chain was off the door handle.

Through the glass, she couldn't see any sign of Whitman or Turpin in the store. The aisles were enough to hide them from view. She figured Whitman counted on that fact. He knew the procedures a SWAT team would use to enter the building—and where to position himself to make it appear he was being held by Turpin.

Emily held the shotgun in her right hand and pushed the door open with her left. She'd forgotten about the door chime sounding as she stepped inside. The door closed and a quick glance behind her revealed the SWAT team members ready to burst in.

"Help me!" a voice called out from the far end of the store. Emily recognized it as Whitman.

"Come out. Now!" Emily commanded.

"Turpin's lost his mind. He's got a gun."

"Frank? Is that right? Are you armed? Throw the gun out into the aisle."

No response came back from either of the two men.

Emily took a few steps deeper into the store. The only thing she could hear was the hum from the old fluorescent lights above her. Her shoe stuck on a gummy spot on the worn linoleum and gave off a slight ripping sound as she lifted her foot.

"Get him. Take him out now!"

Emily placed the voice from two aisles ahead and to the right. There was nothing other than Whitman's voice. No struggle, no pulling against restraints, and most notably, nothing from Frank Turpin.

From the corner of her eye, Emily caught movement. It was her reflection in a large convex mirror mounted in the back corner near the bank of refrigerators where cans of cheap beer and soda lined up, waiting.

Mr. Singh must have installed the mirror after the last robbery, probably when his glass barrier around the cashier's counter went up.

Emily took a few steps back and to the left, and there he was. Whitman came into view. He crouched in the last aisle with Turpin held in front of him. He gripped the man by the back of his collar. It was clear who was in control here.

Considering how to play this, Emily called out: "Frank, let Whitman go. We can work this out."

She saw Turpin struggle against Whitman's grip. Turpin didn't answer her, and the mirror revealed why. Turpin had a length of black tape over his mouth. More black tape was on his right hand. Emily couldn't make out what was in Turpin's restrained hand.

Emily played along. "Frank, come out. It's time to end this."

She watched the mirror as Whitman pushed Turpin down the row to the end of the display case. With a last shove, Whitman ripped the tape off Turpin's mouth and the man stumbled out into the open facing Emily.

Wide-eyed with a gun in his hand, Turpin froze as the SWAT team streamed in the door behind Emily.

"Drop the weapon! Drop it!" one of the SWAT officers ordered.

Turpin put his hands up, but the gun clung to his outstretched hand

"Don't do it."

Another officer yelled a command to toss the weapon to the floor. Turpin was breathing hard, and anxiously stepped forward.

Emily heard the SWAT officers move into position to take out the armed assailant. She called out, "I've got him."

She raised her shotgun and pulled the trigger, sending Turpin stumbling back against the glass refrigerator doors. He slumped to the ground, dazed from the beanbag round fired from her shotgun. She racked the slide, chambering another round.

When Turpin fell, Whitman popped up and came around the corner of the display. A smirk crossed his face when he locked eyes with Emily.

"Hands!" Emily said.

Whitman stepped closer.

"Don't take another step."

With his right hand, Whitman pulled a pistol from his waistband and wheeled toward Turpin. "Gun!" the ex-lieutenant yelled.

Emily swung her shotgun barrel and sent another beanbag round at Whitman, striking him in the chest. Whitman collapsed, trying to catch his breath, and a black pistol fell from his left hand.

The SWAT team moved in and took custody of Turpin and Whitman.

From behind Emily, the SWAT commander said, "We rarely shoot the hostage."

"Some people need shooting."

CHAPTER FIFTY-EIGHT

"YOU SHOT THEM both?" Lieutenant Hall asked.

Emily made it back to the detective bureau and faced mounds of paperwork after the shooting. Even though she used less-than-lethal force—beanbag rounds from the shotgun—there would be reviews and second-guessing by the Rubber Gun Squad and the Public Safety Accountability Board.

"I had to put Turpin on his ass because he was panicking and coming at us with a gun in his hand. It was taped there. Whitman set him up, and I didn't want to take the chance one of the tactical team would take him out."

"And Whitman?"

"He deserved it."

"You should probably rephrase that when they ask you."

"Whitman was preparing to shoot Turpin. He'll try and claim Turpin was going to shoot him—the gun still in his hand and all. Whitman's also a suspect in the bombing attacks against our officers."

"That's better. But can you make it stick? Fingering him for the bombings."

"We're close—"

Javier knocked and leaned against the lieutenant's doorframe.

"I think I can help nail it down," he said.

"Did you find it?" Emily said.

Javier took a chair next to his partner. "Emily was right. Whitman was covering up what he's been doing—selling stolen guns to street gangs."

"Run it down for me," Hall said.

Javier ticked them off on his fingers. "The church bombing—the donation box where Sergeant Conner was injured. Whitman was destroying any evidence of weapons dropped off in the donation box. He couldn't risk guns he stole—and claimed were destroyed—coming back to life. He didn't know which weapons were in the drop-off box, but he couldn't take a chance. The attack at the intersection got rid of a gang shot caller who had purchased a weapon from Whitman and was preparing to work with the police on a neighborhood peace deal. Peace means no gun buyers—bad for Whitman's business."

"What about the second bomb at the church?"

"That was a little tougher to figure out," Javier said.

Emily leaned forward. "It was what the shopkeeper saw the night at the mini-market shooting—after the incident."

Javier smiled. "You were right on."

"The ballistics on the slugs taken from the Turpin family didn't match the weapon recovered at the scene," Emily said.

"No, they did not. A NIBN hit on the slugs came back on a gang-involved shooting four months before the murders in the store. And"—Javier opened a file in his lap—"they came back to this weapon—one of the batch we confiscated from Reverend White's church."

"How did it end up in the reverend's hands?" Hall asked.

"Because it's one of the weapons Whitman stole from the academy. A Smith & Wesson Model 19 revolver. Sold it on the street where it was used in a couple of robberies. McCracken bought it and used the gun in the Turpin family murders. How Whitman knew it was one of his guns, I'm not sure."

"I think we do know the answer. Whitman knew he sold the gun to McCracken. He might have even set it in motion. The shopkeeper said Turpin would take his family there for ice cream once a week. Javi, do you have the list Cindy, your church lady girlfriend, gave us?"

"She's not my girl—yeah, hang on."

Javier flipped through a few pages until he pulled the list he'd gotten—an inventory of weapons dropped off at the church donation box.

He ran his finger down the page and laid the ballistic report next to it. "Here it is—the serial numbers match the weapons stolen from the academy."

"Whitman stole them, sold them, and the good reverend was reselling them?" Emily said.

"You've seen that church. Looks expensive to maintain."

There were unconnected links in this chain Emily needed to bridge. The councilman? Why did Whitman orchestrate the standoff in the market?

"Em—"

"What? I'm sorry, Lieutenant."

"You kind of drifted off on me there. I said the chief's office called and he wants a word."

"What about? Why does he want to see us?"

"Not us—you. And I think it's about your shooting rampage tonight," Javier said.

"It was not a rampage, Javi."

"A temper tantrum with a shotgun?"

"You weren't there," she said as she tossed a paper clip at him.

The lieutenant cleared his throat. "The chief is getting pressure from the mayor's office. The attack on a member of the clergy and another hostage standoff. She's positioning herself to run on a platform showing she's cleaned up the city."

"I'm not here to be the mayor's PR flunky," Emily said.

"All I'm asking is you exercise a little tact . . ."

"Have you met Emily?" Javier said.

She tossed another paper clip at her partner.

"The chief will probably put you on ATO while things cool off," Hall said.

"ATO? Bullshit. I didn't use deadly force."

"You discharged a firearm while on duty. You know what that brings. A shooting review board won't be needed, but Professional Standards will look at the application of force and make a determination if it was within policy, or not."

Emily stood and gathered the file Javier had given her. "Maybe a little time off wouldn't be a bad idea. I have—"

"Issues?" Javier said as he stood to join her.

She backhanded his shoulder.

"I'll let you know what the chief says."

She left the office and Javier followed in her wake.

"Where do you think you're going?" she asked.

"I'm in this with you."

"Nah, I'll take the heat on this. Speaking of heat, why don't you make sure Turpin and Whitman are feeling a little heat in the interrogation rooms."

Javier pulled his cell from his pocket, silencing the Pat Benatar ringtone. He grimaced. "Speaking of heat."

"Jenny?"

"Yeah."

"She make a decision on that job offer?"

He shrugged. "I dunno yet."

Emily rolled her eyes. "Go park your ass and call her. I'll expect a full report when I get back from the chief's office."

"If you get to come back . . ."

Emily turned on her heel and left the detective bureau. The chief was about protecting his officers from external political pressure. But there was only so much he could do without breaking policy, or jeopardize putting the entire department at political risk. Other mayors and city council types had done it before, and this mayor could use the department and Emily's career as a scapegoat for her political shortcomings.

She'd find out soon enough as Sandy, the chief's secretary, waved her in while she was on the phone. The look on Sandy's face was a warning of what was to come.

CHAPTER FIFTY-NINE

EMILY PUSHED IN through the chief's office door and he wasn't alone.

Chief Clark perched behind his desk and Mayor Carsten stood in front of him, hands on hips. She abruptly stopped speaking as Emily came into the room.

"Detective," the mayor said.

"Mayor. Chief."

Chief Clark pointed to a chair opposite him. "Take a seat, Emily."

She lowered herself into the seat while the mayor pivoted to face her.

"Detective, we need to have a word about your future."

Emily's stomach turned, and she glanced over at the chief with his noncommittal stare.

"Madam Mayor, I—"

"You are a one-woman wrecking crew, aren't you? A church leader gets firebombed and you're there. A hostage situation at a local mom-and-pop market and you're there. You, if I have my facts straight, shot the hostage?"

"It was a beanbag round—"

"Now I hear you're rescuing runaway kids, getting them away from gang influences," the mayor said.

"Yes, but—what?"

A grin spread across the mayor's face. "I'm here to thank you, Detective."

"Thank me? I thought you were going to put me on parking duty."

Chief Clark leaned forward. "What the mayor is getting at is there is probably a better opportunity for you than meter maid—is meter maid PC?"

"Parking enforcement officer, Chief," the mayor said. "And yes. I have a proposal for you. I'm starting an Office of Public Safety in the mayor's office, and I want you there—to run it."

"Me?"

Emily was at a loss for words. She wasn't getting tossed on Administrative Time Off. Instead, the mayor was offering her a job?

"What's this about? A task force?"

"Yes and no. I want someone who knows the city, knows where to apply pressure to get the job done, and I know you have the skills to make that happen. I've been the subject of that pressure."

"I'm sorry. I—"

"Don't be sorry. Take the job."

"What—will I still be a Sacramento police detective?"

The chief shook his head. "No. You'll be under the office of the mayor. You'll be a peace officer, but not working for me."

"Now, Chief, don't paint it like that. You'll be a peace officer—in fact, you'll be the chief of this new unit, and we'll take officers from the sheriff, highway patrol, Elk Grove, Rancho Cordova, and Citrus Heights assigned to you. We need better coordination and communication between the agencies."

"Chief Hunter does have a ring to it," Clark said.

"Trying to get rid of me?" Emily said.

"The choice is yours. But I will say it's one hell of an opportunity, Emily."

"Can I think about it?"

"Yes. Not a problem. Don't wait too long, though. I need to move on this. You've set a lot of this in motion based on your recent 'activities.'"

"I need to wrap up the investigation into the bombings, the murder of Councilman Davis, and how the gun trafficking connects them."

The chief excused her, and Emily retreated from the office feeling uncertain. The mayor's offer was unexpected, and she needed to figure out what it meant. Was it to pull Emily away from the high-stakes investigations to relegate her to a sideline role as a political operative? Or would it let her tackle some of the larger crime issues plaguing the region, like human trafficking, fentanyl mills, and the rise of domestic terror groups?

She stopped in her tracks. Terror group? A church bombing would be a page out of their racist playbook. The Molotov cocktail was a step down from the nitrogen phosphate–based bombs Whitman had been delivering.

He hadn't run out of the more sophisticated explosives.

Emily found Javier on the phone when she returned to the detective bureau. He wheeled around so he could face Emily, trying to read her expression after the summons to the chief's office.

"I don't want you to rush into anything," he said, cupping his hand on the phone.

He listened and swiveled his chair around to put his back to Emily.

"No, I understand. How much time are they giving you?"

Emily overheard the light buzz from the other end of the conversation, and it sounded like Jenny. Javier had followed up with her and it seemed like she was about to decide her—and their—future.

"That's not fair. They should give you time. It's a big ask."

While Javier talked with Jenny, Emily shoved aside two files on her desk. Her partner was busy and had collected the information after he'd left the hostage scene. One contained the booking information on Frank Turpin, the technical details on the "messages" he had delivered to her on the radio-controlled cars that didn't explode, and the one that chased her at the cemetery with a noisemaker payload.

At the back of the file was the academy investigation where Turpin was a witness to the gun theft by Whitman before his family was murdered.

Setting the file aside, she scooted Whitman's file in front of her and everything pointed to Davis's electronics store, then Frank Turpin, and then Richard Whitman, one after the other—each with their own connection to the Turpin family massacre. Her theory that Whitman was trying to eliminate anyone who witnessed his failure to rescue Turpin wasn't holding up. No one seemed to care—other than Turpin. Turpin was only interested in Whitman.

Complicating the picture was Whitman's deal with the district attorney, where he acted as an informant when he was caught selling the guns to street gangs. The deal protected him from the old gun theft charges. He had no reason to cover up what happened—unless . . .

Whitman was still selling them. She shoved the file away. Getting enough to convince a jury was going to be tough.

Javier hung up the phone and rubbed his temples.

"Couldn't help overhearing. Jenny's got a choice to make," she said.

"Can't I have a private conversation?"

"Not here you can't. Did you tell her how you feel?"

"More or less."

"Which is it? More or less?"

"We're gonna talk tonight. The new place in Portland is offering her a signing bonus and housing stipend if she accepts in the next week."

"That's some high-pressure sales tactics."

"Yeah. I can't be the reason she gives that up."

"Put your cards on the table. It's still her decision, but you'll both know and maybe fewer regrets over what might have been."

Clearly eager to change the line of this conversation, Javier handed her a report from El Dorado County.

"The sheriff's office up there searched Whitman's compound. They took custody of twelve semiautomatic rifles, twenty pistols of various makes and models—none of which matched the list of guns taken from the academy. They are tracing the purchase history to see if he obtained them legally."

"Any evidence of his explosive workshop? His barn would be my bet."

"No. Nothing."

"Damn. We've got to find him with a smoking gun or a jury could let him walk."

From behind her, an officer approached. "Hey, Detective Hunter, I've got someone who says they need to talk to you."

"They give you a name?"

"Some gangbanger. Goes by Doggy or Red something."

"Red Dog?"

"Yeah, sounds about right. I shook him down. He's not packing. You wanna see him, or do I gotta chase him off?"

"Yeah, we'll see what he wants."

A minute later, the officer escorted the young gang member to the detectives. Emily gestured to a chair.

"What's up, Red?" Emily said.

The gangster plopped down in the chair and leaned back trying to look casual.

"First off, I ain't no snitch."

"Yet here you are," she said.

"Yeah, against my better judgment. Danika said I should come talk to you."

"Danika? I hope you're not trying to drag the girl back into your little circle of fools."

"Nah, it ain't like that. She called me. Wants me to tell you about some old White dude selling guns to my crew."

Emily leaned forward. "We've been hearing. How come you wanna talk about it?"

"Let's say there's too many damn guns out there. Both sides are armed to the teeth and if someone gets disrespected, people gonna get hurt. Rockhead was trying to broker a peace deal. We're still down with that."

Emily unclipped a photo of Whitman and handed it to Red Dog. "This the guy selling weapons out there?"

He handed it back. "Like I said, I ain't no snitch."

"Then what are you doing here?"

"Listen up. I want to keep my crew safe. My family safe. You might want to go take a look at a storage locker out off Northgate. You know the one."

"I do," Javier said.

"Good. Might find what you looking for in unit 535—it's what I heard. That's all."

Red Dog got up to leave. "You gotta, like, escort me out or something?"

Emily caught the set of his jaw. The young thug wanted to say more but needed to talk privately.

"Yeah, I'll take you. This way."

While they waded through the detective bureau, Red Dog whispered. "Cindy at the church wanted me to give you this."

Emily took a folded paper and opened it.

The document was a ledger of payments and deposits on church accounts. Many of them were noted as cash deposits.

"She said you'd know what it was."

"Tell her thanks—and I do."

Emily walked Red Dog out of the building and watched as he climbed into a car parked behind a dumpster. The guy wanted to keep his visit away from prying eyes.

She returned to Javier and tossed the document on his desk.

"You know what this is, don't you?"

"Your budget for self-help groups for the month?"

"It's from your church lady girlfriend, Cindy."

He glanced at the handwritten ledger. "It's her accounting for the gun buyback. It's bigger than we thought. And there are names here . . ."

"Look at the last line."

"Whitman. He was buying the guns back so he could sell them again."

CHAPTER SIXTY

EMILY AND JAVIER pressed into the interrogation room where Whitman waited. He was in handcuffs attached to a belly chain.

"It's about damn time." Whitman leaned back in his chair and looked down his nose at Emily across from him. Javier leaned against the wall to Whitman's right.

"Let's go back to where this started," Emily said.

"I've called my lawyer."

"I haven't asked you anything."

"Don't bother. I'm waiting for my lawyer."

A knock on the door. Javier opened it a crack and spoke with someone out in the hallway. Javier turned to Emily and his tight jaw told her he wasn't happy with his discussion in the hall.

"His attorney is here and she's checking in," Javier said.

"Good. We can move this along."

The door swung open and former DA Allison Warner, now private defense counsel, sat next to her client.

"When did you start representing Whitman?"

Former elected DA Warner folded her hands neatly on the table. "That's none of your concern."

Emily dropped a digital recorder on the table, clicked the power switch, and hit RECORD.

"Fine. This is detective Emily Hunter interviewing Richard Whitman. Also present in the room are Detective Javier Medina and Allison Warner, counsel for Mr. Whitman. The date is August 12th and it is 1535 hours."

"Mr. Whitman, let's begin with the weapons at the public safety academy."

"Excuse me, Detective, my client will not be talking about the firearms removed from the academy. He had an agreement from the DA's office he would not be prosecuted if he worked with them as a confidential informant. He did. And these charges are ancient history. The statute of limitations has expired."

"You would know about that agreement, wouldn't you, Ms. Warner?"

"You know full well I signed off on his confidential informant contract."

"As part of that contract, was your client directed to sell firearms to known gang members?"

"What are you getting at, Detective? My client played a minor role in a larger anti-gang initiative run out of my office."

Emily let the silence suck the air out of the room. It was an effective interrogation technique. A squirming suspect needed to fill that space and often blurted out an incriminating morsel for the patient detective. Emily figured the attorney opposite her would feel the need to explain herself.

The former DA buckled. "My office addressed gang violence across the county. The gun buys marked the players in specific gangs and we could track where these guns landed, who used them, and we obtained criminal convictions with gang enhancements as a result."

"Let me get this straight. You armed known criminals and then let them carry out violent offenses?"

"They were killin' each other. No harm done," Whitman said.

Warner put her hand on her client's arm, urging him to remain silent.

"No harm done? Like the murders of Monica, Taft, and Millie Turpin?"

The attorney began, and Emily shut her down. "No—I want to hear it from him."

"He doesn't need to answer. Thomas McCracken shot and killed those people. It has nothing to do with my client."

"It has everything to do with him. He let those innocent people die."

"He was investigated by your department and found not responsible for their tragic deaths."

"The allegations of misconduct were not sustained. Largely because the victims were dead and couldn't offer testimony. He wasn't exonerated."

"This is the bullshit that made me leave and retire. People like you who have no business second-guessing what really happens out on the street. You've weakened the department with your liberal woke nonsense."

Emily tilted her head at the odd response. "People like me?"

"You and him." Whitman jutted his chin at Javier. "Neither of you deserve to wear the badge."

"Oh, I get it. Detective Medina and I aren't White men like you."

"Don't respond to this, Richard," Warner said.

"You said it, I didn't."

"Explains you hanging out with your militia pals. You sell guns to them, too, right?"

"Where are you going with this, Detective?" the attorney asked.

Emily drew out a copy of a document, the church ledger provided by the reverend's assistant, and laid it on the table between them.

"The questionable decision to let your client play in your own version of a *Fast & Furious* gunrunning operation ended two years ago if I'm not mistaken—after you left office."

"My successor chose policy options in a different direction."

"Then your client wouldn't have any reason to continue selling firearms to known felons and gang members."

"That operation ended." Warner eyed her client and tightened her jaw.

"Whitman, can you explain how these transactions took place in the last six months?"

Whitman leaned in and glanced at the ledger page from the church.

"I don't know what that is."

"It's a record of payments from Reverend White, each time he sold a recovered firearm. You were getting a commission and buying them back too."

"You have no proof of anything of the sort."

"Really, Detective, I think this has gone on long enough," Warner said.

Emily pulled out another document, the list of guns recovered, listed by date and serial number. "Here's the confiscated weapons listed by date received and serial number. Interesting here—some of these were the same weapons you stole from the public safety academy."

"That proves nothing," Warner responded.

"What it proves is you are still in the gunrunning business and these weapons ended up on the street."

Emily tapped a line on the list of weapons.

"This one here—it's perplexing. It keeps showing up. It's a weapon you stole from the academy. You sold it during your time as a snitch. Then it shows up here on the church log because someone turned it in. Then, once more, it shows up on the church log—a week after Turpin's family was murdered. Can you tell me how that happened?"

"How would I know?"

"How you would know is—you sold the weapon to McCracken. We have a witness identifying you walking into a crime scene where the Turpin family lay in their own blood and the first thing you do is take the suspect's weapon."

"We needed to secure the weapon. You should know that, Detective."

"Do you always replace the suspect's gun with a throwaway?"

Whitman grew pale.

"Detective, I need to—" Warner said.

Emily continued pressing. "The ballistics didn't match the weapon you left behind. You didn't think we'd even look because . . . everyone was dead. Well, almost everyone."

"You don't have anything."

"Richard, don't say anything more."

Emily dropped a photo on the desk.

"What I do have is this. This is the weapon McCracken used to kill the Turpin family. We ran the ballistics on it. What I don't get is why you didn't toss the gun somewhere—the river—somewhere it wouldn't be found. What do you do but sell it again to a small-time thug who goes by the name Red Dog. He ID'd you as the one who sold the gun to him."

Whitman dropped his chin. The realization that he'd screwed himself over the sale of a cheap handgun set in.

His attorney cleared her throat. "All this is very interesting, but the statute of limitations is well past on anything to do with these weapon violations. You can't possibly be suggesting my client is culpable for the tragic loss of life in that store."

"Morally, he is. Legally, that's up for debate. But he is a murderer. Let's talk about Councilman Davis."

"Wait one minute. My client will not respond to any fantasy you may have over the attacks on the councilman, or the other attacks in the city."

"Fantasy? Well then, let me tell you a story. Councilman Davis, for all of his faults, did want to make the community a safer place. We differed in our approach, but he did start a dialogue with community leaders, gang leaders, and clergy.

"It wasn't long until Davis found out about how the guns were getting on the streets. Davis, and a gang shot caller by the name of Rockhead, were getting ready to out you. In fact, they'd left a meeting with a police department representative, Officer McKinley. You took Rockhead out because he knew too much, followed by Davis because he was going to blow the whistle on your operation."

"You can't prove any of this," Warner said.

Whitman didn't respond but his face reddened, telling Emily she was on the right track.

Javier's cell blasted the opening chorus of Pat Benatar's "Hit Me with Your Best Shot." He silenced the ringtone and held the phone to his ear. He nodded to Emily and hung up.

"We've finished a search of your storage unit off of Northgate."

Before Warner could object, Javier placed a copy of a search warrant on the table in front of her. The attorney picked it up, studying the scope of the warrant, and Javier showed her his phone, which displayed a photograph of warrant return left at the scene listing dozens of bomb components, a shop table packed with electronic components for his car bombs, and two crates of weapons, one with PUBLIC SAFETY ACADEMY stenciled on the side, full of Glock handguns.

"It's over, Whitman."

Warner pushed the warrant document across the table. "I no longer represent Mr. Whitman."

"You can't do that," Whitman said.

"I can and I do. You had immunity on the old gun charges. Not these fresh developments."

"I want another deal. I can turn over where the militia stockpiles their weapons. But I didn't have anything to do with no bombs."

"I did that dance once before. I'm done," Warner said.

The attorney left the interrogation room and Whitman tried to act hard, as if the discovery of his weapons cache was simply a bump in the road. "You can't make a case on those old guns. You can't even prove I put them there. They don't belong to me."

"I think we can. But I'm more interested in the bomb components our team found. The quick down and dirty is they match the bombs you used—the ones injuring six of our officers—officers you used to work with."

"I didn't—"

"I don't want to hear any denials. You were trying to clean up your mess. Davis and the others were going to expose you and you were determined to make sure they couldn't tell. From the city councilman all the way back down to where it began with Frank Turpin."

"Turpin—that weak punk. He deserved what he got—should have died along with his pathetic family."

"Because of him, we found out you switched out the gun McCracken used. Turpin exposed you and wasn't going to give up after what you did to his family. You let them die in that market and you hoped Frank bled out, too, to keep your secret."

"I can give you the street connection for the gun operation," Whitman said, with an edge of anxiety creeping into his voice.

"We already have Reverend White and his role in the deal. You have no leverage left. You're going away for a long time. The councilman's murder, attempted murder of Frank Turpin, and Reverend White. Then there's the assault with Great Bodily Injury cases from your explosives—attempted murders, if the DA gets frisky."

Javier knocked on the door and two uniformed officers entered, both wearing SWAT uniforms. They looked eager to book the fallen commander.

CHAPTER SIXTY-ONE

WITH WHITMAN ON his way to booking, Javier and Emily entered the second interrogation room where Frank Turpin was resting his head on the table.

He raised his head as the detectives entered. A purple bruise welted above his left eye.

Emily reminded him of his Miranda rights and asked him if he'd agree to talk.

He nodded and Emily placed the digital recorder on the table once more and stated who was in the room.

"Mr. Turpin. I'd like to clarify a few things. Let's start with the list of officers Councilman Davis had. Where did they come from?"

"From me."

"Why? What did they do to you?"

"Do to me? They were there the night my family was taken away from me. They saw what Whitman did."

"What was Davis going to do with the list?"

"What he was supposed to do was get each of those officers to come forward and admit what they saw Whitman do. Then he changed his mind and said he was going to use the information against the mayor

369

in his bid to get elected. He forgot what this was all about—my family." Turpin was breathing hard.

Emily saw he was ready to break. "That's why you killed the councilman? He forgot about your family."

"What? He did, but no—no, I didn't kill Davis."

"You used the radio-controlled car to slide it under his car, just like you did at the church bombing, and on West El Camino."

Turpin's eyes went wide. "No. You've got that wrong. I—I didn't do that."

"Come on, Frank. We saw you at your family's graves yesterday when you sent a car after me—"

"I wasn't there yesterday. I swear."

"We saw you. You have any proof at all you can offer to say it wasn't you?"

He fell silent. "I don't. I've been living outta my truck since I came home and found my place had been messed up. There was a trip wire on the stairs."

"At Mrs. Galvin's place?"

"Yeah. I live over the garage. Someone had been there, and I nearly hit that wire on the stairs. I'm being set up. I haven't gone after anyone but Whitman. That, I fully admit."

"Tell us what you admit. You and Whitman," Emily said.

"Whitman had to pay for what he did to my family."

"McCracken killed them."

"McCracken wouldn't have been able to kill them if Whitman hadn't sold him the gun. A gun that he stole from the academy. I forced Whitman into my truck and took him to the store where it happened."

"What were you planning?"

"It was going to end. I was going to shoot him exactly like he shot my wife and kids. He needed to know what that felt like."

"What happened?"

"I—I got careless. I got too close, and he managed to get untied. He took the gun from me." Turpin pointed to his bruised forehead.

"There was another list—the one you tucked next to your wife's headstone. It was different and had other names on it."

Turpin glanced up at Emily. "What list? I didn't put anything like that near my wife's marker."

"You did send me the academy investigation file, though?"

"I did. I needed you to know Whitman started this. His guns."

"We saw you speeding away from the church in that gray Ford Taurus after Reverend White was attacked."

"I was following Whitman. I saw him. He wanted to take out the reverend because he knew too much about selling the guns to anyone who wanted one after they were donated by the public. He waited out front after you two entered the church. I think he was hoping to get all three of you."

Turpin paused, clearly thinking of something. Then: "Wait. I don't have a gray Ford. I have my Toyota truck. It's red and, like I said, I've been kinda living in it."

"But you were there? You saw Whitman toss the Molotov cocktail?"

"I did."

Emily nodded.

"Is it over?" she asked.

"It'll never be over for me. But if you're asking if I'm done with Whitman for what he did, then yeah. He's going to suffer a worse fate where he's going. A snitch and an ex-cop—he won't have any easy time in prison."

"We'll get you processed. It'll take some time. You're gonna have to answer for the kidnapping, maybe even attempted murder on Whitman."

"I don't have any place else to go."

"I'm sorry for what happened to your family, Frank. I really am."

He nodded.

As the detectives readied to leave the room, Turpin said, "Thank you—thank you for believing me."

Back at her desk, Emily found a phone message. Brian had called. "Discharge from hospital. Any room at the inn?"

She smiled and felt a warm sensation in her cheeks as she reread the message. A thaw in his demeanor? There was a chance the man she loved was reclaiming his personality. She knew there might be mood swings because of the TBI, but this was a positive sign.

She called the number on the message slip, a number she didn't recognize. Emily was surprised when Brian answered.

"Hey, you. Where are you? I got your message."

"They're kicking me outta here. Said I can recover in a rehab facility. I don't need a rehab place. Is your bed-and-breakfast offer still open?"

"If breakfast of a stale bagel and some K-Cup coffee machine brew qualifies, then yeah, I think I can fit you in."

"I was expecting more of a five-star experience—but I'll gladly exchange the hospital food for a bagel."

"When are they putting you out on the curb?"

"You know how they work. They say they're getting ready to discharge me, but it's going to take an hour or three. They need to round up my prescriptions too."

"I'll come by and pick you up. Can you call me when you're ready? I'm at the office with Javi, so I'm only a minute or two away. What phone are you calling on? I didn't recognize this number."

"Mine got damaged and I lost track of it when they brought me into the hospital. I got a cheap replacement until I can find a new one. The nurse here helped me set it up."

"Oh, she did, did she?"

"Yes, *he* did. You sure you don't mind me taking up space at your house? I mean, I'm kinda a big lump of nothing right now. I'll have PT appointments, and if you're okay with them coming to the house . . ."

"That's fine. Everything's set. I have that downstairs guest room. It'll work so you don't need to take the stairs."

"I don't want to put you out, Em."

"You're not. Call me when you need me to come get you. Javi and I are wrapping up reports on Turpin and Whitman—looks like Whitman was your bomber."

"Whitman? No way."

"Way. It involved gunrunning and I'll tell you about it when I pick you up."

"No, Em. It can't be him."

"We have him dead to rights on the gun dealing, and the bombings tried to cover it up. The donation bin that hurt you and your partner— the church was using it to collect firearms from the neighborhood as their own version of a gun buyback program."

"No. I don't accept that." His tone had changed. There was an edge to it again. A quick flip of a switch.

"We'll talk about it later after you're settled."

"I'm telling you, it's not Whitman."

"Okay, okay. I hear you. He made those radio-controlled cars and everything. We found them . . ."

"Emily—Whitman couldn't program his microwave—"

"Call me when you want me to pick you up."

She disconnected the phone and tossed the cell on her desk. Brian was certain, absolutely certain, his former lieutenant wasn't behind the bombings. She figured it was some remnant of loyalty he had toward his old commander. Blinders—unless . . .

Had Emily been the one with blinders on this whole time?

CHAPTER SIXTY-TWO

EMILY STARTED TYPING up the reports tying Whitman to the bombing attacks and the pieces fell together in a tight fit. A cover-up to eliminate anyone who knew about his failures that fateful night, and the gunrunning scam behind it. Too tight and too perfect.

The electronic components traced from the councilman's electronic store. Officer Milton pointed at Turpin and then called out Whitman as a student who took adult education classes. First Turpin and now Whitman. Which was it? Emily wrote it off to the young cop's passion to deliver. She reminded herself to follow the evidence . . .

The components, the servo-what's-it that Officer Milton identified, the records, and the storage unit Whitman rented as his workshop. All locked down tight. Whitman was coming into focus as the figure behind the bombing attacks. Turpin and Whitman going after anyone involved in the hostage situation.

Why, then, did Emily feel a ball in her gut? Was it from Brian's steadfast certainty his old unit leader wasn't behind the attacks? Whatever the source, Emily felt compelled to cross doubt off this scorecard.

"Hey, Javi? What do you know about your pal Officer Milton?"

"Like what? You want to ask him out?"

"No, ass, I mean, like, what's his story? How did he get involved in our case? He's going to be a primary witness because he's been the link in the origin of the electronic components, the documents from Davis's store, he turned us onto Turpin, ID'd Whitman at a class, and searched the storage unit."

"Yeah, he's been in the middle of it from the start," Javier said.

"Where did he come from? He showed up on my doorstep after Brian was injured. What do we know about him?"

Javier pushed back from his keyboard. "Em, where is this coming from? Your spidey-senses tingling again?"

"Something's not—it feels too—I mean he led us to the councilman's business, he led us to Turpin, then connected Whitman to the devices."

"What are you saying?"

"This case will rest heavily on his testimony. I'd feel better if we do a little vetting so there aren't any surprises down the road."

"What's brought on this recent bout of paranoia?"

"Something Brian said. I want to make sure we haven't been working this case with blinders on."

Emily stood from her desk and grabbed a file. "Could you pull Milton's personnel file?"

"Sure, what am I looking for?" Javier said.

"Maybe nothing."

Emily turned and strode out of the detective bureau. She felt bad she didn't share more about the source of her growing paranoia about Officer Milton, who "happened to be" there whenever a key piece of evidence was found or processed.

Emily pulled the storage unit address from the file and entered it into her phone for directions. The yard on Northgate seemed a strange place for Whitman to use for his base of operations. He lived forty minutes away in a compound isolated from the city forces he felt worked against him. Red Dog gave her the unit's location.

She called the number Red Dog had given her and left a message to meet her at the storage facility.

———

The Northgate storage yard was a vast line of orange doors with at least a hundred rental units. She pulled her SUV into the slot by the office and there wasn't anyone at the desk when she entered.

She spotted an older man with gray hair shooting out from beneath a Jets ball cap driving in her direction in a golf cart. He pulled the cart to the open door and didn't bother to get out of the vehicle. Instead, he yelled, "If you're looking for a unit, we're full."

Emily flashed her badge. "I think you have one that'll be empty soon. Show me 535."

The man grimaced. "Come on, then. I don't got all day."

Emily hopped into the cart and they lurched back down the path and found the unit in question. She spotted it easily with the crime scene seal on the door.

"You here when they searched this place?"

"I got no responsibility for what people do in the unit they rent. Says right in the contract they ain't supposed to do nothing illegal. No drug labs, runnin' hookers, or hiding stolen property. I don't know what this guy was up to, but the business ain't liable for none of it."

"No one's saying you are, Mr. . . ."

"Billson. Stanley Billson."

"You ever see what was going on in that unit? I mean, before the police showed up?"

"Wasn't none of my business. When the guy came, he'd go'n pull the door down behind him and did whatever it was he was doing."

"But you saw the man? The man who rented this unit."

"Of course I did. He had to sign the contracts and whatnot."

Emily stepped from the golf cart and sliced the seal with a pocket-knife. She drew up the orange metal door and peered inside.

Evidence of bomb components, explosives, and the crate of academy weapons had been seized and removed. Milton's report of the search had included parts for at least three more radio-controlled cars, traced back to purchases from Full Charge Electronics. There was still a fully functional workbench with tools, wire, soldering irons, and burn marks on the work surface where the devices were assembled.

Emily took her phone out, opened the photo app, pulled up Whitman's photo, and handed it to the storage yard manager.

"This the guy you rented to?"

The man squinted so hard the lines on his forehead came together.

"Yeah. That's him. The last few months, he had another guy coming almost every day."

Emily reached across and scrolled to another photo. "That's the one." He handed the phone back.

Emily glanced at the phone once more. It wasn't a photo of Whitman. It was a photo of Officer Milton.

The roll-up door came crashing down. Emily and the old man were shut inside. The click of a padlock on the door told her they were trapped in the dark.

CHAPTER SIXTY-THREE

THE STORAGE UNIT manager fumbled near the front of the space, banging against the metal door. He found a switch and turned on a light hanging in the center of the unit.

Emily took another look around the storage unit. Small tools and a few remnants were all the crime scene unit had left behind. Nothing that could cut through the door or break their way out of the enclosure.

"You have a way to bust us outta here?" she asked.

"Nuh-uh. I usually unlock these from the outside."

Emily slapped a hand on the metal door. "Anyone out there?"

Nothing came back in response. As much as Emily hoped it was kids getting a thrill out of locking people in a storage unit, this felt more sinister. Milton. He locked the door after they ventured inside.

She pulled her cell phone, and it showed zero bars. She was cut off from calling for help.

A shuffling sound reverberated through the roll-up door.

"Detective? You in there?"

Emily recognized Red Dog's voice through the metal.

"Hey, Red. You need to help us out of a jam here."

"How did you—never mind. What do I gotta do?"

"You have any bolt cutters with you?"

"No. Why? You think I'm gonna carry around burglary tools so you people can send me away?"

The storage unit manager elbowed Emily and whispered. "I got a set of bolt cutters in the office if you can trust this guy."

"I don't see much of an option, do you?" Emily said. Then, through the door: "Red, go back to the office; there's a pair of bolt cutters—" She turned to the manager. "Where are they?"

"Behind the counter. Drawer on the left."

"In the office, behind the counter, drawer on the left."

"Aight . . . lemme go check it out."

"Think he's coming back?" the old man said as he settled against the workbench.

"I'm usually not the trusting type—but I think we gotta—"

A chime sounded.

"What's that?"

"The motion detector in the office. It's how I knew you were here."

A moment later, they heard rattling on the metal door. A *ca-chunk* sound echoed through the surface.

The door rolled up and Red Dog stood in the opening with the bolt cutter in hand.

Emily stepped from her temporary prison.

"Thanks, Red. You see anyone leaving the yard when you got here?"

He shook his head, and his braids swung back and forth. "Didn't see nobody. You told me to come here, so I guess you're glad I did."

"Something like that."

The manager scowled at Red Dog in his red hoodie sweatshirt and red bandanna.

"Now what does this fool want?"

"I can lock you back in there."

"He's with me," Emily said.

The older man sneered and skulked off to his golf cart, zipping off toward the front of the complex.

"You're welcome," Red called after him.

"Hey, Red, thanks for coming."

"What you need me for? You gotta move a couch or something?"

"You told me about this place. Unit 535. How'd you come by this information?"

"I know things," Red said.

"You're about to know my boot," Emily said with a grin.

Red gazed into the storage locker.

"Ain't much in there. Nothing worth this drama," Red said.

"Red—how'd you hear about this place?"

"Okay, okay, don't get it twisted. Like I said, people talk. Word on the street was if you had the cash and needed a gun, this was the place. Well, not here, exactly. They didn't want a bunch of thugs lining up. You saw that old man's reaction. You made a deal and the gun would come from here. Or that's the word on the street. And the best part about it was—no one was gonna get busted for buying a piece."

"Why's that?"

"On account of the dude that was selling them was a cop."

"A cop was selling guns from this locker?"

It fit with the narrative they'd put together. The storage yard manager identified Whitman as the one who signed the contract. If Whitman was the one selling guns, not Milton, then what was the connection to this storage unit?

Emily showed Red the photo of Milton on her phone. "Know him?"

"Am I supposed to?"

"He's not the one selling guns outta here?"

"No—it's a crusty older dude. You ain't the only one been asking about him."

Emily scrolled until she found a photo of Whitman. "Him?"

"Yeah, that's the dude. Kinda high strung and usually had some White boy muscle with him. I think he was afraid of getting ripped off."

That fit with what Emily knew about Whitman and his militia ties. But Milton's connection with the storage unit and Whitman made little sense.

"You knew to tell me this specific unit number. Red, who told you?"

"I ain't no snitch. I keep telling you."

Emily pulled a set of handcuffs from her belt and dangled them in front of Red.

"I come to your rescue and you treat me like this?"

"Turn around."

"All right, all right. I'll tell you what I know."

Emily tucked the handcuffs back in her belt.

"I heard about this place this week. Everybody knew there was a place, but until now, no one knew where it was."

"Red—"

"Okay, some pasty-assed White boy told me. Made it seem like he had some axe to grind about guns. Wanted to get them off the street or some such. Rumor was his whole family got gunned down."

A chill swept up Emily's neck.

"You get a name?"

"Uh-uh. It was the other picture you showed me."

Emily snagged her phone once more. She scrolled back to the driver's license photo of Clay Milton.

"That's him," Red said.

She pocketed the phone and told Red Dog thanks. She strode back to her SUV.

"Don't I earn some reward for telling you what you wanted?"

"I thought you weren't a snitch?"

"I ain't, but I deserve a taste."

"Consider yourself paid with the moral credits you earned by getting guns off the street."

"Moral credits. Unless they can be turned in for cash, it ain't gonna get me my Egg McMuffin."

"I'll buy you an Egg McMuffin." She pulled the roller door down and closed the storage unit. She'd ask the manager to throw a new lock on the door.

As Emily turned toward her SUV, she stumbled over four discarded cigarette butts. She flashed back to a similar pile on the roof of the bank building on West El Camino. Milton. She fumed over the connection between Milton and how he pointed at Frank Turpin and then Whitman at every turn.

She'd been manipulated from the beginning.

CHAPTER SIXTY-FOUR

EMILY PULLED INTO the hospital lot and trotted to the entrance. Brian hadn't called her yet, but she was eager to bring him home. Anxious was probably more accurate.

She made it to his room, where he was parked in a wheelchair, stuffing his belongings in a plastic hospital bag.

Her sudden appearance startled him, and he dropped the bag.

"Em. You're early. I didn't call you."

She kissed him on top of the head and came around to face him. "I thought I'd come and bust you out of here."

"I'm more than ready. The nurse was in here a few minutes ago with the discharge forms. She was getting someone to run down to the pharmacy to pick up my prescriptions. We won't have to."

"That was nice of them. I was thinking, we'll get you to my place and—"

"I'll be fine on my own. Isn't that what you wanted anyway?"

Emily blinked at the sudden shift in Brian's attitude.

"Brian, that's not fair. I want to you to be—"

"You didn't want me at all a couple of days ago. What am I now, some charity project? I don't need you to take me back to my place. I can get a ride."

He reached down to gather his bag with his good arm and it was just out of reach.

Emily bent and took it from the floor.

He snatched it from her and put it in his lap. "I can take care of myself."

She sat on the bed across from him.

"Brian, tell me what's going on."

"Nothing. Nothing's going on. Leave me alone."

She tried to understand why he was pushing her away. She said she needed more time to decide when he sprung the living together question on her. It was sudden, and his reaction now was deliberately hurtful. Was this a mood swing from his TBI, or did the injury simply reveal what he really felt?

"Brian, talk to me. I want you to come stay with me. If you don't want to be with me, tell me why."

"I think you made it clear it was you who didn't want us to be together, Emily."

"I was just surprised you asked. I—I didn't have a chance to think about it."

"It's not something you should have to think about. I know I thought I didn't—maybe I was wrong."

"Brian, let's get you taken care of first. You need time to heal, then we can figure everything else out." She reached a hand out to him.

Brian twitched when her hand drew near, and his eyes welled. "I'm scared, Em. I don't know what to do. You don't want me anymore—I get it. I'm broken. I'm not the guy you knew before."

Brian wheeled his chair away from her, facing it toward the hall so he didn't have to look at her.

"When you told me you weren't ready to move in together, what did you really mean? Are we through? If we are, fine. I. Deserve. To. Know." The last four words were punctuated with a punch to the wheelchair arm with a fist on his good arm.

"We'll figure it out together and get you what you need."

The anger welled from him.

A nurse entered with a clipboard and, with a cheerful tone, said, "Here's your discharge and your prescriptions." She held a small white paper bag.

"You take care of our patient. You want me to have an orderly come and wheel him out?" the nurse asked.

"I can manage. I know you're busy. Besides, I need to have a word with this patient," Emily said.

Emily stepped behind the wheelchair and shoved it out into the hallway.

"Emily?" Brian said.

She didn't respond and pushed the chair down the corridor to the elevator, where she stabbed the button.

"Em?"

The doors opened, and she shoved the chair into the empty elevator car, bouncing the leg extensions off the back wall.

Two hospital employees started to enter the elevator, and Emily cut them off. "This one's full; take the next one."

They eyed each other and backed out of the car. The doors slid closed, and when the car started, Emily jerked the wheelchair around so Brian faced her.

"Where the hell do you come off?" she asked.

"Where do I come off? Do you ever listen to yourself? It's always about what you want. What I want is to be left the hell alone. Did you even think about what this is like for me? I'm fucking useless."

"No, you're not. Don't make excuses. You really want to be on your own? Just say the word and we're done."

Emily could read the struggle on his face. A mix of hurt, shame, and desperation. He started to speak, and Emily cut him off.

"If you're gonna tell me some bullshit about how you're broken and useless, I swear to God, I'll leave you parked in this elevator."

She pulled the STOP button on the control panel and the car lurched to a halt between floors.

"You got something to say? Spill it."

"Em, I don't know what I want. I keep replaying the explosion over and over and I can't make it stop. I can't do anything about it and I'm stuck in that loop. It's all I see—the only thing I think about."

"I'm sorry."

"I don't want you to feel sorry—don't you get it? You don't know the way it makes me feel. Weak. Broken. Worthless. I'm not going to burden you with that. I'll figure this"—he gestured to his arm and shaved head—"out on my own. I don't need the physical therapist treating me like I'm a child, or the doctors who tell me I might not get my life back."

"You don't have to do it on your own. That's what I'm saying. You're angry—"

"Damn right I am—"

"And you should be. Be pissed off at the person who did this. Not the therapists, or the doctors, or me. Did you tell any of the doctors how you felt?"

He shook his head. "No. I couldn't. What was I gonna say?"

"That you needed help."

"I thought I'd be able to pull through it on my own."

"You could have come to me. Ask me for help. Unless you blame me for what happened."

"And let you even think less of me? I mean, look at me. I'm a broken mess. I may never be the same. I don't want you to be saddled with that. No, I don't blame you for that."

She knelt near the chair. He struggled to look at her.

"I get to make that decision for myself. We're in this together. You need help and we'll find you help."

"I don't need anyone—"

"You do. The flashbacks, the anxiety—it's PTSD from what you experienced. People who go through what you did find ways to cope or ignore the pain. Some find ways to deal with it that are more self-destructive than helpful."

"What am I supposed to do now?" he said. Emily noticed the fire was burning out in Brian's eyes.

"We are going to figure this out together."

"You're still willing to be with me, even though I'm broken?"

She got back to her feet and pushed the elevator button.

"We're all broken in one way or another. It's how we put the pieces back together that counts."

Emily wheeled Brian out of the hospital and helped load him into the front seat of the SUV. An orderly collected the wheelchair and Emily got her passenger settled.

"I'm sorry," Brian said in a low voice.

"What was that? It sounded like you said you were sorry, but I couldn't really hear it over the pity party of one you're holding over there."

"You aren't gonna make this easy, are you?"

"Did you expect anything else?" she said as she pulled the SUV in gear.

"What do we do next?"

"The only way out is through."

"Listen to you, Zen Master . . ."

Emily's cell buzzed in her pocket and she hit the SPEAKER button and tossed it on the console between the seats.

"Hunter here."

"It's Javi. Where you at?"

"I picked up Brian from the hospital."

"How's he doing?"

"I'm good—now," Brian said, glancing at Emily.

"He's a work in progress. Hey, I got a nugget to drop on you about—"

"Milton," Javier said, finishing her sentence.

"Exactly. He and Turpin—"

Javier interrupted again. "Milton is Turpin's brother-in-law."

CHAPTER SIXTY-FIVE

"MILTON—OFFICER MILTON was Frank Turpin's brother-in-law. Our personnel records. They have his sister, Monica, listed as Milton's emergency contact," Javier said.

"Milton's been playing us this whole time. Dammit. I should have seen it," Emily said.

Her anger flowed through her foot as she pinned the accelerator to the floor.

"Where is he now?"

"He's not with the crime scene team. They don't know where he went."

"I think he locked me in a storage unit off Northgate."

"He what?"

Emily felt the pieces fall into place with the solid connection between Frank Turpin and Milton. The events were orchestrated to set up Davis, Turpin, and Whitman. She knew Whitman was a slimeball and was up to his neck in gunrunning to street gang factions, but the bombings, the attacks on other officers, the murder of Councilman Davis, and the arson attack on Reverend White were all Milton.

Milton didn't happen to show up at Emily's door after the first church bombing, where Brian was hurt. He was there right from the start to make sure the attacks happened and, unless Emily was way off, he was the one who piloted the device to its target. He knew how. He even bragged about teaching robotics at an adult ed class.

He'd been under her nose this whole time. He was responsible for what happened to Brian.

"Javi, we need to find him. Whitman and his brother-in-law are both in custody. What's his next play?"

"He's gotta know we're onto him. I think he's gonna take another run at them. The scenario he put together to get revenge for Monica is falling apart."

"He's got to understand Whitman and Turpin will walk on the bombing and murder charges. He'll want to finish the job."

"Whitman and Turpin are still in lockup while the DA tries to figure out how to clean up the mess they made with their gun sting operation."

"Milton went through a lot to get in a position to act against Whitman. He's not going to give up now," she said.

"Agreed. But would he risk taking a run at him in jail?"

"We have to make him think it's his only shot."

"Yeah, okay, but how can we send a message to Milton?"

Emily told Javier she had an idea and disconnected the call. "You mind finding the SPEED DIAL button for Kari Hardison on there?"

Brian picked up her phone. "The reporter?"

"Milton listened to her accounts of the attacks and seemed to get off on how she covered the crimes. Now I know why. If we can convince her Whitman is being moved to higher security somewhere, it might force Milton's hand."

"Will she do that?" he asked.

"Find her number and I'll ask."

Brian hit the SPEED DIAL button. The reporter picked up on the second ring.

Emily ran down the events and asked the journalist to issue a report that Whitman was being moved out of the jail to higher security in an undisclosed location to force Milton to act.

"Emily, I can't do that. It's not ethical. I can't knowingly make a false report. It would violate every rule. I can't be viewed as an instrument in a police operation. The press has to remain independent."

"I get that. What if you made a statement that the most serious charges against Whitman may be dropped and there is talk about putting him into witness protection?"

"Is there? Talk about witness protection?"

"We're talking about it now, aren't we?"

"Emily—"

"Kari, it's likely Whitman will be called to testify against Frank Turpin and Milton. Witness protection wouldn't be off the table."

There was a pause on the line, which told Emily she was considering it.

"I'll run it up the chain."

"Thanks. That's all I can ask. Would you call me if it's a go?"

"You giving me an exclusive on this?"

"As far as I'm concerned, you've got it."

Emily thanked her and disconnected the call.

"You up for a little socialization?"

"What do you mean?" Brian said.

"I'd like to drop by the detective bureau and let the lieutenant know what's up."

"I—I don't know."

"Might be good to see some familiar faces."

"Maybe drop me off at your place."

Emily didn't want to leave Brian alone. Sure, he needed help to move around in her space. But maybe it would do him some good to see other officers who didn't think he was as broken as he believed.

It was going to take some time to rebuild what they had. Trust was a gigantic piece of it, and having Emily looking over his shoulder every moment would not go over well. She knew the fix.

She snagged the phone this time and dialed another number by heart.

"Hello?"

"Lucinda. I think I need your help again."

"Your mom? Is Connie okay?"

"Connie's fine. Brian is coming home and I think he might need a little looking in on."

From the passenger seat, Brian squirmed. "I'll be fine, Emily."

"He's putting up a bit of a fight, but I think he could use a little help getting around—at least for a couple of days."

"I can do that. When do you want me to start?"

"How about tomorrow? I think I have today lined up."

"Fine. I'll be back in town by morning. What does that beautiful man of yours like to eat? I'll make him something special. Javier told me what he's gone through."

"Don't spoil him."

She hung up. And Brian chided her. "I don't need a babysitter."

"Only for few days. Make sure you eat, take your meds, and rest. Besides, I think she's a bit smitten."

He shook his head and grinned.

They pulled into the police department lot and Brian moved gingerly. It took effort, but he was determined to make his way on his own.

Once they made it into the detective bureau, Brian saw a few familiar faces and the warm greetings made him smile. He parked at Emily's desk while she grabbed Javier and herded him into the lieutenant's office.

After an update to her boss, Lieutenant Hall leaned back in his chair and rubbed the back of his neck. "This happened in our house? One of our own orchestrated this entire attack on our people and we never suspected a thing? This is not a good look."

"It looks like Milton joined the SPD in the weeks following his sister's murder. He's been planning this all along," Javier said.

"The psych eval didn't catch anything. And he was biding his time until he and Turpin could convince the city councilman to start making noise about Whitman's ongoing gun deals. The impact on community safety and all that."

"No wonder the councilman didn't trust the police department," Hall said.

Emily's cell vibrated. "It's Kari." Then, into the phone: "Hey."

"The editor says it's a go. I reached out to Channel 9 and they're going to give me a breaking news segment. I wanted to see when you want to run it?"

"Give me thirty minutes."

CHAPTER SIXTY-SIX

EMILY DISCONNECTED THE call and noticed Brian in conversation with another detective, Art Brady. It looked serious, and Brady was doing most of the talking. Brian was nodding occasionally.

What to make of that?

"You think your reporter friend can flush out Milton?" Hall said.

She was distracted with Brian and the other detective. There was a handshake before Brady turned away.

"Yeah, yeah, I think she can pull this off. Milton has been focused on taking everyone apart and if he thinks Whitman is going to get off light, he won't be able to resist."

"You're going to use Whitman as bait?" Hall said.

"Let's hope it won't come to that. We'll take him down before he has a chance."

They left the lieutenant's office, and Emily perched on the corner of her desk next to Brian.

"You gonna be okay here for a while? Javi and I need to run and take care of Milton. Turns out you were mostly right about Whitman. He's an ass, but not a murderous one."

"Yeah, I'll be fine here."

"I didn't know you knew Detective Brady."

"I didn't. He came over to introduce himself. Seems he's in a group for officers who've been through things like this."

Emily recalled Brady was shot during a domestic violence call a few years ago. She wasn't aware of any group or therapy Brady was involved with, though.

"Turns out there's a few others. Might be good to hear how they've adjusted and what they did to manage the flashbacks and stuff."

"I'd be happy to go with you."

Brian held her hand. "I think this is something I need to do on my own."

When he pulled his hand away, he'd left behind a brass key.

He read the confusion on Emily's face. He used his good hand and softly caressed the crease in her brow. "It's a key to my place. I don't know if my place is right, but it's what I've got right now."

"It's perfect," she said. Her voice was soft and it trembled a little.

"I know I get angry and fly off the handle. I'll try to do better. I'll figure it out—with you."

Emily bit her lip and nodded. She understood his need to feel like he was reclaiming his life. It was going to be a long road back to reclaim what they had. She leaned over and kissed him softly and didn't care who in the detective bureau noticed.

———

Emily and Javier left for the jail. True to her word, they found Kari Hardison in front of a camera in mid-report. The detectives scooted behind the reporter and slipped inside the jail.

They displayed their badges to the deputies at the entrance.

"I need to have a word with your watch commander," Emily said.

One deputy dialed an extension on a plain black desk phone.

"Lieutenant, two Sac PD detectives here for you."

The deputy listened and hung up.

"She's busy right now, but she said if you want to hang out in her office, she'll meet with you when she has a chance. You guys need to coordinate your visits better."

Emily stiffened. "Coordinate what visits?"

"The other detective."

Emily knew officers and detectives interviewed inmates regularly. The timing of this visit struck a sharp note with Emily.

"The detective give you a name?"

The deputy at the desk flipped through the log. "Where . . . oh yeah. Ten minutes ago. Detective Milton."

It struck Emily that she'd operated under the belief that Whitman was the man responsible for the Turpin family massacre. Then why did Milton finger Frank Turpin at every opportunity early on?

"Shit. Did he ask for Whitman? Or Turpin?"

"Turpin."

"Dammit. He's not a detective. You gotta lock this place down and find him."

The deputy picked up the phone again and dialed an extension.

"Hey, Tomlinson here at the front desk. That detective—Milton— he meeting with inmate Turpin? Yeah, right, thanks."

He hung up the phone, looked at Emily. "Your detective is in the visiting area. He asked for a conference room where he could meet with the guy away from the other inmates. He's there now."

"With Turpin?"

"No. Not yet. That's where the lieutenant is. Turpin is refusing to come out of his cell. We're getting ready to do a cell extraction and pull him out."

"Tell the lieutenant to leave Milton where he's at. Can you lock the conference room?"

"You mean lock your guy inside?" Emily nodded. "Yeah. But why?"

"Take me there. But don't let that man out of the conference room. Especially not in contact with inmates Turpin or Whitman."

Emily and Javier secured their weapons in a locker along with their cell phones. They followed the deputy to the elevator and shot up to the fourth floor.

"What's the deal with him sneaking in to see Frank Turpin?" Javier asked.

"I thought it was so they could get their stories straight. It doesn't feel right. He wanted us to believe Turpin was behind the bombings."

The unit where Milton waited was 4-B. The lieutenant waited at the unit entrance.

"Detectives, you saved me a whole lot of paperwork. Mind telling me why you want to keep inmate Turpin from your detective?"

"He's not a detective, and Turpin—I think he blames Turpin for getting his wife killed—or he holds him responsible, anyway. He means to do him harm."

"So much for a lack of paperwork. What you need me to do?"

"Let us have him and the only paperwork you'll have is down in booking."

The lieutenant shrugged. "Follow me." A short distance away, a door marked for visiting opened and three women were escorted out and to the elevator. Inside the visiting area, an array of glass-paneled partitions were arranged for visiting. To the left, two attorney conference rooms were visible with glass panels in the doors.

Emily pulled open the first one.

"About time—" Milton said, then stopped when Emily and Javier appeared.

"I hope you like small rooms like this one."

Milton pulled a plastic squeeze bottle from his jacket and aimed it at Emily.

A deputy snapped a Taser from his belt and sent two darts into Milton, one clipping the bottle before finding flesh in his chest.

The first spark from the Taser ignited the fluid in the bottle and engulfed Milton's arm.

He screamed and flung his arm, fanning the flame, sending it lapping up his neck. "Let me finish this," he said in between cries of pain.

The fire alarm in the visiting area sounded and a flurry of coordinated activity escorted visitors out the main area. A team of deputies with fire extinguishers rushed in and emptied their cannisters of white powder on Milton, putting out the blaze.

Four responding deputies pinned Milton to the floor and applied handcuffs while he tried to fight them off.

"He was going to burn Turpin," Emily said.

Milton struggled under the deputies. "I need to finish this. It's all Frank's fault. He needs to pay for what he did to my sister. She'd still be alive if he minded his own business and didn't try to make himself a hero. He killed Monica and her kids."

"What about you? Who pays for everything you did?"

They hefted Milton to his feet, and the man radiated anger. "You can't stop me. I'll find him. I'll never give up. I'll kill him—and you too. All of you. I should have ended you at the cemetery . . ."

He was at the Turpin family gravesite. Milton was the one who tucked the note next to his sister's marker. He'd blamed Frank for their deaths and promised to make it right. Everything he did was to steer the investigation—with his planted evidence—to his former brother-in-law and then everyone else who was at the scene when they died.

The deputies dragged Milton out of the room to the jail's medical unit, where he'd be treated before he was booked and locked into a cell of his own.

A cop, even a deranged one, wasn't going to have an easy time of it inside.

CHAPTER SIXTY-SEVEN

Emily stood on a levee near Cal Expo. Javier was a few feet down the earthen barrier, carefully making each step on a pathway cut into the embankment. He used a rope secured to the SUV bumper to make his descent.

"See it yet?" Emily asked. A homeless camp across the river was quiet at this time of the morning, an hour after sunrise. One woman stood on the opposite bank and pointed to Javier's left, guiding him to where a body was spotted.

"There's a cave here."

"Cave? You're not Batman, Javi."

"No. It's dug into the levee bank. Got a blue plastic tarp over it. Some of the earth is slipping away."

"Careful down there."

"Is that concern I hear?"

"I don't want to housebreak another partner."

The rustle of plastic sounded from below when Javier pulled the tarp from the hole in the earthen levee

"Got a body here. Male. Can't see much from here. Looks like he's been gone for a while."

"All right. Come back up and we'll have the CSI team help extricate him for the ME."

Javier pulled himself up the rope, hand over hand. "Looks like the call made to 911 was right. A homeless guy built his burrow in the levee. Gonna need ropes, pulleys, and a stokes to get him out."

"Sounds like a job for the fire department," Emily said.

Her cell phone chirped in her pocket. She recognized the number on the caller ID.

"Chief? Hunter here."

"Emily, the mayor called. She hasn't heard back from you on her job offer."

"That's because I haven't called her back."

"I know. I got an earful from Her Honor, blaming me for stonewalling you."

"Sorry, Chief, wasn't my intent."

"She needs an answer, Emily."

"I know, sir. I need time."

"You've got twenty minutes."

"Twenty—what?"

"We've been summoned to city hall."

Emily told the chief she'd meet him there and pocketed her phone.

"Trouble in paradise?" Javier asked.

"Something like that. Speaking of paradise—you going up to Portland this weekend?"

"That's the plan. We'll see how the long-distance thing works. Jenny's got her hands full with this new gig. It's hard to coordinate time off."

"You got this? I need to go meet Chief Clark."

"Yeah, I can manage this. Chief getting pressure from Mayor Carsten on her job offer?"

"Yeah. I haven't made any decision."

"Sounds like you will. It does sound like a great opportunity. No more middle-of-the-night callouts to fish a floater out of the river. Although, you will miss me."

"You sure know how to sell it, partner."

Emily slipped behind the wheel of the SUV and backed off the levee road. Javier and a uniformed officer stood vigil, waiting for the CSI team and the medical examiner's crew.

Would this be her last crime scene as a homicide detective?

———

Chief Clark waited for her in the mayor's waiting room. He looked uncomfortable on the politician's home turf. He stood when he spotted Emily.

"Chief."

"Detective. The mayor's in a mood. Just to be forewarned."

"Because I haven't given her an answer?"

"That might be a small part. But she's found out Councilman Davis's widow filed paperwork to run against her in the upcoming election."

"That's over a year away."

"Still, it has her stirred up a bit. The nature of the job, I suppose. Something you should be aware of when you take on this new job."

"She expects me to do opposition research for her campaign?"

"Not so much. In fact, I think there are firewalls where city employees are prohibited from campaigning."

"Then what does she want me to do?"

"Let her tell it."

They stepped to the door and Chief Clark took Emily by the elbow. "Listen to her. This is an opportunity that doesn't come around but once."

Emily nodded and entered behind Chief Clark.

Mayor Ellen Carsten removed her reading glasses when they came through the door.

"Chief, I didn't expect you. Emily, good to see you."

"Mayor," Emily said.

Carsten rose from behind her desk. The surface was covered with files, budget reports, talking point memos, and other ephemera of political office.

She gestured to a small coffee table with low, thinly padded chairs. Emily thought they were designed to keep meetings short.

Mayor Carsten sat and directed Emily to a chair on her right. The mayor turned at an angle, so she spoke directly to Emily.

"Given some thought to my offer?"

Emily cleared her throat, which had suddenly gone dry. "I'd like to know more about what you have in mind."

"As we mentioned, I'm establishing an Office of Public Safety here in the mayor's office. I want you to head up this new organization."

"That much I recall. But what is it you hope this new office will do that the existing police agencies don't already offer?"

"Coordination, for one. These departments—no offense, Chief— tend to operate as their own little kingdoms. Siloed off from one another. We need someone to bring that together—to focus public safety efforts where the city needs them. As we've seen recently, we need a special investigative unit to conduct inquiries without potential influence from internal, or external, sources."

"This unit would report to you directly?"

"Yes. What do you think?"

"You mentioned there was to be a task force staffed by officers from different departments . . ."

"We're still working on that. Each chief, or the sheriff, will appoint personnel from their department."

"No. That won't work. If I'm to run this new office, I need to select the staff. I need people I know I can trust, and they aren't hand-me-downs from other departments when they need to get someone out of the way. No offense, Chief."

"None taken. It's what I'd do if given half a chance."

"Now, Emily, I need you to understand how work is done here. We have to compromise—"

"I don't. When it comes to public safety, there is no room for compromise."

"This is the real world, Emily. We work for the people. That means we represent the needs of many different interests."

Emily tipped her head at the mayor's comment.

"I don't know if it's the real world or not, Mayor. It seems—I don't know—artificial. You always have to compromise your position to pacify the special interests and political action committees who fund campaigns."

The mayor smirked. "Do you ever pull your punches?"

"Not that I've noticed," Chief Clark said.

"You're not wrong, Emily," Mayor Carsten said.

"You're up for reelection in two years—"

"Fourteen months and fifteen days."

"What happens to the mayor's Office of Public Safety then? If you aren't reelected?"

"Emily, I don't know if that's—" Chief Clark said.

Mayor Carsten put her hand up. "No, no, she's right to ask. If I'm not in office, there are no guarantees. The next mayor might not see the same value in the office."

"They could eliminate it?"

The mayor nodded.

Emily leaned back in her chair.

"Mayor, I appreciate the offer. I have to decline."

"Emily, are you sure?" Chief Clark said. "If the office goes away, I can promise your job will be waiting for you."

"Chief, I think I can do more for the city in my current position—like we did with Whitman and Milton and the poison they spewed. I'm afraid living in a political world will make me less effective. Mayor, no disrespect to you—I couldn't keep my sanity in check dealing with what you do. I believe I can do everything you're asking me to do within the boundaries of my current position with SPD."

The mayor's lips thinned and she shook her head. "I understand what you're saying. I don't like it, but I understand."

She stood and extended her hand to Emily.

The mayor didn't release Emily's hand immediately. She bore down her eyes into Emily's. "I reserve the right to call you if your unique—somewhat direct—services are needed in the future."

"Like a bat signal?"

The mayor shook her head. "You're—"

"Impossible," Chief Clark said.

"I was going to say, you're refreshing."

"When you need me, I'll be here."

The chief paused at the photograph on the mayor's wall once again—the one capturing Davis after he was sworn in. He tapped his finger on the image he couldn't place the last time he was here.

"Recognize him now?"

Emily leaned in. "Turpin. He'd been here all along."

CHAPTER SIXTY-EIGHT

Emily's front door slammed, and she popped out from the kitchen. Brian was bent over, hands on knees, panting.

"A letter came for you," she said.

She threw a dishtowel at him. "You're sweating all over my hardwood floors."

"The mail doesn't usually come until the afternoon," he said as he picked up the envelope from the maple side table near the front door.

"Messenger delivered it."

Brian scanned the return address. "From the department—personnel services."

Emily leaned on the doorway while Brian tore open the envelope. She already knew what the message contained. He was being reinstated full-time now that his improved medical condition made him fit for full duty.

It was his mental condition that worried her the most. The aftereffects of the TBI had dimmed greatly. Fewer headaches and mood swings. There were ongoing nightmares and anxiety around being in open spaces like where the bomb attack took place.

The group meetings with Detective Brady were helping. The flashbacks were there, and loud noises could trigger a response, but Brian seemed to experience them less often. Exercise, like the run he'd taken this morning, kept them at bay.

Brian unfolded the letter and scanned it. He tossed it on the table surface.

"Back to work?" Emily asked.

"No. They want to medically retire me."

"What? That can't be." Emily snagged the letter and looked for herself. "What's this about? I don't know what they're thinking."

"I know what they're thinking. I'm damaged goods, a liability. They don't trust me to do the job anymore."

"I'll call Chief Clark. He obviously didn't know about this."

Brian tugged on her elbow. "Don't fight my battles for me. If I want this—to go back to my old life—I need to jump through their hoops."

"Okay. I'm pissed they took this approach." She glanced at the signature on the letter. "I don't even know who this is—Sandra Rath. This is how they treat their officers? I think Sandra is about to get her car impounded. I wonder if any of the other officers who were injured in Milton's bombings got the same letters?"

"Good question." Brian took his phone and sent a quick text to Robinson, the officer who was hurt along with him at the first church bombing.

His phone lit up a few seconds later. "Sure enough. Robby got one—so did McKinley and Tucker."

"Dammit. There's an appeal process. Probably a fitness for duty exam."

"That's what Robinson said too. I'm not ready to retire yet."

"Good. I've got to get ready for court."

"Today's the day Whitman testifies?" Brian said.

"Yep. Wanna come along? The DA mentioned his testimony already buried Turpin for the kidnapping. Now it's his turn in the box. Seems Whitman is making good on his deal with the prosecution to get the immunity he wanted. He's still a dirtbag who set this in motion."

"Yeah, I'll come. Let me make a couple of calls first."

———

Two hours later, Department 9 of the Sacramento County Superior Court was in session and the clerk called the matter of the *People vs. Clay Milton.*

The judge asked counsel if they were ready to proceed.

"Tami Lewis, for the people, and we're ready, Your Honor."

Behind the deputy DA, Brian, Robinson, Simmons, Tucker, McKinley—all the officers injured in the attacks—were in their dress blue uniforms; and next to them, Chief Clark.

"Call your witness, Ms. Lewis."

The defense counsel rose. "May we approach Your Honor?"

The judged waved the two attorneys to the bench for a sidebar conversation. Members of the jury were intent and tried to listen to the whispered conversation.

The attorneys returned to their tables.

"I understand there has been a plea agreement reached?" the judge said.

"We have, Your Honor," the DA said.

Over the next ten minutes, Milton, who needed to be restrained during the hearing, entered guilty pleas for the murders of Councilman Davis and Rockhead, along with multiple counts of attempted murder for the bombing attacks.

Emily leaned toward Brian. "Wonder why the change of heart?"

"I heard he took the deal because it's the only way he might have a chance to make good on his promise to take out Turpin. Things happen in prison, and he'll have a lot of time to figure out how."

The judge slammed the gavel down, dismissed the jury, and Milton glared at Emily while two bailiffs forced him from the courtroom.

Chief Clark made his way over to the group of officers, and Emily handed him a note. He read it and his jaw tightened.

He cleared his throat. "I understand some of you received some administrative bullshit about clearing you for full duty."

Heads nodded.

"Sergeant Conner, you've gotten this too?"

"Yes, Chief. The bean counters want to medically retire me—most of us, actually."

The chief craned his neck and let out a deep breath. "It's handled. If you're medically cleared and if you want to return, your job is waiting for you."

McKinley, whose legs were slow to mend, leaned on a cane. "What about those of us who can't return—yet?"

"You'll have a place in the department. We owe that to you."

Handshakes began and Brian pulled Emily aside. "This is your doing, isn't?"

She shrugged. "You know how much the chief supports his own. I appealed to his instincts."

"What did the note say?"

"Oh, I don't recall exactly. Something along the lines of 'do the right thing.'"

"Which means he didn't know what the admin weenies were doing."

"Looks like it."

"You can't stay out of it, can you?"

"Nope. Sometimes we all need a nudge." Emily felt the caregivers group appointment card burning in her pocket. "Others need a swift kick."

THE END

ACKNOWLEDGMENTS

The inspiration for ***Illusion of Truth*** came about from an incident which occurred many years ago when an officer reported that he was shot at on his way to work at the prison. This came on the heels of the wife of a prison gang leader accessing hundreds of Department of Motor Vehicle records listing prison staff home addresses. A weeklong search of gang members, their cells, and work areas followed with organized resistance and violent behavior directed at staff members.

For ***Illusion of Truth***, I wanted to consider the outcome if that original report was fabricated or shifted to place the blame on someone else. We expect our law enforcement officials to meet the highest standard of integrity. I saw enough to know that unfortunately that's not always true. The actions of a few make the job harder for the good cops on the line.

A novel like ***Illusion of Truth*** might be written in isolation but can only come to life with a fantastic team pulling together. I'm forever grateful to Bob and Pat Gussin who originally saw promise in Emily's story. The incredible team at Oceanview who brought the book to life earn my undying gratitude—Lee Randall, Michael Fedison, and Christian Storm put this book in your hands. Thank you.

Thanks to Elizabeth K. Kracht of Kimberley Cameron & Associates for not giving up and finding the perfect home for this series. Thanks, Liz, we did it again!

A special thanks to my advance readers, especially Jessica Windham, Janis Herbert, and Megan Cuffe, who are never shy about telling me what works and what doesn't.

The book community is incredible, and I appreciate the support of independent bookstores like Face in a Book (Tina Ferguson and Janis Herbert) and Book Passage (Kathy Petrocelli and Luisa Smith). They make a bookstore feel like home.

Sometimes words of encouragement came when they were most needed. Lisa Scottoline, J. T. Ellison, Wendall Thomas, Karen Dionne, Baron Birtcher, Matt Coyle, Bruce Coffin, Alison Gaylin, Rachel Howzell Hall, Wendy Corsi Staub, Lou Berney, T. Jefferson Parker, Margery Flax, and Shawn Reilly Simmons, I thank you endlessly.

A special shout-out the incredibly talented Mystery Writers of America Board, to my 2:00 a.m. ThrillerFest road crew, and my fellow Capitol Crimes Chapter of Sisters-in-Crime members for the love and support.

Thanks to my kids: Jessica, whose snarkiness may have influenced Emily's character, and to Michael—I love you guys.

I wasn't always alone at the keyboard, and I owe Emma and Bryn the corgis extra treats for all the plot points they helped me work through on countless walks. The corgis are finally happy to get recognition in Illusion of Truth! Then there's #NotMyCat who now demands extra catnip because of her newfound celebrity. The book would have been done months earlier if not for her walking on my keyboard.

A special thank-you to Ann-Marie L'Etoile for tolerating my nonsense over the years. You let me disappear behind my keyboard and still love me when I come up for air. Love you.

And finally, thanks to you, dear reader. It's only possible because of you.